The Earl's Enticement

Highland Heather Romancing a Scot: Castle Brides
Book 3

Collette Cameron®

Attn: Permissions Coordinator
Blue Rose Romance® LLC
info@collettecameronbooks.com
eBook ISBN: 978-1-954307-09-4
Print Book ISBN: 978-1-955259-86-6
collettecameronbooks.com

★★★★★ "Collette Cameron is at her sparkling best in this, the third in the Castle Bride Series. Beautifully defined characters (Adaira is a treat and Roarke just dreamy) interact with Ms Cameron's typical sparkling wit and lively dialogue. A fast-moving plot sweeps you along in its wake." ~ *Sarah Hegger*

FREE BOOK!

JOIN MY EXCLUSIVE MAILING LIST
Collette Cameron Newsletter

AND GET A FREE EBOOK!

https://collettecameronbooks.com/freegift

Plus Sneak Peeks, Giveaways, Contests, Exclusive Content, and More... P.S. I promise only good stuff ∼ **no** spam!

Dedication

For every woman who's given her heart to a hero.

One

Late June 1817

Roark, Earl of Clarendon, led his limping horse toward a partially constructed building at the edge of the bustling village. The mare, the only horse available for hire at the inn he'd lodged at last night, had gone lame a half-mile back. He rubbed her velvety muzzle, and she blew into his hand.

The gentle, loyal creature had done her best.

He should've taken his coach the last leg of the journey from London. Yet, he loathed confinement. Enclosed spaces stirred childhood memories better left buried. He arched his spine, wincing as familiar tautness twinged from shoulder to hip.

A man, his words indistinguishable, called to a lad standing in the building's doorway.

The boy glanced over his shoulder. "Aye, I shall."

He bounded across the porch, then down the steps in front of the structure. A piece of straw poked from his mouth, and he wielded a riding crop in one hand like a sword.

"Young chap." Roark waved, as with long strides, he closed the distance between them.

Ducking his head, the lad yanked the knitted cap lower on his brow. The Scottish bonnet was far too big for the boy. And tugged nearly over his eyes, he looked rather like Roark's one-eyed Old English sheepdog, Guinevere.

The crop stilled mid-air. Shoulders hunched and eyes lowered, the youth removed the straw from his mouth. He tossed it onto the packed earth. "Are ye speakin' to me, sir?"

"Yes, I need direction to a livery stable." Roark brushed his hand down the horse's warm neck. "This nag's gone lame."

The youth was taller and older than he'd first thought. Mayhap as much as five and ten. "What's your name, lad?"

"Ad—er—Addy, sir." Addy's voice was soft, and his brogue rather melodic for a lad that age. He appeared painfully shy, or perhaps, embarrassed at being caught pretending swordplay. He had yet to lift his gaze from Roark's dust-covered Wellington's.

Trickles of sweat trailed down Roark's back as he scanned the busy street, searching for a stable. "Where might I find a horse for hire?"

His gaze trained on the mare, Addy approached the horse instead of answering the question. He stood with his head cocked, assessing the horse. Rubbing the bridge of his nose, he leaned forward a fraction.

Ire pricked at the lad's audacity, but Roark swiftly stifled his irritation. It wasn't as if someone anxiously awaited his arrival. In fact, truth be told, he wasn't expected. It was gauche to come for a holiday unannounced, but there was nothing for it.

Whispering something unintelligible, Addy tucked the whip beneath one arm before running his hands along the mare's right shoulder. He squatted and trailed fine-boned fingers to her ankle. "I'd bet my sainted grandmother, a bowed tendon is causin' her pain."

Roark quirked a half-smile in grudging admiration. Addy was right. "You know something of horseflesh?"

Eyeing the tip of the crop peeking from beneath the youth's arm, Roark tensed, and his smile faded. He never took a whip to his horses. Or other animals for that matter. He had no respect for anyone who did.

Addy shrugged, still hunkered over the mare's lower leg. "Aye, a wee bit."

Roark scrutinized him. He'd originally thought the boy a village urchin. The well-made breeches and fine boots Addy wore belied that assumption. His jacket hung loosely but was of the highest quality. And, unless he toted the whip around for amusement, he had a horse.

Was he local gentry?

Weren't the only aristocrats in the immediate area the McTavishs and Fergusons, both of whom resided at the castle?

Roark rubbed his brow. Was this boy one of them? Ewan McTavish, the Viscount Sethwick, had a brother about six and ten, and sisters, too, didn't he?

Blast. Roark couldn't remember precisely what his stepsister, Yvette, had written. Except that McTavish's mother and stepfather, Hugh Ferguson, along with a throng of other family members, lived at the keep.

Removing his hat, Roark lifted a crisp, white handkerchief from his coat pocket. He dabbed his sweaty forehead. With one last wipe across his face, he folded the handkerchief before tucking it back inside his jacket. His fingers brushed the irregular scar on his forehead—one of many marring his body—as he swept his hair backward. He donned his hat once more.

Despite his cap and coat, the lad didn't appear the least affected by the rising temperature.

Lifting his gaze, Roark examined what he could see of the flourishing township. No doubt Addy was the son of a prosperous merchant, and the structure was a—

Roark angled his head, studying the odd two-story building with its L-shaped additions. The new lumber glowed wheat-gold in the sunlight. The pleasing scent of freshly cut wood permeated the air. He had no idea what the odd structure was.

An inn, perhaps?

"Where are ye headed?"

Addy's question reined in Roark's musings. He swung his attention to the boy, still gently kneading the mare's leg. The lad made low, crooning noises in the back of his throat.

"Craiglocky Keep if I can acquire a horse."

And even if Roark couldn't, blister it. He didn't relish a lengthy trudge in this infernal heat. He gestured to the building. "What is this meant to be?"

Addy's hands stilled. "An orphanage."

Keeping his back to Roark, the lad slowly stood and grasped the crop once more. He edged around to the other side of the nag, caressing her with his free hand. His nails were clean and square. "Ye are a stranger to Craigcutty. What business have ye at the keep?"

Irritation surged through Roark at the lad's dawdling. He was anxious to see Yvette. Why hadn't she contacted him prior to returning to England? Why did he have to learn of her homecoming by way of the gossipmongers and the letter she posted from Scotland?

Scrutinizing the top of Addy's head, all that was visible above the horse, Roark suppressed his exasperation. He exhaled a long, controlled breath before answering coolly. "My stepsister, Yvette Stapleton, is in residence there."

The mare heaved a gusty breath and shifted her weight.

Before Addy dipped his head behind the nag again, Roark caught a fleeting glimpse of deep brown eyes framed by thick sable lashes. Was that surprise or alarm in the lad's gaze? He still hadn't answered Roark's question about acquiring a confounded mount.

"*Ye* have a stepsister? At the keep?" Skepticism riddled Addy's voice. He stopped patting the mare's neck, then twisted to look at the building. "I canna..."

The boy slapped his crop against his boot.

Meshing his lips together, he flicked Roark a contemptuous glance. The lad stared at the structure while tapping an irregular rhythm on his palm with the whip, frowning all the while.

What was he thinking?

"Yes, I'm—" By God, why was Roark explaining himself to this impertinent whelp?

Rivulets of sweat trickled between his shoulder blades. He examined the hamlet once more. Occasionally, he left off his title when traveling—especially when he wanted to remain anonymous. He'd found it very useful in determining peoples' genuineness.

He wasn't about to tell this cub his title.

"I'm Mr. Marquardt." Marquardt was his surname, although everyone addressed him by his title, Clarendon.

A snort followed by another muffled oath greeted his words. "Blast it to Hades."

"Pardon?" Roark skirted around the ancient horse's head.

Addy stood near the mare's rump, his nose crinkled in distaste. "Nothing. I stepped in—"

A small footprint was clearly visible in the middle of a steaming pile of horse droppings. Roark set his mouth against the grin that threatened. He patted the horse to hide his smile. Instinct told him the lad wouldn't appreciate his amusement.

Roark turned his attention to the well-used forked road. Parallel ruts, formed by innumerable wagon wheels, lined the parched earth. One lane led directly into town, and the other hugged the village perimeter. Most likely, the latter was the route to Craiglocky. "Does this village boast a livery?"

"Aye, there's a livery, but nae horses are available to ye."

Roark swung his gaze to Addy. He seemed to have overcome his bashfulness and stared intently at him now.

"And why not?" Roark tightened his grip on the reins. The mare jerked her head sharply. "Shh." He rubbed her neck. "It's all right."

"Look around." Addy waved the whip in the air. "Ye can see the building and carts and all. Every beastie is already in use."

From where Roark stood, he observed three other buildings in various stages of construction. Hammering, sawing, boards banging, and calls from the workmen carried to him on the inadequate breeze. At least four wagons had rumbled into the hamlet while he'd spoken to the boy.

"Perhaps one of the wagons is continuing on to the

keep?" Roark spoke more to himself than Addy. Another laden wagon creaked by. "Mayhap I could share a ride?"

"Nae likely." Addy shook his head, his cap promptly sliding to his nose. "Bugger me," he muttered, shoving the cap up his forehead.

Roark grinned.

Taking a couple of steps backward, Addy settled the bonnet higher on his head. It still obscured the top portion of his narrow face. "The castle's within walkin' distance."

Roark didn't relish a trek in this heat.

The lad pointed the crop at the outlying road. "It's a wee bit more than a mile along there."

He spun on his heels and started to dash away, but after a few strides, he slid to an abrupt halt. Little puffs of dirt spiraled around his ankles. Half-turning toward Roark, he said, "Take the horse with ye. There's someone at the keep who knows how to treat the animal."

He turned away and took no more than a dozen more steps before stopping again. He faced Roark, staring past him with impossibly dark eyes.

Roark arched a brow. "Was there something else?"

Addy's unnerving gaze met his for an instant, then flitted to the road behind Roark.

"Aye. When ye come to the fork, 'bout half-mile yonder, make sure ye keep to the right. Ye canna miss it. A monstrous old willow tree splits the path." Addy shook his right forearm back and forth for emphasis, and his short jacket rose and fell with the motion. "If ye dinna, ye'll find yerself sinkin' in the bogs."

Something akin to antagonism glinted in the lad's eyes. *Curious.*

Beneath winged brows, they were unusual eyes, too: oval, not round, and coffee-brown, almost black.

A Highlander's coloring, to be sure.

Addy stood, hands on his hips, tapping the toe of one boot. He peered at Roark expectantly. Even with a few feet between them, Roark could see flecks of citrine in the boy's pupils. Impatience also glimmered in their depths.

"Ye un—der—stand?" Addy spoke slowly as if speaking to a simpleton. "Keep to the right. Nae. The. Left." He made three sharp jabs with the whip in Roark's direction.

Roark clenched his jaw.

He typically kept a tight grip on his temper, yet this slip of a boy had managed to rouse his displeasure four times in less than ten minutes. And that damn whip. If Addy pointed the crop at him one more time, Roark was going to snatch it from him and—

Roark gave a curt nod, his patience at an end. "Yes, I understand. Stay to the right at the fork in the road."

"Aye." With that, Addy flicked a cocky salute. One hand holding the oversized cap atop his head, he tore off down the street as if the hounds of hell nipped at his heels.

Roark released a frustrated sigh. From the sting biting on one heel, he'd sport a blister or two by the time he arrived at the castle. That was what came of hiking in new boots with the leather not broken in.

He didn't mind the walk.

He did, however, very much dislike the sweltering temperature. Besides, the nag worried him. The mare was far too old to have carried him this distance. She should've been put to pasture long before now.

Roark shook his head as a new wave of guilt assailed him. He'd caused her lameness, albeit unintentionally, and remorse left a bitter taste in his mouth.

They both could use a drink.

Cool water for the faithful horse and something significantly more substantial for himself. Dunderhead. He should've heeded the innkeeper's offer of a flask of wine when the man suggested it this morning. Roark's stomach rumbled. He smiled ruefully. He'd also skipped breakfast—a decision he now regretted.

There was nothing for it, then.

He'd have to take his time leading the mare. Likely, there was some fresh water along the way. Addy mentioned nearby bogs. No need to hurry. Yvette wasn't expecting him. He'd come without an invitation, but his visit was warranted.

"She was only wearing a filmy chemise. And he was naked as a robin under the toweling when my sister discovered them in his chamber at Banbury Inn."

Roark shook his head to dislodge Lady Clutterbuck's shrill gossip from his memory.

What *had* Yvette been doing in McTavish's chamber?

A shout, followed by cursing, drew Roark's attention to the village center. Addy had plowed straight into a Scot carrying an armful of boards. In the ensuing turmoil of waving arms and crashing wood, the cap slipped from the lad's head.

A cascade of long, chocolate-colored curls, tied at the nape with an emerald ribbon, tumbled free.

Two

Adaira Ferguson threw a fretful glance over her shoulder.

Bother and blast.

Mr. Marquardt stood staring, or rather glowering, at her. Even across the distance, she could see the pinching of his well-formed mouth and his angry, narrowed glare. She'd bet her father's best tartan that sky-blue sparks spewed from Marquardt's eyes. Apparently, he didn't tolerate deception well.

She snorted. Ironic given *his* history.

She didn't know why she hadn't corrected him when he'd first called her lad. Or why she'd thickened her brogue when she could speak the King's English perfectly.

No, that wasn't true.

She'd done so because he was a stranger to Craigcutty, and something about him had unnerved her from the moment she'd laid eyes on him.

Then, when he'd revealed his name was Marquardt...

There, it happened again.

The fine hairs on Adaira's arms and the back of her neck rose as a chill skittered over her.

Och, someone walked over my grave.

She shuddered.

Rot and bother. Marquardt.

The cur had tried to kidnap and despoil his stepsister, Yvette when she lived in America.

Adaira fingered the topaz cross resting at the juncture of her throat. She'd been unable to suppress her oath when he revealed his name. Yvette was Adaira's sister-in-law now, and the thought of what that monster had attempted—

Clenching her riding crop, Adaira envisioned thrashing him with it, the ruddy *bastart*. She bent over, snatching her cap off the ground. "Sorry, Seamus. I was in a hurry and wasn't paying attention."

Settling the hat on her head, she stuffed the mass of hair inside, aware of the baleful blue glare boring into her back. "Did I injure you?"

Bending again, she retrieved the crop.

Seamus crouched. "Nae, Miss Adaira." He began to gather the scattered boards. "Ye're unharmed?"

"I'm fine. Can I help?"

He chuckled, shaking his grizzled head. "Nae, lass. Any fool can see ye're in a great hurry." His arms full, he grinned good-naturedly and gave a quick jerk of his head. "Go on with ye."

"Thank you!"

Offering an apologetic smile, she waved and ran to the rear of the blacksmith's where she'd tethered Fionn. Named after Fionn Mac Cool, legendary for his great strength and bravery, the huge horse was Adaira's dearest friend.

She really should help Seamus with the lumber, but she didn't have time to dawdle. She made short work of mounting the pewter-colored stallion. With a click of her tongue, a squeeze to his sides, and a nervous peek over her shoulder, she tore from Craigcutty.

She didn't have to look behind her to know Marquardt's fuming gaze remained riveted on her. The icy tingling along her spine was evidence enough. Every instinct in her screamed he was dangerous.

Once he realized she'd sent him directly into the woods bordering the bogs, and the castle lay a good three miles away instead of one, he'd be even more furious. God help her if he discovered there were at least two serviceable mounts stabled in the village livery.

Adaira shivered, recalling his scowling countenance. Her heart kicked against her ribs in a mixture of anxiety and anger. She urged the gray onward, bending low over his neck, his coarse, black mane whipping her face. "Come on, my brave friend. We've no time to lose."

With luck, perchance Marquardt would become lost on one of the numerous rambling trails leading from the branch in the road she'd told him to take. It wouldn't take him long to realize most of the tracks eventually led back to the main road, however.

A niggling thought burgeoned into a scheme. Ewan was still in London, although he was due to return any day. What if she kept Marquardt away from Yvette until Ewan returned? Then, her brother could deal with the blackguard.

She flicked a glance at the sky, checking the sun's position. She had an hour, perhaps a mite more before Marquardt emerged from the woods on the far side of the castle. Right where she wanted him to be. Adaira hoped he didn't encounter her family or a clan member headed to or from the castle. *She* must be the one to intercept him.

It wasn't likely he'd meet anyone if he stayed on the route she'd suggested. Thankfully, the pathetic mare was sure to slow his progress.

Adaira wrinkled her brow.

Was the man daft, riding the ancient nag?

Couldn't he afford a better mount?

Marquardt's clothing had been fine enough. Buff colored pantaloons hugged long, muscular thighs, and his boots, albeit dusty, were Wellington's. His soft fawn-colored hunting coat hugged his upper body, hinting at a muscular torso.

She'd noticed his long, slim fingers when he'd dabbed his forehead with his perfectly starched handkerchief. Were they as soft as they looked, or were the pads and palms calloused?

An unexpected prickle of awareness skittered over her.

Which would feel better on bare skin?

Stop it, goose.

Adaira hadn't expected him to be handsome. His chiseled, aristocratic features were quite easy on the eye. A scapegrace such as he should have a pockmarked face, beady swamp-colored eyes, and thin, curling lips dripping spittle. He should smell horrid too, not faintly of sandalwood and something spicy.

From what she'd heard whispered of Marquardt, she'd expected a trow, a Scottish troll. A short, grotesquely ugly monster, bent on making trouble.

Adaira knew the latter to be true of him. She'd eavesdropped on the hushed conversations at the keep between her father, Ewan, and their other male relatives. Ewan said Marquardt spied for the enemy during England's war with France. Her brother suspected Marquardt was also involved in the murders of several Domestic Corps agents connected to the Home Office.

At nearly twenty, she'd no interest in tedious political discussions. However, when the conversation turned to Yvette, and the men's voices dropped further, Adaira had shamelessly eavesdropped. As if assault and abduction weren't enough, Yvette had confided to Ewan that she suspected Edgar Marquardt had poisoned her father and stepmother. The mulled wine Edgar's mother had drunk, he had intended for Yvette to drink.

The man was unhinged. He'd thought to inherit Yvette's fortune because he was her stepbrother. Of course, Marquardt didn't know Ewan and Yvette had since joined in an irregular marriage under Scottish law. Still, when someone was touched in the upper works, rational thought was beyond them.

Unease scraped along Adaira's spine, and she nudged the horse with her heels. "Faster, Fionn. Come on, laddie."

Legs extended, he raced across the meadow.

A flock of doves took to flight as she pounded past the oat field where they fed. She smiled upon hearing the familiar whir of their wings. Once imported and raised as a favored food source, many flocks now flew wild in Scotland. She was fond of the sweet-natured birds which mated for life.

Silvery and resplendent, the castle rose into view, its smooth, rocky face bathed in the slanting rays of the late morning sun. Dating back to the sixteenth century, six-foot defensive walls surrounded the keep. Two towers rose majestically on the northern and southernmost points of the structure. Their mullioned windows competed with four turrets for the most magnificent view from within the keep.

The lowered drawbridge allowed a glimpse of the bailey and gatehouse beyond.

The McTavish banner waved proudly in the gentle breeze. The flag paid tribute to the McTavish clan and its chieftains. Ewan, the current laird, and his father, who'd drowned over twenty-five years ago, were included amongst those noble warriors.

She leaned to the left as Fionn rounded a bend in the road paralleling River Falkirk. By Hades, but it was hot. Slowing Fionn momentarily, Adaira released the top fastenings of her jacket and shirt before yanking the hat from her head and jamming it inside her coat.

Eyes closed, she tilted her head upward, relishing the cooling breeze on her face and rippling through her streaming hair. Her French mother would scold when she saw the hint of new freckles across Adaira's nose and cheeks.

Father, on the other hand, would tease her.

Dratted Scot's complexion and my easily freckled skin.

As a child, she'd refused to wear a wide-brimmed straw hat or carry a parasol when outdoors. Her face became so covered in blotches, she'd resembled the dumpies, speckled Scots chickens, roaming about the keep's outer bailey.

Adaira didn't care about a few freckles, and she'd grown accustomed to censured looks. She wore breeches, after all. How else was she to ride Fionn astride? Climb trees? Swim in the loch or explore the multitude of caves nestled in the foothills beyond the keep if properly attired? Wearing breeches made adventures possible.

Besides, she had a valid reason for spurning skirts. In short, it was much harder to yank off a pair of breeches than it was to flip up a gown's hem.

Mother said that Adaira had inherited her unruly

nature from her paternal grandmother. Father typically chuckled and agreed before launching into another tale about his unconventional mother.

Adaira knew she was an oddity amongst her kin and clan, especially her sisters, Isobel and Seonaid. She didn't possess Isobel's stunning beauty or quick wit, nor was she gifted with the second sight or ability to heal animals as was Seonaid.

Even her brothers raised their hawkish eyebrows at her antics. Ewan, her seven and twenty-year-old half-brother, and Dugall, at six and ten, were guilty of far more outlandish behavior than she. Yet, rarely were they chastised.

There'd been no repercussions whatsoever to Dugall for the snake or bunny incidents at the Bretheridges' house party. Adaira knew everyone believed she'd released the creatures in the house, and the guests blamed her for the disappearance of the chamber pots, too.

In truth, she'd had nothing to do with the snake or rabbits.

The tea voiders, however—

Remembering hoity-toity Margaret Shrewsbury's frantic dash to the bushes to relieve herself still caused Adaira to snicker. That was what Margaret earned for referring to the Ferguson sisters as, "Highland bumpkins with dung on their slippers," to a group of her tittering friends.

Adaira, on the other hand, had been confined to her room for two days after challenging Brayan McVey to a horse race. True, she was wearing a ball gown hiked to her knees, but her riding boots had covered most of her legs. She'd been perfectly decent. Or so she'd argued to her parents, to no avail.

There was *no* justice.

Oh, how she loathed the contradictory standards for men and women. Such bloody hypocrisy. Her scowl shifted into a smile. It had been worth it, for Brayan had lost the race. He had to kiss Mistress Peeble's prize sow—after the enormous pig indulged in a highly fragrant roll in the muck.

"Addy!"

Opening her eyes, she swung her gaze to the river.

"Addy, here I am, by the rocks." A fishing pole clenched in one hand, Brayan stood beneath a grove of alders heavy with summer foliage. He waved furiously at her.

Adaira didn't have time to chat. *Unless...*

Slowing Fionn, she chewed her lower lip. Brayan was half in love with her—had been since she was barely able to walk. Just over three years older than she, he was her closest friend, aside from Fionn. Brayan wanted to be more than that. He never spoke of it. But she could see the affection glimmering in his eyes and heard it in his soft sighs.

He'd do anything she asked.

But this?

She reined the stallion around and trotted him over to Brayan.

A hopeful grin split his boyish face. "How are ye, lass?"

"Very well. And you?" Adaira smiled against the wave of guilt sweeping her.

"I canna complain." At three and twenty, Brayan was not overly tall, but he was well-muscled. Actually, massively muscled.

She'd seen him carry a ewe under each arm as if he were toting week-old kittens. Nose wrinkled, she eyed him as he wiped fish scales on his vest. Adaira drew in a deep breath, barely suppressing a grimace. She abhorred fish.

"Brayan, I need your help." She hated to ask this of him, but what choice had she? "I'm sure you've heard of the abduction attempts on Yvette, both in America and England."

She gently tugged at the chain around her neck, fingering the prongs holding the citrine-colored gemstones in place. Grandmother had given her the necklace for her twelfth birthday. She'd said the stones reminded her of Adaira's eyes.

Brayan's gaze touched hers before dropping to the necklace. "Aye."

Squatting, he lifted a wriggling fish from the gravel. With his thick fingers, he threaded a thin rope through the brown trout's gill. He added the fish to a dozen others, then tossed the lot into the icy river.

They landed with a splash.

Pulling her cap from her jacket, Adaira hid a wince.

After squirming for a moment, the fish lay still.

Attempting a smile, she met Brayan's cheery gaze. "Her stepbrother, the suspected spy, is in the hamlet. He's looking for her. I sent him along the wrong path to the keep. Still, he'll be at the castle within the hour."

A breeze blew by ruffling the alders' leathery leaves, and she caught a waft of sweet fragrance from the nearby heather. Adaira brushed at the hair blowing across her face. "I want to delay him, to lock him in the keep's dungeon until Ewan gets home."

She cast Brayan a sidelong look, garnering his reaction.

His calm gaze studied her expectantly, his russet hair moving with the wind.

Laying the crop across her lap, she gathered her hair into a knot, then crammed it beneath the cap. "Ewan can decide what to do with Marquardt, and Yvette won't even know he's here."

Neither would her parents, and they wouldn't be

pleased. Nevertheless, she squelched the unease jabbing her. Adaira paused, emotion roughening her voice. "Brayan, you should see Yvette when anyone mentions Marquardt's name. She's utterly terrified of him."

Brayan rubbed his face and slowly nodded.

Adaira tried not to stare at the fish scales glistening on the tip of his sunburned nose or the one balanced on his upper lip. Poor Brayan. His large lips resembled the fish he was fond of catching.

"Aye, lass, I'll help ye."

"You will?" Her gaze flew to meet his.

She'd expected to have to persuade him or have him tell her, *Yer aff yer heid.* Mayhap she was off her head, but she loved Yvette. Adaira wasn't some simpering lass afraid to take matters into her own hands.

"Did ye doubt it?" Brayan spoke softly, adoration in his sandy-brown eyes.

Dash it all.

Guilt bathed her once more.

She shook her head. "By now, Marquardt should be nearing Kirk's Craig. I hope to stop him before he reaches Loch Arkaig."

Fionn pawed the ground and pulled his head toward the tempting water. She bent forward and patted his sweaty neck, breathing in his familiar scent. "Sorry, my friend. No water until you've cooled down. We'll be off soon."

Adaira scanned the road ahead. "Can you meet me at the abandoned crofters' cottages? I haven't quite decided how to apprehend Marquardt. I'll hatch a scheme by the time we meet, though."

"Aye, I can stash my fishin' gear there." Brayan retrieved the squirming trout, neatly cutting the excess line. The string dropped to the ground atop his boots. Tying the remainder of the rope into a loop, he extended the wriggling fish to Adaira.

From the pride shining on his face, he might've been presenting her a prized jewel. "Ye take them. They'll spoil by the time I bring them to Mother."

Adaira's nose twitched. Only by biting the inside of her cheek did she keep a look of horror off her face. Couldn't he at least kill the revolting things first?

"I ken yer mother likes them," he said, stepping forward.

Remorse lanced her. Did Brayan know she didn't?

Plastering a smile on her face, she wedged the riding crop into the front of her coat before taking the string of trout. She slipped a hand through the loop. "Thank you. Mother does enjoy fresh-baked trout."

Personally, Adaira couldn't stand them. No matter how trout was prepared, the meat always tasted of mud and weeds.

The cold fish flapped against her thigh, and queasiness tightened her stomach. At least they gave her a reason to use the kitchen entrance. A smile played around the corners of her mouth. Indeed, they did.

The fish provided just the excuse she needed. She could enter the keep through the kitchen and take the rear stairway to the upper levels. If anyone saw her, she'd claim she was ridding herself of fish stink. Once above stairs, she could gather everything she needed to keep Marquardt imprisoned for a few days.

She smiled at Brayan, this time genuinely happy. "Brayan, thank you for your generosity. Mother will be well-pleased."

He picked up the length of rope and wrapped the strand into a neat coil. He tucked the length into his vest pocket before making his way to his horse tethered under the trees. Swinging into the saddle, he said, "I'll meet ye at the old Brodie cottage."

"Aye, leave your horse by the castle ruins. I'll not be more than half an hour." She turned Fionn toward the road.

"Addy?"

Adaira twisted in the saddle to look at Brayan.

He grinned like a buffoon. "I dinna ken any other lass with yer courage." He shook his head. "Takin' the bugger prisoner." His words carried to her on the soft breeze as he trotted away on his roan. "Nae, there be none other like ye, Adaira Ferguson."

Adaira chuckled to herself.

Abducting a stranger *was* beyond the pale, even for her. A surge of pride thrummed through her, and confidence emboldened her. Marquardt deserved this. He was a blackguard and an irredeemable scoundrel, after all. She was simply assisting in his capture.

Her smile faltered. However, the repercussions could be dire. She drew in a hefty breath, holding it in her lungs. Even though Marquardt was a traitor, could she be charged with abduction?

Could Brayan?

Grasping Fionn's reins, she weighed her choices against the consequences. Tilting her chin, she stiffened her spine. So be it. She'd take full responsibility for what she was about to do. Yvette must be kept safe.

Even if it meant she would go to prison.

Three

Adaira scanned the keep's kitchen gardens as she cantered Fionn into the enclosure. *Good.* Only Clyde was about, tending the vegetables on this side of the castle, blessedly shaded from the late morning sunlight. She swung her leg over the saddle, then hopped to the ground. The fish banged against her thigh, leaving a trail of scales.

She grimaced.

"Clyde, will you please walk Fionn for me? I'll be but a few minutes?"

Clyde set aside his hoe. "Aye, be happy to, Miss Adaira."

"Thank you." She eased her crop beneath the edge of the saddle.

The kitchen was situated at the rear of the keep. A walled area to the left boasted a flourishing vegetable and herb garden surrounded by a well-kept lawn. The pungent aroma of sun-warmed sage, rosemary, and mint permeated the air. Violet, pink, and white clematis hung in great drooping clusters from a trellis framing the kitchen door.

Fionn wandered the few feet to the grass beyond the paving stones, and with a soft snort, began nibbling contentedly. Clyde took the horse's reins and patted the stallion. "Not yet, ye great brute."

Adaira rushed into the warm kitchen, bumping into her cousin, Aubry Ferguson. On her way out the door, Aubry jumped backward, jerking her skirts aside to avoid the swinging fish.

"Watch where you're going, Adaira," she snapped. Folding her arms across her chest, she scrutinized Adaira's attire and the fish dangling from her hand. She shook her auburn head. "You're utterly hopeless. Dressed like an urchin." She sniffed, wrinkling her nose. "And smelling like one, too."

Pushing her way past Adaira, Aubry flounced out the door, leaving it gaping open behind her. Aubry should talk. There was more to being a lady than dressing the part. She'd treated Yvette abominably from the day the other woman arrived at Craiglocky.

Adaira couldn't fathom what maggot had given Aubry the notion Ewan regarded her romantically. She'd been furious when Ewan had come home with a bride. Aubry tried to conceal her feelings behind false smiles, but she continued to harbor spite and jealousy toward Yvette.

Closing the door, Adaira sniffed in appreciation. Fresh bread and rolls cooled on a long table, and other marvelous smells tickled her nose: vanilla, lavender, and heather.

Sorcha must be making soap.

Adaira dangled the brown trout. They didn't smell half so lovely. "Brayan sent these."

Stirring a pot, Sorcha smiled and angled her head toward a counter.

"Ye can put them over there. Baked fish for dinner then,

aye? Will ye be havin' any, Miss Adaira? Mayhap ye fancy that nice fat one?" the cook teased, a knowing twinkle in her eyes.

Adaira laughed. "No, fat or not, I shan't, as you well know." She spread her hands, looking at her breeches and scrunching her nose. "Aubry is right. Look at me. I'm covered in fish slime."

Sorcha chuckled as she eyed Adaira up and down. "Ye'd best wash and change. I'm surprised ye even agreed to deliver them."

Adaira made quick work of washing away the odor. Then she grabbed an apple and a couple of carrots for Fionn from a basket atop the counter. After tucking them into her coat pocket, she helped herself to a pair of oat rolls off the table. She took a bite and grinned.

"Mmm, I do love your rolls, Sorcha."

"I'm no' surprised ye're ravenous. Ye dinna break yer fast this mornin'." Sorcha pushed the pot to the rear of the stove and eyed Adaira toe to top. "Ye want a bite of cheese and chicken to go with those?"

Adaira nodded. "If it wouldn't be too much trouble. Would you mind packing enough for Brayan too? Your oatcakes and Scotch pies are favorites of his."

"Aye." Sorcha beamed, patting her ample hips. "Ye be sure to eat some, too. Ye need some meat on yer bones, lass."

Adaira took another bite of the roll to hide her smile. Sorcha believed every woman should possess as generously rounded curves as her.

Sorcha was well-acquainted with Brayan's appetite and the amount of food necessary to fuel his muscular body. Adaira was counting on Sorcha providing enough food to feed a small army. That way, there'd be plenty for

Marquardt for a day or two. Adaira had no intention of starving the cur, though he deserved to go hungry.

She hurried to the stone steps beside the kitchen's enormous soot-edged fireplace. Tossing a glance over her shoulder, she asked, "Can you have the food ready in fifteen minutes? Oh, and some wine, too, please?"

Already busy slicing cheese, Sorcha didn't look up. "Aye, lass. And my shortbread. The lad does like shortbread."

Adaira wrinkled her brow. Had she given herself enough time?

She ticked off a mental list: Change. Pilfer one of Ewan's dueling pistols—thank God he was still in London. Gather the other supplies—blankets, buckets, matches, candles.

Taking the stairs two at a time, she bolted up the narrow stairwell. Were the keys to the cells still hanging from the peg in the stairway alcove? A chill surged over her. She'd not been in the dark maze below the castle for three—no— four years.

Gripping the cross at her throat, she determinedly stifled the memory, something she'd become adept at doing. *Never mind.* This must be done. She pressed her lips together, ignored her roiling belly, and sprinted up the remainder of the stairs.

Vengeance is the Lord's.

She tilted her chin, determined to disregard the voice whispering in her conscience. She'd see to it Yvette never had reason to fear Marquardt again.

～

Holding her breath, Adaira crept past the kitchen door. She hurried on silent feet along the back corridor. Her lungs burned in protest, but she didn't release the pent-up breath until she reached the entry to the lower levels.

Casting one last look over her shoulder, she opened the heavy door. She deftly nudged the bulky bundle onto the landing with her foot. With the two buckets' handles looped over one arm, she made quick work of lighting the lantern. Then, she shoved her way through the partially open doorway. Seldom used hinges squeaked and groaned in protest.

She swallowed.

Had no one opened it since—?

Grimacing, she laid a shaky hand across her knotted middle. Quite possibly not.

Adaira edged the thick wooden slab shut. It closed with a portentous *thunk*. One hand on the cold, stone wall for balance, she turned and peered into the blackness. The heavy air settled around her, its cool dampness thick and suffocating. For a moment, she couldn't breathe, and she closed her eyes, fighting to draw air into her lungs.

The lamp sputtered and hissed, and her eyes flew open. Her heart thudded loudly in her ears.

Please, don't go out.

The flickering stopped, and the weak flame leaped to life. The orangey-red fought against its glass constraints before yielding to the inevitable. Adaira's nose twitched at the acrid smell of burning oil.

She'd not be surprised if bats weren't hanging by their horrid little curled toes on the beams far above her head. She cast a hurried glance upward. *Nothing.* Thank God. Rats and mice she tolerated. But bats? No. Not since she'd hidden in a cave when she was eight and disturbed a colony of the little flying devils.

Her gaze raked the stairwell once more. Blast, but it was black as the Earl of Hell's waistcoat. There was a time when the darkness hadn't bothered her. Back then, she used to visit the lower chambers regularly. Well, truth to tell, she'd sneaked into them to avoid her lessons from the time she was twelve until four years ago.

She'd managed to turn a chamber near one of the outer doors into a rather comfortable sanctuary. Granted, a nasty fall hauling a skirted armchair down the narrow stairs had nearly broken her arm. The bruise had lasted a full month. She'd also stashed a small table, a discarded candelabrum, a straw tick and quilt for napping, and even a stack of books purloined from the library in her secret hideaway.

Only, it hadn't been entirely secret.

She'd learned that too late.

Adaira released a long, slow breath. She was wasting precious minutes. After hanging the lamp on a rusty hook beside the door, she adjusted the buckets. She bent and retrieved the bundle.

Holding the lamp aloft, she eyed the steep stairway. "Och, one false step, and I'll be tumbling head over arse."

She whispered a quick prayer and stepped off the landing. With infinite care, she descended the stairs, taking care to stay close to the fusty wall despite its numerous hairy-legged residents. A shudder rippled down her spine. Lord, how she loathed spiders.

As she stepped onto the dungeon floor, a nervous giggle escaped. It echoed throughout the network of passages before fading away.

She shone the light along the stones.

Where were the keys?

A thick maze of cobwebs covered the opening. Adaira placed the bundle and buckets on the floor. Patting her pockets, she searched for something to move the mass of dusty threads.

The carrots.

Wielding the longest one like a small dagger, she swirled it around the opening first, then inside the slot to collect the webs. A fuzzy brown spider skimmed across her hand and onto the carrot.

Yelping in alarm, she jumped away and heaved the vegetable against the opposite wall.

Adaira shuddered. Whether from the chill of the chamber or the fear she refused to yield to, she couldn't be certain.

What a ninny.

She often walked the woods alone at night with far more dangerous creatures than a few spiders and bats.

"You must do this for Yvette," Adaira scolded herself.

Gritting her teeth, she reached in and snatched the key ring. A wave of relief washed over her. She released a long hissing breath before she grabbed the bundle and buckets off the floor. Then, shoulders squared, she resolutely marched along the passageway. The cloying smells of stagnant air and damp earth encircled her.

Long since forgotten barrels and crates littered the sides of the passageways. Rustic metal brackets were positioned every few feet along the walls. When the torches glowed with flames, the bowels of the keep weren't nearly as ominous.

She'd not dally to light the torches today, however. She wanted to prop open the outer door exiting by the loch, one of two entrances undetectable from the outside. That would help expedite getting Marquardt inside. And she still had to return to the kitchen for the food Sorcha was packing.

Grandmother had shown Adaira the stone doors years

ago. She'd whispered of prisoners, enemy clan members, and even aristocracy smuggled in and out of the keep's bowels. A half-smile curved Adaira's mouth.

Grandmother was the bravest woman she'd ever known.

The occasional rustling of small feet as a rodent scurried ahead of Adaira didn't slow her pace. She was going to be late. Brayan would wait, of course, but that wasn't what worried her. No, it was the knowledge that Marquardt might very well be nearer the castle than she'd calculated.

She held the lamp higher and hurried down another passageway. Her steps faltered as she reached her former sanctuary, and she reflexively swallowed against the wad of fear lodged in her throat.

"Grandmother, I could use some of your courage right now," she whispered into the gloom.

As she stared into the cell, its door hanging wide open, time stood still. Everything appeared exactly as she remembered.

Exactly the way she'd left it four years ago.

Four

Riding low across Fionn's back, Adaira raced the stallion to the cottages. The bag of food slung across her shoulder, bumped against her spine in an annoying rhythm. The pounding tempo of his hooves matched her frantic heartbeat as she'd torn from the keep's lower levels several minutes ago.

Fear and memories surged to the forefront of her mind, and she swallowed, ineffectually trying to force both to subside. When she stood before the cell, she'd panicked—renewed horror overwhelming her.

She'd been terrified once more, her only thought, *escape.*

Dropping everything she'd brought for Marquardt, she sprinted away. Just like that horrific day the blacksmith's apprentice, Godwin Wallace, had attacked her. When she'd regained consciousness, she found her skirts shoved high on her thighs.

She'd flown from the dungeon then, too.

Today was the first time she'd returned.

She closed her eyes, trying to block the memory. Father,

Ewan, or one of her other Scot relatives would've killed Godwin. The man was as good as dead. Knowing that certainty, he'd fled Craiglocky after violating her, never to be seen or heard from again.

Except, Adaira had told no one of the assault. Humiliation and self-castigation muted her. She blamed herself for his attack. She shouldn't have been sneaking in and out of the dungeon. If she'd been in the schoolroom where she belonged, where her parents trusted her to be, she'd never have been accosted.

Thank God she'd fainted before he—

Gulping against the bile burning her throat, she closed her eyes.

She ran a trembling hand over her thigh. She'd begun wearing Dugall's castoff breeches that very day. He'd grown so fast that she had a stack of his barely worn garments in her wardrobe.

The old keep's burned-out shell came into sight, and she shook her head to wipe the haunting memories from her mind. Only the pressing need to keep Yvette safe could compel Adaira to go into the Craiglocky's lower levels again.

Reining in Fionn, she walked him to a grove of alders situated a short distance from the ruins. Peering around the clearing, she frowned.

Where was Brayan?

Perhaps he'd been delayed.

What excuse could he have given Marquardt for waylaying him at the cottages anyway? A discussion about the pleasures of trout fishing would no doubt have commenced.

Brayan and his fishing.

What would she do without him? He was a kind and

faithful friend despite his clumsy, sometimes maddening, attempts to win her affections.

Adaira dismounted and loosely knotted the horse's reins to a low-hanging branch. Rubbing Fionn's nose, she crooned, "I'll be back."

He nudged her pocket, and she grinned. "Smell those, do you?"

It was her love of horses that compelled her to plead with—well actually, it had been more begging and nagging than imploring—Father to learn about horse breeding. He'd objected it wasn't proper for a well-bred woman to know of such things.

Claptrap and balderdash, she'd argued. By whose measures?

Today, she owned over two-score of the sturdiest draught horses in Scotland. Her reputation for breeding horseflesh was growing. Fionn was an enormous Flemish stallion at eighteen-three hands. She'd bred him to carefully selected mares at Craiglocky. The mares had been chosen for their larger than average size, as well. He'd sired twenty foals.

Once Father and Ewan saw the unusual size and strength of the mild-tempered horses, they encouraged her venture further.

Adaira smiled. She'd gifted Father with a colt two years ago. Dand, a massive but gentle beast at eighteen hands, was Father's favorite horse.

Fionn prodded her with his nose again, as if to say, *I've been a polite chap long enough. Do hand over my treats.*

She chuckled. "Patience, my sweet friend."

Adaira pulled the apple and carrot from her vest pocket and extended both hands, the apple in one, the carrot in the other.

"Which do you prefer?"

Fionn wrapped his soft lips around the fruit balanced on her flattened palm.

"I'm not surprised, greedy beggar. You've always did have a sweet tooth." She dropped the carrot to the ground. He rolled his great brown eyes at her as he crunched the juicy apple.

"I'm already later than I told Brayan I'd be. You'll have to make do with the carrot yourself," she admonished.

Holding the riding crop between her knees, she slid the sack off her shoulder. The dueling pistol, swaddled in a pillowcase, lay beneath the food. After unwrapping the gun, she shoved the pillowslip into the thick bag. One she'd tied the top, she hung the sack on another branch. Fionn or the squirrels were sure to help themselves to the contents if she left the bag on the ground.

Adaira gripped the gun's smooth handle, balancing its weight in her hand. She'd never held a gun before. It was awkward and bulky, nothing like the svelte blades she usually wielded. The pistol wasn't loaded, but Marquardt wouldn't know that.

Was he a gambling man? Would he risk challenging her with a gun pointed at his heart?

With a shrug, she slipped the pistol in the waist of her breeches. Brayan would be there to help convince Marquardt to cooperate. If the lout resisted, she'd use her crop. Holding the whip before her, she removed the plaited leather casing, revealing a rapier-sharp blade.

Ah, now this, she knew how to use.

She smiled in smug satisfaction. One way or another, Marquardt would be residing in Craiglochy's dungeon today. After a quick pat to Fionn's shoulder, she darted down the path to the crofters' cottages.

Adaira emerged from the forest edging one side of the loch. A half-dozen abandoned huts dotted the landscape. Twigs, pine cones, and rotting thatching littered the ground around the dwellings. Anxious to find some relief from the sun glaring down on her bare head, she strode to what had once been the Brodies' cottage. Sweat trickled between her breasts and dampened the fabric beneath her arms.

She'd foregone her cap and jacket. Not merely because the temperature had mounted to an uncomfortable high, but because she needed to be able to move agilely.

Especially if Marquardt proved uncooperative.

She grinned, well-pleased with herself. Not likely with Brayan about. Marquardt wasn't a small man, but she'd no doubt which of them would be the victor if the men grappled. Brayan was an accomplished wrestler. She'd seen him lift more than one opponent, and in a few, quick moves, pin the man.

Adaira glanced behind her and puzzled her brow. Still no Brayan.

A wave of nerves coursed through her, settling in her stomach. Ducking beneath the cottage's drooping doorframe, she sighed as the coolness engulfed her. She wiped the perspiration from her upper lip with her forearm.

Marquardt must be nearing the cottages—unless he'd truly become lost. Or mayhap, out of consideration for the old mare, he was taking his time. The thought didn't sit well with Adaira. She preferred to believe he was vile to his foul core.

Stepping over piles of rotten straw and broken rocks from the collapsed roof and fireplace, Adaira made her way to the sagging window facing the path from Craigcutty. She'd rather not confront him alone. But she couldn't risk him reaching Craiglocky.

Patience gave way to irritation.

Where *was* Brayan?

He hadn't gone to the village and told her father what she was about, had he? She leaned out the window, and a piece of the rotten wood frame crumbled beneath her. She grabbed the sash to keep from falling, and a sliver impaled her finger. Swallowing an oath, she lifted the splinter-free, then wiped the droplets of blood on her vest.

No, Brayan wouldn't do that to her.

He still harbored hope she'd return his misplaced affection. The warmest sentiment she could muster for him was that of a bothersome older brother. One who teased and played pranks on her, but was there if she needed him. The notion of a *tendre* for him disquieted her, and she grimaced.

She could never set her cap for him. For anyone, for that matter.

With her gaze fixed on the clearing, Adaira rested against the dilapidated wall. As she often did, she ran the tips of her fingers the length of the crop's handle. The braided leather was worn smooth from thousands of strokes. She scanned the path and the trees before returning her attention to the trail once more.

She'd spent many hours traipsing in these woods and exploring the abandoned cottages and burnt ruins of the original castle. She'd enjoyed an equal number of hours riding Fionn across the heather-covered hills and meadows when she should've been studying Latin or learning new embroidery stitches.

She'd nearly died from the tedium of boring lessons and ladylike endeavors. Truth to tell, she rather enjoyed music, animal husbandry, archery, and fencing lessons. She'd begged for six months straight before Father agreed to the latter two, on the condition she commit herself to her other studies.

Heavy footfalls crunched outside the cottage reining in her musings.

Finally.

Brayan had arrived.

Her gaze still on the path—Marquardt should be here any moment—she smiled and said, "I'd begun to give up on you."

"Indeed?"

Mocking. Cryptic. Scornful.

Adaira whirled away from the window.

Marquardt stood illumed in the door's opening.

"*You!*"

She grasped the pistol as panic tripped an uneven staccato across her nerves. More than heat caused the sweat dripping between her breasts.

"Come now, don't feign surprise, Miss Ferguson." He bent his neck slightly to enter the cottage.

"How do you know my name?" Adaira searched behind him, vainly hoping Brayan would appear.

"Did you think I'd obediently toddle down the path you directed—no—insisted I take?" Like a predator with cornered prey, Marquardt crept forward.

Adaira searched his eyes, recoiling slightly at the cold fury glittering in their depths. Already touching the wall, she was unable to retreat further. She pressed flat against the rough surface as dread seized her. Terror squeezed her chest in a crushing grip.

His searing gaze lowered to the gun in her waistband. A humorless smile twisted his lips at the corners. "I'm sure you can understand my desire to make some inquiries after I discovered you weren't a lad."

With arrogant confidence, he strode forward a pair of steps.

Was he limping a bit?

"*You* made the assumption I was a boy."

"And you did nothing to correct me, did you?" His volatile gaze swept the room. "I cannot help but wonder why?"

Her stomach plummeted sickeningly when he eyed the gun once again.

Jesus, Mary, and Joseph. Where the bloody hell is Brayan?

She wouldn't have time to yank the pistol from her breeches and aim. She'd wager from the cynical skewing of Marquardt's mouth, the knave knew it.

Fine. Adaira would use her riding crop, then. With calm determination, she released her grip on the gun.

A fine sheen of sweat glistening on his face, he advanced a few more inches. "I assume you also knew horses were available."

After a paralyzing moment when Adaira couldn't exhale due to the fear hammering against her ribs, she released a measured breath. She raised her chin in defiance and refused to answer.

His piercing, indigo eyes skimmed her from her hair to her boots.

She scowled when his focus lingered for a moment on her hips and chest.

He lifted his disinterested glacial gaze to meet hers once more. "Which leads me to question why you deliberately deceived me?"

"*Deliberately?*" She asked, stalling.

She cast a swift glance beyond him. Brayan must've

decided he wanted no part in the abduction, not that she blamed him. Even she was having second thoughts.

What of Yvette, then? No, this must be done.

Her scheme could still work. True, capturing Marquardt would be more difficult to carry off. All right, a great deal more difficult, but she was confident she could do it.

He ran a finger across his damp upper lip. "I confess, the blame is partially mine. It's quite obvious to me now that you're a skinny female." He cocked a superior eyebrow. "Although your attire suggests otherwise. No doubt, you're a hoyden, to boot."

Everything he said was true, so why did his words rankle?

Adaira raised the crop and settled into a defensive stance. "I care even less about your opinion of me than I do the horse shite I stepped in earlier."

His dark eyebrows swooped together. "And she swears like a common harlot," he muttered. "A lack of Godly discipline and moral upbringing, to be sure."

Furrowing her forehead, she turned her mouth downward in displeasure. "Do you do that often? Talk to yourself?"

Wasn't that a sign of madness?

Ewan had hinted Marquardt was unbalanced.

He waved his hand languidly at a fly buzzing near his face. "Your parents failed to instill in you the qualities a lady of gentle breeding ought to possess."

"Och, you pompous, Sassenach cur." Fury bubbled up from her stomach, sluicing through her veins. She pointed the crop at him. "I don't care a trow's hairy bum what you think of me, but you'll not disparage my parents."

He swatted at the insect again. Even that movement

was performed with controlled precision. One crisp wave right and another crisp wave left. "They've done a shabby job of raising you so far, I'd say."

Adaira lunged and jabbed the whip in his direction, then danced a few steps backward. "You dare to speak to me of appropriate behavior?" She snorted in derision. "*You?* A known spy?"

His pupils dilated in surprise. Or was it irritation?

Thrust. Retreat.

"*You* who tried to attack Yvette and abduct her?"

Jab, jab. Retreat.

The last lunge brushed his arm.

Instantly Marquardt's demeanor changed. His face hardened into chiseled lines, and his body went rigid, his eyes narrowing to furious slits. "I've had enough of your confounded whip and false accusations."

Adaira faltered, and fear dried her mouth.

She'd only managed to tug the crop cover off a couple of inches before he was upon her. In one swift movement, he lunged for the whip. His hand met air, as she reared back and swung with all her might. The crop slashed across his left shoulder, the tip rendering a stinging slap to his jaw.

"You bloodthirsty termagant!" He gritted between his teeth as he dove and seized the crop, giving it a vicious yank.

She held on, both hands wrapped in a fierce grip about the casing. The concealed blade was her only means of getting Marquardt to the dungeon. The only means of keeping Yvette safe from this fiend.

My only means of protection.

The force of his jerk unbalanced her. With a soft cry, she stumbled and slipped on the stones littering the floor. With a cry, she fell, pulling Marquardt atop her.

Relinquishing her hold on the crop, she twisted and bucked. "Get off me."

She pounded at his head and shoulders with her fists as the pistol wedged between them, digging into her stomach. His weight pinned her to the floor, and waves of panic engulfed her.

He seized her hands in one of his before hurling the whip across the room. It thumped against the wall.

Adaira could scarcely breathe from his crushing weight molding her against him. Sharp-edged stone fragments bit into her buttocks and shoulders as she squirmed and wiggled, trying to dislodge him.

"Hold still," Marquardt ground between clenched teeth, reaching between them. Her shirt had worked itself loose from her breeches during their struggle, and his hand brushed against her abdomen.

Sheer terror gripped her.

Not again.

"No! Let go, you *bastart*." She tried to bite his ear.

Sensing her intent, he angled his dark head away. "Oh no, you don't, you hellion."

As he grasped the pistol, his fingers trailed across her bare skin once more. He tossed the gun aside, its clank against the stones, ringing of finality.

"No!"

Terrified, she fought harder. All reason had flown with the discarded whip and gun. Nothing but escaping mattered anymore. Kicking and twisting, she hauled one hand free, managing to rake Marquardt's neck with her nails. The room began to close in around her.

Again.

"Get. Off. Me!"

Struggling and screaming, she fought him with every ounce of strength she possessed.

He wrapped her hand in his crushing grip. Fury contorted his features, and he pressed the length of his body atop hers, rendering her helpless.

"I said," he growled, "hold still." He gave her a shake for emphasis.

Adaira's stared into his unyielding gaze.

The devil has blue eyes.

His nostrils flared like an enraged stallion. Could he smell her terror? Even amid this nightmare, she dimly registered his scent: Sweat. Sandalwood. Leather.

Her vision narrowed, and grayish spots floated before her eyes. The rumbling in her ears crescendoed to a deafening roar.

"Let me go. *Please.* Let me go." Adaira hated the pleading in her voice, but she couldn't endure ravishment again. She'd go utterly and completely mad.

Marquardt's maleness pressed against the juncture of her thighs, and she couldn't breathe.

"God, help me!" From a distance, she heard an unholy, animalistic cry.

Was that her?

Suddenly, Marquardt slumped atop her. Beneath his suffocating weight, she sucked in tiny, rasping puffs of air. Then, miraculously, blessedly, she was somehow free of him. Rolling to her side, she cast-up her accounts.

Just like before.

Five

daira slowly opened her eyes.

Brayan hunkered over her, lines of worry etching his broad face. Sliding his hands around her, he lifted her to a sitting position.

She trembled as reason returned.

"Addy, are ye all right?"

"I am now." She nodded and offered a tremulous smile. "Thank you."

Nausea still thrummed in her stomach, and terror yet choked her throat. The cottage was stifling, and she wiped her damp forehead on her sleeve. What she wouldn't give for a drink of water to wash the foul taste from her mouth.

Her attention fell on Marquardt.

He lay unconscious, face-down on the dirt floor. His once snowy white collar sported a large scarlet stain.

"Oh, my God!" Adaira gasped, crawling to him.

She untied his neckcloth with shaky fingers. Pressing the fabric to the gash at the base of his skull, she glared at Brayan. "What did you hit him with?"

"Yonder rock." He pointed to a fist-sized stone near

Marquardt's dark head. Brayan hunched his shoulders and clenched his hands, reminding Adaira of a bad-tempered bull. His voice lowered to a fierce snarl. "The *bastart* was attackin' ye!" Brayan gave Marquardt's leg a vicious kick. "He deserved it."

"Stop it." Never taking her attention off his enraged face, she canted her head toward Marquardt. "He's already hurt. How are we supposed to move him to the keep if you injure him worse?"

Brayan lifted his booted foot to kick Marquardt again.

"Don't, Brayan!" She scowled, appalled at his vehemence and hatred. "He might need a surgeon as it is."

Not that there was one to be found nearby.

"I can dispose of him for ye."

Adaira jerked her head up, her mouth gaping in disbelief. She searched Brayan's eyes and face.

Was he serious?

A peculiar glint shone in his eyes. Something hard, cold, and disturbing shimmered in their depths. Something she'd never seen in him before. Something she didn't think him capable of possessing.

Aye. He is absolutely serious.

The knowledge sent a vile jolt to her center. "Are you off your head?"

She lifted the cloth, bending to peer at Marquardt's wound. How badly was he hurt? She knew how to treat horses, but little about doctoring humans.

Ewan's cousin, Gregor, possessed that talent. Adaira couldn't very well ask him to take a gander at Marquardt's head. There'd be the devil to pay if her family caught wind of her scheme before Ewan returned. He'd do anything to protect Yvette. He would understand why Adaira had taken such rash measures.

She examined Marquardt's gash. The laceration was barely an inch long, and the bleeding had almost stopped. However, a good-sized knot had already begun to form. He'd have a headache nasty enough to match his foul temper when he awoke.

How soon would that be?

His chest rose and fell in an even rhythm, but he appeared pale under the light stubble covering his jaw. A vivid crimson streak marred his face where the crop had lashed him.

That, she regretted.

She'd seen the damage a whip could inflict on human flesh.

Craiglocky's blacksmith, Niall, bore the scars from a lashing as a youth. She winced every time she saw the four puckered stripes across his burly back. What kind of a barbarian did something so malicious to another human? Especially a child?

Even a man as evil as Marquardt didn't deserve such treatment.

Casting Brayan a quick sidelong glance, she pressed the bloodied cravat to Marquardt's wound again. "Abducting him to keep Yvette safe is sinful enough, but you're talking murder. I'll be praying for forgiveness for weeks as it is."

Ducking his head, Brayan offered a sheepish half-smile. "Och, I was but teasin' ye, lass."

The shallow remorse lacing his voice didn't convince her.

Marquardt stirred. Groaning, he lifted his head and half-opened his eyes. His chestnut hair fell back, revealing a three-inch scar near his hairline. Full of pained confusion, his gaze held hers for one brief moment before he sank into oblivion once more.

Her conscience twinged as a surge of pity engulfed her.

Stop it. He doesn't deserve your compassion.

He's a traitor, a defiler of women, and a suspected murderer. Each was a heinous crime. In her mind, all were wholly unforgivable and deserving of an eternity in hell.

Adaira inhaled deeply, gathering her equanimity. God was his judge, not her. She carefully levered to her feet, still slightly lightheaded. She swayed and stumbled a couple of unsteady steps.

Brayan was at her side in an instant. He gently took her arm in his huge hand and steadied her. "Are ye sure ye are fine?"

He brushed her cheek with his thumb. It smelled of fish. Of course, it did. He smiled. "Ye had a wee smudge of dirt on yer cheek."

His gentleness and the concern in his voice touched her. How he could switch from murderous fiend to considerate friend so quickly was astonishing—and a bit disconcerting.

"Aye, I am." Her gaze swept Marquardt. "We'd best move him to the keep while he's still unconscious."

Brayan nodded. "Do ye want me to tie his hands?"

He reached for the length of rope he'd crammed in his vest pocket earlier.

Eyeing Marquardt, she gave one sharp nod as she bent to retrieve her riding crop. "Aye, it's a good idea for his safety, as well as ours. He'll probably be furious when he awakens." Sliding the cover securely over the rapier, she pointed the crop at Marquardt. "You better search him for a weapon. I'm certain I felt a knife inside his coat. He's a traitor. He'll slit our throats, given a chance."

~

Roark forced his eyes to open the merest bit. Shadows, barely visible in the gloom, wavered on the rough ceiling. He shivered and reached to pull his coat closed. He was lying on his back with a light blanket draped atop him.

Where the hell am I?

He licked dry lips. Why did his mouth taste of dirt?

Surveying the small, dimly lit chamber, he spotted a torch flickering in a crude bracket on the stone wall across from his chamber. His gaze whipped past the bars barricading the cell door, then shot to them again.

Bars? Cell?

Enraged, he bolted upright and sucked in a gasp when agony speared his brain. Waves of pain cracked against the base of his skull. Groaning, he pressed a hand to his head and encountered a walnut-sized knot crusted with dried blood. Ignoring the insistent pounding in his head, he clambered to his feet. The dampness of the floor seeped through his stockings.

Dammit. Miss Ferguson had taken his boots, which meant she'd found the knife hidden inside the left one. He slipped a hand inside his coat. No knife there either.

Roark bolted to the door and gave it an angry shake.

Locked.

Bloody hell.

He was imprisoned. From the dankness and cold permeating the air around him, he'd wager he was in a dungeon.

No, not *a* dungeon. Craiglocky's dungeon. Though, how Miss Ferguson managed to move him here was an enigma. She was much too petite to lift him onto a horse or drag him here herself.

Someone had helped her then. That explained his throbbing head. Semi-conscious, he vaguely recalled a male voice in the cottage. Some bugger had landed him a fierce blow.

But why? What was Adaira Ferguson up to?

She'd sent him on the rabbit trail to the keep. She'd lied about the horses at the livery. And she'd imprisoned him in this cell, after muttering some drivel about spies and abducting Yvette.

Yvette was the main bloody reason he was here in the first place. She'd spent a small fortune in the past few weeks. The unusual expenditures had aroused his curiosity, one of the details prompting his visit.

The other was of greater concern—*on dit* of a scandal and a possible betrothal. Not that marriage to McTavish wouldn't be a brilliant match for her. The man was laird of this castle, the prosperous village, and the surrounding area. He bore the English title, Viscount Sethwick, as well.

No, Roark's unease arose from the vulgar whispers that had reached his ears. If Sethwick had compromised Yvette, Roark would call him out. He didn't relish the notion. The man's reputation with a blade was well-known. Nonetheless, family honor mandated pistols at dawn if Sethwick had compromised Yvette.

Roark's honor demanded it.

Between his degenerate of a father, his coquette of a wife, and his blackguard of a brother, Roark's and his family's reputations were unalterably tainted.

He would tolerate no further smears against either.

Glaring at the bars imprisoning him, he scowled. No one knew he was here besides that addled chit and her abettor.

He stomped back to the pallet, angrily kicking aside the neat pile of blankets stacked near the makeshift bed. Lowering himself to the straw tick, he let loose a string of oaths. He leaned against the stone wall, taking care not to disturb the bump on his head.

A rat scurrying along the corridor paused as if surprised to see him sitting there. It sniffed the air with its pointy nose, twitching its scraggly whiskers before scampering on its way.

No doubt to inform its hundreds of relatives.

Roark closed his eyes and drew in several deep breaths. He told himself over and over: *The walls are not closing in. The walls are not closing in.*

The pounding in his head finally subsided to a subtle thrum. The straw tick rustled as he stretched his legs before him, crossing them at the ankles.

The last thing he remembered was trying to control the frenzied virago wriggling beneath him. The chit had come at him with the whip, and he'd lost his sense of reason. He'd been taken aback at his immediate arousal when her soft curves pressed intimately against him. Especially given the circumstances. He wasn't in the habit of ravishing reluctant misses.

Adaira Ferguson's hysteria had been unnerving in its intensity. His face still stung where she'd clawed at his face. He touched his jaw, tracing the large welt raised there. Inching his fingers downward, he tentatively touched the scratches along his neck.

Never in his six and twenty years had Roark felt such a desire to paddle a backside until it was rosy. That would teach her a lesson.

No. He fisted his hands until the nails cut into his palms.

He'd *never* hit a woman. *Never.*

Not even his late wife, and by God, if ever a woman deserved a firm hand on her posterior, Delia had. She'd died within minutes of confessing the stillborn boy lying beside her, both of them ghastly pale against the sheets, wasn't Roark's.

There'd been no opportunity for retribution or emotion other than utter devastation. For the past two years, he'd resolutely transformed the desolation into bitter cynicism and rigid control.

The pitiful infant had been a by-blow of one of Delia's many indiscretions. She claimed she didn't know who the father was. Roark assumed she lied in that regard. She'd known he'd call the rake out. He was quite sure he knew who the infant's sire had been, too.

The Marquis of Hedonford.

A womanizing, gambling, debauched, opium addict.

After the funeral, standing beside the two mounds of fresh earth, Roark had vowed he would never again be enticed by a lovely face or luscious body.

His neighbor, Helene Winthrop, a voluptuous widow, possessed a healthy sexual appetite and was eager to accommodate him when he needed physical release. Or for that matter, when she had an itch she wanted scratched. Full breasted, pleasingly plump, she was all feminine suppleness and not the least bit shy about her carnal cravings. He'd enjoyed many an amorous late-night visit from Mrs. Winthrop via Cadbury's discreet back passages.

Theirs was an ideal arrangement. In her early thirties, and widowed for four years, she was perfectly content to remain unwed. Neither expected anything from the other except what an hour's company might provide. They had a perfect understanding.

Helene knew and accepted, thanks to his sire's perverse need for control, even after the old squeeze crab long lay dead in his cold grave, that Roark was obligated to marry well again. He must produce an heir by his second and thirtieth birthday, or his brother, Edgar, would inherit everything not entailed.

By God, Roark's next marriage would be an advantageous business arrangement with a biddable, mousy wife. Before exchanging vows with her, he'd have the surgeon examine her and verify her purity. Mayhap, he'd keep her confined at Cadbury Park. He would not be cuckolded again.

Pinching the bridge of his nose, he released a pent-up breath.

Hell and the devil.

He'd sworn he'd never again be subjected to the humiliation of the *haute ton* whispering behind his back as yet another scandal besmirched the earldom. Or, for that matter, ever succumb to a woman's wiles or trickery again.

He'd been successful until now. But Adaira Ferguson was unlike any woman he knew.

She was no lady, to be sure. Then again, Delia had been sorely lacking in that arena. Oh, his wife had been society's model of decorum and propriety. At least she'd played the part to perfection, publicly. But Delia's string of infidelities portrayed her true moral character.

He'd been an addlepate to trust her beautiful face and immaculate manners. The moment he looked away, she'd hitched her skirts and spread her thighs for every handsome rakehell who came sniffing around. And there'd been dozens.

"Adaira Ferguson, you bloody she-devil. When I get my hands on you—"

"You'll what?" She stepped into the torch's muted light and gave him a withering glare.

He stared pointedly at her slim hips. "I'll give you the thrashing you deserve."

Miss Ferguson laughed, a light, musical sound echoing against the rocky confines before fading into the vault's passageways. It grated along his nerves. Not the laugh itself, but that he'd noticed its melodic quality.

No, that it beguiled him. Enticed him.

She raised her hand and jingled the large ring strung with dangling keys. "Thrashing? Not likely. I possess the only keys to your cell."

She stood staring at him, confidently like a cat with a cornered mouse.

Closing his eyes for a moment, Roark raised a hand to his pounding head. Sweat beaded his brow. He hated being confined. Opening his eyes, he checked the growl of frustration rising to his lips.

Her expression shifted subtly as she pulled a brown vial from her vest pocket. She smiled, a graceful tilt of her full, rosy mouth and set the bottle on the floor outside his cell. "I brought you laudanum for your head."

He blinked several times rapidly.

He was acting like the young misses who batted their moon-eyes at him.

Egads, she was exquisite in the subtle lighting. How could Roark ever have believed her a boy?

What would she look like naked, candlelight caressing her ivory skin?

Good God, where did that come from?

In one fluid motion, he shoved to his feet.

She retreated a few steps.

Wise wench.

He *had* considered reaching between the battered bars and grabbing her.

"You do know,"—his gaze roved the tidy cell, noting the fat, black spider weaving a web in the corner above the cell's door before returning to her—"you could go to prison for a very long time for abducting and imprisoning a peer of the realm."

"Ah, but then you're not a peer, are you?" She smiled again, her row of neat white teeth shining bright in the shadowy corridor. "In fact, I do believe I've done the Crown a tremendous favor. I've apprehended a known spy."

Roark's gaze captured hers. Her eyes appeared black in the meager light, except for those unusual jewel-like gold specks reflecting in her irises. He fisted his hands, the only outward manifestation of his fury.

"That's twice you've accused me of being a traitor. If you were a man, I'd call you out for it."

She raised a perfectly arched brow and grinned. "Swords or pistols?"

Roark raked his gaze over her, shaking his head in disapproval. "Don't tell me you're trained in weaponry?"

"Of course." She struck a fencing pose. "*En garde.*"

He closed his eyes in a long blink. "Was there ever a more unladylike woman of refined breeding?"

Miss Ferguson dared to inch a bit closer. Bold as brass, she pointed at him and chuckled. "You did it again. Spoke your thoughts aloud. My, but that must be aggravating."

She leaned in a fraction, assessing him with her keen gaze. Her subtle fragrance wafted past his nostrils. Something with lilies? He resisted the urge to inhale deeply.

"Can you keep secrets at all, or does everything gush from your lips like milk from a teat?" she asked with a wry grin.

Mouth slack, Roark gawked at her. "Did she truly say teat? To a man, she doesn't know?"

Mischief danced in her eyes. "Yes, I did. *Teat.*"

Hounds teeth. He'd done it again, spoken his thoughts aloud. It only happened— *Dammit.* It hadn't happened since he was five years out of short pants.

She laughed, pointing at him. "You should see your face," she gasped, holding her stomach.

She's adorable when she laughs. Roark's gaze gravitated to her mouth. *And her mouth— perfect for kissing.*

Adorable? Kiss her?

What was wrong with him? He flexed his hands, itching to lay them on her tight *derrière.* "What an incorrigible, ill-mannered hellion. I'll see to it she is turned over my knee for the spanking she deserves."

Miss Ferguson flinched but met his eyes head on. "Rather difficult to do as you're locked behind bars."

Ah, hell.

His thoughts rolled off his tongue like a man well into his cups.

She had courage. Roark would allow her that. He stalked to the cell door.

Toying with her necklace, she retreated a step.

He ran a finger the length of one rusty bar. "But," he cast her a sideways glance and offered a benevolent smile, "I believe I know why you've made the error, and I'm in the mood to be charitable."

Like hell, I am. I'd say anything to be released from this accursed box.

"Indeed?" She eyed him from his stockinged feet to his mussed hair. Was that self-satisfaction curving her full peach-tinted lips?

He smiled widely, relishing what was to come. He'd wipe the smug expression from Adaira's face. The little vixen was about to receive what was due to her. He could all but hear her groveling an apology. He'd decide her retribution later. Right now, however, he must get out of this tomb.

He nodded and gave her his most charming, seductive smile.

Her eyes widened, and she swallowed, stumbling backward, her entranced gaze riveted on Roark's mouth.

He knew how he affected young misses. Older ones too. Hadn't they been throwing themselves at him since he'd come into his title? And even before? *Long before.* He was scarcely past three and ten when a buxom upstairs maid introduced him to the pleasures of the flesh.

He wasn't vain and knew he had nothing to do with his physical features. That was God's hand. However, the looking glass he looked into daily was objective. He was an attractive man. Even the scar on his forehead didn't deter the matchmaking mamas or their moon-eyed daughters.

"You've mistaken me for my younger brother," he announced with gratified confidence.

Edgar, the scapegrace. One of the reasons Roark was intent on restoring the family's honor was his brother's treasonous behavior.

Recovered, Miss Ferguson crossed her arms. The keys clanked against each other with her movement. She arched a brow and smirked. "Indeed?"

There it was again—unfettered cynicism.

"*Indeed.*" Roark swept her a mocking bow. "I'm Roark Vance Philippe Marquardt, the Earl of Clarendon."

Miss Ferguson's incandescent smile faltered. Fingering the topaz cross at her neck, a look of uncertainty flitted across her face. She studied him for a long assessing moment before a grin spread across her lovely features.

He stared, entranced once more.

She was exquisite when she smiled.

"*Of course*, you are," she quipped sarcastically, dipping a half curtsy. "And I'm the notorious Countess Lieven."

"No, you most assuredly are not. I'm acquainted with the countess." He narrowed his eyes, struggling to control his temper. This wasn't going at all as he'd anticipated. "I, however, *am* the Earl of Clarendon."

"Do you think I believe you're the earl?" She snickered. "No, in the hamlet you gave yourself away. You said you were *Mister* Marquardt."

"I sometimes leave off my title when traveling." Something he now regretted whole-heartedly.

She shook her head, sable hair billowing about her shoulders. It gave her an exotic appearance—an untamed beauty. Delia had been a perfectly coiffed, never-a-hair-out-of-place, blonde. At no time had Roark seen her hair loose, not even during their intimate encounters. Delia's hair had always been plaited into a tidy braid.

Miss Ferguson was the type of woman one took in full daylight, splayed atop his emerald-green counterpane, the sun and his hands stroking her naked, ivory limbs.

Ye Gods, man. Enough of the lurid imaginings.

He itched to put his hands on her all right, but it wasn't to enjoy the sweetness he'd no doubt her body could provide. He shifted uncomfortably, blood flooding his cock. He'd visit Helene immediately upon returning to his estate.

Miss Ferguson stood with her hands on her hips, tapping the toes of one foot. Pausing, she puzzled her forehead. What was she thinking? Her gaze dropped to the ground before she brought it up to meet his.

"Yvette hasn't mentioned anything about a visit from you."

"And she apprises *you* of all her business?" He wiped

his damp palms on his coat. He couldn't take much more of this. "Miss Ferguson, I'm warning you. Release me immediately. It will go far better for you if you do."

He'd go mad if she left him in here.

She cocked her head. "That, I cannot do."

Had he given himself away? Could she sense the terror building in him? Hear it in his voice? See it etched on his face and simmering in his eyes?

"I do hope you find your accommodations comfortable, *my lord*." Her emphasis on the last two words clearly revealed her skepticism. She looked past him. "There's food, wine, and wash water on the table."

He followed her gaze to a small table nestled in the corner. "What, no caviar? Truffles? Champagne?"

A stack of rat-chewed books was piled atop the table, along with a bulging linen cloth. A shabby, skirted armchair and two buckets were the only other items in the chamber.

He twisted his mouth into a sneer. "No tooth powder, shaving brush, or razor strap?"

"No," she scoffed. "You're not on holiday." She lifted the torch from its bracket before turning to leave.

"Wait! Are you taking the torch? What am I to do for light?" Could she hear the fear in his voice? He couldn't bear confinement, especially in the dark.

It conjured memories of his sire beating him nearly senseless and then locking him in a small wardrobe throughout the night. If Roark were fortunate, *Maman* would sneak in and let him out. That ceased when the old earl caught her one night.

He'd whipped her and Roark, too. From that day onward, his father kept the key so that she couldn't release Roark. She'd risked further thrashings by creeping in and staying beside the wardrobe until dawn. She sang to him, prayed with him, and told him in her soft French accent how brave and strong he was and how much she loved him.

Pain wrenched his gut. She and his stepfather had died this past December after attending a soiree. The doctor suspected food poisoning, although none of the other guests became ill. Not even Yvette or Edgar.

"I need the torch to return above stairs." Miss Ferguson's light brogue jerked him back to the present.

Roark stared in disbelief. She wouldn't dare leave him here in the dark. *Would she?* This far below ground, not an iota of natural light penetrated the blackness

She quirked a brow at him, then turned her mouth down in exasperation. "There are candles, a holder, and matches in the bundle."

With that, she abruptly spun away and hurried from his sight, taking the meager light with her.

Seizing the bars before him, Roark shook them, unleashing his rage on the unyielding iron. "Curse you, Adaira Ferguson. You cannot keep me locked in here! You will live to regret this, so help me God. When I am out of here, I'll send you to prison!"

Six

Adaira's heart knocked so violently against her ribs, the organ threatened to burst from its confines. *Prison.*

The notion terrified her.

She'd seen vengeance on Marquardt's striking face, burning in his wintry eyes. He'd bring charges. Not that she believed the cur's claim he was the earl. Even with his mahogany hair neatly combed, chiseled jaw shaved, his hunting jacket unsoiled, and his long, manicured fingers grime free—when he'd actually looked the part of an attractive nobleman—she'd not believed him.

Now, rumpled and unkempt, he resembled the cull she knew him to be.

She snorted. *Bah.* She lied to herself.

He was still deucedly attractive. Yet, there'd been something else deep within his gaze, something vulnerable that tore at Adaira, washing her in guilt and remorse.

She began to run, though she suspected she ran from her thoughts rather than Marquardt's outraged curses and threats echoing eerily in the keep's bowels.

Though he'd tried to hide it, she'd seen his dread. Her heart twinged with regret. How could she feel pity for *him?* He was the monster, not her. She was preventing him from wreaking more havoc.

Climbing the slick stairs, she muttered sourly to herself. "How dare Marquardt make *me* feel guilty, the sinful wretch? He brought this on himself. As God is my judge, I'm only doing this to protect Yvette until Ewan comes home."

Her conscience chastised her.

And to punish Marquardt in your quest for personal revenge.

In her bedchamber the next evening, Adaira slipped a new gown over her head and then angled her arms into its sleeves. She sighed, enjoying the sensation of the cherry silk softly caressing her body as it slid to her ankles. She smoothed the fabric over her hips, frowning at her lack of curves.

She'd inherited Grandmother's slender shape. Adaira grimaced as she turned this way and that before the full-length cheval mirror. It was no wonder Marquardt mistook her for a boy. She hadn't the height or the curvy hips and bosoms of her sisters. Isobel and Seonaid had Mother's womanly figure, all rounded softness and curves to tempt a man. Ewan and Dugall were tall and muscular.

Only she was petite and *willowy.*

That was what Father called her, a lissome willow. To her mind, the comparison wasn't altogether flattering. The singular benefit Adaira garnered from being slim was less male attention than her more curvaceous sisters.

That pleased her no end. "Maisey, please help me with the sash."

"Aye, Miss Adaira." The maid gathered the ends of the ribbons. "Are ye wantin' the gold silk slippers tonight?"

"Yes, and the ruby combs." Next to her topaz necklace, the combs were Adaira's most cherished possessions, excluding Fionn, of course. They'd been a gift from her parents for her eighteenth birthday.

Maisey finished tying the bow, then retrieved Adaira's embroidered slippers. Holding onto the maid's arm, Adaira tucked her feet into the shoes.

She only wore gowns for dinner and celebrations. Mother forbade her to wear breeches for either. Adaira knew her mother didn't understand her eldest daughter at all. She accepted Adaira's peculiarities just the same. Now and again, she'd see Mother studying her with a frown gathered between her fine brows as if she sought to see into her daughter's mind.

Adaira had been terrified Seonaid, with her gift of second sight, would do exactly that. It had been four years, and her sister had never hinted she knew anything about the attack. To Adaira's recollection, no one had ever been able to keep a significant secret from Seonaid. Her second sight made it nearly impossible.

And yet, Seonaid knew nothing of what had happened to Adaira.

With a dismissive roll of one shoulder, she straightened a turned-up ruffle on her sleeve. She shook her skirt, and the flounces shifted into place with a soft swish. It was a lovely gown. She'd have to thank her parents again. Truthfully, she enjoyed wearing the exquisite garments more than breeches. The gowns were the very latest fashions from

London, and she quite liked the fripperies, fallalls, and jewelry Mother and Father provided her.

Adaira had never explained to anyone why she'd started wearing breeches around the same time she'd started the horse breeding venture. Many had hinted it was because of her new unladylike interests or a rebellious phase she was going through. She never set them right on their inaccurate assumptions.

She couldn't, lest her secret was revealed.

As the maid twisted and pinned a curl in place, Adaira flinched. She wasn't fond of this part of her *toilette*, or the pulling and tugging involved in acquiring the latest Grecian coiffeur. Maisey was sensitive to criticism, so Adaira bore her maid's ministrations with good grace.

After fastening her pendant around her neck, Adaira scrutinized herself in the looking glass. The necklace's stones were an exact match to the golden ruffles edging her dress. The transformation in her appearance when she cast off boy's attire and donned the trappings of a lady of quality still unnerved her. She had no desire for men to find her attractive. She had all she could handle fighting off Brayan's unwanted advances.

Dabbing a drop of iris and lily perfume behind each ear, she inhaled the fragrance. There was no reason she shouldn't enjoy her favorite scent.

Thank God she'd been spared the ordeal of a coming out, although Ewan and Mother tried to persuade her to at least venture to London once. That was one advantage of being a Scot. There was no pressing need to present oneself at court before being put on display on the Marriage Mart, much like prime cattle at Tattersall's.

Donning a pair of ruby and topaz earrings, she smiled imagining the ridiculous scene. The marriageable misses assembled side-by-side, simpering and preening, as the eligible gentlemen lifted their quizzing glasses and inspected each eager damsel in turn.

I say, Lord Nincumpoop, Miss Birdwit appears delightfully healthy overall. Her breathing is normal, not the least exerted. Her eyes are clear, bright, and free of discharge. Her hair is thick and shiny, and her complexion is free of blemishes, too.

Except for that wart on the tip of her nose.

I suppose for five thousand pounds annually, I could be persuaded to overlook the blemish.

My dear Miss Rattlepate, may I have a look at your teeth?

Oh, would you look at that, Lord Falderal!

Not a tooth missing. Nice and straight, too, Though the garlic and onions you ate at dinner are lingering overlong, my dear. I advise nibbling a sprig of parsley.

What about her disposition?

Is she obedient and compliant?

Does she kick or strike? Nip or bite?

Adaira grinned. If only the misses had to hoist their skirts to permit the inspection of their hips, legs, and feet like her horses before she sold them. What a sight that would be.

Maisey stepped back, eyeing her handiwork. Her blue-gray eyes beamed with approval. "Miss Adaira, ye're right bonnie tonight."

"Thank you." Smiling, Adaira started for the door. "You needn't wait up for me."

Maisey's face puckered into a confused frown. "Again?" Her gaze sank to the floor. "Have I displeased ye in some way?"

Adaira hurried back to the crestfallen maid. Laying a

hand on Maisey's arm, Adaira reassured her. "No, not at all. It will be another late evening, and I know you're helping your sister with her bairn."

A look of relief settled on the maid's plump face. "Aye, he's still not sleeping through the night. The laddie wants the teat all the time."

An image of Marquardt popped into Adaira's mind when she'd said teat. She firmly shoved it aside. "He'll be a fine strapping lad like Niall, then." Adaira grinned. "Perhaps, he's another blacksmith in the making."

With another encouraging smile, she quit the room. Brayan would be at dinner tonight. Her smile faded. Although he'd made several attempts to see her, she'd managed to avoid him until this afternoon. Thank goodness Marquardt didn't know who'd helped her. She'd never reveal her accomplice, especially with Marquardt's continued threats of imprisonment.

Unfortunately, Ewan had yet to return home. Two days she'd dealt with that lout in the dungeon. Days of Marquardt ranting about her inadequacies as a gentle-bred woman. Days of doubting her ill-conceived decision to abduct and imprison him. Days of allowing her imagination to run wild about prison.

The horrors of Newgate's conditions were infamous. Would Marquardt have the power to demand her imprisonment there? Even more alarming was an unbidden thought yesterday morning, which sent her head spinning.

Have I committed an offense punishable by hanging?

Roark prowled his cell. Ten irate paces to the wall. Ten fuming paces back. The lone candle flickered but valiantly continued to burn despite being scarcely more than a nub.

His last one.

The weak flame cast meandering shadows across the rustic walls. On a stone above the table, he'd discovered one hundred and seventeen etched marks. Some pitiable sot had spent almost four months locked in this cell.

What time was it?

Miss Ferguson promised to return after dinner.

Where was she?

He shot a glance to the candle before returning his gaze to the sooty darkness beyond his cell. At most, it would burn another hour.

He tried to conserve the tapers. His fear of the dark, particularly the inkiness caused by being a good twenty feet beneath the keep, had him burning a light constantly. Roark wrinkled his nose. They stunk too, worse than he did. Likely they were made of mutton fat. He sniffed. The whole place reeked of mildew and dank, musty dampness.

Sleep had eluded him. He'd only been able to doze off by repeating in his head the scriptures *Maman* had recited to him or the lullabies she'd sung in French. They'd not brought him much comfort. Despite his vow to never strike a woman, daydreams of paddling Miss Ferguson's backside brought him a great deal of satisfaction.

When he did nod off, the squeaks and squeals of rats and mice fighting over the remnants of his meal woke him. He'd taken to resting with his food tucked near him, after throwing crumbs or leftovers outside the cell. Still, the more brazen of the black-eyed rodents had ventured within.

A shudder scuttled up his spine. He'd dozed off a bit ago and awoke with a grayish-brown rat the size of his three-legged cat, Achilles, perched on his chest, grooming itself.

Instead of scampering off, the rodent had reared onto its haunches and wiped at his nose and ears with his front paws. Grizzled whiskers twitching, the bugger stared at Roark with his black-button eyes.

Then casually, as if it were an everyday occurrence to bathe on a human, the scraggy rat had ambled across Roark's abdomen and down the length of his leg. After giving him a cursory look, the little beast hopped onto the pallet and scampered from the cell.

Roark had remained stock-still throughout. He hadn't a desire to be bitten by the daring rat or the fleas it no doubt hosted. In the medical books he'd studied, he'd read of numerous incidences of humans contracting typhus, cholera, and the plague due to exposure or bites by infected vermin.

Another black mark against Miss Adaira Ferguson.

No doubt, she hadn't considered the dangers of close association with rats. Likely, the addlepate was unaware of the hazards, not that she'd care. She was obsessed. No matter how many times he told her she had the wrong man, she adamantly insisted he was Edgar and, therefore, posed a risk to Yvette.

Roark cocked his head.

Were those muffled footsteps in the distance? She was coming—at last, thank the divine powers. And none too soon, either. The candle would last scant minutes more.

The glow announcing her progress grew in size and intensity as Miss Ferguson neared, moving rapidly. Where was the familiar click of her boot heels?

Then, she was there.

Roark gaped awestruck at the vision before him. Her coffee-colored hair piled into an intricate Grecian knot atop her head displayed her slender ivory neck exquisitely. The deep scarlet gown clung to her slim figure, and the jewels in her hair, earlobes, and around her neck sparkled in the lantern's light.

Petite perfection.

He glimpsed the creamy swell of her bosom as she struggled to slide on a slipper. Her subtle perfume filled the air, and desire speared him. His groin tightened involuntarily

Blister and damn.

Roark cursed inwardly at his body's betrayal. Adaira Ferguson was the last woman on earth he wanted to be attracted to.

Seven

Halfway through the after-dinner entertainment, Adaira pleaded a fierce headache. She promised to return as soon as she took some powders. The moment the drawing room was out of view, she rucked her skirts to her knees. She sprinted upstairs to fetch the candles, food, and other supplies she'd hidden in her chamber.

Tiptoeing back downstairs, she peeked into the great hall. It was deserted, except for Brayan. He took a long drink from a silver flask before snatching a confection from a plate atop the sideboard. He stuffed the whole pastry into his mouth, and a dab of clotted cream lingered at the corner of his lips.

"Brayan, whatever are you doing here?"

He grinned helping himself to another pastry. "I excused myself to use the necessary. I couldna resist helpin' myself to a few more of Sorcha's pasties."

Adaira hurried to the cabinet and retrieved a half-full bottle of wine.

Should she also take another?

No, she'd plenty to carry already. As she snapped the cupboard closed, the cork popped off the bottle, and the stopper rolled across the floor. "Dash it all! I don't have time for this."

Wiping his mouth with the back of his hand, Brayan stopped the cork with his shoe. He swayed the merest bit and whispered, "Do ye need help carryin' supplies to yer prisoner?"

He winked conspiratorially.

"No, Brayan. I only told you I was venturing below so you could cover for me if I'm delayed in returning."

He set the flask on the sideboard before bending to retrieve the stopper. His kilt tilted dangerously high, revealing whisky brown hair on his muscled thighs.

Adaira quickly averted her gaze, something every Scotswoman was accustomed to doing. She'd seen a goodly number of men's buttocks over the years, and on several uncomfortable occasions, other manly attributes as well.

She couldn't, for the life of her, understand their pride in such a peculiar looking appendage. To have to walk about with that *thing* dangling about, swinging back-and-forth—

Well, it had to be most annoying and cumbersome. Especially the larger ones when a man engaged in physical activities like wrestling. Whatever had the Good Lord been thinking?

Thank God she was a woman.

"Here ye are." Brayan reached for the wine bottle. He pressed the plug firmly into the top before handing it to her. He took another long draught of whisky. After replacing the cap, he tucked the flask into his coat.

"Thank you." Adaira speared a worried glance toward the entrance. "You'd best hurry back to the others. I'll return as quickly as I can."

Once she reached the lower levels, she all but ran the entire way to Marquardt. She'd no doubt her slippers were ruined, but there wasn't time to change them. Her family expected her to rejoin them straightaway.

Just as she reached his cell, one shoe slid off her heel. "Confounded slipper."

Breathless and hopping awkwardly, she tried to shove her foot back inside. A difficult task with a bulky sack wedged beneath her other arm and a lantern hanging from her hand.

"You're late," Marquardt snapped, his gaze riveted on her chest, and a scowl distorting his handsome face.

She managed, at last, to tug the silk edge over her heel. She straightened and leveled him with an exasperated glower.

"You needn't sulk. I came as soon as I was able." Adaira resisted the urge to yank her bodice higher.

She was daft for wearing this gown tonight. She'd known she'd have to venture below the keep. No doubt, the cur had enjoyed a generous view of her breasts while she struggled to put on the slipper.

Her nipples puckered at the thought.

Blasted, traitorous body.

Her reaction was due to the dungeon's coolness, not his heated gaze on her flesh. *You lie,* whispered an annoying little voice in her head.

Adaira couldn't deny Marquardt was disturbingly attractive. She knew him to be a scoundrel, yet every time he looked at her, something in his eyes caused a peculiar physical reaction. One she refused to examine. The tingling ache in her breasts and lower, *much lower,* was most irregular. She'd no romantic interest in any man, least of all him.

He reached through the bars. "The candle's nearly burned out."

Adaira glanced beyond him to the table where the stub flickered and sputtered. *Gads*, but the man went through the tapers. What did he do, burn them at night?

Did he never sleep?

From his haggard appearance, she'd wager not a whole lot.

A mere foot separated them, and she scrutinized him for a long moment. Dark stubble shadowed his jaw, giving him a rakish, pirate-like appearance. The mark her crop left had faded to a bruised ribbon. Bluish circles rimmed his eyes.

She'd never seen eyes his shade of blue before. The color of sun-bleached hydrangea blossoms rimmed in cobalt with silvery flecks embedded in them. When he was angry, they darkened to midnight. An icy shiver chased across her bare arms and shoulders at his unblinking glare.

After hanging the lantern on a hook beside the door, she turned her attention to the bundle. Opening the coarse sack, she rummaged inside. She paused and looked at Marquardt, then stared pointedly at the mussed pallet.

He knew the routine.

She wouldn't budge until he was seated across the cell.

"Insufferable shrew." He stomped to the makeshift bed. He sat, lolling against the wall, his forearm resting on his bent knee.

Adaira squatted, her gown billowing about her ankles. After setting the pistol on the ground beside her, she removed the candles. With one eye on him, she retrieved the gun before approaching the cell. She set the candles a couple of inches beyond the door.

"I brought you some tooth powder and a brush."

She placed them alongside the candles. She swiftly laid

out the other items: two large flasks of water, the bottle of wine, a basket of food, along with a washcloth and a bar of spicy soap she'd pilfered from Ewan's bathing chamber.

In one swift, agile motion, Marquardt angled to his feet. Adaira withdrew several steps as he stalked to the door. Smirking, he seized the candles. He strode to the table, and using the flame from the nearly extinct taper, he lit another. Its amber flame sprang to incandescent life.

Securing the new one in place, he cast her a sidelong glance. "Might I have a lamp instead?"

"Do you take me for a dimwit? A lamp won't pass through these bars." She fluttered her fingers at the iron rods. "Once I opened the door, you'd be on me like filth on a hog."

Hands on his lean hips, he heaved a gusty sigh. "How long do you intend to keep me imprisoned?"

She eyed him. Even disheveled and in stockinged feet, he exuded confidence and strange charismatic power.

His well-formed lips tightened when she didn't answer. "I assure you, the longer I'm kept locked in this hellhole, the harsher my retribution will be."

With nary a word of thanks, he gathered the food from the basket and, after depositing it on the table, collected the rest of the goods she'd brought.

The entire time, she kept well beyond his reach. She also kept the pistol leveled at him. He gave it a cursory glance. Did he suspect it wasn't loaded? He appeared more cynical than alarmed when she'd pointed the gun at him.

"I..." Adaira clamped her mouth shut so hard, her back teeth ached. She regarded him for a long moment.

His features were unyielding. He might as well know the truth.

With a slight shrug, she said, "I shan't be letting you out. Ewan will."

Marquardt stiffened. He slowly straightened, his gaze riveted on her. "Sethwick?"

Scowling, he cast a swift glance upward as if he thought to see Ewan through the ceiling. A corded vein in Marquardt's throat stood out beneath her scratches.

"He knows I'm caged here? Does your father also know?" Marquardt ground through clinched teeth. He clenched and unclenched his hands.

Adaira had no doubt he itched to hit her. It came as no surprise. Striking a woman was child's play to a man who'd attack women, commit murder, and betray his country.

After several seconds in which Marquardt visibly struggled for control, his expression softened, and he relaxed. He shook his head. A strand of wavy hair fell across his forehead. "I don't believe you. You see, I know Sethwick well."

Selecting an apple from the store of food she'd brought, he took a bite and ambled across the cell to stand before the door. "*His* honor wouldn't permit it."

Honor. Something Marquardt made perfectly clear she lacked. What did he know of honor? She glared at him. "No, I mean, yes, Ewan's an honorable man. But no, he doesn't know you're here. Father isn't aware, either."

A barely discernible noise sounded from somewhere in the dungeon. A rat? Frowning, she glanced over her shoulder and nervously fingered the cross at her neck. Nothing but shadows shrouded the passageway.

"Pray, tell me, Miss Ferguson, why, if he doesn't know I'm here, will he be the one to release me?" Marquardt enunciated each word as if speaking to a simpleton.

Another noise echoed. No doubt about it. Something or someone was moving about the keep's lower levels.

How far away?

Adaira hoped it was a rodent or a weasel.

Marquardt heard the sound, too. He suddenly straightened to peer past her. His frigid gaze dipped to hers, then skipped beyond her once more. He dared a satisfied grin. "Halloo," he hollered. "Is anyone there? I'm the Earl of Clarendon, and I'm being held prisoner."

She shook her head, sending him a contemptuous scowl. "Stop shouting, you dolt. It's but a weasel or a stoat, perhaps even a squirrel. They come in through the drains or gaps where a stone's gone missing in the wall."

She motioned with the pistol for him to move away from the door once more. "I'm surprised none have visited you as yet. As for Ewan, he's away in London, just now."

With what could only be described as a derisive grunt, Marquardt obliged her and sauntered away from the door. He rested against the far wall, ankles crossed, crunching on the apple.

A muffled thud, as if someone had bumped into something, echoed through the lower chambers.

He perked up. "That was no pest."

Adaira whirled to peer into the gloom.

"I say, can you hear me?" he shouted. "I'm locked in a cell."

She spun back around.

He'd moved to the door, his hands fisted around the bars. *Drat it.* She was losing control of the situation. His presence mustn't be known to anyone other than Brayan yet.

She bent to retrieve the sack. No doubt, Brayan had come looking for her at one of her parents' behest. Marquardt absolutely must not see him for he was well into his cups, and Brayan would boast he'd helped lock the man up. From the sound of the crashing about, he'd sampled the flask a good deal more and was utterly bosky.

"Blast and da—" She stopped as Marquardt's eyebrows flew to his hairline in obvious disapproval. Lowering her voice, she hurried onward. "Ewan's expected back any day. When he returns, I'll tell him I apprehended you. He can do with you what he wants. I'm quite sure it will involve the authorities."

"Apprehended?" He shook his head. "You're still sticking to the absurd notion that I'm Edgar?"

He tossed the apple core between the bars. It bounced before rolling to a stop barely three feet beyond her. A rat promptly appeared, scrambling to snatch the core in his pointed, yellow teeth. The little beast raced down the passageway with two other rodents squeaking their outrage in its wake.

Marquardt had done that on purpose, the lout.

What did he expect her to do?

Scream and swoon?

The women whose company he typically kept, no doubt, would have done. It was expected of delicate, well-bred young ladies.

Another mark against her lack of social graces.

She lifted a shoulder. What did she care what he thought of her? *He* was no saint. Ironic that such a despicable knave as he was concerned with society's expectations.

She draped the sack over her arm.

"Leaving so soon?" He arched a cynical brow at her while quirking the corners of his mouth in disdain.

"I must return above stairs."

And stop Brayan—please, God, let that be who's causing the racket—from reaching the cell.

"It's a wonder no one has become suspicious of your sneaking about. Tell me, why does your negligent family take such little interest in you? Are you so irredeemable they truly don't care?"

He accused her of being irredeemable?

Pompous prig.

Adaira faced him. "You know nothing of me, Mr. Marquardt. Believe what you will. I truly don't care that someone of your ilk has a low opinion of me."

She took a step closer and aimed the pistol straight at his heart. "But, hear me, and hear me well, you...you horse's arse. Say another word against my family, and I'll leave you to starve here in this," she swept the pistol in an arc, "pit until Ewan returns."

Seemingly unperturbed, Marquardt unwrapped a serviette holding oat rolls. Palming one, he crossed to the door and lounged against the bars with one shoulder. His gaze resting on the gun, he took a bite of the roll.

Cocking his head, he curved his lips into a sensual smile.

Adaira's toes curled in her slippers, and bumps covered her skin from her forearms to her shoulders. Her traitorous nipples hardened once more. She had the oddest urge to press her thighs together, *tightly*, to still the strange fluttering at their apex.

She squeezed her eyes shut.

It was the cold. The dampness. Nerves. Worry. Fright. Hunger.

Hunger?

"I'll admit, properly attired, you're not unbecoming," Marquardt murmured.

Her eyes flew open.

His gaze made a visual journey over her. "I'd never have

believed you were a beauty beneath that boy's garb. One has to wonder why you go to such lengths to hide your womanly assets. Though, in truth, I prefer a fuller bosom and more curvaceous hips to warm my bed."

Adaira stiffened.

He was speaking his thoughts again, and his words were more on spot then she cared for him to know. Faith, didn't the man hear himself? Her threat to abandon him hadn't appeared to disquiet him in the least. He stood there, munching the roll as if he hadn't a care in the world. His gaze brimmed with cynicism and something else.

That unnerved her more than his cutting remarks or blatant hostility.

She deliberately relaxed and affected a nonchalance she didn't feel. Placing the gun inside the bag, she knotted the end. Visualizing Marquardt trussed like a goose, she tried to decide on a fitting punishment.

Mayhap pouring honey over him and inviting a colony of ants to a picnic. Or tarring and feathering the twiddle-poop and parading him about Craigcutty, still bound like a goose.

Yes, that would do nicely. With that image firmly set in Adaira's mind, she met his indolent gaze straight on.

She shook her head in exasperation. "I'm not hiding my womanly assets, as you crudely put it."

She was, but she'd eat worms before she admitted it to him.

"And hell would bloody well freeze over before you ever found me warming *your* bed." *Or, any man's, for that matter.* "I'd sooner sleep with an adder."

A sardonic grin twisted his mouth as his hooded gaze hovered over her breasts. "Oh, there'd be *something* wiggling about the sheets."

Heat scorched her face. How dare Marquardt make such a vulgar innuendo? Was he raised in a cow-byre? Gentlemen simply didn't speak of such things. Ever.

Ninny, he's no gentleman, and he doesn't know he revealed his thoughts again.

Adaira laughed softly before turning the tables on him. "That must be rather embarrassing, blurting your thoughts aloud."

She couldn't keep the mockery from her voice.

His nostrils flared, and his eyes narrowed to slits.

"Egads." She pointed at Marquardt. "It's a good thing you're not an agent for the Corps like Ewan. You'd be unable to keep state secrets and spill all sorts of confidences."

His lips firmed. He squashed the roll in his hand into a lump of dough.

Oh, that had set up his bristles.

"Not nearly as maddening as being locked in a cage by a foul-mouthed hoyden." Vehemence, sharp as thorns, laced his voice.

"Blame me all you wish, Mr. Marquardt, but your depraved actions have landed you here." She snatched the lantern from the hook, then turned and ran down the corridor. She had to stop whoever was below before they reached Marquardt's cell.

Eight

"Addy? Addeey? Where are yeee, lasssh?"

Yes, definitely Brayan, and most assuredly, ape-drunk by the sound of his slurred speech. The yoke of guilt and regret for involving him in her scheme weighed upon Adaira. Marquardt couldn't see him, but she had no doubt the fiend would also exact his full vengeance on Brayan.

She'd only known Marquardt for two days. Yet, she was certain of one thing. Mercy was not a virtue of his. He'd threatened her each time she'd ventured below. Not that she blamed him. She'd be furious, too, if someone confined her and took away her freedom. She knew full well the horror of being controlled and held powerless by another.

A shiver slithered the length of her spine. She wrapped her arms around her shoulders. There was a remote chance —very remote—she kept telling herself that he *was* the earl.

God help her if that proved true.

She swallowed against the lump of fear wedged at the back of her throat. Yvette seldom spoke of her stepbrothers. Adaira knew both had dark hair and blue eyes, but little else regarding them. She scrunched her brow. Had Yvette ever mentioned anything that would positively identify either man?

Rushing around the corner, Adaira plowed full-on into Brayan's broad chest. "Oomph!"

He staggered backward, one muscled arm wrapped around her and lifting her off the floor.

"Let loose, you great oaf!" She shoved against him. "I cannot breathe."

Gads, but he was strong.

He released her, and air rushed into her lungs.

Rubbing her side, certain she'd sport a large bruise in an hour, she leaned toward him and sniffed. She crinkled her nose. He reeked of whisky.

"Blister it, Brayan, are you touched in the head? Why are you down here?" She grabbed his arm and started towing him in the direction from whence he'd come. "Did you take care to make sure no one followed you?"

"Of coursssh. Yer mother was ashkin' after ye." He tripped and swayed unsteadily.

Adaira tightened her grip on his arm. Her fingers barely went halfway round his massive bicep.

"I tol' 'er one of yer mares was due to foal." He sniffed and wiped his nose with the back of his hand. "An' ye'd probably los' track of the time when ye'd gone to check on 'er."

Stopping, Adaira smiled at him. "That was brilliant! Vala is due soon."

Brayan beamed at her, a lopsided grin on his face.

"Now," Adaira said, hauling him along, "I shan't have to explain my ruined slippers. We need to hurry, though. Let's use the other door and circle around to the stables. We'll have to enter the keep through the gatehouse, but that shouldn't raise any suspicions."

He hiccuped. "Nae, it shouldna."

She gave him a quick hug. "What would I do without you, Brayan?"

"Addy...?"

The seductive timbre of his voice alerted her, and she nearly groaned aloud.

Drat, not now. *Not ever.*

She couldn't let him declare himself, especially when he was in his cups. She didn't want to break his heart. Why couldn't he simply be satisfied to remain friends?

"Come." She grabbed his hand. "This way. Hold your lantern aloft, will you? It will be much easier to see our way."

Jabbering on, she didn't allow him an opportunity to say a word as she wended her way through the maze of passages.

He lumbered along beside her, weaving from side-to-side.

How much had he drunk, the fool?

She glanced at Brayan. "Mother will be miffed."

He puckered his face in concentration as he strove to place one big foot in front of the other without toppling over.

"I told her I was going to take headache powders and return at once. Of course, knowing my penchant for horses, especially the foals, she'll forgive me." Adaira hustled him along another corridor. "Here we are. Help me with the door, please."

"Aye," he said.

With a powerful yank, he forced open the stone door. It grated across the floor, sending shivers the length of her spine. Warm air swept across her, and given the dungeon's penetrating chill, she welcomed it.

The perfume of nearby roses wafted into the entrance. As she whisked through the doorway, her gown caught on a thorn, and Adaira stifled an oath. Before she could detach the material, Brayan plowed into her from behind. She stumbled and nearly fell. The delicate fabric tore, and a good length of scarlet cloth remained on the bush.

"Oh rot, this is a new gown, too!" She bent to inspect the damage and huffed, "It's ruined."

"Ye dinna need fancy gowns, Addeey. Mother always says, 'A preddy face suits the dishcloth.' Ye're so bonnie, it disna madder what ye wear." He bashfully ducked his head.

Jaw slack, Adaira gaped.

Was he actually blushing?

Impossible to tell for certain even with the two lanterns. Blast, he was truly trying to court her. That explained why he was in his cups—to bolster his courage.

He waggled his eyebrows. "I like ye in breeches myself." A silly grin on his face, he stared at her hips.

Oh, this was outside of enough. She'd speak to him when he was sober, make it perfectly clear, once and for all, she harbored no romantic feelings for him.

However, there was a fetching lass in the village who'd welcome his attentions. More than once, Adaira had seen Megan peeping at Brayan from beneath her lashes and giggling behind her hand.

Yes, she'd better play matchmaker. And soon.

She pointed to the door. "You close the door, and I'll douse my light. We don't need both of the lanterns." She blew out the flame. "We'd best hurry—"

Suddenly, Brayan gripped her shoulders. Before she had a chance to utter a squeak in protest, he mashed his wet, whisky-tainted lips against hers. The coarse stubble of his beard scratched her face as he tried to shove his tongue between her firmly clamped lips.

Wrenching free, Adaira slapped him. Hard. She staggered backward several steps, holding her stinging hand against her middle. "Ye'll not be taking liberties with me, Brayan McVey, ye great drunken sot!"

Her voice wavered with fury.

She wiped her mouth with the back of her hand as a shudder rippled through her. *Disgusting.*

Throwing his head back, he laughed.

The sound lodged in the pit of her stomach.

"Aye, lass, I shall." He tilted his head toward the door. "If ye be wantin' me to keep yer secret."

With that pronouncement, he dug a flask from his pocket and stumbled away.

Adaira wasn't sure how long she stood staring after Brayan. Except that it was long after his enormous form wobbled from sight, and his drunken singing faded into silence. An owl's hooting roused her from her stupor. With a great deal of grunting and swearing, she managed to shove the keep's door closed.

She cast a glance skyward. The full moon shone nearly as bright as dawn's violet-gray light. A hot tear spilled from the corner of one eye and trailed over her cheek. She rubbed it away, refusing to cry. She loathed waterworks. Besides, this mess was entirely her making.

Yes, but Brayan....

A shaky huff escaped her. She'd never have believed him capable of such treachery.

Mentally shaking herself, Adaira set a course for the stables. She still needed to check on Vala. Though the mare wasn't expected to foal until next week, foaling a fortnight early or late wasn't uncommon. In any event, it wouldn't hurt to make a showing in the stable in case anyone questioned her whereabouts later.

What hour was it anyway?

She'd not descended into the keep's belly until a quarter to ten. She raised her face to the heavens once more. Thousands of stars cheerily blinked back at her. The moon was just right of straight overhead. It was well past eleven o'clock—closer to midnight, actually.

The grooms were already abed, then.

A thought riveted her in her tracks, and a wide smile bent her mouth.

Brayan's threat held no merit.

Once Ewan was home, the entire castle would know she'd abducted Marquardt. They'd also know why. She'd be vindicated and absolved of all blame.

Her grin faded as quickly as it had appeared.

Unless, of course, she did, indeed, have the wrong brother.

God, help me.

Nine

Adaira cautiously entered the hall a bit past noon two days later. She'd dressed in her comfortable buckskin breeches, a white shirt tucked into the waistband, and a leather vest secured across her chest.

Since the night before last, when Brayan had threatened her, she'd stayed sequestered in her room. The day afterward, she'd claimed to be indisposed. She hadn't even gone to the lower levels to check on Marquardt. He had plenty of candles and food. He might be starved for company besides rats and other pests, but he wouldn't go hungry.

Unless, the vermin invaded his rations.

Blast, why hadn't she considered that before?

She should've provided him with a storage container of some sort. However, that would've meant opening the door to his cell, and the archangel Michael himself couldn't have persuaded her to do that. If only there'd been shackles attached to the walls.

Moving farther into the hall, she released a pent-up breath. Only Mother and Isobel were present. They sat at a smaller table placed before the hall's gargantuan unlit fireplace. Mother's midnight tresses and Isobel's caramel-tinted curls were bent close together as they read a letter her mother held.

Adaira released a sigh of relief. At least she didn't have to deal with Aubry.

Adaira had never been particularly fond of her female cousin, unlike Callum, Aubry's brother, who was well-liked by all. They had come to live at Craiglocky ten years ago after their parents were lost at sea.

Since Ewan threatened her with banishment for her horrid treatment of Yvette, Aubry had been rather scarce. Although Aubry had begged Yvette for forgiveness, Adaira didn't trust her surly cousin.

Mother and Isobel glanced up at Adaira's entrance. Duplicate pairs of aquamarine eyes framed by thick charcoal lashes greeted her. Mother smiled a warm welcome. The corners of her eyes crinkled, the faint lines the only indication she was old enough to be the mother of a man seven and twenty.

"From my sister." She waved the paper. "Once again, she's issued an invitation to visit her in France."

Mother's mouth swept upward. "Floressa is persistent if nothing else, *non?*"

The paper crackled softly as she folded the letter and set it aside. She skimmed her astute gaze over Adaira. "It's good to see you up and about, Addy. I thought to have Gregor examine you if you hadn't improved by today, *ma chère.*"

Adaira heard the relief in her mother's soft, French accent, and she forced a cheerful smile. "I'm feeling much better."

It was true. Knowing she could soon turn Marquardt's

care over to Ewan was a tremendous relief. A day or two more at most, and then she'd never have to see the blackguard again. The lout had caused her more self-doubt and self-recrimination than anyone else ever had.

"Are you?" Isobel tilted her head to the side, her intelligent gaze scrutinizing Adaira. "You're still rather pale."

Her sister knew her far too well. Their dispositions were as different as summer and winter, yet Adaira was very close to Isobel. After kissing their mother on the cheek, Adaira took a seat.

"Truly, Isobel. I am recovered." Adaira smiled and accepted the china plate covered in blue roses her mother handed her. "As you know, I never remain ill for long."

Isobel poured Adaira a goblet of claret.

"Here, *ma chére.*" Mother nudged a plate of Scotch pies and oatcakes her direction. She thought Adaira was too thin as well. The truth was, she was afraid to put on extra flesh. Men seemed to prefer women with amply rounded bosoms and hips. At least Scotsmen did.

And one profusely annoying Englishman she could think of.

She placed a steaming chicken pie on her plate and made a mental count of the remainder. Nine pies and seven oatcakes. She scanned the table quickly, assessing the other food: apples, strawberries, oat rolls, bread, and assorted cheeses. Her stomach growled at the mixture of delicious smells. She smiled, genuinely pleased. There was plenty of food to pilfer for Marquardt.

"Strawberries, Addy? I know they're your favorite." Isobel held a bowl practically under Adaira's chin. Isobel really needed to wear her spectacles. She couldn't see past the end of her nose clearly without them.

The fresh, sweet scent of ripe, just-picked berries

hovered above the fruit. Dutifully plucking three from the bowl, Adaira set them on her plate. Taking a bite of the Scotch pie, she chewed it slowly.

Her thoughts reluctantly returned to Marquardt. A traitor wouldn't hesitate to lie about his identity. She'd found no identifying papers on him when she'd searched him for weapons after Brayan knocked him out. Wouldn't an earl have something on his person for identification? A signet ring at the very least?

She toyed with a strawberry.

She dared to venture from her chamber today after watching Brayan and her brood of male relatives thunder from the bailey midmorning. As if sensing her presence, Brayan turned to peer at her window. She'd promptly ducked behind the heavy velvet draperies.

Traitorous bounder. Rotten knave. Bloody trow.

How she wished she were a man. A huge, grossly muscled man so that she could pummel Brayan soundly.

He'd dared to send her a note yesterday. She'd stared at her name scrawled on the creased paper before slowly unfolding the page. She grimaced upon spying telltale finger smudges and fish scales.

Addy,

Please forgive me. I was talking rubbish. It was the whisky. I tell ye true. I swear, I'd never hurt ye.

Ever yours,

Brayan

She'd crumpled the note and thrown it into the fireplace.

Balderdash and hogwash.

He wasn't going to be absolved by blaming his threat on spirits. No, indeed. What was spoken came from the heart and revealed a person's true character. The fact that he could recall his despicable threat meant his faculties weren't as impaired as he'd have her believe.

Brayan's actions revealed much about him. Things she wouldn't have believed if she hadn't witnessed them herself. Perhaps she'd approach Ewan or Father about her concerns. However, that would have to wait until after Marquardt's presence was revealed.

"You're not acting yourself." Isobel's concerned tone dragged Adaira's attention back to the table.

"Addy, is all well with you?" Mother asked. "You're certain you aren't feeling indisposed?" She rested the back of her hand against Adaira's brow like she had in years past. Back before the *ugliness* happened and changed Adaira forever.

"You don't feel feverish." Mother's gaze dipped to the mutilated berry on Adaira's plate.

Adaira forced a cheerful smile. "Nae, I'm well."

To give credence to her claim, she speared another strawberry, and raising it whole to her mouth, took a large bite. A commotion in the hall's entry drew her attention. A beaming Ewan strode into the room with an equally glowing Yvette on his arm.

Adaira gasped, choking and gagging on the strawberry. She snatched her goblet and took a gulp, trying to wash the berry down. Instead, she snorted into the vessel and sprayed droplets of wine all over her face.

She seized her serviette and peeking over the edge, dabbed at the wine dripping from her cheeks and chin.

When had he arrived home?

Last night? This morning?

After kissing Mother on the cheek, and offering Adaira and Isobel a warm smile, Ewan took a seat. "Where are the others?"

"Your stepfather's at the mill." Passing Yvette the bowl of strawberries, Mother smiled. "The rest are working in the village at the orphan asylum. Except for Seonaid. She's doctoring a dog that injured its shoulder yesterday."

Ewan and Yvette piled their plates with food. One would think they hadn't eaten in a week. If they took much more, there'd be little left for Marquardt.

Adaira bit the inside of her cheek to keep from smiling at the irony. For pity's sake. She was begrudging her brother and sister-in-law their meal for fear the knave in the dungeon would go hungry.

Fork raised, Yvette eyed Adaira. "Addy, you're unusually quiet."

Adaira's gaze flicked to Yvette's before darting away. "I am? I'm sorry. I've something weighing on my mind." *Weighing?* More like suffocating her.

"Is it anything I can help with?" Yvette asked kindly.

Guilt wracked Adaira at the concern in new sister-in-law's eyes. A lovely blonde, Yvette was every bit as generous and kind as she was wealthy and beautiful.

Adaira glanced around the table, discomfited to find everyone's attention fixed on her. Seizing the first thing that popped her head, she blurted, "I'm simply trying to behave with a bit more decorum. I need to be an example for my sisters. I know I've been a hellion, uncouth and all that. I've not demonstrated the behavior one would expect of a lady of quality."

Ewan's eyebrows shied high on his forehead in obvious disbelief, and Mother stared at her as if she were addled.

Isobel snorted. "And a zebra can change its black stripes to orange spots."

Adaira couldn't very well explain what was really going on, now could she? She lifted a shoulder slightly and offered a half-smile. She added two more Scotch pies, three oatcakes, a pair of apples—as Marquardt seemed to like them—several wedges of cheese, and two rolls to her plate.

Staring at the mound of food, Ewan raised his eyebrows again but said nothing.

She rapidly added six flaky shortbread biscuits to her stash. "In case I run into Brayan," she explained.

She peeped at Ewan from beneath her lashes.

Should she tell him she held Marquardt captive below?

Ewan smiled at Yvette, adoration in his eyes. It was quite obvious they'd shared a joyful homecoming. Of course, she wasn't supposed to know of such things. Her family would be surprised at precisely what she knew about relationships between a man and a woman. Truth to tell, they'd be appalled at her knowledge, and even more so, at how she'd come to acquire the information.

Adaira took a careful sip of her wine and then began piling the food from her plate onto her napkin.

No, she decided, she'd wait until tomorrow to tell him. She'd give Ewan and Yvette this day to celebrate their happy reunion.

Marquardt could wait one more day. He'd be exchanging one prison for another in any event. Compared to Newgate, his Craiglocky accommodations were luxurious.

"I think I'll take my luncheon with me and eat it later, if you don't mind, Mother. I need to speak with Father. You said he's at the woolen mill?" She loathed lying to her mother.

Mother waved her away. "I believe so. Either there or the orphanage. Do be careful, *chére*. With all the construction in town, there is an unusual number of wagons and carts on the roads, not to mention strangers wandering about."

Truer words were never spoken.

Gathering the corners of her napkin, Adaira covered the food. "I shall."

After grabbing a crust of bread, her favorite part, she left the great hall and headed directly for the lower level. She'd gone but a few steps along the hallway when Yvette's words halted her mid-step.

"Would it be an inconvenience to have the earl underfoot for a few days?" Yvette asked.

Making her way back to the hall's entrance, Adaira idly slid the cross at her neck from side-to-side while unabashedly eavesdropping.

"By all means," her mother said. "Write the earl a letter, and ask him to pay us an extended visit."

"I did suggest a visit when I wrote him a few weeks past," Yvette said. "But I never issued a formal invitation. Rory's a stickler for propriety."

What? Adaira inched closer, cocking her head to listen.

Yvette continued, "He'd never impose without a written invitation." She gave a soft chuckle. "I've never known anyone with a more rigid sense of honor or who adheres more strictly to society's dictates."

Hadn't Yvette invited the earl yet?

That meant the deceitful cur below *was* Edgar Marquardt. *I knew it!* A millstone lifted from her shoulders, and the noose loosened around her neck.

Thank God.

She heard a bit of rustling, and she dared to peek around the doorframe. Yvette was embracing Mother.

Adaira smiled.

Her new sister-in-law fit into their family very nicely.

Standing upright, Yvette murmured, "Thank you. Rory's nothing like Edgar. My stepmother told me that as a boy, the old earl whipped Rory. He bears the scars to this day. He has a soft heart and is very compassionate toward those less fortunate than himself."

No doubt about it—none indeed. Adaira had captured the right man. There was nothing soft-hearted or compassionate about the ill-tempered brute prowling about below the keep.

Adaira's smile widened into a gratified grin.

The off-tune singing of Iona, one of the orphans who lived at the keep and helped Sorcha, rang the length of the hallway. Careful to walk on her toes, lest her boot heels rap on the stone floor, Adaira crept from the door. She resisted the urge to kick her heels together like the wee folk.

The red-haired moppet skipped into the entry, a feather duster in her hand. She wore a faded yellow dress. "Pleased, I am to see ye, Miss Adaira."

Iona grinned, exposing her missing front teeth.

"Ye are all better now?" She brandished the feather duster like an enraged rooster flapping his wings. Dust particles flew everywhere. Above the keep's entrance, streams of sunlight slanting through the leaded glass window depicting the McTavish crest illuminated the floating bits.

Adaira smiled and tousled the urchin's hair. "Aye, that I am."

Indeed, she was much better. She nearly rubbed her hands together in glee. Oh, she couldn't wait to see the look on Marquardt's face when she told him Ewan was home. And that Yvette had confirmed she'd never sent the earl an invitation to visit.

Marquardt, the rotten imposter, was done up, by Jove.

Ten

daira hummed a cheerful tune as she made her way to Marquardt's cell. She popped the last of the savory crust in her mouth and merrily chewed. Things had turned out splendidly. In less than a day, she'd be heralded as a hero for detaining him.

There was still the awkward business with Brayan, though. She wasn't certain how to remedy that situation. Their friendship had taken an uncomfortable turn. She couldn't fathom a way their relationship could be repaired. Truth to tell, she didn't want the friendship restored. She would never trust him again. One didn't threaten a friend with extortion.

There was darkness in his soul.

However, she'd keep his threat to herself. There was no reason for anyone else to know, although she'd been sorely tempted to tell her father. But he, of course, would tell Mother. Then Adaira would have to lie to cover up Brayan's involvement with Marquardt.

Her footsteps slowed, and she found herself tiptoeing as

she neared her prisoner's cell. Odd, it was unlit and eerily silent. Unease skidded over her, causing her scalp to tingle.

Had the fool truly used all the candles?

How was that possible?

She'd left him more than a dozen. Each one burned for at least six hours. She quickly calculated in her head. A trifle over thirty-eight hours had passed since she'd left him. He should have a few candles remaining, even if he burned them around the clock.

Holding her breath, she edged closer to the cell, afraid of what she might see. "Mr. Marquardt?"

"You're a vindictive wench, aren't you?" His voice was scarcely more than a hoarse growl.

Adaira peered into the gloomy chamber.

Where was he?

She lifted the lantern higher, casting the light wider.

Oh, my God.

He sat wedged in a corner, the table propped before him. Or rather, what was left of it. He'd broken the legs off. The armchair lay on its side, jammed against the destroyed table.

Good Lord.

He'd built himself a makeshift fortress.

Adaira's mouth fell open. "What in heaven's name?"

Marquardt rose, slowly unfolding his tall frame from a hunkered position. His expression savage, he held a battered table leg in his hand. "Do you have any idea, you heartless bitch, how vicious and brazen rodents become when there's no light?"

What?

Dumbstruck, she dropped her attention to the floor. Twenty or more rats lay dead, their thrashed bodies strewn across the ground, some in puddles of blackened blood. A wave of revulsion engulfed her, immediately followed by swirling dizziness. Inky spots flickered before her eyes.

Stop it! You will not faint, Adaira Brenna Georgene Ferguson. You. Will. Not!

Closing her eyes, she pressed her fingers to her forehead and sucked in a gulp of clammy air. She started, her eyelids popping open in alarm when Marquardt viciously kicked the table aside. It skittered across the cell and crashed into the wall, splintering into several pieces.

He's gone mad. Off his head, he is.

"I had a hard enough time keeping the vermin at bay with a lit candle." He stalked to the cell door. Fury fairly radiated from him. He no longer wore his coat. His muscled arms and chest strained against the confines of his once-white shirt. He'd torn the coat into strips and wrapped several lengths around his forearms.

To ward off the rats?

"Dear God," Adaira whispered, utterly horrified. Even he didn't deserve such treatment. For every predatory stride Marquardt advanced, she retreated a leery step.

"You drugged the wine. Laudanum, I'd guess from the effects. While I was unconscious," he waved the hand holding the table leg, indicating the dead rats, "the little demons ate every morsel of food." He snorted contemptuously. "And the candles too, I might add. After all, rancid mutton fat must be quite a treat to these vermin."

She shook her head, trying to make sense of his ranting.

Marquardt pointed at the dead rats again. "A few decided to have a go at me."

Appalled, her gaze flew from him to the rats, then back to him once more. "I..." She swallowed against a wave of sickness. "I had no idea..."

She stuttered to a stop, gaping at him in disbelief.

"Drugged? Did you say the wine was *drugged?*"

"It's too late for half-hearted theatrics, my dear." His lips curled into a sneer. "Don't insult my intelligence by feigning ignorance." He stared at her hard. "Who else but you had access to the wine?"

Brayan. The scurrilous lout.

Adaira willed her thrumming heart to stop its assault on her ribs. She clenched her jaw against the unpleasant emotions assailing her. Fear. Guilt. Remorse.

"I came to tell you Ewan's returned home." Holding the bag to her chest, as if it offered her protection from the fiery darts spewing from Marquardt's rage-filled gaze, she lifted her chin and boldly met his eyes. "I'll tell him you're here."

She'd intended to wait until tomorrow. But given the half-mad look in Marquardt's eyes, and the ghastliness of what he'd undergone defending himself against the rats, her Christian conscience wouldn't allow him to suffer further. Never mind, he'd brought this on himself or that according to rumor, Newgate's conditions were far harsher.

Adaira had never deliberately caused another to suffer mental or physical anguish. A bit of discomfort perhaps, if she'd no alternative. But prolonged torment? No. She knew too well some things haunted one for the rest of one's life.

Except, as noble as it sounded, the sentiment was drivel. She'd imagined all sorts of fitting punishments for Godwin, and each included various forms of severe, often prolonged suffering.

Shame beset her. "Ewan out as soon as I return above."

"How very *generous* of you." Marquardt haughtily looked down his straight, aristocratic nose.

She resisted the urge to touch the slight hump on hers.

He tossed aside the table leg before beginning to unwind the fabric from his arms. He paused and glared at the bundle she clutched to her chest like an improvised shield. "Well, are you going to continue to starve me?"

Adaira shook her head. "No, I..." Her stomach coiling into a sickening knot at the stench of blood and dead vermin, she set the lantern on the floor. She knelt beside it and rested the sack on the top of her thighs. "If you'll move away from the door—."

"Bloody hell! Still playing that game, are we?" Glowering, Marquardt raked his hand through his hair. Righting the armchair, he flopped into it, then continued to unwrap his arms. "I don't suppose you brought anything to treat wounds?"

In the act of removing his food, Adaira froze. "They bit you?"

Swiftly skimming him from head to foot, she searched for evidence of blood or small puncture wounds. She relaxed the tiniest bit upon finding no obvious injuries. Frowning, she scrutinized the dead rodents. "There never used to be so many."

He cocked an arrogant brow and scoffed, "Oh, and you're accustomed to spending a great deal of time in this abyss?" His angry blue gaze roamed the cell. "Little witch that you are, somehow that doesn't surprise me."

He tossed off the last scrap of material, then rotated and flexed his wrists. "I hope you brought fresh water. At least I can clean the scratches."

Crossing his legs, he relaxed into the chair. Casually, as if he were carrying on a cordial conversation in the finest drawing room, he said, "I've decided to rescind my vow of never striking a woman."

Adaira rested her rear on her heels. "What a surprise," she quipped in a futile attempt to cover the frisson of fright freezing her blood.

His hooded gaze sank to her buttocks. "A spoilt, troublesome termagant like you deserves a firm hand on her enticing posterior."

Leaving the sack by the door, she stood. "As you'll never be alone with me, or for that matter, see me again once I go above, the likelihood of you ever touching me is less than a snowflake's chance of surviving in hell."

She lifted the lantern from the floor, and with her spine ramrod stiff, marched away, her boots clicking rhythmically on the stone floor.

"I'll send Ewan straightaway," Adaira called without turning around. She'd no desire to lay eyes on that scunner, Marquardt, ever again. He'd been nothing but a troublesome nuisance.

She'd send Ewan—if she could find him.

This time Marquardt didn't scream at her for taking the light. Evidentially he'd grown accustomed to the dungeon's hellish gloom. Fitting since he was a spawn of the devil. She could feel his evil glare on her. What other reason could there be for the peculiar fluttering in her belly and tingling along her nerves?

Consumed with her thoughts, Adaira trudged along the corridor.

Was Ewan still within the castle?

He'd been absent over three weeks. He also had responsibilities in Craigcutty. He might well be out and about the estate.

"This way, Yvette."

Aubry?

Her cousin's distant voice carried far in the dungeon's silence.

Adaira stumbled to a halt. After the grief Aubry had

caused Yvette, what was her sister-in-law doing in the keep's bowels with her?

Aubry had lied to Yvette, claiming Ewan was her betrothed, and he'd only married Yvette for her fortune. Complete and utter nonsense, of course. Aubry's vicious fabrications had nearly destroyed Ewan and Yvette's love. Aubry was every bit as wicked as the fiend Adaira had left stewing in his cell moments ago.

Sensing something was afoot, Adaira extinguished her light. She crept along the passageway on her toes, the leather of her boots, making little scuffing creaks. Dratted boots. Impossible to walk quietly in them.

She took a couple more tentative steps, then stopped to listen.

Whatever was Yvette thinking, accompanying Aubry into the dungeon?

She advanced another half dozen strides.

Adaira knew Yvette couldn't abide Aubry and had made a point to avoid her these past weeks. Something was too smoky by half.

Was there someone else in the dungeon? Someone waiting for Aubry? Possibly.

But who?

Adaira bit the inside of her cheek.

"Where, exactly, is Seonaid?" Yvette asked, her voice quivering slightly. "Are you certain this is the shortest way?"

Adaira sucked in a silent gulp of air. *Seonaid?*

"I told you, near the wetlands. And yes, this route is far shorter than going around the outer wall," Aubry said.

Wetlands? Adaira went rigid. Aubry lied.

Seonaid was tending a wounded dog unless she'd gone to the wetlands for herbs.

Adaira stole forward another pair of steps. Her confounded heels announced each movement. She sat down, then pried off the tight boots, refusing to contemplate what she might be sitting in. Soundlessly, she scrambled upright. Her progress, now silent, she hurried along the passage in her stockings.

Every instinct told Adaira her contemptible cousin was leading Yvette into a trap. Adaira didn't dare run for help. She'd risk losing them if she didn't stay on their trail.

Throughout the belly of the keep, lay a labyrinth of passageways, dozens of chambers and doors, and at least as many subchambers. If Adaira lost track of the women, she'd have a deucedly wicked time finding them again.

She strained to see in the blackness.

A light glowed faintly in the distance, coming closer.

There they were.

A few moments later, Yvette and Aubry walked past the end of the long corridor Adaira occupied. Should she shout and warn Yvette?

What if Aubry had a weapon?

Would she use it on Yvette? Aubry had been trained in weaponry right alongside Adaira and her sisters. And if her cousin had an accomplice, Adaira wanted to know who it was.

She flattened herself against the wall, accidentally kicking a loose piece of stone. It rattled noisily. Holding her breath, she crouched low and pressed against the cold, dank stones.

Gasping, Yvette stopped and looked directly into the corridor where Adaira squatted.

"Just rats," Aubry assured her. "Hurry, we're almost there."

Yvette and Aubry continued to talk in hushed tones as

the soft rustling of their skirts and the swish of their slippered feet faded away.

Adaira crept forward, intent on following them. A door clicked closed in the distance, and she heard them no more. Feeling her way along the wall, she paused at the end of the passage. She strained her eyes for the slightest trace of light.

She took a hesitant step forward. Confound it. She needed a match to relight her lantern.

A muffled sound rent the stagnant air.

Was that a scream?

"Dear God, Yvette!" Adaira choked out, the hair on her nape rising. Without hesitation, she turned and, in the lightless gloom, felt her way along the wall. Half-running, she awkwardly rushed back in the direction of Marquardt.

He had matches.

A faint flicker of amber glimmered ahead. Sprinting, she tore back to his cell, scraping her hands along the rough wall. She slid to a stop at the sight before her.

He stood washing, naked from the waist up.

Holy Mother of God. He's beautiful.

At Adaira's inarticulate sound, surprise, quickly followed by discomfiture, swept his face and lingered in his eyes. Fine chestnut-brown hair covered his glistening muscled chest and disappeared into the vee of his unfastened pantaloons.

Her gaze involuntarily whizzed the length of his body. A hot flush rushed from her neck to her forehead. She gawked, jaw gaping. She was certain the sensation whipping across her senses was pure lust. Astonishment widened her eyes. Marquardt might be a knave of the worst sort, but he had the form of a Greek god.

More's the pity.

"What the hell are you doing back here?" he snarled.

"Matches," she gasped, thrusting the lantern at him. "I need matches. Aubry tricked Yvette."

"*Aubry?* Who the blazes is Aubry?"

"My cousin on my father's side." Adaira's lower lip began to tremble. "I saw them together, and then…I heard a scream." Tears trickled over the rims of her eyes, and she scrubbed at them angrily. She hadn't the time for waterworks.

"A *scream?*" Marquardt went rigid. He threw the washcloth aside and bolted to the door. Grabbing the bars, he shook them. "Unlock this door, Adaira."

"No." Adaira shook her head. "Just give me the matches." She thrust her hand out, palm upward.

He had the temerity to reach through the bars and gently grasp her outstretched hand in his much larger one. A jolt of sensation lanced from her fingers to her breast. Her heart and lungs did all manner of irregular things.

His chest was but a foot from her nose. The scent of his spicy maleness drifted between the bars. "Adaira, please. You must trust me. Yvette's life may depend on it."

Trust him? *Trust him?*

One didn't become a spy without being a master of deception. Why next, he'd be trying to convince her that a monster lived in the depths of the loch or fairy cats roamed the woodlands behind the keep.

No, she'd never trust him.

Adaira yanked her hand free and rubbed it against her thigh as if burned. "Just give me the bloody matches!" Panic churned her innards. "If you have a shred of decency in you…" Her voice caught on a sob. "Please, I'm begging you. Please, give me the matches."

"And what, pray tell, are you going to do alone?" Marquardt struck the wall with one hand. His bicep bulged.

"Dammit, I told you, I'm *not* Edgar! You're wasting precious minutes arguing with me."

Adaira stared into his piercing eyes. She could find no trace of subterfuge in their depths. She wanted to believe him, wanted to trust him. All that mattered now was helping Yvette.

He raked a hand through his mahogany hair, leaving the damp strands sticking up at awkward angles. The scar on his forehead stood out, a white beacon of ire.

"With every passing minute, the danger to Yvette increases." Whipping around, he rushed to the corner of the cell and snatched his shirt from the arm of the chair. Puckered pinkish-red scars crisscrossed his back, resembling a ragged quilt of human flesh. He yanked the soiled garment over his head.

God above, how he must've suffered.

"This delay could cost my sister her life," he said, his voice low and gravelly.

Adaira swore he swallowed against ragged emotion, clogging his throat.

Yvette's gentle voice echoed in Adaira's mind.

"As a boy, the poor man was whipped by the old earl. He bears the scars to this day."

Choking on a horrified gasp, Adaira couldn't tear her attention from his back. She clutched the door to steady herself against a sudden rush of faintness.

"Oh, sweet Jesus in heaven."

Marquardt looked over his shoulder, a quizzical expression on his face.

Lifting her reluctant, appalled gaze to his, she pointed a shaking finger. "You're the earl."

Eleven

Adaira fumbled with the keys, and her hands shook as she tried to slide the key into the rusty lock.

"Bloody hell! Let me do it." The earl snatched the ring from her. Angling his arm, he tucked the skeleton key into the lock. With a quick twist of his wrist, the latch clicked loose.

She shoved past him, and stepping over the dead rats, she ran to his supplies. Tossing items aside, she fought back tears as she searched for the matches. "We'd best find help. I think Aubry was taking Yvette to one of the outer doors."

She speedily lit the lantern, then blew out the match. "Ewan will…"

His lordship's hands closed over her shoulders, and she gasped when he spun her around to face him, his features hard.

"I don't have the leisure at the moment to give you the spanking you deserve." He snared her hand in his, towing her to the door. "But, rest assured, things aren't finished between us. There will be consequences for locking me in here."

Roark unceremoniously hauled Adaira into the great hall. Sethwick, several Scotsmen, as well as a handful of ladies and a small red-haired urchin, stood huddled together. From the distressed looks on everyone's faces, he presumed they knew Yvette had gone missing.

At his and Adaira's appearance, a shocked hush cocooned the room.

Surprise, followed by confusion, then anger flashed across several faces, including Sethwick's. A flush of humiliation surged over Roark. He'd never appeared in public, or private for that matter, this unkempt.

Several days' growth of beard on his face, in his shirtsleeves and with filthy stockinged feet, he stood before them wholly disheveled. His clothes were so soiled that despite his hurried bath, he could barely abide his own scent. He knew his appearance bordered on scurrilous.

Adaira gave a tentative tug on the arm he had wrapped in his grasp. When he didn't release her, she slanted him a hesitant glance. Face flushed, her eyes—the pupils dilated and black as coal—were wide and anxious. Her sable hair, an unruly mass, hung to her waist, and her rumpled shirt was untucked, the top gaping open.

His chest tightened as realization struck.

Good God, she looked like she'd been thoroughly compromised. He shot a quick glance at the others. Their gazes reflected a concert of negative emotions. There would be hell to pay if they jumped to that ridiculous conclusion.

Adaira's pink tongue darted out and traced her lips, and a painful surge of blood rushed to his groin.

Ye gods.

Had she done that on purpose, to disarm him in front of

her family? Her kind knew how to use their tears and wiles. Delia had perfected the art of manipulation. The thought of his late wife cooled his ardor and inflamed his ire.

Adaira swallowed several times.

Was she nervous? Good. She should be.

Roark's gaze perused those assembled.

An attractive middle-aged, dark-haired woman bounded to her feet. She rushed across the room to grip an enormous, fierce-looking Scotsman's arm. The parents, Lady Ferguson and Sir Hugh, no doubt.

Lady Ferguson's expression held a blend of alarm and uncertainty. Her eyes met Roark's, then sank to his hand encircling Adaira's arm. Scrutinizing her daughter, her eyes widened at the rumpled shirt, and her gaze flew to meet Adaira's. "Addy?"

The one word asked several questions, namely, *Has this rake ravished you?*

"What be the meaning of this? Unhand my daughter," the Scot bellowed, taking a threatening step forward.

His wife's hand on his arm halted his progress.

"Clarendon?" Sethwick's eyebrows rose in astonishment before crashing together in a harsh glower. "Where the hell did *you* come from?"

Roark gave Adaira a slight jostle.

She didn't protest, only stared mutely at the floor. So, she was capable of holding her tongue. Would wonders never cease?

Sethwick's mouth thinned, the half-moon scar on his cheek standing out boldly against his clenched jaw. "Clarendon, you'd better have a bloody good explanation for your treatment of my sister."

The father and an equally huge young man greatly resembling Ewan growled dual warnings.

"*Now*, you're silent?" Roark sliced a glance at Adaira. "You've been blathering inaccurate, irrational balderdash for days."

He shook her lightly again.

"*Days?*" Lady Ferguson looked from Adaira to Roark and back to Adaira. "I don't understand." Lady Ferguson raised perplexed eyes to her husband.

"My apologies, Lady Ferguson, sir." Roark made a leg, his clasp on Adaira never relaxing. "I'd hoped our introduction would be under different circumstances. Your daughter...," He leveled Adaira with a blistering glare. "Has kept me as a forced *guest* in the dungeon."

"*What?*" A chorus of voices rang out in incredulity.

Her voice unsteady, Adaira finally spoke. "I thought—" She peeked at Roark.

Firming his lips, he stared back at her unrelentingly. He'd offer her no quarter. He was the victim—she the criminal.

She averted her eyes when her gaze collided with his merciless stare. Shoulders slumping, she mumbled, "I thought he was the other one. The one who wants to hurt Yvette."

Roark did not attempt to hide his fury. "Even though I insisted she'd had the wrong man, she kept me caged below."

"Oh, Addy, *non*," Lady Ferguson gasped, flattening a hand to her throat. "Tell me you didn't!"

Adaira nodded as a pair of tears made parallel journeys over her high cheekbones. "I met him in Craigcutty, and he asked directions to the keep." She raised her eyes to his, her expression pleading and desperate. She pointed at him. "You were traveling alone, and you said you were *Mister*

Marquardt." Her gaze dropped to his hand. "You're not wearing a signet ring, either."

Her tone rang with accusation. She dared to blame him?

Roark resisted the urge to take her other arm and shake her until her teeth rattled. Or turn her over his knee. Or kiss her until she was breathless and admitted her wrongdoing, stubborn chit.

He met Sethwick's gaze full-on, silently challenging him to object. "I often leave off my title," he raised his bare hand, "and signet ring when traveling alone. I find it eliminates a great deal of, shall we say, undesirable attention? Surely *you* understand."

Sethwick gave one crisp nod. "I do, but can we discuss this," he made a sweeping gesture that included Roark and Adaira, "later? There's a much more critical matter at hand." He turned his piercing gaze on his sister. "Go to your chamber and stay there."

She huffed out a breath, tilting her chin defiantly. "But, Ewan, I don't..."

"Cease!" The expression on Sir Hugh's face was a mixture of anger and worry. "Have ye nae idea the seriousness of what ye've done, lass?"

He tossed a glance at his wife. Lady Ferguson continued to stare at her daughter in appalled disbelief.

"Yer mother and I shall speak with ye later. Go to yer bedchamber and stay there. Ye are no' to leave it." Giving his wife a swift hug, he moved toward the exit.

"Yes, Father." Ducking her head, Adaira made to escape as well. She tugged against Roark's hand, still holding her arm.

He wouldn't release his grip. "Miss Ferguson?"

She raised her gaze to his, a question in her doe-like eyes.

"This isn't over," he murmured for her ears alone.

Her eyes darkened and rounded wide as the center of sunflowers. The green-gold shards glittered. In fear? The color drained from her face, the freckles smattered across her nose and cheeks vivid against her pale skin.

"But...but...you wouldn't dare—" She darted a glance at the others and swallowed. Her voice a rasping wisp of a sound she added, "Spank me."

He smiled a wholly self-righteous smile. "Wouldn't I?"

She shook her head.

He bent his neck a fraction, and his breath caressed her ear. "Who was your accomplice?"

"Miss Adaira," Maisey huffed as she hurried into Adaira's chamber carrying a tray. "I rushed here to tell ye the good news. Lady McTavish is safe, praise be! That's why yer dinner is so late."

Late?

It was half-past eleven. Adaira had assumed her punishment included going to bed without eating.

Maisey set the tray on the table with a slight thump. The dishes rattled and clinked together, and she grinned sheepishly. "Sorry about that. The laird and clansmen have returned. She's with them."

Hearing a commotion in the bailey hours ago, Adaira had looked out a window. Her eyes had misted in relief. The torches held by several mounted clansmen revealed Yvette sitting before Ewan on his horse, wrapped safely in his arms.

Adaira closed the book in her lap. Worry had kept her from reading a single page. "How is she?"

"She is verra shaken but unharmed. Except for a wicked knot on her head, that is," Maisey said. "The laird found her in the bogs. Praise the saints she dinna fall in."

"Did they capture Edgar Marquardt, too?" One could count on servants' tattle to know what was happening in the keep, and Adaira had seen a dark-haired man surrounded by burly Scots as he was escorted to the gatehouse. She dragged her thumbnail back and forth across the volume's closed pages.

"Aye, Laird McTavish captured him," Maisey said with satisfaction. "He's bein' kept in one of the guest chambers on the third floor. Under guard, too."

"As he should be. He's a dangerous man." Adaira set the book aside.

"Och, that he is. My heart aches for the earl, it does." Maisey turned back Adaira's bed coverings. "He found out tonight his brother poisoned their mother. Poor man." She made a *tsking* noise in her throat, and after smoothing the counterpane, she toddled to the wardrobe.

Adaira gaped at the maid.

Hadn't the earl known?

It made sense.

He'd been in England when his mother and stepfather had died in America. After a two-year absence to expand Gideon Stapleton's shipping enterprises, Yvette and her parents were preparing to return to England. And Lord Clarendon hadn't seen Yvette since she returned.

Her arrival at Craiglocky had been secretive, too. After her parents' sudden death and Edgar had tried to abduct her, she'd fled Boston in the middle of the night. She'd been so terrified of Edgar, no one but her cousins, Lord and Lady Warrick, had known she was coming to England.

Adaira wished she might see the younger Marquardt in person. Did his wickedness show in his appearance, or was he as handsome as the earl? Her stomach reacted to the notion with a most uncomfortable quivering. She'd felt that way once before when Mother had insisted she drink whisky-laced hot possets after coming down with a beastly cold.

"Maisey, what of Aubry? Wasn't she with Yvette?" What would Ewan do with *that* traitor? Adaira rather hoped Aubry would see the inside of Newgate.

Maisey shook her head and clucked her tongue. "Nae, she wasna. I dinna have the whole of it, but there be somethin' about her deliverin' Lady McTavish to spies, and then the banshee fled the keep with Campbell, the blackguard."

Campbell? Another conspirator in their midst.

Her face flushed with her agitation, Maisey ducked her head. "I'm sorry, Miss Adaira. I am speakin' out of turn."

Adaira waved away the apology. "Not at all. The circumstances have been distressing for us all." She wrapped a curl behind her ear. "You said, spies. Didn't they capture the others?"

Maisey paused, scrunching her eyes in deep thought. Bringing her hand to her chin, she rubbed it. "Nae. I heard Sorcha sayin' Laird McTavish found two dead—a man and a woman—in one of the cottages."

Two?

She dropped her hand. "It's queer, too. Edgar Marquardt shot them. *He's* the one who saved her ladyship from the spies."

"Are you sure?" Adaira tilted her head to the side and drew her brows together. That didn't make any sense.

Drat, she needed to talk to Yvette or Ewan. There must be someone who could tell her the truth of the matter.

"It's bafflin', to be sure, but that's what Sorcha said, Miss Adaira."

And Sorcha usually had the right of it.

Maisey bustled around, setting the meal on the table. "I fear it's mutton tonight, and tough from sittin' so long." She offered an apologetic smile.

Adaira eyed the silver plate topper. She barely tolerated mutton. Blasphemy for a Scot. She sighed. At least it wasn't trout.

Maisey set the serviette and utensils beside the covered plate. "There are some lovely seasoned tatties. Baby carrots, cheese, and rolls, too. Oh, and bread puddin'."

Adaira wandered to the table and eyed the food. In truth, she hadn't much of an appetite. A knotted mass had replaced her belly. Yvette's return and Marquardt's capture had dispensed a good portion of her disquiet. However, his lordship's question about her accomplice continued to churn her innards relentlessly.

She sank into a chair, then poured herself a cup of tea. Steamy tendrils drifted upward from the hot liquid. Adaira placed a hand on her stomach and released a sigh. A long soak before she retired might be just the thing to ease her taut nerves. "Maisey, will you have a bath prepared for me, please?"

"Aye, miss. I'll see to it while ye eat. Ye want it brought up straightaway?"

"Yes, please. It's very late already." Adaira poured cream into the tea before adding two lumps of sugar. Lifting the silver spoon, she stirred the brew.

Maisey turned to go, then stopped abruptly, slapping a

hand to her forehead. "Och, I almost forgot. Jocky told Niall to tell me to tell ye that Vala is foalin' tonight."

"*Tonight?*" Adaira sat bolt upright, dropping the spoon against the fragile china with a loud clink.

Maisey sucked in a deep breath and rattled on. "He says all the indications are present." Lifting her hand, she ticked them off, finger by finger. "She's twitchin' her tail, pacin' in her stall, and stampin' her feet."

Adaira jumped up and rushed to her desk, quickly penning a note. After folding the foolscap, she extended it to the maid. "Please deliver this to Father immediately."

Excitement in her eyes, Maisey grabbed the message and tucked it into her apron pocket before dashing out the door. A smile twitched the edges of Adaira's mouth at the unmistakable sound of the maid running pell-mell down the corridor.

She returned to the table, and once she'd inspected the eggshell-thin blue rose teacup for cracks, took her seat once again. Sipping the tea and nibbling a roll did help settle her stomach.

Five minutes later, a knock echoed on her chamber door. She gave her father a wary smile as she opened it. "You received my message?"

"Aye." He stepped further into her room.

She didn't remember the last time he'd been in her chamber. It seemed to shrink around his great size. She laid a hand on his arm. "Please let me go to Vala, Father. This is her first foal. She needs me."

Though Vala was a large horse, Adaira wanted to be present in case there were complications. More than once, she and Niall had needed to assist with one of the mares' birthings.

Her usually jovial father stood in the center of her

room, more somber than she'd ever remembered him. He shook his head, the thick mane of his too-long black hair brushing the collar of his shirt. Worry glimmered in his serious gaze. "Nae, lass. Ye will stay here."

Disappointment tightened her throat.

He skimmed the room with his gaze. "Until Ewan and I can meet with the earl." His broad shoulders slumped, and he sighed. "Clarendon is verra angry and rightly so." Father rubbed his forehead with his great paw of a hand, and his troubled cinnamon-colored eyes met hers. "This is verra, verra serious, lass. Ye're a Scot, and ye imprisoned an English nobleman. He could bring charges against ye."

"I know," Adaira whispered.

What if he did?

She could hang.

Her father shook his head again. "I dinna even want to think about what could happen to ye if the Regent or some other English peer gets wind of it. The English are always wishin' to teach us Scots a lesson. We're hopin', now that Ewan is the earl's brother-in-law, his lordship will be lenient with ye."

Adaira stretched out her hands, imploringly. "It's not like I tortured him. He was well-cared for."

Except for that ghastly business with the rats.

"And I was trying to protect Yvette. Surely you—" She pulled in a steadying breath. "He understands that."

"Lord Clarendon's no' a man to trifle with. He's a verra powerful lord with a strong," her father paused and shook his head, "nae an unyieldin' sense of justice." Father moved to the doorway. "Stay in yer chamber, do ye hear me?" He pointed a large finger at her. "I dinna want the earl to see ye before we can reason with the man. I'll lock ye in here if need be, daughter."

Lock me in?

Had it truly come to that?

He stepped into the corridor, his serious gaze boring into hers. "Yer mother and I are verra disappointed with ye."

"I'm sorry." Adaira's voice shook as a wave of remorse engulfed her. Her eyes filled with tears, and she wrapped her arms around her middle to still her trembling.

Father extended his arms, and she ran into them, desperately needing his reassurance. She was terrified, wondering what the earl would do. Her father's soothing embrace eased her tremors but did nothing to lessen her fears.

Resting her head against his comforting chest, she asked, "Can you ask Niall to tend Vala? He's helped with the last several births."

Thank God for the blacksmith. Strong as an ox, he was also gentle as a lamb.

"Aye, lass." Father's voice was gruff with emotion. He patted her back, then released her. "See that ye remain here."

"I shall, I promise."

She had fully intended to keep her word, too.

Twelve

short while later, Maisey poured a draught of lily scented oil into a copper tub in Adaira's bedchamber. The maid swirled the water with her hand. "Ye'll be pleased with this foal, miss. Niall says it must be verra big. The mare's havin' to work to birth her babe."

Adaira paused in the process of piling her hair atop her head. "Vala's struggling?"

"Aye, but Niall says yer no' to worry. He has someone to help."

Help? Who?

Adaira secured a couple more pins and glanced at the window facing the stables. This wasn't good. She swallowed, forcing herself to remain calm. "How long has she been in labor?"

Births were usually swift. Delays could be deadly.

Maisey shrugged. "No' that long. Niall says she'll deliver soon."

Soon?

What if a hoof was stuck?

What if the foal was breech?

What if— What if the baby was just too big?

Adaira had been so careful to select the largest mares to breed with Fionn. She'd reduced Vala's feed to make sure the foal would be smaller during the last month. Still...

She had to find out what was happening. But she'd sworn she'd not leave her room. Hurrying to the window, she nudged the heavy velvet draperies aside. There was little to see in the deepening night. Thousands of glittering moonbeams glistened on the loch's surface. Light blazed from the stable's open doors and windows, beckoning her.

Dash it all.

"Maisey, I'll not need you to stay." Adaira turned her head and offered the maid a wobbly smile. "This day has been fraught with emotion, and I need time alone."

The catch in her voice and the moisture pooling in her eyes were real. She'd jailed an earl and created an enormous bumblebroth. Yvette had been abducted, and now, Vala was foaling without her.

Adaira was on the verge of caterwauling like a wee bairn.

"Ye've had a time of it today, that ye have," Maisey agreed sympathetically. She efficiently gathered the remnants of Adaira's dinner. "Ye dinna eat much."

"I know. I've much on my mind, and my stomach's unsettled."

"I'll bring ye a hearty meal to break yer fast in the morn then" The maid smiled on her way out the door. "Sleep well, Miss Adaira."

Though Adaira thought she might go mad from the wait, she delayed ten minutes before daring to open her door and peek into the hallway.

Silence.

Boots in hand, she hurried along the corridor, listening for the slightest sound. Muted snores penetrated two of the doors she slipped by. Tiptoeing down the front staircase, she nibbled her lower lip. She couldn't take the time to use the back stairs into the kitchen. The stables were much closer if she exited through the gatehouse.

She sent up a silent prayer that she'd not encounter anyone.

The castle was silent as she made her way below. At least five and seven people lived here, but it appeared everyone was already nestled in their beds. An odd sense of loneliness permeated the keep.

The monstrous front entry whisked open and closed with nary a sound as Adaira slipped into the cool night air. She donned her boots, furtively watching the bailey for anybody that might be wandering about. Except for shadows contorted by a soft breeze, nothing moved.

As she cast a swift glance over her shoulder, her breath caught. A meager light shone through a crack in the drapes covering the window of Ewan's study. Raising her gaze, she spied two more lit rooms, one directly above the other.

Not her family's chambers. It seemed neither Marquardt brother could sleep tonight.

A guard on watch lifted his hand in a casual wave. Adaira waved back. No sense in raising his suspicion. It wasn't unusual for her to visit the stables at night. She squinted into the darkness. No light glimmered in the blacksmith's cottage on the far side of the courtyard, but a dim glow filtered from an open stable door.

She descended the stairs on silent feet. Sticking to the shadows, she dashed to the stables. No one had sent further information about Vala. All Adaira knew was what Maisey had told her over a half an hour ago.

Mares generally delivered in under an hour.

Was Niall still with the mare?

Adaira prayed Vala wasn't yet in labor. It didn't bode well if she was. She slowed her pace just outside the west end of the stables, and apprehension gripped her. What if there'd been no word because something awful had occurred? Why hadn't that occurred to her before?

As she had requested for the past several evenings, the twin doors stood open to allow the chill of the night to cool the livestock. The days had been beastly hot, the heat lingering long into the night hours.

Adaira cast a worried glance at the keep.

The study light had been extinguished.

She'd sworn to stay in her room and couldn't bear to add to her mother's and father's disappointment. Her impulsive actions had disgraced the entire family this time. When the earl announced she'd imprisoned him, the matching expressions of hurt disbelief on her parents' faces had wrenched her heart wide open.

How was she to breach the chasm between them? There was no one to blame but herself. She'd made a mull of it, plain and simple. If she'd only gone to Father upon first meeting his lordship in the village instead of acting impulsively and letting her emotions rule her. Her misguided quest for vengeance had led her astray.

Adaira closed her eyes against the wave of despair coursing over her. Grasping her cross necklace, she bowed her head.

Lord, what have I done?

At that moment, when she'd accosted the earl, her life had irreversibly changed. Something unidentified had been set in motion. There was no putting things aright or going back. The fear of an unknown future was suffocating in its intensity, and for a moment, dizziness seized her.

Sagging against the door, she drew in great pulls of air.

I know I don't deserve your help, Lord, but please. Show me your mercy. Let Lord Clarendon be forgiving.

Fionn nickered softly in welcome, reeling her back to the present. Straightening, she shook off her melancholy and smiled at the horse. A lone lantern hung by a hook on a post near Vala's stall.

Adaira took several cautious steps into the building, her boots crunching on bits of straw and oats littering the smooth stone floor. She released her breath with a slight huff. Vala stood in her stall. Her head lowered, and then slowly moved up and down. She licked her foal, no doubt.

Adaira cast a glance around. No one else was here. She'd take a peek at Vala, say hello to the foal, and return to her room straightaway. No one would be the wiser.

She stopped to greet Fionn and took a moment to rub his forehead. "You've become a father again, my friend." Pressing her head against his, she breathed in his familiar scent. With a last pat on his neck, she said, "Forgive me, but I'm anxious to see your foal. I'll say good-bye before I go."

He nudged her shoulder, and Adaira chuckled. "I promise."

Striding to the mare's stall, Adaira murmured her name. "Vala." She unlatched the box's door. "How's my beautiful?"

The mare whinnied softly. Standing beside Vala was the largest foal Adaira had ever seen. He had to be over twelve or thirteen stones. "My goodness. No wonder you had a time of it."

She caressed the mare's dark bay neck. "You've done

well, Vala. I'm so pleased with you, my bonnie lass. So, do you have a son or daughter?"

Adaira stepped around the mare and ever-so-gently touched the foal. Was the new addition a laddie or lassie? Skimming her hands over the newborn, she bent to take a peek. *A colt.* The sheen of his coat glistened in the muted light. Other than a white face and leg markings, he was the color of rich Turkish coffee.

"Ooh, you're magnificent!" she breathed in awe.

"He is, indeed," rumbled a harmonious baritone.

Gasping, one hand at her throat, she whirled around.

The Earl of Clarendon leaned across the stall door, his forearms resting on the top edge. He clasped a silver flask loosely in one hand. Shirtsleeves rolled to his elbows, he'd discarded his waistcoat and jacket. He'd unfastened the top of his shirt, too.

Just perfect.

She wasn't supposed to be anywhere near the earl, and here he was, in *her* sanctuary. She ought to be afraid, after his parting words, but she sensed something altogether different.

No, she wouldn't stare at the crisp dark hair on his forearms or peeking from the collar of his open shirt. *Bugger it.* She curled her hands into fists against the oddest urge to run her fingers through the curly hair on his chest. A bolt of unease speared her, though whether from his disquieting presence or her awareness of him as an attractive man, she couldn't be certain.

Clearing her throat, she asked, "What are you doing here, my lord?"

And more on point, why are you dressed indecently?
Father would be furious.

"What are *you* doing here?" Lord Clarendon raised the

flask to his lips, then paused. "I distinctly heard your father tell you to stay in your chamber." After taking a swallow, his lips tilted into a boyish grin, and he shook his head as if amused. "Not that I'm surprised to see you. Truth to tell, I was expecting you."

He was?

Well, that didn't bode well.

Adaira eyed him uneasily. The rakish tilt of his lips and the glint in his eyes caused another flicker in her belly.

She ran a hand along the length of the mare's back. "I had word Vala was struggling to deliver. It's no wonder. He's the largest foal yet."

Adaira glanced at the colt, then in the earl's direction. He looked relaxed, almost boyish. Shifting her gaze to the door, rather than focusing on his lordship, she dared a couple of steps toward him. She needed to leave. Now. Not another inkling of impropriety must occur.

"I should be going—" She shouldn't be talking to him at all.

For a moment, she thought he'd refuse to move. He slowly straightened to his full height, and after tilting his head and closing his eyes, Lord Clarendon took a hefty swig from the flask.

He swallowed and gave a low satisfied sigh.

How on earth could taking a drink be sensual? And why, in heaven's name, was she aware of him in that manner?

He moved away, his lips skewed up at the corners.

Thank goodness. She must return to the keep. Swinging the door open, she blurted, "Really, though, what are you doing here? I'd have thought you'd be eager to seek the comfort of a nice soft bed tonight."

Her tongue seemed to have a mind of its own, dratted

thing. She was sorely beginning to regret her tendency to speak frankly. Heat suffused her face. What was she thinking, rattling on about soft beds?

With her back to him, she latched the bolt. "My lord, I'm sorry—"

He snorted loudly. "I'll wager you are."

She sent him a sharp look. "I'm sorry about your brother."

Pain pinched Lord Clarendon's face for the briefest of moments. A flash, then it was gone. He masked the emotion so swiftly, she almost thought she'd imagined it.

"Don't be. Edgar received exactly what he deserved for his illicit conduct." The earl took another short swallow. Holding the shiny container before him, he shook it. "Empty, blast it."

He sank to a stool, setting the flask on the stone floor beside a pile of soiled straw, probably from Vala's foaling. The flask promptly fell over, clanking against the stone.

Adaira slid an uneasy look to the door.

"Tell me about these." He motioned to the stalls, his attention on the horses. "Niall said this is your doing. I've never seen such colossal horseflesh. They're truly beautiful steppers."

Pride surged through her. "Yes, they are spectacular," she said softly.

Sweet-goers, everyone.

"How long have you been at this?" His lordship seemed genuinely interested.

Returning her attention to him, Adaira regarded him for a lengthy moment.

He'd crossed his legs before him and lounged against a support beam. His coat and waistcoat hung on a nail. He stared moodily at her from under hooded eyes.

Was he foxed?

His speech wasn't slurred, and his gaze was as intense as ever. If she didn't count his partial state of undress, he was neatly groomed once more.

The stables were warm, and he must've become over-heated. But that didn't explain his presence here in the first place. Unless he was in the habit of quaffing back a dram or two while sequestered with livestock.

"My lord, I'm not supposed to be in your company. Please excuse me." Chin tucked to her chest, she made to move past him.

"Surely you can answer my questions." He straightened and began to unroll a sleeve. "After all," he sent her a side-long look, a lock of sable hair falling across his forehead, "if it wasn't for me, it's possible the colt and his mother would've perished."

Adaira went rigid. She was sure from the odd quivering in her chest that her heart skipped a beat or two. She grasped her cross as if it could give her some strength. She flung a look to Vala and the foal, then blinked at the earl.

"Truly?" she whispered, emotion closing her throat. "They would've *died?*"

He gave a curt nod before turning his attention to his other sleeve. "The foal's head was turned aside, blocking the birth canal. I simply manipulated his muzzle into the canal, and everything proceeded as normal."

Simply?

"But Niall—" She drew in a trembling breath, hating how her voice shook.

"Only knew how to assist in drawing a stuck foal from a mare. He had no idea how to proceed with one that wasn't even in the canal yet."

For the first time, she noticed the dark stains ringing the

earl's shirt cuffs. He'd had to reach deep inside Vala. Adaira acknowledged a flicker of admiration for him. "How did you know what to do?"

Standing, he yawned and stretched his arms overhead. His shirt strained tautly across his muscled chest. "I've had a bit of surgical and medical training. I also spend a great deal of time with animals, mainly livestock."

He wasn't the dunderhead she'd thought him to be. There was considerably more to this man. He *might* be a decent person. The notion piqued her interest and flooded her with contriteness.

"I..." Adaira pulled her chin to her chest again. Shame kept her from meeting his gaze. "Thank you." She blinked against the moisture burning in her eyes. Turning her head to hide her tears, she moved past him, hurrying to Fionn's stall. "Goodnight, my—"

Lord Clarendon snaked his arm around her waist. Catching her unawares, he hoisted her off her feet.

Thirteen

daira released a yelp, her heart surging to her throat. Though she struggled against him, his embrace remained unyielding. She fought the band of steel, squeezing the breath from her. "What are you doing? Put me down!"

With both hands, she pried at Roark's arm, as she twisted her neck to glare at him.

His gaze clashed with hers, and a self-satisfied smile—no, it was more of a snarl—curled his firm mouth.

"I'm giving you the spanking you deserve."

"*Now?* Are you off your head?" Adaira clawed at him and kicked her legs furiously. One heel connected with his shin, and he grunted. "There's no time. I have to return to my bedchamber," she hissed between clenched teeth.

"You little hellcat. You can spare a minute so that I can teach you an overdue lesson." In one fluid move, the earl tossed her over his shoulder.

Adaira wriggled and jerked, pounding his back with her fists. "You pigheaded oaf, put me down! A groom will hear us and tell my father."

"Good," the earl said. "I've already had one discussion with your father regarding you. I've no qualms about having another. Especially since you're not supposed to be here, and you still haven't revealed your accomplice."

And I never will.

He rendered a stinging slap to her buttocks. "That's one."

"*Ouch.* Get your hands off me. Ewan will kill you. Father will kill you. *I'll kill you!*"

His hand was so large, the entire right side of her bum throbbed. She didn't dare scream. Instead, she beat his back with all her might. He didn't even flinch. She could feel the rough ridges from his scars through his fine linen shirt.

Roark chuckled deep in his throat. The foxed lout was enjoying this. "I think not, vixen."

He plopped onto the stool with such force that the air whooshed from her lungs, and her knees bounced against his chest. She reared up to keep her head from smacking the post behind the stool.

He deftly swung her from his shoulder, and she caught a glimpse of his face before he turned her over his knees. He looked pleased as Punch, the rotten bugger.

"You damnable merry-begotten cur." She struggled against his unyielding grip, condemning him to every sort of punishment in hell. Her curses would've burned the ears of the most hardened Scot. Turning her head, she caught the curious stares of the horses.

Where were the blasted grooms?

Surely someone had heard the commotion.

As if reading her mind, his lordship drawled, "The stable hands shan't be coming to your aid. I paid them quite handsomely to—er—be *discreet.*"

"I'll tell Ewan they did nothing while you assaulted me," she vowed, overcome with fury.

"You're going to tell your brother that you disobeyed your father and went to the stables? I'd wager he won't object overly much to a mere spanking considering what I could've done—still can do—to you for imprisoning me."

She shoved against Lord Clarendon's marble hard thighs.

"You're a strong little thing." A chuckle rumbled through his chest again. He pressed her shoulders into his lap with his forearm and struck her again. "Two."

Four more sharp blows fell on her *derrière*.

Tears flooded her eyes.

"There, that should teach you a long-overdue lesson," he said, his tone oddly gruff.

Surely that wasn't remorse in his voice?

Adaira rolled off his lap, then curled into a ball beside the soiled straw. Burying her head in her arms, she sobbed uncontrollably from humiliation and pain; because no one had come to her aid; because she couldn't tell anyone about the spanking; because Vala and the colt might've died; and because she'd imprisoned the wrong damned man.

She could very well hang for her foolishness—*if* the earl were determined, she receive her due.

"Oh, hell." Suddenly she was swept into the earl's arms and cradled across his lap.

Adaira pressed into him, needing this comfort. Although, why she sought it from him was wholly baffling. Perchance her wits had flown. Trying to staunch her tears was futile. The dam had broken. She could no more contain her rasping sobs than she could harness the moon.

Except for the attack four years ago and when Grandmother died a year later, she hadn't been this desolate.

Lord Clarendon tucked Adaira's head beneath his chin and cuddled her like a wee bairn. "It's not as bad as all that. I but swatted you a half dozen times."

"Vala—" She snuffled noisily against his chest, soaking his shirt. A scrumptious trace of sandalwood lingered on the fabric, and his chest hair tickled her cheek.

"Is fine, as is her foal." His lips moved against her hair, warming her scalp with little huffs of air as his hands rubbed the length of her spine.

"You're not Edgar."

He stiffened for a moment, then released a gusty sigh. "No. I told you I wasn't."

Utterly terrified, Adaira whispered against the curly hair poking from the vee of his shirt. "I could go to prison. I..." She choked on a low moan of anguished regret. "Could hang."

His hands stilled. With his forefinger, he tilted her chin upward until her gaze met his. No trace of his prior fury remained. The tenderness on his gorgeous face took her aback.

"You'll not go to prison or hang. I give you my word, vixen." He wiped the tears from her cheeks with his finger. "But I shall out your co-conspirator."

His gaze sank to her lips, then dipping his head, he kissed her.

The earl's lips were soft, warm, and tasted of whisky.

He smelled heavenly: horse, and leather, and sandalwood.

Why wasn't she afraid?

She had no urge to pull away. In fact, his mouth wreaked all sorts of havoc with her thoughts and her body. Her pulse kicked to a rapid staccato, and her stomach tumbled and churned in an unfamiliar fashion.

His tongue grazed her lips as his hand brushed the side of her breast. She gasped against his mouth. The next instant, she was abruptly, and none too gently, planted on her feet.

"Fiend seize it! What am I doing, kissing *you?*" His voice hardly above a whisper, self-loathing colored Lord Clarendon's tone. His prior curtness had returned in full force.

Stunned, Adaira stared at him, her mind a whirl of confused emotions. One moment he was swatting her bum. The next, he kissed her like a man long-starved. Then he thrust her away as if oozing pox sores covered her.

"You need to return to the keep." Roark surged to his feet. He shoved past her to snatch his waistcoat and jacket.

She tottered unbalanced for a moment.

He stomped several steps along the stable before swiveling back to her, impatience stamped on his face. "Come along. Stop dawdling."

Adaira started for him, still wobbly on her feet.

Blasted kisses.

She was all muddled, and he stood there seemingly unaffected, except for the return of the sour scowl to his face. Not the reaction a woman wanted when she'd been soundly kissed. Mayhap he'd found her kisses unsatisfactory.

Another mark against her.

She stopped before him, her gaze resting on his mouth. She started to lick her lips. Catching herself, she closed her mouth and met his mocking gaze. Heat swept her cheeks.

Och, it was certain he knew what she was thinking.

His brows arched, and one corner of his mouth inched upward cynically. "Stop acting as if you've never been kissed before. No *chaste* maid kisses in the manner *you* just did."

His insinuation snapped her out of her befuddled state. Fury raged through her and exploded into a red haze. Adaira punched him.

~

Father bursting into Adaira's chamber awakened her. Head muzzy, she fought to remember the lovely dream she'd been having. Someone had been holding her in his arms, kissing her senseless. Oh, it had been beyond wonderful.

Intense blue eyes filtered into her memory.

No! Now the scunner is invading my dreams.

She dared to open her eyes a crack.

Father was in high dudgeon, seldom seen wrath flashing in his dark brown eyes. Before she could sit up or wipe the sleep from her face, he demanded an explanation.

"Why did ye leave yer room last night, Adaira, after ye gave me yer word?"

She caught her breath.

How did he know?

Had the earl told him?

What explanation had his Royal Pomposity given for his split lip?

Not the truth, for certain.

Scooting to a sitting position, she brushed her hair away from her face. "I only—"

"Nae, daughter! Ye were no' to leave yer room." Her father threw up his hands and turned from her in angry frustration. He spun back around to face her, his hands planted on his hips. "Arena ye in enough trouble already, damn it?"

Her breath left her in a whoosh.

Father had cursed—in the presence of a woman.

Adaira stared at him, stunned. He was livid. Oh, but she'd done it up brown this time. She was in suds to her neck.

"Did ye think I'd no' find out? Brayan saw ye and the earl leavin' the stables."

She'd just bet he did. *God rot the rat.*

What was *he* doing prowling about in the wee hours?

Spying on *her?*

Her breath hitched. Had Brayan seen—?

Lord help her if he had. The notion was too horrid to contemplate.

Father ranted on. "When I questioned his lordship, he said ye'd been desperate to check on yer mare. Mortified to have been caught soused and half-dressed with a cut lip from plowin' into a post, he begged *my* pardon."

What?

Plowing into a post?

She clenched her bruised hand. What a pile of horse— *codswallop.*

"The man needed some privacy, and I dinna blame him for tossin' back a few." Father brushed a hand over his eyes. "For the love of God, Addy. Last night, he learned his brother killed their mother!"

Adaira winced, and unwarranted compassion for Roark beset her.

She flung aside the sheet, then swung her legs over the side of the bed. She hopped to the floor, completely uncon-cerned about appearing before him in her chaste white nightgown.

"Father, I—"

He held up his hand, although it wasn't the gesture that

effectively silenced her. No, the glint of unyielding steel in his usually warm eyes did. Ire darkened his gaze to obsidian. Despite the lingering heat of yesterday, a chill gripped her. This was a side of her father she'd not seen before.

"Lass." He leveled her with a penetrating look.

She swallowed, suddenly wary.

"Yer mother and I are done up with ye. We tried to be understandin' when ye started paradin' about in men's breeches. We even encouraged yer unladylike interests in horse breedin' and fencin', hoping ye'd eventually find yer own path to happiness."

Blowing out a gusty breath, he broke eye contact with her. He sank his focus to the floor while he rubbed the back of his neck. "Ye've been discontented and troubled for nigh on four years."

Adaira padded to him on bare feet.

He lifted his weary gaze to hers.

Laying her hand on his solid arm, she searched his eyes. "I know I shouldn't have gone. It was foolish of me."

The memory of his lordship's kiss was far more disturbing to her than the blow she'd landed him. Or the swats on her bottom.

Pray God, his lordship hadn't revealed that, too?

No, that would paint him in a less than admirable light. His lordship's sole purpose seemed to be to ridicule and disparage her. She reluctantly conceded she'd given him sufficient fodder to fuel that fire. Dash it all, enough to fuel a conflagration for the annual Guy Fawkes Bonfire Night celebration.

Father stared at her, his expression pensive. Melancholy softened his craggy features, and a sad half-smile skewed his mouth.

"Ye are always sorry afterward, lass. It's time ye act yer age. Yer mother was married, bore a child, and was widowed by the time she was one score, scarcely five months older than ye are now. Seonaid is more mature than ye at times."

Inwardly, Adaira flinched. That stung. Her sister was but six and ten.

He stepped to the door and withdrew the key from the inside lock.

"No!" Adaira gasped, immediately comprehending the significance.

Once he slid the key into the outer keyhole, he moved back to the center of the room.

Grasping his thick forearm, she begged. "Don't do this."

She'd stay in her room, but there was something about being locked in.

She shuddered. It was too much like a prison. The whispers of Newgate's horrors still haunted her even though the earl had given his word that she wouldn't go to jail.

In some small measure, she understood how he must've felt as her prisoner. The helplessness. The powerlessness. Entirely at someone else's mercy. Her father was her jailor, and she hadn't a doubt he loved her wholeheartedly. She'd been a hostile stranger to the earl when she imprisoned him. He'd also been injured—an injury she'd caused.

"I give you my word. I'll stay here. I..." She gulped past the lump pressing the back of her throat. "I know I made a mistake."

Father slowly shook his head. "Nae, ye've made one unfortunate choice too many. Now yer mother and I, Ewan, and Lord Clarendon, too, will contemplate a solution."

Nibbling her lower lip, she plucked at her nightgown.

She sent her father a hesitant glance. "Does *he* have to be involved?"

The earl would demand full accountability without a jot of mercy.

Do I truly deserve any?

It was evident Father knew without asking who *he* was. He angled his head. "Aye. It's his favor we seek. Ye'd best hope he's no' a vindictive man, Addy. It does no' bode well for ye if he is."

He strode to the door, and with a hand on the latch, said, "Even though Ewan's a viscount and laird of Craiglocky, the Earl of Clarendon wields far more power. He's a very influential peer, and he kens it."

She nodded in reluctant agreement.

Why couldn't the earl have been some plain, unremarkable milksop, more interested in insects and tide pools than conventions or decorum? Why did the man have such a rigid sense of propriety?

And such lovely lips?

A movement behind her father caught her attention. Following her gaze, he half-turned and, upon seeing Maisey, motioned for her to enter. Her gaze lowered, she scurried into the chamber, carrying a tray. She made straight for the table before the window seat. Uncovering the food, she began noisily arranging Adaira's breakfast.

Her stomach growled as the aromas of fresh cinnamon buns and ham drifted to her nose. Worry had prevented her from eating most of her evening meal.

Father glanced at Maisey, then met Adaira's gaze square on. His voice a low rumble, he said, "His lordship has us at Point Non-Plus. Any reasonable suggestion he makes for yer punishment, I fully intend to agree with."

She pursed her lips and narrowed her eyes. "I see."

Why did she feel betrayed?

She'd brought this on herself. Every action she'd taken, every choice she'd made, she'd known the consequences.

At least she'd thought she had.

Drawing in a deep, fortifying breath, she gave him a shaky smile. "How long am I to be confined?"

"Two weeks." He shifted his gaze to Maisey once more.

She paused in straightening the bed covers, looking to him expectantly.

"I'll leave the key in the lock." Father motioned to the key protruding from the door. "Attend yer mistress, and when ye're done, see ye bring me the key. I'll be in the library."

Maisey, her blue eyes round as dinner plates, bobbed her head. "Yes, Sir Hugh."

She darted Adaira an apologetic glance and tried to smile. It looked more like a sickly grimace.

Adaira followed her father to the doorway. "Is he still here?"

"Nae, he left at first light to convey his brother to Newgate and deliver Ewan's letters to the Secretary of War."

She furrowed her forehead.

How would his lordship confer with Father and Ewan about her sentence, then?

Perchance, once the earl was back in England, he'd find it too inconvenient to communicate about the matter. For certain, Lord Clarendon wouldn't return to Craiglocky. He had no more liking for her than she did for him.

What about that kiss? taunted a voice in her head.

It meant nothing.

Lord Clarendon was half-foxed, and she, well, she'd allowed her fear about Vala and Maximus—for that was what she'd named the colt—to overcome common sense.

The kiss meant less than nothing. It wasn't worth a blink.

Liar, whispered the same mocking voice.

"Do hush!" Addy muttered crossly while sweeping her hair behind her shoulders.

Father gave her a quizzical look. "Pardon?"

"Nothing, Father. I was scolding myself aloud."

He angled his brow in obvious suspicion. Pausing beyond the door, he said, "Ye canna have visitors, either."

He inclined his head in Maisey's direction. "She'll attend ye twice a day, but she willna stay to dress or talk with ye."

Adaira's shoulders slumped in resignation. From habit, she fingered the cross resting on her breastbone. How would she endure two weeks of isolation?

"Would you send some books on animal husbandry from the library, please?" Not that she was overly fond of reading, but she had to have something to occupy her time. She wasn't about to take up embroidery or tatting. "You'll see to my horses? Fionn needs exercise daily. He prefers me to ride him, but will tolerate Jocky or Ewan."

Father's features softened. "Dinna worry about yer beasties. We'll see they're well cared for."

He smiled then, the first hint of happiness she'd observed in him since this whole debacle began yesterday. "The earl is mighty impressed with yer horseflesh. He's of a mind to purchase some of the yearlin's and spoke of a joint breedin' endeavor."

Adaira gaped.

Was he serious?

As if she'd *ever*—as long as she had breath in her body, as long as the Church of Scotland sanctioned marriages at Gretna Green, as long as...as Dugall gobbled down Sorcha's shortbread like a man long starved ever—agree to such a ludicrous scheme.

Ever.

She stifled a hysterical giggle when her thoughts turned to discussing breeding procedures with the earl. How ridiculously discomfiting. Surely the heat infusing her was caused by outrage, or—she cast a glance to the windows, yes, the sun was pulsing off the pane—the temperature outside.

Maisey approached them, wringing her hands in her apron. "Yer breakfast is prepared, and I made yer bed." She sliced a nervous glance toward Adaira's father. "Do ye need anythin' else, Miss Adaira?"

There was a hopeful tone in her voice.

She was such a loyal dear.

Adaira sighed. "No, Maisey. I can manage well enough on my own, thank you."

The maid dipped a curtsy, and Adaira bit the inside of her cheek to stop the smile that threatened. Maisey only curtsied when Father was present.

He stepped aside to let the maid pass, and she continued down the hallway.

"Dinna be too hasty to say no to the breedin' venture, lass. Clarendon has some remarkable horseflesh himself." He gave her an intent look. "Ye'd do well to remember whose keep this is, and why ye have been allowed yer discretion with the horses, Adaira. The earl may very well make a contract between the two of ye a contingency of yer retribution."

"Never!" she vowed, fists clenched. Blackmail her,

would his lordship? He had no right to her new line of horseflesh.

Father scowled. "Ye'll have nae say in the matter if it's what he demands."

With that dour declaration, he closed the door. Metal scraped against metal as he turned the key in the lock.

"We'll see about that," Adaira muttered mutinously.

Fourteen

The deed was done.

Three days after leaving Craiglocky, traveling day and night, Roark delivered Edgar to Newgate. They'd stopped at Cadbury Park for thirty minutes enabling Roark to exchange the borrowed horse for one of his own. He'd refused to ride in the carriage with Edgar. Without a backward glance, he left his brother to rot and made for the Home Office straightaway.

Maman's words, spoken to him when he was but eight years old, echoed in his mind as he rode the few blocks.

"You must guide and protect your brother, Rory. He doesn't have your wisdom or ability to make right choices."

May Maman, God rest her soul, forgive him.

He was good and done with guiding or protecting Edgar. Roark clenched his teeth against remorse and grief as he dismounted Tenacity. He handed the reins to an overheated groom in primrose and emerald livery.

Edgar was reaping what he'd sown, ensnared by his evil deeds. Removing his gloves and hat, Roark shook off the guilt niggling him. His brother was well beyond redemption, at least here on Earth.

Roark ran up the steps to the Home Office, Edgar's mocking words still ringing in his ears.

"There's no proof, Rory, damn you to hell. I'll not hang. You wait and see. I'll be a free man again, and soon. When I am, you had best watch your back. I'll not forget your betrayal, *brother*."

Proof or not, Edgar had let a jot of the truth slip. Roark needed no more convincing. He knew his brother.

The venom in Edgar's voice, and the hatred radiating from his wintry eyes, raised the hairs on the back of Roark's neck. Edgar looked and sounded like the old earl.

Roark strode down the musty corridors of the Home Office. He had one intent—delivering the missives Sethwick sent to the Secretary of War, Bartholomew Yancy, the Earl of Ramsbury. Then, Roark planned to return to the relative peace and quiet of his estate, Cadbury Park, for the remainder of the summer.

How ironic that his conscience plagued him more for swatting Adaira than it did for abandoning his brother to Newgate. One was more deserved than the other, that was why. He couldn't blame his actions in Craiglocky's stables that night on being half-sprung either. Yes, he'd had a bit to drink. Hell, a great deal to drink, but he knew perfectly well what he was doing when he'd spanked her.

Guilt thrummed through him. He'd taken his ire out on her, although her irascible behavior was to blame in part. He still didn't know what possessed him to kiss her. She'd been so pitiful, sobbing on the stable floor. Once he held her in his arms, rational thought had fled. As had his desire to find who'd helped imprison him.

The despair in Adaira's voice when she'd sobbed she

might go to jail or hang had lodged in the pit of his stomach. He'd been unable to keep from comforting and reassuring her.

And, by God, he'd enjoyed every moment.

When the hot-blooded vixen began returning his kisses, he'd been hard-pressed not to tumble her in the pile of straw. He might've if the bedding had been clean and fresh. Her passionate responses were not those of an innocent.

His groin stirred at the recollection.

No, he was confident it wouldn't have been her first time, and the notion rankled.

After two wrong turns amongst the miles of corridors in Whitehall, he forced himself to sequester those memories and focus on the task at hand. At last, he reached the secretary's office. Roark gave a sharp rap on the ornately carved double door.

"Come." The thick wood muffled Yancy's clipped command.

Opening the heavy door, Roark paused for a heartbeat before stepping through the entrance. Yancy sat hunched over his desk. He held several papers in one hand and a quill in the other. He glanced up, his green eyes widening, and a grin split his face.

"Clarendon! What a pleasant surprise."

He reared up, dropping the papers and setting the quill aside. Yancy strode across the room and seized Roark's hand in a firm grip. Pumping his arm, Yancy slapped him on the shoulder. His astute gaze studied Roark.

"I say, you look like bloody hell."

Roark offered him a rueful smile as he handed the packet over. "From Sethwick. You're to read them at once."

At Yancy's raised brow, Roark explained. "I just came from Craiglocky."

"Ah, yes, I knew Sethwick was there. Something to do with escorting Miss Stapleton, I believe. Care for a drop of brandy?"

Yancy made for a small cherry-wood cabinet, tossing the packet onto his cluttered desk as he passed by. "You look like you could use a stiff drink, old chap."

"Yes, well, as to that, I've spent the past three days traveling here in rather a hurry. One of Sethwick's sisters mistook me for Edgar. She locked me in the keep's dungeon for another few days." He pointed to his cracked lip. "She also gave me this."

A vision of Adaira's swollen pink lips, moist from his kisses, widened his smile. By Jove, the chit kissed like a wanton.

Yancy's jaw dropped, the brandy decanter poised in midair. "The devil she did!" He poured a generous splash into the glass, glanced at Roark, and added a dab more. "Which sister?"

"You've met Sethwick's sisters?"

Yancy nodded before taking a drink himself.

"Yes, at a house party given by the Marquis and Marchioness Betheridge two, perhaps three, years ago. I believe you're acquainted with their son, Flynn, the Earl of Luxmoore. They're distant relations to Giselle Ferguson if I recall correctly. I believe Luxmoore's paternal grandmother was also Scots and is somehow related to McTavish."

Roark nodded. "Yes, I know Luxmoore well. We were boyhood chums. His father has a hunting lodge a few miles from my estate. The chap's an eternal optimist with a perpetual grin on his face and a curvaceous woman on his arm."

Yancy chuckled. "Yes, that's him. As to the daughters, one was quite young and painfully shy. Another had eyes like Sethwick's." A far-off expression flitted across his features. "'Pon rep, truly the most exquisite woman-child I've ever seen," he murmured.

Roark gave Yancy a sharp look.

The secretary raised his glass and grinned. "And the eldest, a dark-haired, petite hoyden who let a snake—a rather large snake I might add—loose on the dance floor amid a waltz."

Yancy laughed. "The ladies were not amused, especially since the night before, someone had released a dozen baby rabbits in the music room. Earlier in the day, she'd hidden all the chamber pots."

He topped the crystal decanter. "Come to think of it, she never confessed. She just glared daggers with those black eyes. A hostile bit of fluff."

"That would be Adaira," Roark said.

And her eyes aren't black. They're coffee brown with citrine flecks.

Damn his eyes. Had he said that aloud?

A sharp glance at the secretary told him he hadn't.

He was neither surprised nor entertained by Yancy's revelation. Neither did it please Roark that he remembered what color Adaira's eyes were. He fingered his lip. The swelling was gone. Only a small scab at the corner indicated he'd been clobbered recently.

How old had she been two years ago? Seven and ten? Eight and ten? Old enough to know better. He rubbed his forehead. Yes, she most definitely needed instruction in proper decorum.

Yancy picked up the second glass, his signet ring clinking against the crystal. "Adaira, was your jailor?" Humor laced his voice. His gaze dipped to Roark's lip, and he flashed another sardonic grin.

"Yes." Roark's clipped response was harsher than he'd intended at the reminder of his imprisonment. He unbuttoned his coat, grateful for the cooling draft wafting in through the open window behind Yancy's desk.

He wrinkled his nose.

Unfortunately, not only did the din of the city carry into the office, London's summertime stench, the putrid Thames, and rotting refuse and excrement piled along the streets did as well. He yearned for the freshness of Cadbury Park.

Or the balmy heather-scented air of Craiglocky.

"By-the-by, my stepsister is Viscountess Sethwick now," he said.

Yancy's russet brows shot to his hairline. "Indeed?"

He chuckled, a low delighted rumble. "Sethwick, married." He shook his head and chuckled again. "You'll have to fill me in about that *on dit*, and that dungeon bit, too. Sounds most intriguing."

A sly smile teased the secretary's mouth.

Roark's lips twitched. "Undeniably."

"And a blow to your male pride, I imagine." Yancy did not attempt to hide his delighted snicker.

Taken aback, Roark stared at his friend. By God, Yancy was right. Roark's pride *did* sting. He'd been taken in by a slip of a girl. He arched a brow, then shook his head, chuckling in agreement. "Indubitably."

"Ah, do I detect a smattering of derision, my friend?" It was the secretary's turn to arch his brows.

"You do know you'll be mocked when word gets out, Clarendon." He crossed to Roark. "And it will. You cannot keep something like that a secret, old chum. Too many parties involved."

"I'm aware. Sethwick and I hope to keep the murmurings to a minimum, nonetheless."

"I assume there'll be no complaint filed?"

"Not by me, and I've not authorized anyone else to do so."

Yancy nodded. "Good. A female relative of a peer having charges laid against her, and Scotswoman to boot—" He swiped a hand through his hair. "Ugly, complicated business, that."

"Indeed, which is precisely why I've negotiated a different recourse with Sethwick," Roark said.

At least he'd been saved the task of calling Sethwick out, although the circumstances surrounding the viscount's marriage to Yvette were highly unusual, to say the least.

Canon Law proved to be quite convenient when an expedited marriage was necessary in Scotland. Now that Yvette was married and her honor was intact, he chose to ignore the tongue-wagging surrounding the betrothal. Compared to Edgar's imprisonment as a traitor to the Crown, the betrothal gossip was trivial.

Roark swallowed an oath.

So much for preventing further smears against the family name, though.

"Here." Yancy handed Roark his brandy.

"Have a seat." The secretary waved, indicating the black leather wingback chairs before the room's unlit fireplace. "And I'll take a look at Sethwick's missive."

Roark sank into the comfortable chair with a welcoming sigh. Raising the glass, he took a long drink. The brandy stung his injured lip, then burned a welcome trail of heat to his gut. He closed his eyes, barely noting the crackle of papers as Yancy removed them from their leather covering.

Lord, but Roark was tired. He hadn't had a decent night's rest in nigh on a week. No, it was closer to a fortnight. A pair of saucy dark chocolate eyes and rosy lips interrupted his musings.

"Well, I'll be damned." Yancy's oath yanked Roark fully awake.

"Edgar's finally been apprehended." Staring off into space, Yancy drummed his fingers on his desk. "But is there sufficient evidence to convict him?"

God willing.

His fingers stilled, and his compassionate gaze sought Roark's. "How fare you in this? Must be ruddy uncomfortable, him being your brother and all."

Roark winced inwardly. That was putting it mildly. "Edgar insists there isn't enough proof, and I fear there might well be some truth to his claim."

He took a sip of brandy, savoring the bold flavor and the slow burn to his belly.

"Even Sethwick's sources could find no conclusive evidence of my brother's involvement in either the poisonings or traitorous activities. Hell, Edgar helped the Crown by killing the two Italian spies who held Yvette after Aubry turned her over to them."

"Aubry?" Yancy interrupted, a puzzled frown furrowing his forehead.

"A jealous Ferguson cousin, I believe." Roark crossed his legs and took another swallow of the amber liquid. "The conniving chit fled after the deed was done."

A droll smile tilted Yancy's lips. "You and Sethwick do have some, ah, *interesting* relatives in your family trees." The secretary relaxed against his chair. "Edgar eliminating two spies may work in his favor, blast it."

"Indeed."

He tapped the papers before him with an ink-stained

forefinger. "That doesn't absolve him of his attempts to abduct Miss Stap—er, Lady Sethwick, in America. But, as he well knows, England's courts won't prosecute him for those crimes."

"Or the deaths of Maman and Gideon." Roark shoved to his feet. He lifted his glass. "May I?"

Yancy waved him toward the liquor cabinet, as he sifted through the papers once more. "By all means, help yourself."

Roark crossed the Turkish carpet, his boots sinking in the plush depths. "There was no indication of poisoning, you know. From my medical studies, my guess is he used evening nightshade."

Damnation, how could he stand here talking calmly about the methods his brother used to murder their mother and stepfather?

Yancy nodded. "Sethwick suspected either that or arsenic. Both are undetectable, and their symptoms often mimic those of a fever."

After pouring another dram of brandy, Roark turned and rested his hip against the cabinet. "My gut tells me my reprobate of a brother is responsible, although Yvette and Gideon were his targets, not Maman. With Yvette and her father out of the way, Maman would've been the sole heir to the Stapleton fortune. I've no doubt my brother planned on convincing Maman to bestow a generous settlement on him."

Roark shook his head. "Edgar could always manipulate our mother. As for the treason, who remains to testify against him? Will it make any difference?"

Yancy heaved a gusty sigh. "The English court system is a muddled mess, as you well know, Clarendon. Half the time, an innocent man stands accused of a crime, based purely on hearsay or someone hired to swear the accused committed the crime."

He straightened the papers on his desk, adding, "Punishments as harsh as hanging are administered within hours. Then there are cases of guilty parties greasing someone's fist, bribing their way out of prison, or living in luxury under house arrest for months, even years, on end."

Roark angled his head in agreement. "Money, power, and position are used against the accused as often as they're exploited to exonerate the guilty." He snorted in disgust. "Even suspected of poisoning our mother and stepfather, attempting to abduct and despoil Yvette, and betraying England, I fear Edgar may walk away a free man."

"Damn," Yancy said.

Roark slapped his palm against the cabinet. The crystal ware clinked and tinkled. "It's the injustice of the situation that infuriates me."

How was it possible the same blood ran in his and Edgar's veins?

Was Roark also capable of such dark acts?

He had the temper, though he kept a tight rein on it. Where did such corruption originate?

He wiped his hand across his brow.

Asinine question, dolt.

Roark knew full well.

Their sire. Sherman Marquardt. Satan's spawn and evil personified.

He'd inherited the earldom when his older brother had broken his neck in a hunting accident. *A suspicious accident.* Sherman's first two wives died young, one during childbirth, and one after throwing herself from an upper story window after one of Sherman's terrible beatings.

Maman had been seven and ten when she'd been forced to marry the three and fifty-year-old degenerate.

And she'd died by her youngest son's hand.

May God forgive Edgar for Roark wasn't sure he ever could.

Staring at the floor, he clenched his hands into tight fists. Rage and grief squeezed his chest in a sharp, unyielding vice. He couldn't pull in any air.

God, he was suffocating.

Breathe. That's it. Take a deep breath and let it out. See, the pressure is easing.

Maman's whispered words of assurance carried to him across the expanse of time. The iron band around his ribs relaxed.

Roark gave himself a mental shake. He lifted his gaze to Yancy's sympathetic one. Blister it, had he spoken his thoughts aloud?

Heat crept across his face.

The secretary cleared his throat and directed his attention to the papers he held. "I'll respond to these today." He lifted the letters slightly. "Thank you for bringing them directly here. I know it cannot have been easy for you."

Roark offered a cynical smile and shrugged. "We all make sacrifices." He set the empty glass on the cabinet. "I must be off."

After shaking Yancy's hand again, he left the secretary frowning over Ewan's correspondences.

Stepping onto Horse Guards Avenue, Roark blinked several times against the sun's unyielding glare. He set his hat upon his head before taking Tenacity's reins from the sweating groom. *Poor sot.* He handed the chap a shilling. "Here, purchase yourself something cool to drink."

Wiping his dripping brow and face with a none too

clean handkerchief, the groom bobbed his head. "Thank you, my lord."

Roark swung into the saddle. The mare quivered and sidestepped, as eager to be away from the city as he was. If he left now and paced the mare carefully, he'd make Cadbury Park by nightfall.

Turning in the saddle, he cast a cursory glance at the Whitehall. He bent and smoothed a hand across Tenacity. A thick rope-like scar encircled her whisky-colored neck. "What say you, my beauty? Can we be home by tonight? It's not an easy ride."

Tossing her head, Tenacity nickered, and Roark smiled. The Flemish mare would die for him. He'd saved her from brutal abuse. He'd come across her, bloody and beaten, too weak to stand, and being dragged by the neck. Her owner had been intent on delivering the young mare to the slaughterhouse, all because of a mild stifle injury, no doubt caused by another of the sot's thrashings.

Roark hadn't known if she'd live or die. He'd spent two weeks by her side, sleeping in her stall, and using every bit of medical knowledge he possessed to save her. She'd shown such tenacity in her will to live, Roark had named her thus. Her devotion to him was only outmatched by his to her.

He'd like to breed her, and several other mares, to that stallion of Adaira's. They'd produce a splendid line of horseflesh. That was why Roark had hinted a breeding partnership would do much to appease his ire.

Sir Hugh seemed amenable to the suggestion.

Adaira possessed some exceptional young horseflesh that Roark was determined to acquire. Somehow, he doubted the Scot's saucy daughter would willingly oblige.

What was Ferguson thinking, permitting her to be involved in such a masculine endeavor?

Horse breeding of all things?

It was long past time someone curtailed Adaira's uncultivated ways.

It's none of your affair, whispered his conscience.

It became mine when she locked me underground.

With a shake of his head, Roark headed for home. He trotted Tenacity along the avenue, her hooves clattering over the cobblestones. An idea began to bloom, burgeoning, and growing along with his ever-widening grin.

By God, he'd do it. He would.

He touched his sore lip with his tongue. Adaira's small tongue had touched him there. His length hardened against his thigh. *Confound it*. Merely thinking of her had him aching to bed her.

He had just the thing to bring Adaira Ferguson up to scratch, once and for all.

He'd make a lady of that wild Scottish vixen yet.

Fifteen

Adaira punched the pillow in her lap. Legs crossed, she sat in the middle of her bed.

"I shan't do it. I shan't. They cannot make me. I'll run away to Tante Floressa's. She's invited me to visit her many times over the past two years."

Never mind the French Wars had prevented any such thing. Tante Floressa was somewhat of a flibbertigibbet. The only time Adaira had visited France, her aunt had nearly swooned when she spied the constellation of freckles on Adaira's nose. She hadn't even been six yet.

Wonder what she'd make of my breeches?

A momentary smile hitched the corners of Adaira's mouth before shifting into a scowl. There would be no more breeches. She punched the pillow twice more with sharp hard blows, pretending it was the Earl of Clarendon's smug face. "I'm glad I hit him," she muttered. "Wish I'd hit him harder. Wish I'd broken that perfect, straight, arrogant nose of his."

Whap.

Adaira slugged the pillow again, this time hard enough that it flew across the room. The cushion bounced off an armchair before tumbling to the floor. She knew she sounded like a petulant child and acted like one, too.

She didn't care. What they asked was *too* much.

She hugged another small pillow to her chest and almost moaned aloud.

Father had confiscated her riding crop after his lordship had squawked that she'd attacked him in the crofter's cottage. She hadn't meant to strike Lord Clarendon with the weapon, and the earl knew it. Now, how was she to protect herself? She supposed she'd have to start toting a dagger sheathed to her thigh like Yvette's Romani cousin, Lady Warrick.

Wouldn't that put the stuffy earl in a dither?

The punishment Adaira's parents levied on her, dictated by the earl, of course, was far too harsh for her crimes. He'd suffered no serious injury. His detainment hadn't been torturous or lengthy.

Yet, the sentences imposed on her were both of the latter: A year at Miss Hortensia Doddington's Finishing School or a Season in London.

"Oh, God," she groaned.

Adaira had to choose.

Three months of torture or nine?

Hell or Hades?

She sighed, dropping the pillow to her lap.

No, she'd not blame her parents.

This chastisement was the earl's doing, the pompous prig. He'd hinted at dire consequences if they didn't cooperate. They'd all heard his veiled threats during the meeting he'd insisted upon. The blackguard's demands were nothing short of extortion.

Adaira blinked fiercely against the scalding tears welling in her eyes. She wouldn't cry. She would not. Her throat and head ached from the effort to curtail her tears. She'd not give that interfering churl the satisfaction.

She peered around the bed, seeking her handkerchief.

She lifted the pillow on her lap.

Nope. Not there.

She tilted one muslin clad knee up, then the other. She snuffled loudly. Where was that dratted handkerchief? She spied the wadded lacy square under the chair before the fireplace.

Oh, that was right. She'd thrown it on the floor in a fit of temper.

With a shrug, she wiped her nose on her sleeve.

So there, your lordship.

No more breeches. No more shirts or vests. No more knee-high boots. Just proper lady's gowns. And footwear. And—gads, the worse of it—perfectly coiffed hair *all the time*. No more tying it back with a ribbon or letting it hang loose.

Even a suitable habit for riding Fionn was required now. One of those heavy military-styled atrocities, no doubt. The poor horse wouldn't know what to do with all that fabric draped across him. *She* wouldn't know what to do mounted on him sidesaddle.

Another preposterous constraint used by men to control women. As if seeing a woman's legs were sinful. What drivel. God gave females legs. The only thing immoral about them was what wicked men's minds imagined.

The truth was, even if she had a riding habit, Adaira wasn't confident she could keep her seat in a sidesaddle. It had been years since she'd ridden on one of the ridiculous things, and that had been on a pony. She certainly couldn't ride neck or nothing, much less jump fences or hedges. No, a safe, sedate, *boring* trot or slow canter was all she could expect to be permitted.

In any event, that issue was moot. Thanks to the earl's ruddy meddling, she wouldn't be riding Fionn for some time to come. Not until she had a riding habit made. Not until she learned to ride sidesaddle again. And not until Fionn was trained to carry her that way.

Oh, he was going to hate this as much as she did.

Several fat tears plopped onto her clenched hands. *Drat, drat, and drat.* Confounded waterworks. Confounded earl.

She flopped onto her back, staring at the bed's ivory and blue canopy while toying with her necklace. She had to acknowledge that in the scheme of things, the earl's options were vastly better than Newgate Prison or hanging, but...

At her age, she was far too old for finishing school or a coming out. Plus, the little Season didn't start until the end of August, and Miss Doddington's lessons wouldn't commence until the end of September.

So, the earl had *generously* suggested Adaira's instruction in refinement begin with a round of English house parties this summer to, "*Introduce her to society and allow her a more private environment to acquire the behavior and manners expected of a refined lady of quality.*"

Twaddle and claptrap.

Another pillow sailed through the air, hitting the wall with a distinct thump.

To imply she received no instruction in proper decorum was insulting to her parents.

Why were they allowing his high-handedness?

What leverage did he have over them?

The earl proposed her journey into sophistication begin with a month-long house party at his estate.

Was the man short on wits?

Why, in God's name, would he want her anywhere near him? She'd no desire to be within a day's ride of him—no, a fortnight's ride. Had he made reforming her his personal mission?

To tame her?

To what end?

She toyed with the cross at her neck. After three week's absence, he had the audacity to return to Craiglocky two days ago. This time her confinement was self-imposed. She'd no intention of encountering that lout unless absolutely unavoidable.

A light rapping interrupted her thoughts.

"Who is it?" She wished she'd been able to lock the door, but Father still held the key.

"It's Yvette. May I come in?"

Adaira sat up and muttered a watery, "Yes."

The door opened with a slight swish. Yvette glided into the room. "I've come to help you prepare for your visit."

Adaira swung her legs over the edge of the bed. "*Visit?*" She stood. "Visit?" she repeated. "As in, Cadbury Park visit?"

Even to her ears, she sounded like a simpleton. She cleared her throat and tried to pin several loose curls back in place. "Surely, we aren't to leave for Lord Clarendon's this soon?"

She thought she'd have a few more days to prepare, to brace herself emotionally.

Yvette smiled, her sapphire eyes reassuring. "Not yet, but in a week."

She scanned the room, taking in the pillows and handkerchief on the floor. There was no condemnation in her eyes. "Your mother and sisters will be here shortly."

Before she finished speaking, the three women filed into Adaira's chamber. She ran her hands over her rose and jonquil chintz dress, smoothing the wrinkles from the gown.

"Why must we begin packing this soon, Mother?" Adaira crossed the room to pick up one pillow. Dangling it from her hand, she moved to the other. "Surely a week in advance is not necessary."

She bent and retrieved the second pillow. After tossing them both on her bed, she folded her arms and waited for an explanation.

"We're not packing as yet, Addy, just taking stock," Mother said.

Adaira turned to the mirror in the corner and attempted to straighten her mussed hair. Her tear-swollen eyes peered back at her, taking in her rumpled gown and her stockinged feet peeking from beneath the ruffled hem of her gown.

She looked a sight.

"Ewan and Yvette will leave for London tomorrow. He has pressing business to attend to." Mother swung open the doors of one of Adaira's armoires. She removed a morning gown in the palest lavender. "While they're in Town, Yvette has generously offered to make the rounds and purchase anything we might need in the way of gloves and other fripperies."

Isobel looped her arm through Yvette's and smiled at her. "Hopefully, we won't overwhelm you with purchases."

Seonaid joined them, taking Yvette's other arm. "We don't mean to be a bother."

Adaira sensed her sisters' excitement. Even shy Seonaid was anticipating the extended stay at Cadbury Park, though it meant time away from her beloved pets. Attired in the latest fashions and their hair intricately twisted and pinned atop their heads, Adaira couldn't help but notice how lovely the three were.

Yvette flashed Seonaid a brilliant smile, then patted Isobel's hand resting on her arm. "I shall enjoy making the rounds. I assure you, it will be no trouble. I quite like shopping."

Laying the gown across her arm, Mother pulled out another. This time, a simple white silk adorned with emerald green ribbons and embroidered in green and gold along the hem and bodice. She poked around the bottom of the wardrobe and frowned. "I was sure you had gold slippers."

A stab of guilt sliced Adaira. She cast a covert glance to her bed, beneath which she'd hidden her ruined shoes. She'd meant to dispose of them but forgot due to the ordeals of the past weeks.

Removing four more gowns from the wardrobe, Mother sailed to the bed. She laid them atop the rumpled coverlet. "Yvette and Ewan will travel directly to Lord Clarendon's from London. It takes less than a day, so they'll arrive at Cadbury Park a day or two after we do."

A ray of hope stirred. "Might I go with them?"

Adaira didn't care if Ewan and Yvette arrived one *hour* later than everyone else. It was one hour without the earl's stodgy presence. The shopping she could well do without, but it was a sacrifice she was willing to make.

"No, *chére*, I'm afraid not.' Mother shook her head. "His lordship was most insistent we arrive before the last Friday in July for a ball he's hosting."

Once more before the armoire, she continued to remove Adaira's gowns.

It seemed they had this all worked out, didn't they?

Adaira squashed a surge of bitterness. She wouldn't take her vexation out on Mother, Yvette, or her sisters. They weren't the target of her irritation. She shrugged her shoulders. "Let's be about it, then."

The others bestowed relieved smiles upon her. Evidently, they'd expected a battle. The knowledge caused Adaira a painful twinge.

Was she truly that difficult?

Two hours later, wardrobes had been discussed and planned to the minutest detail. Yvette possessed a rather substantial list of items Mother deemed essential to a successful month-long visitation to the earl's. The women made their way below stairs, all of them, except Adaira, intent on a spot of coffee or tea and pastries.

"Are you sure you wouldn't like to join us, Addy? Sorcha made fatty cutties," Isobel said with a teasing smile.

Adaira nearly groaned aloud. *Fatty cutties?* They were her favorite sweet biscuit, bless Sorcha's heart. Adaira slid her hand into a glove, tugging the snug fabric over her splayed fingers.

"And fresh marmalade," Seonaid chimed. "You know how you adore marmalade on warm scones." Her lips curved in a gentle smile. Laying her hand on Adaira's arm, she gave it a slight squeeze. "We've missed your company."

Gratitude warmed Adaira's heart as she tugged on the other glove. Her sisters were trying to lighten her mood and make her feel included. She'd been rather distant, spending a great deal of time alone, wandering the paths by the loch or secluded in her room.

Anything to avoid Brayan or the earl.

And truth to tell, her family.

She'd disgraced not only herself but her kin, and the full

impact of her impulsive actions weighed heavily on her. Although she was truly repentant, she resented His Royal Stodginess's meddling. He ought to leave the matter of her discipline to her parents.

Adaira gave her sisters a quick hug. "Thank you, but not today. Tomorrow I shall, I promise."

She squeezed Yvette's hand and smiled at Mother to include them. Forcing another upward tilt of her mouth, Adaira left the women at the foot of the stairs. She crossed the entry hall with quick strides. She had just stepped over the threshold when Mother called.

"Addy?"

Adaira half-turned in her mother's direction. "Yes?"

"*Chérie.*" Mother's gaze skimmed Adaira's bonnet and dress. "You're not riding."

It wasn't a question.

She bit back a glib retort. This wasn't her mother's fault.

She wouldn't behave like an *overindulged, cosseted child.* The words the earl had spewed at her in the dungeon.

"No, Mother, I don't intend to ride. I want to spend as much time as I can with Fionn and my other horses before we leave, however. I'll not do more than walk him around the paddock today."

Her mother approached, scooping a lacy white parasol from the stand beside the entry. "Here, take mine. You'd best become accustomed to using one, my dear."

A parasol?

Adaira stared.

Had she ever used a parasol?

Did she even *own* a parasol?

"Thank you. I surely would've forgotten."

And not accidentally either.

She obediently grasped the ivory handle. "We cannot have my fair complexion ruined by unsightly freckles, can we? Do be sure to add a parasol or two to the list of essentials to transform me into a respectable woman of quality."

A momentary flash of pain glinted in her mother's eyes.

Instant remorse pricked Adaira. Would she ever be able to control her rebellious tongue? She must. "I'm sorry. That was hateful of me." Adaira kissed her mother on her cheek. "I promise to use it every moment I'm outdoors. After all, I wouldn't want anything else to compromise me or my standing."

One must obey society's dictates, no matter how preposterous.

Seonaid gasped, pressing a hand to her throat and a shadow falling across her features. She stared at Adaira transfixed, as though she saw something else.

One of her visions.

Cold dread sliced through Adaira. The hairs stood up on her arms, and icy fingers of fear crawled down her spine. After all this time, had Seonaid finally seen something?

What, bugger it?

Her back to Seonaid, Mother was unaware, and Yvette and Isobel had already wandered to the great hall. They hadn't seen Seonaid's reaction either.

"We're having stovies and clootie dumpling for dinner tonight." Mother smoothed a wayward wisp of hair behind Adaira's ear. "We've missed you dining with us."

She gently grasped Adaira's shoulders, looking deeply into her eyes. Adaira recognized compassion and resolve in Mother's gaze.

"Lord Clarendon's not an ogre, Addy."

No, he's a ruddy trow—the devil's spawn.

Mother smiled, knowingly. "He's acting most generous,

and I believe you know that, too. You'll have to face him eventually. It would be best to get it over with, *chére*, sooner than later."

Why? So Adaira could be ridiculed and found wanting? So he could catalog her shortcomings and make her feel more inadequate as a woman? So she'd have to remember their not altogether unpleasant kiss? Fine then, wholly delicious kiss? Her stomach fluttered, and that peculiar quivering began between her legs again.

"I know. It's just that..." She sucked in a shaky breath. "He makes me..."

He makes me feel beneath his touch.

She shrugged lightly and shook her head before lowering her gaze. "I cannot. Not yet. I'm not ready."

She never would be. When did she become a coward?

She peeked at Seonaid through her lashes. Her sister had regained her composure, but her mouth was drawn into a firm line, her amber eyes flashing with indignation.

Seonaid *had* seen something. But what?

His lordship kissing Adaira in the stables?

Heaven forbid, Godwin's attack?

Or, something that as yet had not occurred?

Leaving her mother standing in the doorway, Adaira opened the parasol. Angling it over her shoulder, she descended two steps before sending a forced smile over her other shoulder. "I'll try to hurry so that I can join you for tea."

Mother's eyes brightened. "That would be *magnifique, chérie.*"

After another swift glance at Seonaid's strained face, Adaira made her way toward the stables. Chickens cackled and scampered out of her path.

She avoided eye contact with the clan members going

about their tasks in the bailey. She felt like an outsider amongst the people she'd known her entire life. She tilted the parasol, hiding her face in its protective shadow. The dratted thing was of some use after all. The copious layers of gaudy white lace drooping from the edge shielded her from the most curious stares, yet enabled her to look about covertly.

Niall stopped pounding whatever he was hammering and watched her pass. His kind gaze held pity as well. No doubt, Maisey had filled his ears.

Humiliation heated Adaira's cheeks.

Another bulky form emerged from the blacksmith's lean-to.

Brayan?

She didn't wait to find out but quickened her pace. Never had the stable seemed so far from the gatehouse.

The month away from her horses would be unbearable.

Darts of sadness and despair pricked her. How could she endure an entire Season without them? She'd decided a Season was the lesser, and shorter, evil of the two repugnant choices his lordship had presented her.

Perhaps Father would permit her to bring Fionn to London. Wasn't riding in Hyde Park all the crack? Or, was that Rotten Row? Wait, wasn't Rotten Row in Hyde Park?

She dared a hurried glance around her.

No one else seemed to be paying her any mind.

Venturing to the stables proved humiliating, none-theless. The stable hands treated her no differently since the mortifying thrashing, yet she burned with self-consciousness. Surely they had told others about the inci-dent unless his lordship had paid them not to. She wouldn't put bribery past him.

The earl wouldn't mention it to anyone, and she'd eat

the mire in the hog pen before she whispered a word of the degrading spanking. Father hadn't confronted her, so he must not know. Ewan hadn't breathed a hint that he knew anything untoward had occurred that night, either.

Lord Clarendon had kissed her and laid hands on her, both sufficient reasons to be called out. Ewan was a dab hand with pistols. She was certain he'd be the winner of such a match. The notion didn't bring her joy. While the earl was a prickly thorn in her side, she didn't wish him harm.

Adaira took another peek around her. A couple of women broke into hushed whispers as she passed them. Heat warmed her cheeks again.

Her unfortunate acquaintance with the earl had caused her to become unsure of herself. What was it about that blasted man that filled her with self-doubt? She'd always been confident and comfortable with her choices.

Until he appeared.

Now, she was uncertain. Nothing was clear anymore.

"Addy?" Heavy footsteps clomped behind her. "Addy, wait for me," Brayan called.

Dash it all. Though the stables were still several yards farther on, she didn't slow her pace. He grasped her elbow with a firm hand and forced her to stop or else make a scene. Adaira faced him, tilting the parasol until she met his eyes. She wanted to smack him with it, the rotten bounder.

"You forget yourself, Brayan."

His grip tightened a fraction.

Adaira dropped her gaze to his large grime-smudged fingers encircling her arm before raising her eyes to meet his once more. She arched a brow in annoyance.

Anger flickered in his eyes, and a surly expression marred his features. "Why dinna ye stop when I called ye?

Ye've been avoidin' me for weeks." Raising a hand, he smoothed a rough forefinger along her jaw, his broad features softening. "I've missed ye, lass."

His gaze sank to her breasts.

"What do you want?" Adaira took two steps backward, casting a furtive look around.

What if Lord Clarendon was near?

He couldn't see her and Brayan speaking together.

Brayan puffed out a gusty breath, shoving a hand through his coarse hair. "I told ye. I've missed ye." He gave her one of his familiar lopsided grins. "Ye arena still vexed at me for stealin' a kiss from ye?"

"Yes, Brayan, I am, but more so for your threat." Casting her gaze to the ground, she said, "I never should've involved you. That was wrong, and I need to ask you to forgive me, especially since I abducted the wrong man."

And this man, although not a spy or a traitor, was every bit as hard-hearted. She lifted her eyes to Brayan's.

"The earl can never learn that you helped me." Adaira laid a hand on his forearm, and his muscles contracted at her touch. He must be made to understand. "He's a powerful lord, Brayan, and we broke the law. The consequences for you would be severe."

Brayan scowled. "I'm no' afraid of that dandified prig."

Eyeing his bulging biceps, she murmured, "I'm sure you're not, but that's beside the point. We wronged him. He has every right to be livid. In truth, I'm somewhat astonished his retribution to me hasn't been far harsher."

Not that she was elated with what he required her to do to meet his approval.

Did she want his approval?

She doubted a Season in London could accomplish any such thing. Lord Clarendon had no way of knowing, no one had, that parading herself before the *ton* was akin to running naked as a robin through Hyde Park. Humiliating and torturous.

"Why are ye defendin' him?" Brayan's eyes darkened, and a sinister glint appeared in their depths. "Are ye sweet on him?"

"Don't be absurd."

"I've seen the way the lasses ogle him. I hear their sighs and whispers when he walks by." Brayan grabbed her upper arm again. "Has he kissed ye?"

Adaira jerked her arm lose. "You go too far."

"Nae," he growled. "Nothin' is too far when it comes to ye. I love ye, Addy. Ye are goin' to be mine. I've always kent it."

He lifted his head, staring intently over her parasol.

Is that why he'd made a point of telling Father he saw her and the earl leaving the stables?

Was Brayan that jealous?

Adaira turned to see where he looked. Several grooms were engaged in various activities with horses inside the paddock. After giving them a cursory glance, she swiftly scanned the other men.

Lord Clarendon wasn't present.

At least there was that to be grateful for.

Brayan's hoarse words rang in her ears. "I've been patient, waitin' for ye to realize we're meant to be together. I willna let another have ye."

Adaira swung around to face him. "Brayan—"

She swallowed. Her words would wound him, but they must be said. They were long overdue, truth to tell. He'd become possessive and unreasonable.

"I am not yours, nor will I ever be," she said firmly. "I've loved you like a brother, but naught else."

The stricken look on his face sliced straight to her heart.

"But ye will come to love me." Desperation warped his face and voice.

She shook her head. "No. I shan't."

Memories of another claiming she'd be his erupted to the surface. Her belly coiled, but she shoved the recollection aside. She closed her eyes and took a calming breath. "I don't know if—" She opened her eyes and met his gaze directly. "I don't think I'm capable of loving any man."

Why had she told him that?

"I... Ye dinna..." He slammed his mouth shut.

Fury and hurt fought for supremacy in his eyes. His jaw was rigid with repressed words and emotions. He spun away from her and tromped in the direction of the black-smith's before he switched course and broke into a run. Chickens and geese squawked and flapped their wings in alarm as he sprinted from the bailey, his boots stirring little billows of dust.

Tears filled Adaira's eyes, and she quickly dropped her gaze, blinking against the moisture. She'd lost her childhood friend this day. Her shoulders slumped. No, she'd lost him the day he threatened her. It had become final today. With a heavy heart and equally leaden feet, she resumed her journey to the stables.

Just outside the building, she lifted her focus from the dusty ground and searched the paddock for Fionn. A group of stable hands gathered around a newly broke mare at the far side of the paddock.

Ewan's gargantuan McTavish relatives, his uncle Duncan and cousins Gregor and Alasdair, clustered near the enclosure's gate. Ewan, Dugall, and Callum lounged against the three-railed fence, each with one booted foot on the lowest rung.

His back to her, hands at his hips, Father stood beside them watching the horses go through their paces. It was unusual for all the men to be here. Most days, they were in Craigcutty working on Yvette's foundling house or woolen mill.

A movement caught Adaira's eye.

Ewan waved her over, but she pretended not to see.

She was not pleased with him.

Why was he collaborating with the earl? The enemy? He was *her* brother. His loyalty should be to her.

Idly sliding the topaz cross at her neck to-and-fro, she frowned. This entire misunderstanding was turning into a Cheltenham tragedy. She rolled her eyes upward at the irony. And men accused women of being melodramatic.

She bowed her head. The weight of condemnation and censure, albeit unpleasant, were bearable. And yes, somewhat merited. Less so was her family's disloyalty.

Rotating the parasol, she blocked her view of the compound and effectively obstructed anyone from seeing her face as well.

Fionn wasn't in the paddock. Neither was Vala nor Maximus.

Spinning on her heels, Adaira continued to the stables. Stepping into the hospitable coolness, she blinked several times while her eyes adjusted to the darker interior. A heady mixture of straw, manure, and liniment met her nostrils. After folding the parasol, she tucked it beneath her arm.

Fionn stretched his neck over his stall door and showing his teeth in a horsey grin, whinnied a welcome.

She chuckled. "Missed me, have you?"

She propped the parasol against the wall, then hurried to him. Wrapping her arms around his neck, she whispered,

"I've missed you too. Forgive me for neglecting you. I've made a muddled mess of things, my friend."

To her right, another horse blew a hefty expanse of air before poking its head over the stall in greeting. Adaira ran a practiced eye over the beast.

Not one of hers.

"Well, hello. Who are you, my lovely?" She smoothed a hand over the big mare's satiny neck, coming to an abrupt halt and gasping when her fingers encountered a hardened scar. Adaira peered around the horse's head. Even in the muted light, she could see the rope-like mark encircling the mare's neck.

"My God, you poor thing!"

Fionn nuzzled the mare.

Was she coming into season?

"You became a father again mere weeks ago. Behave yourself. She's not part of your harem, you rogue." She caressed his silky neck, then kissed his muzzle. "I'm going to miss you."

Tears threatened, and he shifted restlessly. "I know. You want to gallop across the moors. I wish we could. I'm not permitted to ride you at present." She laid her head against his shoulder. "Everything has changed. I have to wear gowns now, even when I ride."

Tears spilled from her eyes, streaming down her cheeks. "And I have to use a sidesaddle. You'll not like it, I'm afraid. I shan't either."

Contemptible tears.

Adaira wiped at her eyes with her fingers. She had no handkerchief with her. The delicate cloth still lay on the floor in her bedchamber. "We'll never race across the meadows, *ventre a terre,* belly to ground, again. It's...it's... unladylike."

She gave up trying to stifle her tears. Clinging to Fionn, she gave way to the grief ripping at her heart. "Nothing will ever be the same," she sobbed. "I've made a powerful enemy, and he's determined to destroy me."

Strong arms turned her into a masculine embrace. "Not destroy. Just subdue a trifle."

Sixteen

Roark scrutinized the bonneted head against his chest. Adaira's delicate scent teased his nose. The urge to pull off her hat and kiss the crown of her head was overwhelming.

Why did he feel compelled to comfort her?

He'd seen her approach the stables, head bent, shoulders slumped, a becoming gown swishing about her ankles. A soft breeze ruffled the pink ribbon of her bonnet, and flirted with the hem of her gown, revealing tan half-boots.

Though she walked swiftly, the spring had left her step. She tried to hide beneath the parasol. Yet, he'd seen the despair in her dark eyes and the tension around her full mouth when her gaze roved the paddock.

He'd been standing on the other side of the mare, calming the high-spirited horse. He'd also seen Adaira speaking to a burly Scotsman who'd stopped her halfway across the bailey.

That warranted investigating.

Roark bent his head a fraction and inhaled. She smelled

exquisite like spring rain and lilies and sun-drenched meadows.

He resolutely squashed the guilt prodding him.

She might be despondent at present, but in the end, he was convinced she'd realize the benefits of moderation and decorum. Gentlewomen couldn't gallivant about unchaperoned wearing breeches, brandishing blades, and swearing like fishwives.

And abducting nobility.

It simply wasn't done. For Adaira's own good, for her safety, she needed to curtail her hoydenish ways and follow society's rules.

It was a blessed wonder she hadn't been set upon by some scurrilous cur as yet. A reprobate like Roark's sire, knifed to death by a crazed innkeeper after Father despoiled the man's daughter. That had taken a tidy sum to hush the gossip and provide for the poor girl's future.

Roark had spent his life setting to right the consequences of other people's corrupt choices. Edgar's arrest was the *coup de gras.* Not that Edgar's was the first allusion to treasonous behavior by a Marquardt.

Enough!

Roark deliberately curtailed his reflections and focused on the woman in his arms. It was apparent her parents adored her. In his estimation, they'd been lax in their management of her. It didn't bode well to give an unmarried woman, a young and beautiful unwed woman, too much freedom. Adaira would be in a dither if she knew, but he'd seen the relief on her parents' and Sethwick's faces when Roark stated his demands.

He wasn't altogether sure which pleased them more, however. Roark not laying charges against their daughter if she complied with his stipulations? Or, was it that she'd be forced to curb her uncouth behavior once and for all?

She'd not noticed him in the paddock with the grooms.

He'd been in his shirtsleeves and on the far side of the horse. Exercising horseflesh was one of the very few times he threw propriety aside. That and when he doctored animals. How was one to train horses in an intricately wrapped cravat and snug coat? Both prevented free movement, essential when working with livestock but indispensable when taming unbroken horses.

He'd hurriedly donned his navy hunting jacket and tied a simple knot in his neckcloth before hastening after her.

"Unhand me, my lord." Adaira's kept her tone carefully modulated. She made no effort to leave his arms but stood stiff and unyielding against him, her focus riveted on the floor.

When Roark didn't move and remained silent, she raised her dainty foot to tromp on his boot or kick his shin. He squeezed her to him, preventing the blow. "I think not. It will hurt you far more than me."

He remembered the last time they'd been here together. Her reaction had been wholly different. As he recalled her passionate kisses, blood rushed to his lower regions. God rot him. He'd enjoyed her responses far too much.

Except for the blow to his mouth.

Why did the idea of her locked in ardent embraces with other men make him want to throttle those faceless strangers? To kiss her until she begged him to take her and forget all others?

Ignoring his better judgment, Roark flattened his hands on her back, drawing her closer. Lowering his head, he nuzzled her creamy neck beneath her ear. Her breath left her in a long unsteady sigh. Pressing his nose to her skin,

Roark inhaled deeply, trying to draw her essence into his being.

Her body was unbending, and tension radiated through her.

Anger or arousal?

He flicked the tip of his tongue over her velvety skin, tasting her, and she inhaled sharply.

"So sweet—" Oh, God, to be able to taste all of her.

Raising her palms to his chest, she stuttered, "Y-you, you shouldn't." Even as she angled her neck to give him better access to the silky flesh.

He disregarded her protest.

Her sultry voice beckoned him, belying her huskily whispered words. He covered her neck and jaw with feathery kisses, his manhood growing heavy and pulsating insistently against his thigh. Her scent surrounded him, making him forget all else but the lush woman in his arms.

She gave a pathetic shove against his chest. "My lord, release me before someone sees us."

Her voice was a wispy breath.

He wound an arm about her shoulders, then lifted her chin. "Is that truly what you wish?"

Her chocolate eyes round and pensive, she stared at his mouth. When she wet her lips with her pink tongue, he was undone.

Groaning, he lowered his head and touched her lips. He moved his mouth across their sweetness, cajoling, enticing. Sweeping his tongue across her bottom lip, he urged her to part her mouth. With a whimper, she sagged against him and opened to his tender probing.

At once, he plunged his tongue into the sweet cavern. Timid at first, Adaira soon met his passion, twirling and jousting with her small tongue. Crushing her to him and her breasts smashed against his chest, he ground his erection into her soft belly. She clung to his shoulders, a throaty moan escaping her as he devoured her with his mouth.

Skimming a hand up her side, he cupped a breast, flicking the hardened nub with his thumb. He slid his hand inside her bodice, closing it around the exquisite softness of one warm breast—perfection in his palm.

Her guttural groan of pleasure sent a jolt of pure lust exploding through his veins. Already hard as marble, his knees nearly buckled from the new surge of desire, so intense, the sensation bordered on pain. He clenched his teeth against the exquisite torture. It was all he could do not to lift her skirts and take her against the stable door.

A vision of him buried deep inside her, his hands gripping her bare buttocks, her head thrown back, and her legs wrapped around his waist as he pumped into her sliced through his mind.

Bugger and blast!

What was wrong with him?

He wasn't given to lewd imaginations or undressing women with his eyes. He mightn't be a saint, but he had a distinct moral standard. What was it about her that had him off-kilter?

"*Je ne peux pa vous résister?* Why can't I resist you?"

Startled he'd spoken his thoughts, Roark opened his eyes. Adaira seemed unaware. Her dark lashes fanned her flushed cheeks, her silky mouth parted. Her hands had crept up his chest to clasp behind his neck.

Her kisses were tantalizing ambrosia, making him forget who she was.

Who he was.

Making him overlook the oaths he'd made to remain beyond reproach, to conduct himself as a gentleman.

A thud reverberated against the stable outside.

Adaira went rigid, trying to pull out of his embrace.

"Please, Roark, my standing with my family is already precarious." She angled away from him. "I cannot bear anymore indignity."

Nearby voices carried into the stable. Adaira swung her head toward the entrance.

"Let go!" Panic crept into her voice when he didn't immediately release her.

She flicked her anxious gaze to his. Her beautiful eyes widened, the yellow-green specks sparking in shock before she quickly lowered her lashes. He hadn't been able to disguise his lust. She'd seen it in his eyes.

That, and primordial possession.

Her distress seemed genuine, and Roark wrinkled his brow.

He released her, then stepped away, putting a respectable distance between them.

Confound it, he'd lost control, and it infuriated him. And fiend seize it, he'd spoken his thoughts aloud again. Blasted inconvenient that. With her, he couldn't be sure what precisely would tumble off his tongue. She had him completely out of step.

For all his high talk of propriety, he'd just compromised her. Again. Why did he find her so enticing? Irresistible?

Once free, Adaira raised shaky fingers to her lips, staring at him with her soft brown eyes wide and wary. And alarmed.

He dipped his gaze to her disheveled bodice, a smile curving his mouth at her unintentional display.

You're a lout, Roark.

Indeed, he was. She brought out the worst in him. Foul

family tendencies he'd managed to keep suppressed until she came along were rearing their vulgar heads.

Brow furrowed, her gaze sank to her breasts. The tip of one dusky nipple peeked above the ivory lace. Yanking the material upward, she speared Roark with a barbed scowl, and deep color swept her face. "Duddering oaf."

He chuckled.

Adaira swiveled toward the far doors. She took but a half dozen steps before she stopped abruptly. "Curses." She whipped around and stalked back the other way, muttering under her breath. She ignored Roark when she passed him except for a crossly muttered, "Rutting cawker."

The voices grew louder. Lifting her skirts, she dashed to the entrance, snatching the parasol propped there. Whirling around, she charged in Roark's direction once more.

This spirited woman is preferable to the passive one I first held in my embrace.

The thought took him by surprise. Crossing his arms, he angled his head and watched her march toward him. He chuckled again as she passed by.

She opened her mouth, then snapped it shut, meshing her lips together. Oh, she wanted to ring a peal over his head, to scold him soundly. Roark could see it in the sideways glower she tossed him. Citrine sparks glittered in the depths of her lovely eyes. The nostrils of her adorable, freckled, turned-up nose were flared, and her cheeks glowed with two fetching pink spots.

She'd gone from impassioned to piqued in an instant.

Roark would wager ten pounds that it required all of her resolve not to give him a firm set down. Or wallop him with the parasol she unconsciously held like her riding crop. He made no effort to curb his smile of amusement. She was a delightful conglomeration of transparent emotions.

He rather liked that. He much preferred honesty over the wintry, unreadable facades affected by many of the *ton's* denizens. Delia had mastered the art to perfection. Ice goddess on the exterior while a harlot's heart burned within.

"Adaira, wait." Sethwick strode into the stable, Gregor and Dugall on either side of him.

Adaira threw back her head and issued a low groan, clearly miffed. Without looking behind her, she took a couple of tentative steps forward.

Feigning a cough, Roark barely smothered another laugh behind his hand. He'd no doubt she'd every intention of bolting from the stable, pretending not to hear her brother.

Striding in her direction, Sethwick called to her again. "Adaira, please wait. I wish to speak to you."

Heaving a gusty sigh, she turned. "Yes, Ewan?"

Her voice was soft, resigned. Her gaze skimmed Dugall and Gregor before it settled someplace over Sethwick's shoulder. She'd not meet his eyes. Ah, she'd not forgiven her brother for his role in her chastisement. Roark, she pointedly ignored. He might well have been a fly on dung for all the attention she paid him.

Dugall nudged Gregor hard in the ribs. "Do my eyes deceive me, or is my sister wearin' a pretty gown? In the stables?" Giving her a cocky grin, he waggled his eyebrows at her.

Adaira quirked one brow. "It's not like you've never seen me in a gown before, Dugall."

"Aye lass, we have, many times." Gregor nodded and grinned, his eyes dancing with mirth. "But, ye have to admit, it's the first time ye've boasted long gloves and a lacy parasol when entertainin' the beasties."

Tapping her leg with the sunshade, she muttered,

"*Some* people think it's more suitable. Ludicrous, if you ask me."

Dugall's gaze hovered on Roark for a moment. "Since when do ye care what others think, Addy?" Kindness replaced the humor in his voice.

Pain whisked across Adaira's face before she schooled her features. Roark didn't miss the tensing of her shoulders or her fisted hands. A wounded glint lingered in her eyes.

Roark cast Dugall a sharp look.

Of course, she should care what others thought. That was the problem with society today. Too many men and women casting off propriety and strictures and behaving as they were wont to without consideration for decorum and respectability.

Was Dugall unaware of Roark's conditions? Or, if he was aware, was he encouraging his sister's wayward habits?

Ignoring Dugall's question, she turned her attention to Sethwick. "Ewan, do you need something?"

He grinned at her, his eyes filled with affection. "Here now, why the Friday face? I wanted to tell you, Clarendon," he sent a friendly glance Roark's way, "has graciously agreed to allow Fionn to stable at Cadbury Park. We'll be able to commence with the breeding project while we're his guests."

Adaira's mouth dropped open, and her eyes darkened to ebony. She swung her astounded gaze to meet Roark's, and then back to Sethwick. There wasn't a jot of acquiescence in her stiff stance. Her spine was so taut, Roark feared she'd fracture into pieces if he so much as sneezed.

She squared her dainty shoulders and tilted her small chin stubbornly. "This hasn't been discussed with me."

Still smiling, Sethwick approached her. He brushed

several black strands of hair off his forehead. "Aye, it has. Hugh told me he spoke to you."

Her control snapped.

"Nae!" she spat. "Father said it *might* be one of *his* conditions." She flung a hand in Roark's direction.

Dugall's confused gaze darted from Roark to Sethwick before settling on his sister. "I'll leave ye to yer—discussion."

The giant beside him nodded his blond head and muttered, "Aye, I need to speak with Niall about, uh, somethin'."

The men beat a hasty retreat, casting wary glances at Adaira over their broad shoulders as they rounded the stable's exit.

She paid them no heed but directed an irate glare at Sethwick.

His attention lingered on the door, as if he, too, yearned to escape his sister's wrath.

"I've agreed to all his demands." She pointed at Roark. "I'll attend his confounded house party and any others he dictates I should." She shot him a venom-laced glower. "Though, Lord knows, I'll go out of my mind with the tedium and simpering and posturing."

She drew in a deep breath. Roark covertly watched the rise and fall of her bosom. For one so slight of figure, she was generously endowed.

His manhood pulsed.

Down, lad.

For one horrifying moment, he'd feared he'd said that aloud. Except, he tightly clenched his jaw. He'd learned to keep his lips firmly pressed together when not intentionally speaking to Adaira.

She shoved a stray curl back under her bonnet. "I'll go to

London for the Season, put myself on display like a mare at Tattersall's." She rested her hands on her hips. "Shall I permit the gentlemen to inspect my teeth, Brother? My hair?" She lifted her hem, exposing her petite foot. "My feet?"

Roark's lips curved in appreciation as her gown inched upward another pair of inches.

"My legs?" She turned sideways and stuck out her deliciously rounded bottom. "My arse?"

Oh, my God.

Roark bit the inside of his cheek. He should be appalled. Instead, he fought the urge to laugh. Or reach and touch her tempting *derrière*.

Scowling, Sethwick opened his mouth.

She straightened, cutting him off before he uttered a sound. "What, no? Well, then I'll smile and be gracious and pretend to be dazzled by the glitz and glamour."

Adaira stood with her arms akimbo, tapping her foot. "I'm wearing stays and gowns, Ewan. My hair's been tugged and tucked and pinned until I fear I might go bald. Mother's given me enough lotions and creams to lighten my freckles and soften my hands, I might as well be a greased goose."

Her voice had risen to a shout.

She paused in her tirade and cast a longing look at her stallion. "I'm not riding Fionn, because I don't have a riding habit that fits, and he's not trained to a blasted sidesaddle. I'm wearing elbow-length gloves on in the stables." Tears glistened in her eyes, and she dropped her gaze to her fisted hands. "I couldn't find my short gloves."

"Adaira..." Ewan began.

Adaira stomped to her brother. She wiggled the fingers of her right hand beneath Sethwick's nose. "Fancy gloves,

Ewan. In the stables! I'm even using this preposterous atrocity."

She raised the parasol and shook it.

He ducked when she nearly whacked him aside the head with the flailing sunshade.

"Enough, Adaira," Sethwick growled, clearly at the end of his patience.

"Enough? I'll give you enough." She poked him in the chest with the parasol then poked him again. He jumped backward when she lunged at him a third time.

Sethwick's brows swooped into a dark scowl. "Do that again, and I'll snap that blasted thing in two."

Behind her, Roark choked on a guffaw.

She'd done the same thing to him with her confounded crop.

With a final glare at Ewan and Roark, Adaira stomped from the stables, muttering under her breath.

Zeus, but she was splendid when in a temper. She'd outshine everyone else in London. Why hadn't he seen it before? She was a diamond of the first water. A rough diamond, true, but he'd have her polished to blinding brilliance by Season's start.

She was bound to snare a husband with her exquisite beauty, petite lushness, and soon-to-be impeccable behavior. And she'd a sizable dowry too, he'd learned. Some lucky chap was going to be damned fortunate.

A glower settled on his face.

Bloody hell.

That hadn't been his purpose for taming her at all.

Seventeen

A week later

Drat. The sun valiantly shone, a bright beacon promising an afternoon favorable for a picnic as was planned. Adaira had hoped the outing would be postponed, or better yet, abandoned altogether.

From her chamber window, she surveyed Cadbury Park. The week prior to their departure had flown by with no reprieve. If she hadn't been so disheartened, she'd have enjoyed the bird currently bathing in a puddle and the colorful prisms dancing across the pond's surface.

In the early morning hours, a summer tempest blew by, fierce but short-lived. The parched ground eagerly drank the torrential rain. The wind had whipped its furious fingers through the trees. Leaves scattered and scraped to-and-fro, leaving the ground littered in a verdant blanket. Now, the sun caressed the earth with its calming rays.

The bright beams were already hard at work drying the

few damp remnants of the shower, and beyond the treetops, a vibrant rainbow glowed. Several fountains, mazes, and manicured gardens bursting with flowers of every hue imaginable were visible from her second-story room.

Cadbury Park was a meticulously cared for estate.

No surprise there.

Since Adaira had met the man, she'd learned the Earl of Clarendon insisted upon order and structure. For one still quite young, he was most stodgy. Everything, at all times, must be within propriety's bounds.

How utterly dull and tiresome.

Except for his shameless behavior in the stable.

Stop.

She wouldn't think of it, of his entirely disarming kisses. Why, for pity's sake, did her body betray her at his touch? She responded to him like the wanton he'd called her. Her mind screeched *no* while her traitorous body acted the part of a light-skirt. It didn't help that his chest and shoulders were sculpted with well-defined, oh so, firm muscles that felt glorious beneath her hand.

Stop, dunderhead.

Twice now, he'd kissed her. Passionately. And she'd not resisted. *Resisted?* No, she'd clung to him like a tick on a hound. She'd even allowed her gaze to linger on his long legs and tight bum.

And the substantial bulge in his pantaloons.

Adaira pinched the back of her hand to stop her wayward thoughts.

Enough! What is wrong with me?

It served no purpose to dwell on those moments in the stable. She needed to focus on the present and how she'd endure a month under the same roof as Roark. He didn't think her capable of behaving like a lady. Her ardent responses in the stable hadn't lent to that opinion, now had they?

A smile tugged her lips upwards.

She intended to charm Lord Clarendon's socks right off.

Oh, you just wait and see, your royal pompousness. I'll be the quintessence of tonnish decorum.

Her gaze returned to the zealously attended grounds. Heaven forbid there be a weed or spent flower amongst the groomed beds. No doubt, the earl required the deer and squirrels—even the birds and bees—to ask permission before they were allowed access to the charming gardens.

She could almost hear his condescending voice as he addressed the creatures.

Please do take care not to trod on the flowers or leave any droppings.

Truthfully, the beautiful grounds were a startling contrast to the austerity of the mansion's outer facade.

When Adaira had arrived early yesterday evening, misty rain had bathed the manor. The structure sat beneath the sunless sky, the same dismal shade of pewter gray as the heavens above. From without, the monstrous house appeared unwelcoming, almost hostile. Its dark windows reflected no light, like great soulless eyes.

A shiver had tripped across her shoulders.

She wasn't being fanciful. The place emanated unhappiness.

They were admitted to the manor by a one-armed, stooped shouldered butler. Despite his physical restrictions, the man bore an air of poised dignity. With an infinitesimal bending of his lips, he intoned, "Welcome to Cadbury Park. I am Westbrook."

He bowed deeply. "If you require anything at all, please

let me know. His lordship's greatest desire is that you enjoy your stay."

A stunning circular entry, complete with a glossy black marble floor and eight Roman pillars, boasted a crystal chandelier that was every bit of six feet tall. It loomed overhead, dead center of the entrance hall.

Craning her neck, Adaira suppressed a gasp of astonishment. A domed window atop the entry filtered what light the late afternoon offered. The chandelier's prisms would create a glorious web of color when the sun struck it from above.

Dual ornately carved staircases leading to the upper wings graced the opposite side of the entry. Two pocket doors, one on either side of the entrance hall, revealed a drawing room and library.

A flash of movement had caught her eye, and Adaira had surreptitiously peeked into the library.

Good heavens, was that an owl?

Perched in a large cage, a mottled chestnut brown and white, pigeon-sized bird watched her. It blinked its great dark eyes at her, then rotated its head nearly all the way around.

Two more doors, these closed to curious eyes, flanked the staircases. Beyond the stairs were several more doorways. An assortment of luxurious chairs and glossy tables were strategically placed throughout the grand entrance. Lush bouquets graced several of the tabletops.

In comparison, Craiglocky's furnishings seemed outdated and worn. Comfortable though, and unpretentious. Unlike the room she'd been assigned as her bedchamber.

Decorated in shades of green, ivory, and peach, the chamber shouted opulence from the lush jade carpet she stood upon—the exact shade of the moors at dawn—to the thick peach and cream counterpane. Silk papered walls, resplendent with impossibly detailed images of tropical birds and plants, paled against the gilded gold-framed paintings and mirrors. Even the furnishings, tinted a pale eggshell, were embellished with flowering vines.

"The carriages are waitin', Miss Adaira." Maisey held a straw bonnet. A slew of pale blue, white, and lavender silk roses adorned the crown. They matched the lavender braiding edging Adaira's blue spencer.

Taking the bonnet from Maisey, Adaira twisted her lips into a wry smile. "I look like a great confection."

"Nae, ye look grand." Maisey cocked her head. "Are ye sure yer jacket willna be too hot?"

Would it?

"You may be right. Why don't you fetch my gauze shawl, Maisey? I'll take it along as well. Yesterday was too warm by far. I've no idea how much shade is available along the lake's edge."

Adaira searched the landscape with a blasé eye, noting several tall groves of trees in the distance near the lake. Her gaze lit on the magnificent stables and meadows a good ways from the manor house. Fionn, his sleek ebony mane streaming behind him and legs stretched into a full run, streaked across a meadow.

Braggart.

Three mares, including the one she'd met in Craiglocky's stables, galloped behind him.

Trollops.

Fiend seize it.

She'd lost that battle. Never had she felt so betrayed by her family. Where was their allegiance? Lord Clarendon snapped his fingers, and they fawned all over him.

Forcing her to stud Fionn with the earl's mares was outside of enough. Now, she'd forever be linked to *His Regal Stuffiness.* She ran her practiced gaze over the mares. From here, they looked to be prime steppers.

That rankled.

She'd hoped Roark's horses would be sway-backed nags.

Adaira took the bonnet. Setting it on her head, she loosely tied the wide ribbon to the right of her chin.

After tugging on her gloves, she gathered her reticule, her parasol, and a book of Coleridge's poems. She'd no intention of reading, but the book afforded her an excuse to bury her nose in its musty pages and ignore the earl. Taking the shawl from the maid, Adaira draped it over one arm.

Due to their late arrival last night, she'd been spared dining with her host. Fortune surely wouldn't smile on her as benevolently from this point onward. Most of the guests were arriving for the ball today or tomorrow. His lordship had insisted she be present for the event. It would be one taxing gathering upon another, every day, for thirty bloody days.

With *no* hope of reprieve.

Torturous.

She'd overheard one of the upstairs maids tell Maisey one hundred guests were expected to stay at least two weeks. More than three hundred were invited to the ball.

Adaira cringed.

Did he have to invite *that* many people? It made her head spin.

Firming her lips, Adaira closed her eyes. She inhaled slowly. She could do this. God help her, she must. The perfume from two enormous vases of flowers teased her nostrils, and she sneezed, her eyes popping open.

She sighed. "I'll wear the ivory mull with the silver embroidery tonight, Maisey."

The latest fashion, the gown was modest and sophisticated—the essence of the role she was compelled to assume.

"Aye, miss. I'll hang it to air." The lady's maid dutifully headed to the wardrobe.

"Thank you."

Adaira left her chamber, her contemplation returning to the source of her agitation. She'd insisted on introducing Fionn to Lord Clarendon's stables. She refused to utter more than a half dozen words to his lordship as she did so.

She sighed again while slipping her reticule's drawstrings over her wrist. Surliness was out of the question from this point onward. She was determined to be the epitome of ladylike conduct, and perchance, shorten her term of indenture.

Toward that end, she plastered a demure smile on her face and made her way to the waiting carriages. Not so much as one peevish word would fall from her lips.

She could do it.

All she had to do was avoid Lord Clarendon at every turn.

Leaning against the fence of one of Cadbury's many pastures, Roark extended his hand. The mare greedily snatched the apple from his palm. He'd purchased the ancient nag he'd ridden into Craigcutty and turned her out to pasture. She'd never carry a rider again. She was in good company. A blind mule, a deaf sheep, and two arthritic plow horses were her new companions.

In the adjoining field, Fionn, Tenacity, and two of Roark's largest mares romped happily.

He grinned, recalling how Adaira's eyes had snapped with fury when she led the stallion to his stall in Cadbury's stables last evening. Roark had allowed her the small concession. He didn't need her raising a breeze on her first day here.

A hard knock against the back of his knees made him grip the fencepost for balance. Guinevere's cold nose snuffled his hand, then his coat pocket.

Roark chuckled. "Yes, old girl, I have a treat for you too."

He patted her shaggy head. The dog, tail wagging furiously and tongue lolling, turned her head to look at him with her good eye.

The rattle of carriage wheels on stone drew his attention to the courtyard. Helene's driver expertly tooled the conveyance to the front of the manor, where the barouche joined another pair of barouches, as well as three wagonettes, two wagons laden with picnicking supplies, and a landau.

A frown knitted his brow. Why were the supplies still here?

They ought to have gone on ahead to prepare for his guests' arrival. A maid scurried from the house and handed Westbrook a basket before she climbed into the wagon. Roark smiled as his diligent butler lifted the cloth and peered inside before giving a sharp nod of his head.

Evidently, something had been forgotten. Westbrook returned the hamper to the maid, then spoke to the wagon drivers. A moment later, the vehicles lurched and rumbled down the lane.

Several guests loitered about the circular drive while others had already been directed to their seats by his footmen, Oscar and Thom. Both walked with slight limps, a result of wounds acquired during the war with the French. A few gentlemen, including Luxmoore and the Fergusons, chose to ride horseback rather than in an equipage.

The picnic party was relatively small, perhaps thirty in all. Those present consisted primarily of the local gentry. A few intended to stay at the manor, but most would seek their homes at the end of the day and return for tomorrow's activities. The house would be swollen with guests come nightfall, however.

Roark's gaze roved the monstrosity that was his home. Even washed in sunlight, the place reminded him of a tomb. There had been so little joy within its walls. A familiar pang wrenched his heart.

Just then, Adaira emerged from the entrance, and his breath hung suspended for a moment. Breathtaking in a white and blue gown and blue spencer edged with lavender, a smile lit her radiant face. She lightly skipped down the steps, almost stumbling over a pair of frolicking kittens. She regained her balance and paused to stroke each of their mottled backs. Raising her head, she smiled and headed for the carriage containing her family.

Thom approached her, saying, "Miss, over here, please."

With a sweep of his hunter green-clad arm, he directed her to the landau instead.

Confusion skittered across her beautiful face, but she shrugged and, waving her fingers at her mother and sisters, dutifully followed him. After handing her into the vehicle, Thom bowed smartly before making his way to Westbrook's side.

Once Adaira adjusted her skirts, she opened her parasol and covertly scrutinized the other guests. She almost seemed shy, using the contraption as a protective barrier against the many inquisitive glances sent her way.

A peculiar urge to protect her assailed Roark.

Helene spied him and began waving her handkerchief enthusiastically. She turned and said something to the balding man sitting beside her.

Annoyance pinched his face, as he grudgingly moved to the opposite seat, already occupied by a younger gentleman holding a squirming dachshund puppy. The men must be the Austrian relatives she'd mentioned were coming for a visit.

Roark strode toward the mansion, his lips turned up slightly. Helene expected him to ride with her. He had other plans—discussing the breeding venture with Adaira, to be precise. Confined to the same vehicle for the two miles it took to reach the lake, she'd be forced to hear him out. With the other guests also in open-topped carriages, there would be no question of impropriety.

As he drew closer, the guests not yet in a vehicle scurried to find their places. Helene scooted over, brushing her skirts aside to make room for him. Leaning forward, providing him and any other male within viewing distance a clear view of her ample cleavage, she curled her mouth into a seductive smile.

"My lord, allow me to introduce my cousin, Count Otto von Schnitzer, and his son, Freidrick. Otto darling, this is the neighbor I've told you *so* much about. Roark, the Earl—"

Yelping, the puppy escaped the younger man's arms and jumped to the floor. Head lowered, it cowered in the corner, its entire body quaking in terror.

Roark considered Freidrick with considerable contempt.

From the corny-faced rash covering the lad's face, he guessed the whelp to be about eight and ten. The boy's expression was one of bored arrogance. He regarded Roark with the haughtiness of one who is overly indulged and fully aware of his elevated station.

Helene glared at her cousin. "I told you not to bring that beast along."

Distaste written on her face, she edged the terrified dog away from her with her toe. Freidrick grabbed the pup by the nape of her neck, causing another yap of pain.

"*Stillsitze,*" he growled harshly. He forced the puppy to sit on his lap, his hands clamped around her small brownish-red form. She whimpered, regarding Roark with soulful brown eyes.

His gut knotted, and he fisted his hands.

One more cry from that pathetic animal, and—

As if he read Roark's thoughts, Freidrick made a pretense of gently petting the dog, a cocky smile skewing his petulant mouth. *Insolent cur.*

The count had yet to say a word in reprimand to his son. He stared over Roark's shoulder, a salacious smile curving his thin lips. His bulbous eyes glowed with lust, and Roark followed von Schnitzer's gaze.

Adaira sat demurely in the landau. Her gaze roamed the wagons, locking onto Roark's for a lengthy moment before widening in fright when she met the count's eyes. At once, she dropped her attention to her lap.

Roark didn't miss the flush staining her cheeks, or her hand clenching around the parasol's handle. Odd, she appeared truly disconcerted.

Westbrook passed near the landau, and she spoke to him. He paused, spearing Roark an almost indiscernible look before answering. Even from where he stood, Roark saw her stiffen and strain settle on her face. She jutted her adorable chin upward, and sparks flew from her expressive eyes.

No doubt about it. She'd learned who she'd be sharing the landau with.

Blast Westbrook's efficiency.

Helene stared at the butler making his way to her carriage. "I cannot imagine why you surround yourself with all these...these decrepit souls, my lord."

Her strident voice demanded Roark's attention, and he glanced at her.

She shifted her position, and her breasts heaved upward with the movement. Was it because he'd become accustomed to Adaira's slenderness, or was Helene even more rounded? She stared at Westbrook, the merest hint of distaste etched on her beautiful face.

Count von Schnitzer yawned, making no effort to cover his mouth before muttering, "I'd prefer to not expose my son to *das* undesirable riffraff."

He ran his forefinger along his thin mustache.

Roark had hand-selected every member of his staff. After his sire's death, he'd dismissed the entire household without references. Not once had any of them made a single effort to aid him or his mother. They'd been more concerned with their monthly wages, turning a deaf ear and blind eye to the abuse doled out by their employer.

Instead, Roark offered positions to those no one else would consider for employment. His compassion resulted in a fiercely loyal, as well as competent, household.

Helene wiggled her gloved fingers imperiously at the

butler and footmen. "Surely there are places for their kind," she whispered *sotto voce*.

She'd never voiced this attitude before.

Roark considered her for a moment.

A poised, attractive woman, with no hint of malice in her lovely eyes, looked back at him. Had lust blinded him to her true nature? Was she trying to impress the count by ridiculing others? That spoke volumes about both of them.

Roark adjusted his hat and tugged his gloves on more firmly, lest he say what burned on his tongue. Resting a hand on the barouche's side, he smiled at her.

"You are absolutely correct, Mrs. Winthrop."

She tilted her head and puffed out her chest, basking in her perception of his approval. Meeting her cousin's eyes, she smiled confidently.

"Their place is with *me*," Roark said.

She deflated like a windless sail.

Westbrook reached them, and his impassive gaze skimmed the occupants of the carriage. "Please pardon the wagons' delay, my lord. The eating utensils were overlooked."

"Ah, Westbrook, what would I do without you? I'll be to my conveyance in a moment. Please inform Miss Ferguson."

"Directly, my lord." With a regal nod, Westbrook moved away.

"What? You're not joining us, my lord?" Helene sputtered. She cast a desperate glance at Count von Schnitzer and offered a grimace for a smile. "But I assured Otto, as the highest-ranking peer in attendance, he'd have your undivided attention."

"I'm sorry to disappoint you." Roark's regard moved to include the count. "But, I'll be escorting Miss Ferguson."

Helene's eyes narrowed, and she pursed her lips, casting

Adaira a dismissive look. "Is she another soul you feel the need to rescue? You are far too kind, my lord. Did I detect a limp when she tripped on the stairs?"

No, you did not.

She tossed a glance Adaira's way. "I cannot quite tell what kind they are as she's hiding behind her parasol, but I'm certain there are marks of some sort on her face. Pox, perhaps?"

Roark choked on an oath.

Was Helene serious?

She reclined against the velvet squabs in triumph, satisfaction curving her lovely mouth. "That's it, isn't it? You pity the girl. Come now, it's admirable to be sure, but you alone cannot save all the wretches of the world."

Roark eyed her with aversion.

She'd kept this side of her nature well-hidden. Until now.

She smiled an invitation, desire sparkling in her sky-blue eyes. "Though, I do find a compassionate man *very* attractive."

It would seem Helene wasn't as sweet-tempered and amiable as she'd affected for all of these months. Just as well, he'd already decided to terminate their association before Sunday.

"On the contrary, there's absolutely *nothing* amiss with Miss Ferguson," Roark said.

He spun on his heels and, with a fast-paced stride, marched toward the waiting landau. He'd permit no one to scorn his loyal staff or his other guests.

Guinevere bumped about his ankles, almost upending him more than once as he made his way to his carriage. She anxiously wagged her feathery tail, her bottom wiggling in anticipation.

"Yes, you can come too." He scratched behind her ears. "Miss Ferguson won't dare ring a peal over me with you chaperoning."

Stepping into the landau, he met Adaira's accusing gaze. She lifted her nose, and with the air of a duchess, turned her head the other way, giving him the cut indirect.

Eighteen

Adaira itched to smack Lord Clarendon or box his ears soundly.

He'd manipulated the traveling arrangements to force his unwelcome presence on her. The landau bounced, and his thigh brushed hers. He shouldn't be sitting beside her at all, let alone this near.

A large, hairy dog snoozed on the opposite seat. The animal was the earl's excuse for taking the seat beside her.

And *he* was the one concerned about appearances.

Adaira barely suppressed a snort. Of course, as they were in full view of all, nothing untoward could be suggested.

Another dip in the road shifted the carriage once more, and Roark's hip and leg brushed hers—*again*. Was he doing that on purpose? She sliced him a peek through her eyelashes.

An unrepentant grin framed his handsome mouth.

He is, the lout.

Nevertheless, her stomach fluttered. Why did he have

to be so very dashing and so blasted good looking? It would be much easier to dislike him if he were as ugly as the devil.

Shifting away from his distractingly hard leg, she breathed out a long, slow sigh. Her vexation wasn't aiding her cause and apparently, served to amuse him. She'd prove to the boor she could act the part of a lady if required. She'd do it if it killed her.

By God, he'd not find her wanting.

She inched her gaze upward. Roark's leather-clad hands rested on his thighs. Buff pantaloons stretched across ridiculously muscled thighs and his— She jumped her gaze past *that* part of his anatomy.

A black jacket, so form-fitting she'd no idea how he managed to move about in it, was spread taut across his equally impressive shoulders. A topaz pin glinted in his perfectly tied neckcloth.

Her gaze riveted on his neck, she asked, "What are you about?"

A low timbre rumble began in his chest, his laughter causing the cravat to shift up and down. Funny, Adaira had never noticed it doing that before. But then, she'd never been as aware of a man before either.

"Do you expect my neckcloth or the pin to answer you?" He chuckled again.

Adaira compressed her mouth to prevent the smile teasing her lips from emerging. She met his amused gaze. "I presume you have a purpose for our traveling arrangement?"

He lifted her gloved hand, running his thumb to-and-fro across the top of the fabric. Sparks, darts, tingles—drat she didn't know what they were—streaked up her arm and other places.

Staring at him, she yanked her hand away. She rubbed it on her skirt, trying to make the sensation stop. There was strength of character in those insufferably blue eyes and something she'd never expected to see directed at her.

Attraction.

It rattled her, and she drew in a deep, calming breath.

Good God, how could he be attracted to *her?*

Don't react. It will give him more fuel.

Angling her head, with a great deal more composure than she felt, she met his penetrating gaze and waited for him to answer her question.

He flicked a silk flower on her hat. "You look lovely today."

"Thank you." She said no more, just waited.

He was stalling.

He gestured in the dog's direction. "Guinevere. She's blind in one eye."

"Indeed."

Adaira *would* wait him out. Curling her toes in her shoes kept her from tapping them in impatience. Or kicking him.

"I also have a blind mule and a deaf sheep," his lordship announced proudly.

Adaira clenched her hands, bit the inside of her cheek, and made a strangled choking in the back of her throat, trying to suppress her laugh. It gushed forth in loud peals. She slapped her hand over her mouth, but couldn't control her hysterical giggling.

"A deaf sheep? Are all of your animals needy in some way?" She sat up straighter and gripped his forearm. "Do you have an owl in the library, or did I imagine that?"

"And what, pray tell, is wrong with having an owl in

one's library?" The earl drew himself up and pretended to look down his nose at her. "Are they not wise?"

Adaira shook her head, and between bouts of giggles, said, "You are hopelessly absurd."

She sat back, folding her arms across her chest while trying to balance her parasol. "My, my. It seems you are a fraud, my lord. Why, no self-respecting member of the peerage keeps an owl in his library."

"He does if he raised her from a fledgling. I found her beneath a tree. She must've fallen from her nest. Sophie has deformed feet, and she'd never have survived in the wild. I couldn't let her die," he said softly, his voice low.

Adaira watched him from the corner of her eye. What kind of man surrounded himself with servants and animals others would cast aside? It revealed far more about his character than his rigid adherence to society's rules.

Why, he violated what most members of the *ton* would do every day. The man was a sham. Or else, much more complex than she'd imagined. For some odd, inexplicable reason, the idea was comforting.

She scrutinized the dog.

Guinevere lay on her back in a most indecorous manner. She groaned, and a peculiar squeaky whoosh emanated from her followed by an unholy smell.

Roark's startled gaze collided with Adaira's, and a flush stole up his angular face. "Holy mother of God! *What* did she eat?"

Adaira was too busy laughing and gasping into her handkerchief to answer him. The driver's shoulders shook so hard, she feared he'd wreck the conveyance.

"Well, that certainly is *not* the impression I wanted to make. I cannot very well expect decorum for others when that beast," Roark flicked his hand at the dog, "is causing me to color."

Guinevere opened her good eye, thumped her tail once, and went back to sleep.

Adaira smiled. "She's charming. What happened to her eye?"

"I don't know. I found her beside the road abandoned and starving when I was on my way to London a few years ago." He shrugged. "I inherited my love of dogs from my Aunt Beatry, my father's elderly aunt," he added by way of an explanation.

"She lived at Cadbury but died when I was very young. I've left her chamber untouched. Somehow, it seemed wrong to toss the things she was so fond of, even if they are hideous."

The earl almost looked vulnerable before an aloof mask slid into place. "We're nearly to the lake. There's the matter about which I wanted to speak to you."

Adaira sighed, pretending to inspect the piping at her wrist. "The horses, I know."

"You'll be compensated, of course."

His arrogance was back in place.

"My lord, I'm creating a breed. There's nothing comparable in all of Scotland or England."

"I know, and I'm truly impressed. They're brilliant."

She flicked a glance at him, then focused on the glittering indigo a short distance off.

"Women are allowed very little control over their lives, as you well know. I'm aware you think me completely uncouth, but everything you object to about me truly is about control. What I wear or say. What activities I should participate in. Whom I should or shouldn't associate with."

She spared a glance in his direction.

His face was impassive, although he appeared to be listening intently.

Shifting the parasol, she said, "I've acquiesced to your demands, and to have the one thing, the most important thing in my life simply appropriated from me—"

And even more galling, she'd essentially given his lordship that right when she imprisoned him. With the threat of Newgate, or worse, dangling over her head, he knew it, too. Still, Adaira pressed her case.

She shook her head. "I shan't tell you commandeering Fionn is acceptable. It's not. I'm quite certain you have some fine horseflesh. That's not enough with the line I'm developing. It should've been *my* decision to make. And you, Father, and Ewan stripped me of that choice."

Unbidden memory bubbled to the surface. Just as she'd been stripped of her innocence four years ago, even if she couldn't remember precisely what had happened because she'd fainted.

Fuming inside, she silently rebelled. Her restraint amazed her. Yet, her resolve to act the part of a refined woman of breeding, to prove to the earl she could, helped her keep a tight rein on her tongue and temper. Besides, there'd been no discussion of consequences if she failed to do as he bid and behave with deportment.

What would he do if she botched things?

She waited for him to say something. Silence hung heavy and awkward between them. She turned against the seat to face him more fully. His brows furrowed, his gorgeous lips compressed, he stared at his hands, lost in thought.

At long last, he lifted his gaze to hers. "You're right."

Her eyes snapped to his, and she almost dropped the parasol. "I am?"

"Yes. You are, about the horse breeding, that is. I've been unfair and exploited the situation to my advantage. That was wrong." Roark's mouth slid into a half-smile.

Egads, she did so like it when he smiled. So did her body. All sorts of unfamiliar sensations centered in her womanly place.

Jaw slack, Adaira gawked at him.

Did he truly apologize and admit to being unfair?

Did *he* say he was wrong?

She pinched her hand. This was no dream. Who was this kind, considerate man? Where had the trow got to?

His gaze hovered on her breasts before lifting to her face.

She tried to keep her features serene. Her nipples, wretched things, were pebble hard against her gown.

He chuckled. "Do you know how expressive your eyes and face are? I know exactly what you're thinking."

"You know no such thing." Adaira averted her gaze in embarrassment.

Dear God, he couldn't know the tips of her breasts were hard enough to crack an egg with. And between her legs...?

Well, all manner of odd things were happening in that vicinity. One strong bump of the carriage and she'd skid right onto the floor, so damp was the region. It was mortifying.

With his forefinger, he touched her jaw and gently turned her face back to his. "I do. You are astounded I apologized and admitted I was unjust. You also cannot believe I admitted I acted selfishly."

She lowered her lashes, finding it unnerving to stare in his perceptive eyes. He was too insightful by far. Did he know what her body was doing as well? A fresh wave of heat coursed through her.

She'd bet Fionn he did.

Lord Clarendon's thumb brushed her jaw. "Do I have the gist of it?"

"Yes," she admitted reluctantly.

He had her all muddled, reading her mind, and her body, like a book. Yet, she couldn't find any way inside his stoic facade. It was most perilous to be so vulnerable to one's enemy.

Especially one so attractive.

She drew in a steadying breath, determined to stop her fanciful musings and her suddenly skipping heart. "Well then, what are we to do about it?"

Oh, for the love of God. Must I sound like a breathless ninny?

Roark's eyes glittered with mirth, but he kept his features schooled. "I propose, since the stud is already at Cadbury, you inspect each of the mares I was considering breeding with him. You can say yay or nay as you see fit."

Adaira eyed him doubtingly. "What about the three already pastured with him?"

The carriage slowed, and his lordship swung his head around to view the wagons that followed. Seemingly satisfied, he returned his attention to her. "None are in season. I was but getting them acquainted with Fionn."

The landau rolled to a stop behind the other vehicles beneath a stand of monstrous Oaks. Guests immediately descended, their excited conversations disturbing the once peaceful grove.

Adaira didn't believe him. Skeptical, she challenged, "What if I decide they are all inferior?"

He shrugged. "So be it. I'll be no worse off than I was before."

"Oh."

He'd conceded much too readily for her peace of mind. Bother, but the man blew hot and cold.

He chucked her lightly under her chin. "Now, put a smile on that beautiful face—"

Adaira gasped, her eyes narrowing to irate slits. A young man had tossed a small puppy onto the grass from his barouche's open door. "I'll box his ears!"

Nineteen

Roark hopped to the ground. The gentlest of breezes tickled the trees' leaves, and the soft rustling filled the glen with a soothing refrain. He swiftly followed Adaira across the picnic area.

She snapped her parasol closed, and after unceremoniously clambering from the landau, she dashed toward Helene's carriage. He didn't like the way Adaira wielded the parasol or the look of outraged determination on her face.

Even infuriated, and stamping in her haste, her hips swayed enticingly. Others had begun to take note of her progress. Conversations dwindled before stopping altogether. His guests stepped aside, opening a pathway for her as she bustled toward the barouche.

If the situation weren't so dire, he'd permit the laugh nudging his lips. It was ridiculous. Adaira's petite figure stampeding to rescue the pup or ring Freidrick a peal and everyone edging away was chuckle-worthy.

Where was her family?

Ah, they too were moving as a unit to intercept her.

The women swooped in from the left. The men advanced from the right.

They wouldn't make it in time.

And neither, by God, will I.

How could she move so fast in that gown? Its ruffled hem didn't allow long strides. Light blue stockings, embroidered ivory clocks at the heels, peeped out each time she took a hurried step.

She raised her closed parasol over her shoulder like a knight with a sword.

Oh, hell. Roark didn't like the looks of this.

Her first public jaunt, and she was going to make a bloody scene, devil seize it. He picked up his pace, covering the ground with long strides just short of a trot. He hoped to avert a disaster before it occurred.

All he needed was for her to thwack Freidrick, and there'd be an international bumblebroth to put aright. His gut told him Count von Schnitzer was of a vindictive, vengeful bend.

Roark descended on Helene's carriage, already rehearsing his apology, as well as his verbal reprimand to Adaira. He stopped mid-step, flabbergasted. She graced Helene, the count, and his son with a beatific smile, then popped the parasol open.

He took the half-dozen remaining steps to the group, eyeing Adaira dubiously.

"Please do forgive me." She twirled the parasol against her shoulder, flirtatiously. "I know we've not been introduced. It's terribly gauche of me, although I'm sure Lord Clarendon will do the honors momentarily."

Casting Roark a saucy glance, she flashed a brilliant smile.

His tongue stuck to the roof of his mouth. Not a single

sensible thought made itself known. Confound it, when she smiled at him like that—

His member jumped like a dog eager for a pet.

Damnable tight pantaloons.

Adaira approached the puppy. "But I simply *had* to make this little darling's acquaintance. May I?"

Without waiting for permission, she bent and scooped the pup into her arms. It crawled up her shoulder, then buried its nose behind her ear.

"There's a dear." She cuddled the frightened dog, clucking indiscernible reassurances. Stepping to Roark, she smiled once more.

"My lord, please, won't you introduce us?" She tilted her head in the direction of the barouche. Mischief shimmered in her black-lashed eyes.

He stared at her stupidly.

The count handed Helene out. Her gaze shifted between Adaira and Roark, the merest hint of a pucker on her otherwise smooth forehead.

Roark found his tongue and made short work of the introductions. The other guests, realizing they weren't going to witness a spectacle, began to seek other activities.

Taking a moment to survey his staff, he smiled in appreciation. Some of the menservants were setting up the tables and chairs while others busily set out food, blankets, and other assorted picnic goods.

"*Es ist mir ein Vergnügen, Sie kennen zu lernen.*" Adaira greeted the count in flawless German, prettily telling the count what a pleasure it was to meet him.

A look of surprise crept across his craggy features, quickly replaced by a lecherous gleam in his eyes. "Delighted I pleazoor you, *meine Liebe,*" he murmured suggestively.

Freidrick snickered.

Helene sliced her cousin a look of disapproval. "Really, Otto."

Von Schnitzer offered an oily smile. He lifted a shoulder. "*Meine Englisch* needz vork."

His English had been just fine at the house.

Roark skimmed his gaze over Adaira.

Her face had paled, and her pupils dilated to the size of olives. She remained poised, except for tightening her grip on the pup. She angled her head gracefully before giving the count a tight smile.

Everything within Roark told him she was afraid. He pressed his lips together.

What exactly did the count say to her?

From von Schnitzer's smug expression and the randy glint in his eyes, Roark would bet the bastard said something lecherous. Hadn't Helene mentioned the bugger had business or diplomatic duties to attend to in London? Catching Roark's assessment, the count raised a cocky brow.

Just how long was the pissant visiting?

Roark's good manners were wearing thin, and he'd been introduced to the boor but an hour ago.

"Mrs. Winthrop?" Adaira said. "May I compliment you on your stunning shawl? It has the most intricate needlework I believe I've ever seen. Did you embroider it yourself?"

Roark shifted his attention to Adaira. She appeared utterly enthralled by Helene's wrap.

Helene's gaze raked Adaira from her stylish bonnet to her shoes. She murmured, "Yes, it was quite laborious, but when one has talent..."

Roark nearly choked. One-eyed Guinevere's embroidery skills exceeded Helene's.

Adaira leaned in further, studying the stitches. "My, such astounding aptitude. Oh, I do hope you will take an afternoon and teach me your technique."

Little fraud. She loathed needlework. She'd told Roark so herself. What was she about?

Catching his eye, she sent him a wicked little smirk.

What in hell was she up to?

"Thank you," Helene grudgingly acknowledged, running her fingers across the silk threads. She raised her nose the merest bit as if Adaira was beneath her touch. "But I'm afraid I simply won't have time this weekend to teach needlework."

Adaira snuggled the pup, sleeping soundly in her arms. "Oh, I didn't mean to imply you should do so this weekend. I'd be grateful for an opportunity any time over the next month."

Helene stiffened, her fingers curling into the shawl like talons.

"*Month?*" She hurled Roark a look of hurt disbelief. "This is a month-long event? I do believe you quite *forgot* to mention that, my lord."

Her eyes sparked with accusation.

He'd not forgotten.

Completely unruffled, he nodded. "Yes, the Fergusons, as well as several others, have graciously agreed to be my guests for the next month. Do have your secretary speak to Chambers about the scheduled events."

Roark leveled von Schnitzer an impassive stare. "I'd be honored if you'd attend as well."

Like hell, he would.

He'd sooner invite the devil, and he'd made it a point to cleanse his household of evil long ago.

Adjusting the dog in her arms, Adaira asked, "What's her name?"

She directed her question to Freidrick, sulking in the barouche.

He glared at her, and for a moment, Roark thought he'd refuse to answer.

A sullen pout shadowed Freidrick's features as he grudgingly muttered, "Irmgard."

Adaira's spectacular eyes widened, and her lips twitched. Her throat convulsed three times before she could utter a composed response. "A most—er—*robust* name."

Holy Jesus—robust?

Roark swallowed the guffaws jolting his throat, although one strangled noise escaped him.

She cast him a knowing glance. The humor glinting in her eyes challenged him not to laugh.

Guinevere snuffled around Adaira's ankles, obviously smelling another dog, but having no idea where it had got to.

Adaira laughed softly, earning her a sharp look from Helene.

Squatting, Adaira presented the pup. "Here she is, dear."

Guinevere greeted the sleepy newcomer with a friendly sniff before wandering to plop down in the cool grass beneath a tree. She promptly resumed her nap.

The other Fergusons joined them, and introductions were made once more.

Freidrick roused himself from the carriage, brushing furiously at his pant leg. A damp spot on the young man's thigh explained his urgency to see the pup leave the carriage and his reluctance to do so.

Dugall turned away, his broad shoulders shaking.

Drawn to Irmgard, Miss Seonaid stepped next to Adaira. She petted and cooed to the puppy, who opened a drowsy eye, then went back to sleep.

Freidrick stood gawking, seemingly unable to tear his gaze from Miss Isobel.

She returned his bold appraisal with calm aloofness before shifting her beautiful turquoise gaze to the lake, effectively dismissing him.

Roark didn't miss the flush stealing across the boy's face accenting the already unattractive blemishes marring his countenance. Freidrick fisted his hands and stomped off, leaving the pup in Adaira's care.

She didn't seem perturbed in the least.

Helene laid her hand on Roark's arm possessively. "My lord, surely you can spare a few moments for a *dear* friend. Why, I'm confident the Fergusons are anxious to make the acquaintance of the others in attendance, and I did promise Otto."

By Hades, leave it to Helene to throw a rub in the way. Roark intended to ask Adaira to eat with him, perhaps even row about the lake in one of the skiffs along the shore. He suppressed a sigh.

Perhaps in the interest of pacifying Helene and the count, he'd better play along. He didn't trust this previously hidden and altogether unpleasant side of her character. What else had she deceived him about? She wasn't so very different than Delia in the end.

Was he cursed to always have deceptive Jezebels in his bed?

Roark slanted the count a sideways look. He didn't want von Schnitzer anywhere near Adaira. Even now, the black-guard undressed her with his eyes, a lewd grin on his thin lips. When he adjusted his pantaloons in full view of the ladies, Roark itched to throttle the knave.

Sir Hugh's eyebrows lashed together, and in an overt move of protection, he casually stepped between the count and the Ferguson women. Compared to the burly Scot, the Austrian was rather a scraggy twig.

Roark extended his arm. "Of course, Mrs. Winthrop. Let's do see about sampling some of the delicious food Mrs. Bardy prepared for us."

He met the count's gaze. "Do you like English food? We have traditional picnic fare today. Cold roast, boiled eggs, fruit sandwiches, and I'm sure there are seedcake and short-bread. I told Cook to be sure to include sweet Madeira, too. Oh, and tongue, of course. Do you like tongue, von Schnitzer?"

The count paled beneath his swarthy complexion. Evidently, the Austrian didn't favor the organ. Roark didn't blame him. He refused to touch the stuff himself.

Turning his lascivious attention to Adaira, von Schnitzer asked, "Fräulein Ferguson, can I persuade you to join us as vell?"

Roark almost laughed at the man's audacity. Clearly not taken with the count, Luxmoore and the Ferguson men stood like sentries on either side of their women. Sir Hugh's gaze met Roark's, and an unspoken message passed between them.

Adaira's father knew exactly what was going on in the count's depraved mind. The Scot was having none of it, either. Even Luxmoore's face was devoid of his usual smile. His jade green eyes regarded the count with casual contempt.

"I'm sorry to disappoint ye, von Schnitzer, but my

daughters will be dinin' with my wife and me," Sir Hugh said. "It's a Scots tradition."

Nuzzling the pup, Adaira eyed the count warily. She sliced Roark a sidelong glance with her big eyes.

He cursed to himself.

Strictures required her to acknowledge the count's invitation, and Roark had insisted she adhere to propriety.

"Thank you for the invitation, my lord," she said softly, her focus on Irmgard. Except for a soft whimper and a jerk of her foot, the exhausted puppy didn't stir.

The count smoothed his mustache, but not before Roark saw an angry sneer curl his lips. A vengeful glint lit his black eyes.

Roark yearned to say, "Decorum be damned. Plant the bounder a facer, Miss Ferguson, and do make it a sound one."

Twenty

Less than an hour later, Adaira, her stomach overly full of buttery shortbread, took her cousin, Flynn's, elbow. They made their way along a wide, well-trodden path. He'd asked the group eating with her family if anyone cared to venture onto the lake.

Suppressing the urge to shout, "Dear God, yes!" she'd jumped at the chance.

She was yawning behind her fan, bored almost to tears with the fustian discussions about the spices in the deviled eggs, the latest *on dit* from London, and Prinny's questionable taste in clothing.

Did the Prince Regent truly have a pink cutaway coat and breeches edged in diamonds and rubies? She grinned as she tried to envision the prince attired thusly. At a rumored five and twenty stone, he would resemble a giant, pink pudding.

Hearing laughter, she glanced over her shoulder. Her sisters and Dugall followed. *Wonderful.* They must've been done up with dull conversations and had made their excuses as well.

A feeble breeze ruffled the tall grass bordering the trail and brought a modicum of relief to the day's warmth. A fat bee slowly buzzed about the flowers on Adaira's bonnet.

"Silly thing, they aren't real." Waving her fan, she shooed the insect away.

"A row about the lake should cool us nicely," Flynn suggested. He squinted into the cloudless sky, then turned to wait for the others. "Especially if we stay to the east side where the trees shade the water."

"I do hope so," Adaira said.

She'd done away with her spencer, and for once, welcomed a parasol's shade. Gads, but she was perspiring. Fanning herself, she cast a covert glance at her sisters. In their white embroidered muslin gowns, each looked as fresh as newly opened peach roses.

How did they manage it?

"I'm as wilted as the cabbage in Sorcha's rumbledethump," Adaira declared, waving her fan vigorously.

"Oh, Addy, rumbledethump?" Catching up, Seonaid giggled. "That's one of your favorite dishes."

Adaira raised her brow. "Yes, I enjoy eating the onions and cabbage, but I don't enjoy feeling droopy and baked."

Flynn wiggled his eyebrows and began walking again. "As bad as all that, eh?"

"I'm feeling a wee bit like wilted cabbage myself." Dugall tugged at his neckcloth. "Last year, we had no summer at all, and this year, we are toastin' like bugs on a log."

Flynn nodded his head, daring to unbutton his coat. "You have the right of it. It's beastly warm."

"Do you suppose Mother would be scandalized if we were to remove our shoes and dip our toes in the water?"

Adaira yearned to jump in the lake and swim as she did in the loch at home.

Isobel looked longingly at the tempting water. "That does sound lovely, Addy, but I'm sure it's most improper."

Of course, it was. Everything fun was improper.

Flynn winked. "I shan't tell, dear cousin."

Father hadn't hesitated to allow his lordship to accompany the Ferguson sisters. Flynn was a relative, though Adaira had never quite understood the connection. Somewhere in the family tree, his father's cousin was related to her grandmother. Second cousins twice removed or third cousins once removed? It was of no importance.

Besides, Ewan was related to him on the McTavish side, too.

Fun and irresistibly charming, Flynn was a delight to be around. He and Adaira had always had a special bond.

"Look at the ducklings!" Seonaid pointed to a shallow area near some tall thrushes and cattails. "Oh, there's a whole family of the little darlings."

Flynn tossed a lazy grin at them and flung a look over his shoulder. "What say you—?"

He stopped, his nostrils flaring.

Following his gaze, Adaira smothered a groan. Count von Schnitzer and his son strode their way, the poor pup snared in Freidrick's arms. He'd retrieved Irmgard, all but snatching her from Adaira, shortly after dining.

She'd been sorely tempted to refuse him the dog, but she hadn't the right.

She had no doubt the von Schnitzers intended to intrude upon their excursion. Not that it was private, by any means. But, by George, she was certain as the day was hot, the count would direct his lewd attention toward her.

She picked up her pace. She wasn't about to climb into

a vessel with either Austrian if she could help it. There was something off about them. Something that went beyond her usual leeriness of men.

Reaching the lake, she quickly assessed the trio of sturdy skiffs tied to the small dock. Each was capable of holding three people comfortably. Two menservants hurried from the shady oaks to assist them into the boats.

Her stomach sank as she sent another furtive peek along the path. Mrs. Winthrop and the earl had joined the count and Freidrick. The woman chatted animatedly, pressed so snug against Lord Clarendon's side, her bosom brushed his arm and bounced with every step.

Why, one would almost think she did it on purpose.

Step. Bounce. Step. Bounce. Step. Bounce.

Goodness, it made Adaira dizzy to watch her cavorting breasts. His lordship's arm would sport a bruise from the pounding it was taking. Couldn't he feel them hammering away, or was he simply unwilling to call her attention to the *faux pas?*

Or, was he enjoying it?

Whipping around, Adaira pointed to a skiff. "Seonaid and Isobel, you take that boat with Flynn. Dugall and I'll share another." Adaira lowered her voice. "Quickly, then. Let's put to the water."

She stepped toward her boat. "Look who approaches."

As one, the others, except Flynn, turned to peer down the path.

Oh, that is subtle, featherheads.

Isobel's gorgeous eyes widened, and she needed no further prompting. She grabbed Seonaid's hand and practically dragged her to the waiting footman.

"Prudent to make haste, I should think." Flynn stepped into the boat and took up the oars.

Dugall narrowed his eyes, and taking Adaira by her elbow, propelled her to a skiff. Swiftly settling on the seat, she lifted her parasol, creating a convenient barrier to the intense sun and equally intrusive scrutiny of Lord Clarendon and Count von Schnitzer. Flicking her gaze upward, she eyed the parasol's three-inch fringed edge. It was quite a useful apparatus, after all.

"Hurry, Dugall. Let's be away," she urged.

Her brother promptly obliged, his powerful arms propelling the boat several feet from the dock with one strong stroke. *Safe. Thank goodness.* The tiniest twinge of guilt speared her uncharitable actions. She dismissed it with a mental shrug. The count made her skin crawl. She recognized the look in his eyes. It had glittered in another's.

Her stomach lurched sickeningly.

A single boat remained. One of the approaching foursome, most likely Freidrick, since he held Irmgard, would be required to stay on land.

"Ho there, wait, Dugall," the earl called.

Oh, rot.

"Devil it," Dugall muttered beneath his breath. He met Adaira's gaze, a question in his dark eyes.

She sighed, resigned. Damn her vow to be a gracious lady today. "There's nothing for it. We cannot risk offending his lordship or the others."

She sagged on the bench seat, the once-promising boating venture now ruined. "Turn the craft about."

Which one of the gentlemen would join them?

The count or Freidrick, she guessed for, Mrs. Winthrop was attached to the earl like a barnacle on a ship. Adaira refused to examine why that rankled.

Eyeing the Austrians, she opted for Freidrick. His

father was by far the more disturbing of the two. "Do join us, Freidrick. I should love to have Irmgard's company."

The pup wagged her tail when she heard Adaira's voice.

"Yes, do go along, Freidrick. I'd prefer not to have that creature underfoot in our tiny vessel." Mrs. Winthrop nervously eyed the boat, then the lake. "Just how deep is the water, my lord?"

Lord Clarendon's gaze hovered on Adaira before alighting on Mrs. Winthrop. "It's neck-high until you are one hundred yards offshore. You needn't fear. I'm adept at rowing, and I'm a strong swimmer should the need arise."

Mrs. Winthrop didn't look the least reassured.

"We'll stay to the edges if you're concerned." Was his voice tinged with a trace of impatience?

Relief replaced the strained expression on her face. "You mistake me, my lord. I wasn't concerned for myself. I know how to stay afloat, but do your Scottish guests?"

Like an otter, madam.

Lord Clarendon quirked a brow at Adaira.

Did he expect *her* to answer? *Humph.*

There were three others just as capable. With the thoughts rambling around in her head at present, it was far wiser to keep quiet. Otherwise, she'd say something she'd regret.

She was pleasantly surprised at how well they'd got on today, except for the moment when he'd first entered the carriage.

Dugall grinned and winked at her. "My laird," he said. "We all swim. There is a loch verra near Craiglochy if ye recall."

Why did Dugall insist on speaking with a thick brogue? He could speak the King's English perfectly well.

"Indeed, so there is." Lord Clarendon guided Mrs. Winthrop to their boat. "See, there's no need to fret."

She frowned, worry once again, lining her face. "But, Otto, do you or Freidrick swim?"

Adaira pressed her lips together. The woman was grasping at excuses not to go boating.

Why didn't she beg off, then?

Adaira slid her focus to the earl. Because Lord Clarendon clearly intended to participate whether the reluctant widow did or not. Heaven forbid she allow him an inch or two to breathe.

Stop it, Adaira. It's not like you to be churlish.

With an irritated sigh, the count said, "Yes, Helene, vee do. Either climb in *das* boat or return to *das* picnic. You're delaying our departure. I, for one, am anxious to spend some time with dese lovely *damen*."

Though he'd said ladies, he kept his predatory gaze on Adaira the whole while.

So, this is how it feels to be hunted.

She touched the cross at her neck. If only it could ward off evil. She'd wave the necklace before the von Schnitzers until they sprinted back to their musty tombs in terror.

"Thom, please help me assist Mrs. Winthrop," the earl said, his hand at her elbow.

In a huff, her cheeks red as ripe plums, Mrs. Winthrop allowed Lord Clarendon and Thom to help her into the vessel. Not, however, without several little screeches and clumsy steps that had the boat rocking precariously.

Freidrick wasn't happy. He'd obviously hoped to share a boat with Isobel. With a mumbled oath, he climbed into Adaira's skiff, taking the seat next to her. Irmgard whined, and the pup tried to crawl into Adaira's lap, but Freidrick held her fast.

He speared Adaira a resentful glare.

Lord, but he was peevish and immature.

She dared a peek at Count von Schnitzer. From the scowl shadowing his face, it was apparent he wasn't pleased, either.

He ran a finger the length of his thin mustache, his gaze holding a dark promise.

Another shiver stole over her. Two surlier men, she'd never met. Surely, they hadn't expected everyone else to exit the boats so the seating arrangements would meet with their approvals?

With a sniff, the count took his seat, the earl in his wake. At last, everyone was established in a boat. Lord Clarendon manned the oars of his craft. No surprise there.

Adaira didn't doubt the count was the type who disdained something as menial as rowing a boat. That was for inferiors, though a British earl was of the same rank as a continental count.

Truth to tell, the earl was by far the more muscular of the two. The count tended toward the thin side. A *shotten* herring, skinny fish, as Dugall and Ewan were want to say. Most appropriate. There was something cold and slimy about the Austrian.

Hugging the perimeter of the lake, the three vessels moved leisurely toward the oaks bent over the water. Their height cast cooling shadows a good distance onto the lake's surface.

The earl's boat went first, then hers, and lastly Flynn's.

The bunching of Lord Clarendon's muscles beneath his coat proved most distracting. He caught her perusal, and a cocky grin split his face.

Heat bloomed across Adaira's cheeks. She started to tilt her parasol to hide her flaming face when Mrs. Winthrop threw a flustered look over her shoulder. Her eyes thinned to slits, and she tossed her head haughtily before facing frontward once more.

Adaira suppressed a sigh of frustration. Had it only been her and her family, she might've indulged the urge to dip her feet in the cold water and find a bit of reprieve from the day's heat.

Boating should be great fun, but the brooding presence of the Austrians and Mrs. Winthrop's frequent squeals and nervous fluttering dampened the pleasure. More like dried it to a shriveled token of what it could've been.

"It's blessedly cooler on the water," Adaira said to ease the awkward silence that had settled over the trio of boats.

"Indeed," murmured the earl.

Did she detect the slightest trace of mockery in his low tone?

Seonaid's quiet, "So true," was followed by Isobel's, "Quite a welcome relief."

"Clarendon, 'pon my rep, with the day's heat, you should've scheduled a swimming outing," Flynn said.

"I may indulge in a swim later anyway." Dugall stopped rowing. He dabbed the moisture from his upper lip and forehead with a handkerchief, then deliberately rocked the boat from side-to-side.

"What say you, Addy. Want to go for a swim?"

Freidrick snarled, "*Aus*. Stop!"

He struggled to hold on to the squirming puppy.

Dugall had the grace to look shamefaced. "Do accept my apologies." Perfectly enunciated, there was the slightest hint of distaste in his tone.

Irmgard kept trying to crawl into Adaira's lap, and Freidrick became increasingly irritated with the dog's efforts to get away from him.

"I'll hold her." Adaira reached for Irmgard, who strained toward her. "I don't mind."

"*Nein!* She's mine." He jerked the puppy back, hurting her hind leg.

Irmgard reacted instinctively and nipped his hand.

"*Du Gott verdammten hund!*" He tossed the terrified dog over the side of the skiff.

"No!" Adaira jumped to her feet. "How could you, you despicable piece of sh—"

Tearing at her bonnet's ribbons and kicking off her shoes, she jumped into the water. The last thing she heard before sinking beneath the surface was a chorus of voices.

"*Dummkopf,*" Freidrick sneered.

Seonaid gasped, "Addy!" as Isobel cried, "Adaira, dear God!"

"Silly chit."

"*Das fräulein* will drown."

"Don't worry. Adaira's a strong swimmer," Dugall assured Mrs. Winthrop and the count.

"Not surprised, no indeed," Flynn said, humor ringing in his voice.

And, lastly, Roark's enraged, "Hell and the devil."

Twenty-One

Well, Adaira had her wish. She'd cooled off, quite nicely at that.

Panting and clutching the shaking puppy in her arms, she sloshed the last few feet to shore. Her soaked gown impeded her trudging progress. She stopped just short of the beach. Many of the pins had slipped from her hair, and it flopped onto one shoulder. What wasn't pasted across her face, that was.

Thank God she was an experienced swimmer, and the boats had been less than seventy feet offshore. The weight of her wet gown and undergarments had been far greater than she'd expected. With the pup clutched to one shoulder, she'd fought to kick her legs and swim forward with her free arm. Twice, she'd turned onto her back to catch her breath.

As she brushed a hand across her breastbone, her breath caught. Her necklace. Where was it? With shaking fingers, she searched around her neck. Locating the chain, she tugged the cross loose from her tangled hair, her breath leaving her lungs in a relieved whoosh.

Peeking between the streaming tresses plastered to her face, she saw her parents bolting along the path. Naturally, the rest of the party charged along in their wake, no doubt buzzing conjecture. The *ton's* denizens were worse than vultures on carrion. And she'd unwittingly given the gossips enough fodder to fuel their fires all winter, bother it all.

Adaira pursed her lips to still her chattering teeth as well as belated compunction. So much for not making a spectacle of herself. Sucking in a ragged breath, she glanced down and froze. The gown clung to her like a second skin, and her nipples, pebble hard, protruded through the thin material.

She tucked the shivering puppy under one arm and plucked at the filmy fabric. *Drat.* Sodden, the cloth, immediately hugged her once more.

Oh, she'd done it up brown this time. She might as well be naked.

Never mind the peeresses in London often dampened their gowns to make them cling to their curves. If it weren't for her stays and chemise, there'd be no need for anyone to imagine what lay beneath her gown. The count was most probably staring at her bum this very minute.

Still, what was Adaira to do?

She couldn't let the puppy drown. She shoved wet hair out of her eyes, then snuggled Irmgard against her chest. At least she could hide her breasts that way. By all that was holy, she wouldn't apologize for jumping into the lake. Hurt as she was, the pup mightn't have made it to shore. She was a tiny dachshund too, likely just weaned.

That *bastart* had hurt Irmgard's back leg. The poor dear had a small gash on her side from where she'd hit the boat when the churl tossed her overboard. What other abuse had the dog endured at his hands?

Hot rage surged through Adaira.

Oh, just wait until that spawn of Satan was ashore. She'd—

Blast, her riding crop would come in handy right now. If she were a man, she'd call him out. She whipped around at the loud splash behind her.

Lord Clarendon tromped through the water, pulling his boat the last few feet to land.

His boots are ruined.

He'd an expression she'd never seen on his face before. The sun glared behind him, haloing him in ethereal light like an avenging god.

She ducked her head, hiding her face against the pup. She wasn't up to his chastisement. Not yet. She closed her eyes, sending up a silent prayer.

Please don't let him admonish me in front of everyone.

Cautiously opening one eye, she dared a peek at the count. The bounder was ogling her, lust glimmering in his gaze.

Mrs. Winthrop, a vise-like grip on her bench, sat pale but composed. There was a strained look about her mouth as if she struggled to hold her tongue. No warmth or pity shone in her round eyes. She visually inspected Adaira toe to top. No, gloating satisfaction better described the look on the widow's face.

Unbuttoning his coat, Lord Clarendon slogged toward Adaira. His perusal traveled from the top of her dripping head to her feet, still in the lapping water. The chiseled angles of his face settled into hard lines. The corners of his mouth turned downward, his eyes blazed, but not with anger.

She felt naked beneath his scorching stare. With an odd

pang under her ribs, her heart sank to her soggy stockings. She'd disappointed him. *Again.*

"I'm sorry." And she truly was. She'd meant to show him she could be a lady. That she was every bit as refined as the *tonnish* damsels whose company he typically kept. Why it mattered, she couldn't say. It just did. And it shouldn't, drat it all. "I only meant to—"

"Hush, Adaira."

He shrugged out of his coat, his signet ring boldly gleaming against his tanned hand.

Where were his gloves? His hat?

And whatever was he doing?

He wrapped the jacket around her shoulders. After tugging it closed in front, he secured a button across her arms as she cuddled Irmgard.

Oh, how thoughtful.

She whispered, "Thank you. I am awfully sorry. I..."

He gave an almost indiscernible shake of his head while perusing the gathering crowd through hooded eyes. "Not now."

Daring to meet his gaze, she swallowed a gulp of air. Expecting anger, she was taken aback at the gentleness in his eyes. His gaze lingered on her mouth, almost as if he wanted to kiss her. A different kind of warmth swept her, causing her pulse to thunder.

The other boats docked, and Adaira's family scrambled out of their vessels. Dugall planted his foot on the craft he vacated and gave the bow a mighty shove.

Freidrick toppled onto his bum, his legs waving in the air.

Her brother and sisters rushed across the dock, joining her parents. Worry and concern etched their faces, but none bore disappointment or censure.

His lordship gestured to the footmen with two fingers. "Thom, Oscar, please come assist Count von Schnitzer and Mrs. Winthrop from their boat."

The footmen hurried to do his bidding, leaving an infuriated Freidrick to fend for himself—by deliberate design, Adaira would bet.

She bit back a laugh as the brattling tried to step from the boat, only to fall backward into it again, cursing and flailing. Freidrick finally angled a knee onto the dock, and in an undignified manner, crawled from the craft.

Served him right, *God rot the cur*.

"Addy, come out of the water, at once." Mother hovered on the shore, holding Adaira's shawl.

"Here, let me have the puppy. You have it difficult enough with your soaked gown." Lord Clarendon plucked the pup from the folds of his cutaway coat. He angled his head in the direction of her parents. "Go on. Don't speak of this to anyone other than your parents until I can tell the tale. I'll put everything to rights."

She blinked at him. "How?" Casting a wary glance at the titillated onlookers, she lowered her voice and said, "I've made a merry mess of it."

"Leave that to me."

"And me," Flynn interjected.

The men's gazes meshed, and a silent communication passed between them.

"I couldn't let her drown." Adaira searched Lord Clarendon's eyes. Squaring her shoulders, she jutted her chin out. "I couldn't, Roark. Please understand. I had to jump in after her."

His smile was tender as he pushed still dripping tresses off her cheek. "If you hadn't, I would have done."

The most proper Lord Clarendon jumping into the lake fully clothed? *Scandalous.*

Adaira stared at him, slack-jawed. "You would have? Really?"

"Indeed." He winked. "You're a hero—er—heroine. Now, go along."

He slanted his head at the shore once more, a lock of chestnut hair falling forward rakishly. The scar on his forehead peeked out between the silky strands. Was his hair as soft as it looked? She had the oddest urge to touch it and find out.

"You're staring." His voice was low and gravelly.

Drat, she was, and she dropped her gaze to the pup Roark cradled. She hadn't a doubt that rouged cheeks glowed no brighter than hers at the moment.

Roark bent his head to her ear. "I rather liked it."

A delicious bubble of happiness encompassed her, and she grinned.

"Here, let me help you." Flynn waded to where she stood and wrapped one arm around her shoulders while steadying her with his other at her elbow.

Another pair of boots ruined.

"With Flynn helping me, I can manage the pup, my lord," Adaira said softly.

The earl rubbed the dog's head and earned a lick on his hand. He passed Irmgard back to Adaira.

Once ashore, her family immediately surrounded her. Mother wrapped Adaira's shawl around her front, holding it closed at her nape. Lord Clarendon's cutaway coat, although it hung past her knees, did little to cover the front of her from the waist down.

Freidrick stomped over to her, and lowering his petulant chin, demanded, "Give me *das hund.*"

"No." Adaira straightened her spine, hugging the puppy tighter. She scanned the faces around her, relieved that none held judgment or reproach. "You don't deserve this precious animal. She would've died if I hadn't saved her. Name your price. I'll buy her from you."

"Excellent. If you weren't going to, I was." Roark sent Freidrick a fierce scowl. "There's no way I'll allow an abusive sot like you to leave here with that pitiable animal."

He pointed at the pup, then sent Adaira a reassuring smile before wading back to his boat.

She cast a pleading glance at her father. "Please, Father. You cannot let Freidrick have her."

Father's gaze warmed, and he nodded. "How much do ye want for the *cuilean*?" Seeing the confusion on Freidrick's face, Father repeated, "Name yer price for the pup. I'll no' have ye sayin' we stole the dog from ye."

He leveled Freidrick with a contemptuous glare.

A shriek behind Adaira muffled Freidrick's response.

She swiveled, clutching Irmgard.

Roark carried Mrs. Winthrop to shore, her arms clasped around his neck, and her head pressed against his chest. She met Adaira's gaze, a triumphant smile tilting her painted mouth.

Adaira hid a smirk in Irmgard's doggy smelling coat. My, but the earl was strong. He toted Mrs. Winthrop like she was a toddler. No easy task, given the woman's *full* figure.

A rider galloped into the picnic area, and a man Adaira didn't recognize leaped from his horse and scanned the grove. He handed the reins over to a servant who pointed in the crowd's direction.

What now?

More histrionics?

Perfect.

Perhaps it would serve to divert some unwanted atten-tion from her.

The newcomer strode purposefully to the lake. He was handsome in a severe sort of way. He made directly for Lord Clarendon, barely sparing Mrs. Winthrop a glance, although his attention lingered on Isobel for a moment.

"Clarendon, I've urgent news."

"Yancy, I thought you weren't arriving until later in the week." Lord Clarendon lowered Mrs. Winthrop to her feet. She leaned against him as if too weak to stand on her own.

Adaira rolled her eyes skyward. One would think from the woman's theatrics that she'd been the one to dive into the lake to save the puppy.

The earl smiled at his guests. "It's time we head back to the mansion to rest before the evening's activities. Please make your way to the carriages." He glanced disinterestedly at the woman, clinging to him. "Mrs. Winthrop, I must speak with Lord Ramsbury. Count von Schnitzer, may I impose upon you to escort your cousin to her barouche?"

"Certainly." His lecherous regard never leaving Adaira, the count extended his elbow to his cousin.

Adaira promptly averted her gaze.

The man was a rude cawker.

Mrs. Winthrop reluctantly released the earl's arm and took up the count's instead. She touched Roark's shoulder. "Will you accompany me in my carriage on the return, my lord?"

His gaze traveled over Adaira. "Yes, perhaps that would be best. Lady Ferguson, Sir Hugh, do feel free to avail your-selves of my landau. Miss Ferguson should make for Cadbury straightaway and have a hot bath, lest she catch a chill."

"Thank you, my lord." Mother smiled her gratitude.

"Here, let me have the puppy so that you can hold the shawl yourself." Seonaid took Irmgard and nuzzled her neck as she followed the others to the carriages.

"Let's do hurry, Adaira, *non*? I don't wish for you to fall ill at the beginning of our visit." Mother started up the gentle sloping embankment, accompanied by the rest of the family.

"Yes, Mother." Clutching the shawl, Adaira half-turned to thank Roark once more.

Lord Ramsbury stepped nearer to the earl and lowered his voice. "He's free, Clarendon. Edgar's been set free.

Twenty-Two

Freshly bathed and perfumed, the lake's residue washed from her hair, Adaira stood before the mirror in her chamber. She adjusted the bodice of her gown slightly. Satisfied with the modest expanse of skin above the lacy edge, she fastened an ornate ivory and silver cameo around her neck before donning the matching earrings.

A movement on the bed caught her attention. The tiny dachshund attacked a stack of pillows, growling low in her throat as she tugged and pounced at the satin and lace edges.

Adaira grinned. "Little fiend."

She crossed to the bed, stockinged feet sinking into the plush carpet. The puppy rolled onto her back and wiggled ecstatically on the satin counterpane. Adaira rubbed the dog's belly, and the rascally pup tried to nibble her fingers.

"*Irmgard.* What a ridiculous name for something as adorable as you." Bending, she kissed the puppy's snout. "No, I shall call you Kiki because it means beginning a new life, and this is a new life for you, sweetheart."

"Here are yer slippers and fan, Miss Adaira," Maisey said, extending the items.

Adaira straightened, and her skirts swished about her ankles. This was one of her favorite gowns, and she'd only worn it once before. The silver beaded embroidery work was extraordinary, especially across the neckline. There was a fairy-like quality to the filmy garment and its gauzy netted overskirt.

Even the air stirred with expectancy as if something enchanted was about to occur.

She smiled at her nonsensical thoughts. She didn't usually have a penchant for fanciful musings.

Whatever had come over her?

A handsome face with sensual lips and unsettling blue eyes.

A delicious shiver skimmed her senses.

Yes, that might well be the cause.

She slid her feet into the shoes before taking the fan. "Thank you."

Kiki let out a whimpering woof, and Adaira swiveled to the bed. Curled in a tight ball and her nose tucked beneath her tail, the pup twitched and snuffled in her sleep.

"Maisey, why don't you take Kiki below? Ask an under footman to care for her this evening. I don't want to add to your duties."

"I dinna mind. The pup is a wee nipper," Maisey said.

Kiki growled in her sleep, and Maisey giggled like a little girl with her first pet. "If she wiggles around too much, a couple of lads in the kitchen would happily play with the tyke."

After slipping on her gloves, Adaira hesitated, eyeing the cameo bracelet. It was too bulky for her taste and too big for her small wrist. But Mother expected her to don it tonight.

Setting the clasp, she took one last look in the mirror.

A beaded silver ribbon entwined her dark hair, the strands shiny from a fresh washing and Maisey brushing them dry. Several long curls framed either side of Adaira's face, and a rosy flush of excitement tinted her cheeks. Her lips glowed red from constant nervous nibbling as the maid dressed her hair.

Adaira wanted to be at her best tonight. No one would call her a dowd or frump when she faced his lordship and his guests. A stab of unease poked her. What Banbury tale had Lord Clarendon concocted that could excuse her jumping fully clothed into a lake?

The way he'd stared at her this afternoon caused the blood in her veins to sing. Why, she was truly anticipating this evening's dinner and entertainment. A first for her. Humming a Scottish ditty, she strolled the length of the corridor, then continued to one of the stairway landings.

Fierce whispering under the other arched staircase brought her up short.

Should she continue or return to her room?

Or perhaps make a great deal of noise?

Adaira allowed a mischievous grin to tip her lips upward. The latter ought to do it. She turned, then halted mid-step.

"She locked him in a *dungeon?*" a high-pitched, outraged female voice asked.

"Yes, but it was a case of mistaken identification. So, I was told by my abigail, who heard it from one of Lord Clarendon's housemaids, who heard it from his lordship's valet," another female replied.

A man entered the conversation, his voice laced with

boredom. "How can you be certain it's true? Most likely, it's nothing but servant tattle."

"Oh, no, Sawyer," the second female denied, breathlessly. "When we boarded the carriage to return to the mansion this afternoon, my darling Trask found he was without his cane. He'd left it propped against a tree in the grove of oaks, you see."

Clothing rustled before she continued. "While fetching the cane, he overhead Lord Ramsbury. He and Lord Clarendon were on the other side of the trees. Ramsbury teased Clarendon about Miss Ferguson getting into *another* scrape. Clarendon laughed and said, 'At least she didn't lock me in a dungeon this time.'"

"'Pon my rep! It's illegal to imprison a peer," a man with a nasally voice exclaimed. "Whyever didn't someone bring charges against the chit?"

"I've no idea, except her half-brother *is* Viscount Sethwick." Squeaky woman again. "After her behavior at the lake, I'm quite convinced she's an incorrigible tart."

"I don't believe she was wearing a chemise beneath her gown. Did you see the way the fabric clung to her figure?" snooty lady two asked.

"Scandalous, I tell you. Whatever is Clarendon thinking, inviting those uncouth Scots to his house party?" sniffed the first woman.

Uncouth Scots? I'll show them an uncouth Scot.

Pressing her lips together, Adaira clenched her fan, wishing she possessed her crop.

"I quite liked the gown—" Sawyer started to drawl.

"*Sawyer!*"

The unmistakable *whump* of a whack to an arm or shoulder promptly followed the outraged cry.

"Let me assure you, Helene will hear of this," lady two declared.

"Is that necessary, Lady Bradford?" Sir Nasal whined. "She'll get her back up. You know how difficult she is when in a froth."

"Sir Oliver, you know full well she's been waiting for Clarendon to propose for nigh on a year," Lady Bradford scolded.

"He couldn't very well do so earlier as he was mourning his wife and child," the first lady offered sagely.

Her strident voice grated along Adaira's brittle nerves.

"Helene's my dearest friend, and it's beyond the pale. I cannot in good conscience keep this from her," Lady Bradford said. "She won't be happy he's brought a chit of questionable standing into her future home. No indeed. She fully anticipates Clarendon to declare himself, perhaps this very evening, so that an announcement can be made at the ball tomorrow."

The blood singing in Adaira's veins transformed into a gloomy dirge. Lord Clarendon was a widower, *and* he'd lost a child? How utterly tragic. He was much too young to have suffered such sorrow.

And he intended to marry Mrs. Winthrop?

Unaccountably, Adaira's vision blurred, and she blinked rapidly to clear the moisture.

They'd make a brilliant match. The widow was the perfect example of *haut ton* desirability: cultured, well-spoken, and the epitome of feminine delicacy, fashion, and grace. Not to mention perfectly rounded in all the places a man desired. Precisely the type of woman he'd take to wife.

Not a slender one that chews straw, rides astride, and wears breeches.

A queer ache pinged near the vicinity of Adaira's heart.

Absurd. It was of no importance to her. Compassion for what Roark had suffered caused her eyes to tear. Nothing else.

On tiptoes, she edged closer to the balustrade.

The stairs concealed the gossipmongers' faces and upper bodies.

Why weren't they with the rest of the guests in the drawing room? Had they just arrived?

Craning her neck, she saw Westbrook bidding new arrivals welcome at the entrance.

Returning her attention to the chinwags, she tried to identify them. The men wore almost identical garb—black breeches and shoes with white stockings. No clue there.

The women were a different story altogether. One woman's gown was a travesty of excessive green ruffles, ribbons, and bows. And that was only from her knees down. Adaira half expected vine shoots to sprout from the skirt and begin creeping along the staircase.

The other woman's gown was elegant in its simplicity. A shimmering champagne shade with a gossamer overskirt in the same shade, the garment screeched sophistication.

The voices faded as the gossips moved away, their shoes clicking on the marble floor.

Lady Bradford's last words rang in Adaira's ears.

"You don't suppose the little upstart has designs on his lordship? Helene will be furious, I can tell you."

Little more than half an hour later, Roark sat at the head of the immense dining table surveying his guests. A full fifty sat for dinner, resplendent in their formal finery. Their chatter, the clanking of china and crystal, and the occasional shouts of laughter and feminine giggles created a pleasant din.

Candlelight glinted off the ladies' jewels and the crystal teardrops of the ten evenly spaced polished candelabras on the table.

He sought one guest in particular.

Adaira sat three-quarters of the way down the table.

She was beyond breathtaking in gauzy white and silver. In the candlelight, the gown glowed, the effect ethereal and nymph-like. Her earrings bobbed as she nodded in answer to spinsterish Miss Darlington's question. The cameo teasing the crest of Adaira's breasts repeatedly begged for a leisurely assessment of the ivory mounds.

His fingers and lips itched to touch that same tempting flesh, and his groin pulsed against his tight breeches. Never before had he so appreciated the privacy a tablecloth offered.

Not once had she looked his way, at least not that he'd noticed. He had the distinct impression she was out of sorts, or perhaps, unhappiness subdued her.

She answered the questions posed to her by the charming, but at seven and sixty, completely harmless, Sir Harrison on her right, and the equally delightful Miss Darlington on her left. The gentlemen seated across from her were notorious rogues, however. She'd ducked her head and blushed more than once at some comment they addressed to her.

Roark tapped his fingers atop the table. It was gauche to address anyone other than those seated beside you. Dankworth and Pemberton, the rakes, knew better.

Although it wasn't proper, Roark had seen to it that Miss Darlington was seated beside Adaira. The woman was intelligent and kind. More importantly, she wasn't given to gossip. He was confident she'd do her best to put Adaira at ease.

"Lord Clarendon," Lady Bradford said, rudely peering past two higher-ranking guests to address him. "I've never known you to host such a large, extended house party. And my goodness." She pressed a hand to her breast. "A *ball*, no less. Not even when Lady Clarendon—"

Fork halfway to his mouth, he arched a starchy brow at her.

Faltering, she gave Roark a dazzling smile, fully realizing her blunder, he'd no doubt. Taking a sip of wine, she recovered swiftly. Leaning forward, her scrawny bosom nearly in her food, and Lord Cammish's elbow up her nose, she pressed Roark.

"Perchance there is cause to celebrate, my lord? A special announcement to be made?"

He damned near choked on the peas he'd forked into his mouth. He ended up swallowing them whole rather than spew them like tiny green cannonballs onto the table.

These were the people he'd insisted Adaira model herself after? Was he out of his bloody mind?

Lady Bradford sent a sly smile to Helene seated a bit further along the table. Helene returned the smile before leveling her possessive gaze on Roark.

So, they'd plotted this, had they?

He took a long sip of wine, forcing the glob stuck in his throat to finish its painfully slow journey to his stomach.

He'd speak to Helene tonight, set things straight with her, and make it perfectly clear they were finished. He didn't envy the scene he suspected might follow. He perused her, and his blood ran cold. Helene glared at Adaira, pure venom in the widow's eyes.

The count, seated to Helene's right, openly leered at Adaira. Egads, the boor was practically drooling in his food.

A vision of mashing von Schnitzer's face into his creamed potatoes and peas intruded upon Roark's imagination. He gritted his teeth and lowered his clenched hand to his lap.

Thank God, Sir Harrison commandeered Adaira's attention. At that moment, the chivalrous old flirt winked at her.

She laughed, full and throaty, at something he shared, and then self-consciously skimmed her gaze around the guests. For the briefest of moments, her lovely brown eyes met Roark's before skittering away.

He recognized the confused melancholy pooled in their depths. His conscience twinged. This gathering was truly trying for Adaira. Most women he knew flourished at social gatherings. Not her. She didn't welcome the male attention.

Most intriguing *and* telling.

Roark was having a difficult time reconciling the passionate woman he'd kissed to this one, obviously wary of men.

"My lord? Have you good tidings to share?" Lady Bradford persisted.

Good God.

Lady Arterbury tittered at the nosey question, and Lady Bradford sent an annoyed glower across the table.

Lady Arterbury raised a brow, still grinning like a cat in the cream.

Roark clenched his jaw. Lady Bradford was determined and intrusive. The only tidings he had pertained to Edgar's release from Newgate. Not something Roark cared to share or celebrate. According to Yancy, Edgar had flown to the continent upon his release.

How many guests were aware of his brother's change in status?

Roark considered those at the table. Lady Bradford peered at him expectantly, waiting for an answer to her question. Best to answer her. It was easier to separate green from a leaf than deter the woman once she'd set her mind to garnering *on dit*.

"No, nothing special." He shook his head. "Merely the pleasure of having some friends to visit. It's time I put Delia's memory to rest."

Make of that what you will.

Lady Bradford's hazel-green eyes widened, and she sliced Helene an unsteady half-smile.

Pretending to be absorbed in the glazed duck on his plate, Roark observed Helene through lowered eyes.

A puzzled frown crossed her features, and she angled her head the merest bit in his direction. She looked between Lady Bradford and him several times.

Raising her wine goblet, Lady Bradford lifted a shoulder, giving a small shake of her head.

Roark's focus settled on Count von Schnitzer. Once Helene was informed of her new status, Roark was certain she'd beg off attending the other events at Cadbury. That meant he'd be spared the count's presence, as well.

Praise the saints.

Freidrick, the irritating whelp, had declined to join his father and cousin for dinner tonight. Just as well. Roark wasn't altogether sure Adaira wouldn't have given him a set down. Or drawn his cork. She packed quite a wallop. He pressed two fingers to his lip in remembrance.

The rest of the dinner passed with excruciating slowness. Every time Roark tried to catch Adaira's eye, she glanced away.

Whatever was going on?

Conversations buzzed around him, but he participated little. Flicking his hand, he indicated Thom should fill his wine glass once more.

"I say, Clarendon, what a brilliant bit of excitement at the lake today."

Roark eyed Lord Sawyer. The man was a loutish dolt, but a close neighbor and powerful lord. Slighting the man by not inviting his household to the house party was unthinkable.

Upon hearing the remark, several heads swiveled Roark's direction, eager, he was sure, for a morsel of gossip. He pressed his lips together, then turned his most jaded look on Sawyer.

After wiping his lips with his serviette, Roark nodded.

"Yes, Miss Ferguson is quite the heroine, risking her life to save the pup when the dog fell overboard. The other boats weren't near enough to help, and it would've taken the gentlemen in her boat too long to remove their boots and coats."

He took a leisurely sip of his wine. Those closest to him nodded their heads and smiled, murmuring their agreement.

"Yes, indeed, Miss Ferguson was most brave."

"What an admirable young woman."

"It's fortunate she's a strong swimmer."

"True, and it was the puppy's good fortune that Miss Ferguson was in the same boat."

No one dared question Roark's word. If they had suspicions all was not as he'd suggested, his guests would voice them away from him.

He waved his hand, indicating dessert should be served.

Biting into a strawberry, he cocked his head at an unexpected sound.

What was that?

Thudding footsteps and frantic voices had him out of his seat and halfway across the dining room. Georgie, a stable boy, his face smeared with dirt and smoke, plowed into the room. Westbrook followed inches behind him.

Holding his side and gasping for breath, Georgie blurted, "Fire, yer lordship! The stables are afire."

Twenty-Three

Tossing her napkin on her plate, Adaira sprang to her feet.

The horses. Fionn!

She cast a frantic glance about the table. Chaos erupted. Women screamed and swooned while the men littered the air with oaths.

Panic gagged her as a score of men, including Father, Dugall, and Flynn, charged to the dining room doors.

"A moment, please." Roark held his hand up. His calm voice rang throughout the chamber, and everyone turned anxious gazes to him.

How can he sound composed?

Gripping the table's edge, Adaira squeezed her eyes shut, fighting waves of nausea.

Dear God, we must save the horses.

"Lady Ferguson, can I impose upon you to entertain the ladies in the drawing room? Those wishing to assist, do follow me. Lord Harrison, I leave the other gentlemen in your capable hands."

Adaira's eyes snapped open.

Drawing room?

She wasn't sitting and twiddling her thumbs in a confounded drawing room, listening to inane feminine drivel. She cut a glance toward Mrs. Winthrop. Red-faced, she appeared to be on the verge of an apoplectic fit.

Count von Schnitzer remained in his seat, casually spooning trifle into his mouth.

Unmitigated, cowardly boor.

Roark laid a hand on Westbrook's arm. "Please see to the needs of our guests."

"Of course, my lord," the butler said, angling his head in acquiescence.

From the glint in his eye, Adaira would wager her savings, he would rather be fighting the blaze.

Without further ado, Roark and the other men, including a slew of liveried footmen, stampeded out the door. In the ensuing confusion, Adaira edged to the French windows at the end of the room. Casting a glance over her shoulder, she slipped out unnoticed.

She rucked her gown to mid-calf and tore after the men thundering to the stables. Dozens of others joined them, both the earl's staff and other servants who'd accompanied their privileged employers to Cadbury for the house party.

The screams of terrified horses, men's coarse shouts, and the eerie groans and shrieks of the burning buildings shattered the night's tranquility. Flames, fueled by a brisk breeze, shot to the heavens, lighting the sky with writhing orangey-red and yellow blades.

Hell on earth.

Please let Fionn be safe.

Please let Fionn be safe.

Oh, God. Please. Please. Please. Please.

Gasping for breath, Adaira reached the first of the

buildings. The smoke gushing forth made it impossible to see anything clearly. The cloying heat and stench gagged her.

Flames engulfed two of the larger structures.

Coughing, her eyes watering and lungs burning from the thick acrid smoke, she peered around. Yanking her handkerchief from between her breasts, she covered her mouth and nose.

Where were Father and Dugall?

Where was Roark?

She grabbed the arm of a stable hand running past. Sweat mixed with soot and grim dripped from his face. He whipped around, impatience on his features until he saw who she was.

"The horses? Did the horses get out?" She shoved aside her hair, which had come loose of its pins.

"Yes, miss. We moved all the stock into the pastures when the fire was first spotted." He cast a hurried glance to the fracas taking place beyond them. "We made sure the animals were safe before word of the fire was sent to the manor."

A sob caught in Adaira's throat. "Thank God!"

"Miss, I need to go. I must help."

Swallowing the knot of fear turned relief, she managed a nod. "Yes, of course."

He sprinted off.

"Wait!" She shouted to be heard above the melee. "Where's Lord Clarendon?"

The groom half-turned, yelling a response, but the wind carried it away. She hurried his direction, wincing when she stepped on something sharp with her slipper.

"Pardon?" she called, swiping at her hair, billowing around her face and shoulders. *Dratted nuisance.* This is why she wore her hair tied back. The asinine pins worked loose half the time.

He trotted back to her, pointing to outbuildings on the other side of the paddock. "His lordship and half a dozen men were over there the last time I saw him."

Adaira nodded and smiled her thanks.

She'd been to the stables but once. Closing her eyes, she tried to picture the barns and outbuildings as she'd seen them yesterday. The coach house and the stable hands' quarters were situated on the north end of the paddock, and beyond them lay the pastures.

Blast, if Roark were still in the vicinity, he might see her. Keeping a wary eye on the blazing buildings, she gingerly picked her way around the corral. She must find Fionn. She wouldn't believe he was safe until she'd seen him herself.

Scrunching her eyes against the stinging air, Adaira strained to see the far meadow. This side of the grounds was darker and a scant less frenetic with activity.

She hadn't seen Father or Dugall yet. She searched the area where Roark was last seen. It was impossible to tell if he were part of the throng bustling about over there.

The men weren't trying to extinguish the fires greedily consuming the two larger barns. Their efforts concentrated on protecting the other outbuildings. Startled, she yelped in surprise as one roof, with an eerily human-like shriek, caved in. The impact was deafening as fiery debris spewed far into the gloamy sky.

Mouth dry, she couldn't tear her attention from the snapping and writhing barn as it died a slow, grotesque death. Slapping a hand over her mouth, she stared in wide-eyed horror as the seething bones of three sides of the barn shuddered before disintegrating into a massive crackling mound of rubbish.

A frisson of sorrow spurred her. She could imagine what Roark must be feeling. Another loud thud followed by a shower of sparks and flames shooting every which direction announced the demise of the building's final wall.

This must be similar to what hell was like.

Someone seized her arm, whirling her around. "What are ye doin'? Does yer mother ken ye're out here?"

"Father!"

Adaira ducked her head guiltily. Mother would be frantic and his lordship, if he found her here, no doubt livid. Ladies of quality weren't supposed to plod around stable grounds.

In their slippers.

Unescorted.

At night. With buildings afire.

Her father lifted her chin. Half-wild eyes in a blackened face peered into hers.

"Why arena ye inside where it's safe?" he roared, although whether from temper or the need to be heard above the furious din, she couldn't be certain.

"I must know if Fionn is all right." She wiped at the smoke-caused tears trailing down her cheeks. She scanned the area. "I still haven't seen him."

Wrapping her in his arms, Father gave her a swift, hard hug. "I have, lass. He is fine." He set her away from him. "Now, go inside. I canna be worryin' about ye, and I canna escort ye back."

"Dugall? Flynn?" It terrified her to think her kinfolk were battling this fiery chaos.

"Over there." Father pointed to a bunch of men with shovels and spades.

Adaira made out the shape of her gargantuan brother hunched over, beating the flames. Flynn, she didn't see.

Father gave her a little shove in the direction of the manor. "Go. Now. Scoot."

She reluctantly swung around to return to the house. "Aye, if you're positive—"

"Yer horse is fine, lass." With a final pat on her shoulder, Father rushed to assist some men across the enclosure.

She stood for a few moments more, admiring the dedication, and the willingness of the men to put themselves in grave danger. Glancing down at her gown, she grimaced. She was a sorry sight, not that she cared. Those in the manor would, however. If she used stealth, perhaps she could make it to her chamber undetected.

Strands of hair swished across her face once more, and grimacing, she brushed at them impatiently. They stank of smoke. For certain, sooty filth covered her, and her lovely gown was only fit for the rubbish pile now.

Heaving a sigh, she cast one last wistful glance over her shoulder before making the return trek to the mansion. A coatless man holding a lantern swiftly strode to the carriage house. He lifted the lamp high in the air.

Lord Clarendon's angular face and straight-nosed profile were illumined against the gloomy backdrop. Bathed in soft amber light, he searched for something. He twisted his head this way and that then lowered the lantern and disappeared around the corner of the building.

Adaira's heart pattered unevenly.

He was safe.

She didn't examine the reasons for her profound relief. After all, Roark was the adversary, although this afternoon, he'd been more savior than tormentor. The look in his eyes made her want to snuggle up to him, nuzzle his neck, and run her fingers through his hair.

But he was Mrs. Winthrop's.

Even as she turned to go, a movement caught her eye. A shadow glided along the edge of the coach house. Unease slithered up her spine.

Frowning, she peered around.

Everyone else was busily engaged, and no one paid her any mind. Directing her attention back to the mysterious form, she furrowed her brow.

No one was there.

She bit her lower lip. Perhaps she'd been wrong.

So, why were the hairs on her nape still standing upright, stiff as wild boar bristles? Moisture beaded her brow and upper lip as well as dampened her underarms.

Should she seek help?

Was she overreacting?

She couldn't very well interrupt the important task of fighting the fire to say she saw a phantom looming about the place. She'd met with enough censured looks and behind-the-hand-smiles this evening to last a lifetime. She didn't need to add ghost sightings to her repertoire of faults.

Hands on her hips, she stared in frustration in the direction her father had gone. It couldn't hurt to take a peek. If something nefarious was afoot, there was plenty of masculine help available.

Guilt tripped across her conscience. Oh, but Father was going to be incensed that she didn't obey him and return to the house straightaway. Quickly, before anyone caught sight of her, she sneaked after the earl.

Adaira hastened to the carriage house, sticking to the shadows as much possible—a difficult task with a monstrous building nearby blazing like a mammoth torch. Her heart pummeled her breast, and her breaths came in short little puffs, more from nerves than danger. Once at the building, she pressed flat against its boarded side.

Lord, what she wouldn't give for her riding crop right now.

Instinctively, she reached for the familiar cross at her neck. *Blister it all.* Tonight, of all nights, it lay upon the dressing table.

A sidelong glance told her she'd yet to be detected. That was somewhat troubling. Any manner of person could be prowling about the grounds, and no one would be the wiser. She peeked around the corner of the building.

Nothing.

Straightening, she released a gusty breath. Mayhap, she'd imagined the stalker. The wind was blowing, and with the fire sending all manner of odd configurations into the darkness, the movement may have been something else entirely.

This side of the building wasn't visible to those fighting the fire. Still, Adaira was confident if she screamed, the sound would carry to the men a couple of hundred feet away. She truly was capable of screeching like a banshee. Hadn't her sisters and mother accused her of it often enough?

Intent on Roark's safety, she slipped around the corner. She needed to know if someone had truly been peering in the window, and if so, why?

Reaching the end of the building's side, she again sneaked a peek around the corner. The carriage house doors gaped wide open.

Roark stood between a landau and phaeton, his head and shoulders bowed, eyes closed.

Was he praying? Grieving?

Gone were his neckcloth and waistcoat. His once white shirt was torn and filthy. His hair mussed, blackish grime coated his hands and face.

Never had he looked more handsome.

"Roark?"

His stricken blue eyes, red-rimmed and bloodshot from smoke, met hers. Heartache tinged with wrath hovered in their depths.

Adaira's stomach skidded sideways.

Devastation etched his face.

"Roark," Adaira breathed, moving into the open space, desperate to comfort. She ran her gaze over him.

"Are you...? You aren't hurt, are you?" She touched his smudged cheek where a small cut lay.

He gave her a tired, lopsided smile. "No, vixen."

Covering her hand with his, he closed his eyes. He pressed his face into her palm as if it were the most natural thing in the world.

She studied his features.

How could she have ever thought him cruel? He was a gentle man, a compassionate man. No one surrounded themselves with those less fortunate unless they were generous and kindhearted.

He kissed her hand, then opened his eyes. His gaze dipped to her mouth, and he traced her lower lip with his thumb. An insane urge to lick it welled within her.

"Do you have any idea what you did to my heart when you jumped in the lake? I was afraid, you'd—" He caressed her face, with light, feathery strokes. "Never mind."

Had he been frightened for her? She closed her eyes and raised her lips in an invitation, breathing out a sigh when his firm, warm mouth closed on hers.

This was becoming a habit, a most delectable one.

She tasted the merest hint of smoke on his lips. He gently moved his mouth on hers. Cupping the back of her head with one hand, he held her immobile. His mouth devoured hers like a man long-starved. Moaning deep in his throat, Roark wrapped his free arm around her back, urging her against his hard chest. His tongue sought entry into her mouth.

An intense wave of desire sluiced through Adaira, buckling her knees. She gripped Roark's broad shoulders and leaned into his solidness. Parting her lips, she granted him the access he sought. How was it possible a kiss could cause her to cast aside all thoughts of decorum? She was unprepared for such bliss.

This wasn't proper.

They weren't betrothed or married.

He belonged to another.

And she didn't care.

She floated on a wave of unfamiliar sensation. A dizzying rush of excitement sped along her nerves. He was the cause. He was the only man who'd ever made her feel this way.

Roark's tongue touched hers, and she was undone. If the building erupted into flames, the scorching heat would be nothing compared to the fire thrumming through every fiber of her being. It settled molten and heavy between her thighs.

Appetite whetted, she wrapped her arms around his neck, mashing her breasts against him. This felt absolutely perfect, like the sweetest of homecomings. She couldn't get close enough, was desperate to be a part of him, have him be a part of her. She breathed in his musky smoke-tinged scent, even as her tongue partnered with his.

His mouth tasted of wine and berry. She sighed when

he ran his hands through her hair, the last of the pins pinging onto the floor. What would it be like to have those hands roam over her bare flesh? Desire flooded her, leaving her weak and wanting.

"Feel what you do to me, vixen," he murmured against her mouth, arching his hips into her belly and cupping her bottom, holding her firmly.

His hardness throbbed against her softness. Perfection.

With a tremendous clunk, the door slammed shut, rattling the windows. Wrenching her mouth from Roark's, Adaira spun around.

Brayan loomed before the entry. A drunken sneer contorting his face, he held a bottle of whisky in one giant paw of a hand and an ugly-looking knife in the other.

Twenty-Four

Numbing fear surged from Adaira's mangled slippers to her unbound hair. She shoved the wild strands behind her ears. How she wished she had her crop. Brayan might think twice before engaging her with a blade. He knew her skill, and besides, Roark was prepared to do battle as well.

This tears it.

She was carrying a dagger strapped to her thigh from now on. *If* she managed to extricate herself from this unholy situation alive.

"Who are you, and what business have you here?" Roark edged in front of her, his body rigid. He fisted his hands at his sides, prepared, she was sure, to defend both of them. He scowled. "Didn't I see you at Craiglocky?"

Placing her hand on his arm, her voice low, she said, "He's Brayan McVey of my clan, though I have no idea why he's here."

Roark slid a sidelong glance to the window nearest him. She peered through the hazy glass as well.

The blaze appeared to have diminished a trifle. The

barn that remained standing continued to spew turbulent flames, however. Shadowy forms darted here and there, their shouts muted by the commotion outside and the walls of the solid structure surrounding her.

She looked at Roark. Would anyone notice he was missing?

Not likely, leastways, not for a while. No one had seen him enter the coach house, save her. Had she and Brayan gone undetected too?

Help would not be forthcoming unless God intervened. She sent up a silent prayer.

Please, God. Tell someone.

Without a weapon, Roark stood less than a fox's chance during a hunt against Brayan. *A weapon.* They needed a weapon. She searched wildly around the building. There in the corner, beside the dusty window, was a workbench with tools lying atop it. Surely there was something there that would suffice.

Lifting her chin, she stepped forward. "Why are you here? Are you responsible for the fires?"

Raising the bottle, Brayan took a deep gulp, then shuddered. He gestured in Roark's direction, giving her a drunken grin. "Did ye think I'd let some dandified sot take ye from me, Addy? Ye're mine. I told ye so."

He narrowed his eyes, rage suddenly contorting his face. "I saw ye actin' the *hoore* with him, rubbin' yer teats against his chest, wigglin' yer arse—"

A flush of humiliation scourged her.

She wasn't ashamed of her response to Roark, but having someone watch them together was mortifying. And sickening. What kind of a person did that? Watched people's most intimate moments. It was unnatural.

She shivered.

"Enough." Roark's calm tone belied the indigo fire in his eyes. A vein pulsed in his temple, the only other indication of his outrage. "Don't you dare address her so foully."

Brayan lurched forward a few steps, his nostrils flaring in ire. "Ye think to make me?" Eyeing Roark scornfully, he scoffed. "I can snap yer neck like a twig. I've done it before."

Adaira gasped, clutching a hand to her throat. How could she have known Brayan for so long and not seen this depravity?

Was he bluffing?

Had he truly broken someone's neck?

Whose?

Despite the oppressive heat of the building, a chill stung her. She hugged herself. Had it been an accident? The satisfied gleam in his eyes and the arrogant smirk skewing his mouth told her no.

She took a couple of steps in the direction of the workbench. When Brayan didn't notice, she dared a few more until she stood near the front of the landau. A trickle of fear-induced sweat slid down her spine.

"Did Addy tell ye she's soiled goods?" Brayan wiped his nose on the back of his hand, sniggering. He pointed at her with the knife. "She's been despoiled. I caught her with him, in Craiglochy's dungeon."

A wave of dizziness slammed into her. The dim light swirled, and roaring echoed in her ears.

God in heaven.

He saw? Before? How?

He'd never said anything.

Trembling, Adaira grasped at the carriage, her legs gone weak in remembered terror. She couldn't draw enough air into her lungs. Her breath came in short, painful huffs. Closing her eyes, she struggled to gather her scattered wits.

She wouldn't faint. She couldn't be of help to Roark if she were an insensate lump on the ground.

She forced her eyes open.

Roark also inched nearer to the window.

Was he of the same mind as she?

Brayan took another healthy swig before ranting on. "She taunted Godwin that summer, paradin' around in those tight breeches, carryin' on like a *hoore*."

Bile surged, bitter and hot, to her tongue. She swallowed against the burning in her throat. Holding her stomach, she shook her head and threw Roark a frantic glance. "No, I didn't wear breeches until after he attacked me."

His unreadable gaze skimmed over her, then Brayan as Roark glided closer to the worktable.

"Nae man could stand the temptation." Brayan had the audacity to wink at Roark.

He froze mid-step. Brayan seemed oblivious to Roark's change in position.

Precisely how foxed was Brayan? Or, was he so cocksure of himself, he didn't think Roark was a threat?

"I dinna blame ye, Clarendon, for succumbin' to her wiles."

"You whoreson, shut your filthy mouth!" Roark bellowed, taking a step in Brayan's direction.

No, Roark. Not without a weapon.

Brayan ignored him. "I saw Godwin follow her in the keep's dungeon that day." He took another quaff, then chuckled, a wicked, sickening sound. "Ye had the pleasure of abidin' in the cell he had his way with her in."

An inarticulate sound ripped from Roark's throat. His shock-filled gaze swept her, blanketing her in icy scorn. He was nearly to the window. Three or four more steps and he'd be there.

In his drunken arrogance and intent on blathering lies, Brayan didn't seem to notice.

"I saw most of it," he boasted.

He droned on, sparing no details, ripping down Adaira's carefully constructed barriers. Making her see and hear and smell everything that happened that awful day all over again. Nausea surged to her throat. She gulped, then gulped again.

Oh, God, I'm going to be sick.

Brayan emptied the bottle. He pitched it on the floor. It clanked loudly, a jagged crack splitting the green glass before it rolled to stop against the landau's wheel. "I've had her, too, dozens of times. She's no' discreet with her favors. When she gets the itch, she'll spread her thighs for anythin' in a kilt—or pantaloons, it seems."

How dare he, the bloody liar?

Livid, she shook her head, her hair swinging around her shoulders and back. "No, that's not true!"

Adaira half-turned to look at Roark. A mask of cold fury had settled on his stony face. A muscle ticked in his jaw, and his nostrils flared with rage. It was the murderous glint sparkling in his eyes that sent her breath whooshing from her lungs.

To whom was his rage directed?

Surely Roark didn't think so little of her that he believed Brayan. *Did he?* She turned to Brayan, outraged.

"Aye, my lord. I ken it rips at yer gut. I begged her to marry me. To see her carry on with other men tore out my heart, but what was I to do? I love the lass. I would've tamed her, though. Bedded her often and fiercely. She'd never yearn for another."

Lust tinged Brayan's eyes and voice.

Roark shot her a sidelong glance full of disgust and loathing.

A blow from a blade would've been less painful. Destruction reigned outside while inside, Brayan's insidious lies shredded what remaining dignity Adaira had salvaged.

Roark believed Brayan.

She shouldn't be surprised.

Why did it hurt so intolerably then? Still, she tried to convince Roark otherwise.

"He's lying. I was never with him or anyone else." Lifting her hand in entreaty, she pleaded with Roark. The cold indifference on his face caused something unnamed to wilt within her. She licked her lips. "I don't remember much of the other—"

Oh God, I truly might cast up my accounts. I must make him understand.

"I...When I regained consciousness, Godwin was gone."

She swung to look at Brayan, then frowned, struggling to remember. *The shadowy form beyond the cell.* It had been him. "You were there! Why didn't you stop Godwin?"

Brayan's lower lip trembled. Adaira stood stock-still as his face crumpled like a small lad's. Giant tears seeped from his eyes. "He was hurtin' ye, Addy. I heard yer screams. I couldna let him hurt ye."

"You *did* let him hurt me," Adaira accused. "You let him assault me!"

In an instant, Brayan's demeanor changed to one of outraged condemnation. "Ye brought it on yerself, lass. Ye ken ye did. I thought it would teach ye a lesson."

"You bloody, heartless bastard." Roark was on him in a flash.

Despite his drunkenness, Brayan's swing was accurate. His fist connected solidly with Roark's jaw. The impact flung him against the barouche. His head smacked the side with a horrifying thud, and he slid to the floor, where he lay unmoving.

"Roark!" Adaira screamed, running to kneel beside him. Blood trickled from a cut above his temple. Livid, still on her knees, she rounded on Brayan.

"Are you insane? I'll never be yours. Do you hear me? Never. You're despicable, watching Godwin attack me and doing nothing."

A puzzled look skittered across Brayan's face. He gazed at her, his hazel eyes confused and forlorn. Sweat ran in long rivulets down his wide face. "But, Addy, I stopped him."

His expression cleared. He grinned like a lad redeemed after a scolding. He slapped his forehead. "I forgot. Ye fainted. I killed him for you. I broke his neck with one twist. I weighed him down with stones and dumped him in the loch. That's how much I love you, Addy."

He'd killed Godwin and expected her to be grateful?

"How *noble* of you. You could've stopped Godwin, should've stopped him before he ruined me." She blotted at the blood on Roark's cheek. "And what of your lies about me? Telling Roark, I'd been with you and others." A sob caught in her throat. His betrayal wounded her raw and deep. "Why did you do that? I thought you were my friend."

Brayan's demeanor changed again. He twisted his lips into a nasty grin of triumph. "Because ye never wanted me. I hung around ye like a stray dog, waitin' for a morsel of affection from ye. I've loved ye for as long as I can recall, and ye've always acted too good for me."

He truly was off his head.

Shuffling her way, he nodded and muttered to himself.

"McTavish and Ferguson will see it my way. They'll not want the wench ruined and left unwed. Yes, I'll sample her charms, and they'll be grateful to have me take her off their hands. She's been a troublesome lass, for certain."

Frantic, Adaira shot a desperate glance at the door. She'd never make it.

And what of Roark?

She wouldn't leave him to Brayan's crazed justice.

He lumbered closer, weaving as the alcohol he'd gulped made its effects known. How much more had he drunk? He lifted his foot to kick Roark in the side.

"Don't, Brayan! He's already hurt."

Her memory shifted to another time Roark lay unconscious. She'd spoken those exact words. Except now, she was desperate to protect him. When had her distrust and aversion become, well, she wasn't certain what it was she felt for him, but the emotion warmed her heart and quickened her pulse.

At her cry, Brayan turned rapidly, causing him to teeter unsteadily. His cheeks flushed and eyes glassy, he chuckled. "I think I've nipped a wee bit too mushhh."

He glanced at Roark and glowered. "Ye'll no' be havin' yer fancy English gent."

Adaira scooted backward until her back slammed against the landau. Something nudged her bottom. *The whisky bottle.* Sliding her hand behind her, she grasped its neck.

Brayan staggered closer.

"Brayan, please listen. Don't do this. You've been my dearest friend." She contrived what she hoped was a convincing smile.

Keep him talking and off guard. She braved a sideways glance at Roark. *And keep him away from Roark.*

She edged along the landau, halting like a cornered mouse when Brayan knelt before her. He touched her face with his calloused, dirty forefinger. Adaira forced herself not to cringe as sweat, stale ale, and the ever-present odor of fish assailed her.

"I mean to have ye, lass. Once yer mine, ye'll have to marry me. Ye'll be disgraced."

A dash of hope heartened her.

He was feeling the effects of the whisky. His slurred speech and uncoordinated movements confirmed it. Bending, he tried to kiss Adaira.

Adaira turned her head away, resisting the urge to retch. He didn't stop but rained wet kisses on her neck and shoulder. She shoved her free hand between them. "Stop it! You're no better than Godwin."

Infuriated, Brayan stiffened.

Oh, she'd done it now. Madness glowed in his drunken gaze.

He fell on her savagely, his weight driving the breath from her lungs and a scream from her throat. Her hand lay trapped beneath her, still clutching the bottle. Her shoulder shrieked in protest at the awkward angle and his great bulk bearing down atop her. His bristly stubble scratched her tender skin. His fat lips weaved a sloppy wet trail across her cheek before he slammed his mouth on hers.

No, this couldn't happen again.

God, don't let this happen again.

She yanked at his hair with her free hand, but he didn't budge. He forced his tongue into her mouth, and Adaira gagged. She'd not make this easy or painless for him. She bit him. Hard.

He roared in fury and slapped her face, leaving the coppery taste of blood in her mouth.

With one mighty jerk, he ripped her gown from bodice to waist. Seizing the arms, he shredded the remaining fabric. Her shoulders stung from the force of his violent assault on the gown. He raised the knife, then brought it flashing downward.

"Brayan, nooo!"

He slashed her stays, dropping the blade to fondle her breasts.

Great rasping sobs tore from her throat.

Adaira's filmy chemise offered little protection from his lust-filled gaze. He dipped his head, slathering greedy kisses across her neck before nipping across her collarbone and chest with his teeth. Reaching her breasts, he bit harder. Ragged pain seared her with each sharp tweak.

"Get off me, you bloody *bastart!*" Wincing and her arm twisted beneath her, she struggled to free her hand.

Brayan roughly pawed and pinched at her breasts, grinding his thick hips into hers. His heavy breathing mixed with her enraged cries.

Bucking and kicking, she managed, at last, to slide her arm and the blessed bottle loose. Without hesitation, she brought it down with terror induced fury on the back of his head.

It shattered, and he collapsed like a stone wall atop her.

Grunting, hysteria choking her, she edged from beneath him and crawled away. Curling her knees to her chest, she wrapped her arms around them and buried her face. Sobs wracked her, shock rendering her nearly senseless.

An object burst through the other window. Adaira screamed in renewed panic. At the rear of the long building, a lantern bounced off the coach's coat of arms before exploding into flames. For a moment, she sat stupefied. Her heart slammed against her ribs, and her lungs refused to draw in air.

Had she escaped Brayan to be faced with this? The carriage's glass window pinged and crackled before exploding into a thousand shards, jolting her back to full awareness.

"Roark! Oh, God Roark, wake up!" Clambering to her feet, yelling his name, she raced to his prone form. She shook his shoulder, none too gently. "Roark, you have to wake up."

He remained motionless.

Tears coursed from her eyes. "You great oaf, wake up. Please, wake up." The flames streaked across the floor, igniting the spilled oil before snaking up the wall.

"I'll not let you die in here, you arrogant, impossible man." Clenching her teeth and grunting, she managed to roll him onto his back.

Her hair formed a curtain around his head and shoulders as she bent over him. She swiped at it angrily. "Confounded hair. Should cut it off. Nothing but a nuisance."

Straining and grunting, she shoved at him, maneuvering his tall form so that his head faced the door. She wiped her dripping forehead with the back of her hand. She squatted and slid her hands under his arms. A whiff of sandalwood wafted upward. She stepped backward, tripping on her gown hanging low on her waist.

Annoyed and verging on stark panic, she kicked at the hem. With gritty determination, she lugged Roark inch-by-inch in the direction of the door. Concentrating on saving him, she muttered aloud to force her fear aside.

"Rescuing unconscious lords is *so* proper." Her gaze dropped to her breasts. "Especially with my bosoms practically exposed and touching his nose."

She lugged Roark another couple of inches, her attention trained on him.

"Look at him."

Step. Lug.

"That nose. Perfect."

Grunt. Tug.

The fire roared hungrily, its voracious flames licking their way along the ceiling. The heat was overwhelming, and sweat beaded her brow and trickled between her breasts. Her chemise clung to her damp flesh, her breaths coming in deep, raspy gulps. Her focus sank to Roark's face as she dragged him.

"No man should have lashes that thick."

"Or hair that shiny and soft."

Throwing a searching glance over her shoulder, she moaned. She still had several feet to go. *God, help me.* She must hurry. Sucking in a ragged breath, she jerked him a bit farther.

"And those lips—those utterly delicious lips."

She lurched backward.

"Great pompous, delectably handsome brute."

"You think my lips are delicious, and I'm delectably handsome?" Roark asked groggily.

Startled, Adaira yelped, dropping him and jumping away. Her heels tangled in the sagging gown. She tottered for a moment, arms flailing before careening to the floor. White pain crashed over her, centered at the back of her head.

Blackness zigzagged before her eyes. Squinting at Roark, she tried to lever to her elbows. She needed to save him.

He groaned and rolled to his stomach, then crawled to

her. His eyes widened before narrowing to furious slits. "What the hell?"

Why is he swearing?

Blinding agony radiated through her head. In a daze, Adaira gazed at the stern, bloodied face hovering over her. Fire flickered in the background. Blackness swirled around her. An icy chill deadened her limbs and mind.

I've died and gone to hell.

Twenty-Five

Full, enticing breasts hovered mere inches above Roark's face.

He must be in heaven, and this was an angel.

Did angels go about scantily clothed?

He was going to quite like the place if they did. It seemed at odds with the church's teaching. He scowled. If this was heaven, then why was it beastly hot? And, Christ on Sunday, why were there flames?

The beautiful, lily scented angel suspended over him was mumbling something about delicious lips and delectable handsomeness. He hadn't thought heavenly beings spoke of such things.

He must've voiced his thoughts because full awareness rudely returned when his angel abruptly released him. His head and shoulders hit the ground with a heavy smack.

Holy Jesus.

Groaning, he closed his eyes and raised a hand to his head. Cracking pain surged against his skull. He could hear it snapping and popping.

He dared to half-open one eye. Flames leaped and danced before him. *Fire?* By God, the building was on fire.

Hearing a sharp cry and a thud, his eyes snapped wide open. Fighting the agony in his head, he rolled over. *Adaira!* He crawled toward her, every movement threatening to split his head asunder. Her gown was shredded to her waist, and her hair was a loose mass of snarled curls.

"Damn," he growled, noting the vicious red handprint across her pale cheek and the bruises beginning to—

What the hell?

Were those bite marks marring her chest?

He dragged himself closer until he loomed directly above her. Her unfocused eyes rolled back in her head. The doors exploded open, crashing against the wall where they dangled on broken hinges. He shook his head against the unclear phantoms wavered before his eyes. A crowd surged through the entrance.

Thank God.

Three forms emerged from the melee. Tilting his head, he shouted, "Get Adaira out! I can manage."

Roark attempted to lever to his feet, but swirling blackness stopped him. He collapsed atop Adaira, his face planted on her chest.

"Angel breasts," he muttered as large hands lifted him.

Then there was nothing but oblivion.

Stampeding cattle kicked up their heels as they frolicked around and around inside Roark's aching skull. His mouth tasted like hogs had wallowed in it—after rolling in mire. *Good Lord.* How much wine had he drunk at dinner last night?

He tentatively probed his head.

Wait.

Memories deluged him, one after the other.

Fire. Adaira. Brayan.

"Adaira!" He lurched upright, then groaned, holding his head in his hands. "Holy bloody hell."

"Ah, sir, you're awake at last."

Roark forced an eyelid open. His valet, Pepperhill, stood beside the bed, holding a glass of liquid. He thrust the glass beneath Roark's nose. "Drink this, my lord. It will ease the pain."

Catching a whiff of the murky contents, Roark nearly gagged. What in God's name was it? He started to shake his head, instantly regretting the movement. Pain plowed through his brain. Instead, holding perfectly still, he said, "No, I don't think—"

"You don't need to think, my lord. Doctor Kimball left me instructions. I'll do the thinking for both of us. Now, sir, do drink it. You look horrid." Bone thin and scarcely two inches above five feet, the diminutive former actor never hesitated to order Roark about.

He eyed the valet.

A wholly unrepentant, lofty gaze stared coolly back at him.

"Exceptionally bold this morning, aren't we, Pepper?"

Grimacing, Roark took the glass and gulped the bitter contents. A shudder rippled the length of his spine before he placed the glass on the nightstand. He swung his legs over the edge of the bed, gripping the mattress until the room stopped spinning. Shoving to his feet, he gingerly yawned and stretched.

Pepperhill yanked the draperies open.

A fresh slice of agony pulsated behind Roark's eyes.

"Devil it, man. Are you trying to kill me? Close the infernal draperies."

"No need to be peevish with me, my lord. I'm not the one who passed out with my face pressed against Miss Ferguson's bosoms."

Roark paused in the midst of donning his navy and burgundy striped banyan. He glared at his man. "Pepperhill, you go too far."

The valet shrugged his slender shoulders. "I'm but telling you what the tittle-tattle is, sir. You're sure to hear it yourself. Not that anyone's blaming you. No indeed. What with the fire, and that monstrous buffoon—"

He gave a dramatic sigh and turned a watery glance on Roark.

Were those tears?

Pepperhill swiped at his eyes before attending to the breakfast tray. "Miss Ferguson saved your life by dragging you to the door. Such a tiny, little thing, and she lugged you across the burning carriage house."

Saved his life?

Clasping his heart, Pepperhill sighed theatrically. "My, my, she's got mettle, she does."

Roark tied his banyan closed. He couldn't remember much of what happened after ham-fisted Brayan planted him a facer, except for snippets about Godwin, stones, and a loch. Then Roark had awakened in what he believed was heaven.

There was something about breasts and delicious lips, but the precise details escaped him. A vague image of full nipples pressed taut against damp fabric flitted enticingly across his memory. The scent of lilies teased a corner of his mind, too.

Adaira, he vaguely recalled, had been a bruised and ravaged mess.

Worry consumed him. She was completely compromised. While he'd been unconscious, had Brayan ravished her? The Scotsman's ugly accusations rang in Roark's ears. What was the truth, and what were the ravings of a jealous—no mad—drunk?

Trying to sound casual, he asked, "How is Miss Ferguson?"

"Well enough. She has a nasty lump on her head." Pepperhill clucked his tongue. "You're quite the pair. Doctor Kimball says you're both fortunate not to have split your skulls or perished from smoke inhalation alone."

He unfolded the serviette, placing it beside the plate, and then drew the chair away from the table. "Imagine, such chaos, and you snuggled into Miss Ferguson's chest, mumbling, '*Angel breasts.*'"

Flushing, Roark closed his eyes.

Damn, damn, and damn.

Pepper snickered, and in *sotto voce* continued. "Even Cook was tittering on about how romantic it was when I went to fetch your breakfast tray."

Humiliation and anger converged on Roark. "Pepper, it escapes me why you find this humorous,"

"Of course, it does," Pepperhill said, entirely unrepentant.

"If you value your position—"

The valet ignored him like he always did when he didn't like a topic of conversation or Roark's opinion. Which was often. If Pepperhill weren't impossibly talented at his job, and equally perceptive to Roark's moods and preferences, he'd have dismissed the man for his impertinence long ago.

Roark was tempted to give Pepperhill his *congé* if only to see his reaction. The servant was entirely too confident of his position. It would do him good to be set back a pace or two.

"By-the-by, my lord, your clothing from yesterday was beyond repair." Pepperhill wrinkled his nose in distaste. He eyed Roark. The gleam in his eyes changed from cocky to compassionate. "You'll feel better if you eat something. Doctor Kimball advised the draught should be taken with food."

Pepperhill turned his attention to the table. After arranging the dining utensils, he poured a cup of coffee, and then lifted the dome from the sausage, bacon, poached eggs, and toast. Raising a brow, he waited behind the chair.

Lying down and yanking the covers over his head was much more appealing, but Roark had a houseful of guests to attend to.

And a fire to investigate.

He obligingly sat in the chair Pepperhill held for him. He took a sip of tepid coffee.

Roark fingered the egg-sized knot on the side of his head. He'd have a brilliant headache for a day or two. There was no help for it. Duty called. He couldn't stay abed and nurse his head. He'd suffered far worse at his sire's hand and still functioned.

"Pepperhill, please tell Westbrook to have Sir Hugh meet me in my study." He glanced at the clock. "In an hour."

That gave him plenty of time to bathe and organize his thoughts. They repeatedly drifted to a chocolate-eyed siren. Suddenly he was quite famished. After spreading marmalade on a piece of toast, he took a healthy bite.

"Very good, sir. Will there be anything else?"

"Yes, I'd like a bath, and I want to be informed the moment Miss Ferguson is awake. Did Doctor Kimball say if she'd be able to entertain visitors or be up and about today?"

He took another bite of toast, then forked a bit of egg into his mouth. It was cold, precisely why he preferred eating below stairs. Hunger compelled him to take another bite despite the unappetizing condition of the eggs. Besides, he needed his mind keen today. An empty stomach didn't lend itself to sharp thinking.

"I'm unaware of Doctor Kimball's orders regarding her. I'll check with Miss Ferguson's abigail straightaway, my lord." Pepperhill opened the chamber door to leave.

"Pepper, where's the Scot, Brayan McVey?" Roark paused, a piece of bacon halfway to his mouth. "I assume he's been detained somewhere on the grounds."

The valet sent Roark a searching look. "Sir, he perished in the fire."

Roark stared, open-mouthed.

Pepperhill moved back into the room. "You and Miss Ferguson were barely found in time. The coach house collapsed moments after the two of you were brought out. No one had time to find the Scot, much less rescue him. If it hadn't been for Miss Ferguson moving you as far as she did, and Miss Seonaid's vision, I'm afraid you both would've died as well."

This time, there was no hiding the tears pooling in the man's eyes. He brushed them away but made no apologies for his emotional display.

The Scot was dead.

Adaira had held him in affection, at least at one time. Something told Roark, she'd grieve her friend's death, despite his atrocious actions. The man had been unbalanced, much like Edgar. Why the stupid fool had started the fires, Roark would never know. For certain, Brayan hadn't expected to be a victim of his own demented scheme.

"Where is his body? His next of kin will need to be notified."

"My lord," Pepperhill swung his attention to a window. "The building burned to the ground. There were no remains left."

Roark could muster no sympathy for the Scotsman. What Brayan had put Adaira through was unpardonable.

"You mentioned Adaira saved me by dragging me to the door." Roark furrowed his brow. "But, Miss Seonaid, how could she have known?"

Pepperhill grinned, which so startled Roark, he choked on his coffee, spewing it across the table. Pepperhill didn't grin. Ever. The minutest upward tilt of his lips passed for a smile on extremely rare occasions.

The manservant rushed to Roark and began pounding him on the back, sending shards of pain into his already thrumming head.

"Enough, man! Did you forget my head?"

"My apologies, my lord. I did indeed. I feared you were choking."

Roark waved off the apology, his appetite effectively squashed. "You were saying? Miss Seonaid?"

The valet nodded. "It seems she has the second sight. Prior to this, I'd not believed in such drivel. While we were fighting the fires, she and the other ladies were sequestered in the drawing room. She suddenly went stiff and blurted something about Miss Adaira being in danger."

Pepperhill brushed a speck of lint from his immaculate sleeve before straightening his already perfectly aligned waistcoat.

"But how did you find us in time?" Inexplicably restless,

Roark stood. He crossed the room to gaze on the charred ruins beyond his window. He'd come very close to dying last night. Adaira could've escaped unharmed, but she'd risked her life to save him. His chest tightened with suppressed emotion.

God, he was grateful she was daring and unconventional.

Why had he ever thought to change her?

"I'm given to understand Miss Seonaid sees things. Images. I was told that she saw flames, carriages, and her sister being set upon. If it hadn't been for Miss Adaira maneuvering you near the entrance, you would've died."

Pepperhill made an odd sound in the back of his throat.

Visions?

Thank God her family believed Seonaid, trusted her enough to send help. And thank God for Adaira. How she'd hauled him that far, Roark would never know.

The clanking and tinkling of china and silverware told him the dutiful servant cleared his leftover breakfast. Then he was beside Roark, placing a hand on his shoulder.

"Sir, are you well? Can I get you anything?"

Turning his head, Roark smiled. "I'm fine, Pepper. I need naught else but my bathwater. There's much to put aright today. Please send Westbrook to me after you've delivered the message to Sir Hugh."

"At once, my lord." One he'd gathered the breakfast tray, Pepperhill made a smart half bow, and turning on his heels, left the room.

Roark's gaze skimmed the blackened mounds proclaiming where the stables and carriage house had once stood. His house party was over before it had begun. Although the arrangements were already made, there was no way on earth he could host a ball tonight. He'd not be surprised if half his guests hadn't left for home already.

Blister it. More visitors would be arriving today.

His other barns were sufficient to house their horseflesh, and none of the guests' carriages had been in the coach house. However, there was the magistrate to contact, staff and guests to question, a list of lost goods to prepare, another list of items to be replaced immediately, and still another of building supplies to order.

And, of course, there was the bumblebroth with Adaira and her thoroughly compromised reputation. Those and dozens of other thoughts careened about in his head. If it didn't already ache fiendishly, the turmoil in his mind would've set his head pounding.

A silvery flash caught his eye as he leaned against the window's sash. Fionn, head and tail high, trotted majestically around the pasture, followed by several mares. Even as he watched, the stallion mounted Tenacity.

Well, confound it. She is in season.

Roark quirked his lips.

It seemed Adaira's stallion was destined to sire a line for him, after all.

Adaira. He released a long, controlled breath.

Last night, the passionate woman in his arms had been unequaled. She fascinated him. He'd not deny it. His responses to her were powerful and unrestrained—overwhelming reactions previously foreign to him. Her fervent kisses revealed her desire for him, too.

Doubt and suspicion raised their ugly heads, however.

He hadn't a qualm that Godwin had forced himself upon her. But Roark had kissed her on several occasions, and not once had she responded like a woman afraid of passion. In fact, the opposite was true.

Had Brayan spoken the truth?

Was Roark nothing but another man to her?

Did Adaira revel in her passionate conquests as Delia had?

No.

Adaira wouldn't have jeopardized her life to save him if that were true. His gut told him neither Delia nor Helene would've gone to the extremes the Scottish lass had to protect him.

Brayan's revelations had staggered Roark. Even now, rage boiled his blood.

Adaira had been assaulted—the worst, most degrading, fate for a woman. That knowledge explained much. Her discomfort around men. Her unsuccessful attempts to hide her femininity by wearing boys' attire.

Damn his eyes. He was a bloody, boorish cur, for he'd accused her of that very thing. His ignorance and pride had blinded him to her loveliness.

Lord, what a mess.

He rubbed the nape of his neck, wincing when he encountered a smaller lump low on the back of his head.

She was ruined.

A good score of men had seen her state of undress. The telling marks on her delicate skin didn't leave much to the imagination. There were people in this very house who'd be only too happy to whisper and snicker behind their hands, spreading their version of last night's events.

There was no help for it. The mold was cast, and the outcome couldn't be changed. He sighed, and pushing away from the window, strode to the bell pull.

If Roark hurried, he could have a courier leave for London today with a missive requesting his solicitor obtain a special license.

Adaira Ferguson would be his countess.

Twenty-Six

The moment Adaira awoke, her mother, sisters, and Maisey converged on her like fog on a loch. Their faces marred with concern, she hadn't the heart to object to their fretting over her. Father, Dugall, and Flynn had poked their heads in to check on her health, as well.

Maisey, her eyes red-rimmed and nose suspiciously shiny, flitted from one side of the bed to the other on the pretense of straightening the coverings or rearranging items on the bedside tables. Cheerful mid-morning sunlight bathed the other four women crowded atop the mattress.

Kiki, hind legs stretched behind her, wiggled her way toward the breakfast tray resting on the counterpane beside Adaira

"How are you feeling? You've quite a knot on your head," Mother fussed, her gaze returning over and over to the welts she knew lay hidden beneath Adaira's gown.

"I'm fine, Mother, truly." Self-conscious, she pulled the nightgown's neckline a bit higher. She'd explained the marks last night, but the unsightly tokens reminded everyone of the attack. "My head scarcely hurts at all, but

I'm afraid I've lost the cameo necklace and bracelet. I'm sorry."

"Don't fret about them." Mother patted Adaira's knee. "You're safe. That's all that matters."

Kiki snatched a piece of toast and dived onto the floor. With her prize clamped in her mouth, she scurried under the bed to enjoy her treasure uninterrupted.

Isobel gasped. "Why, the little thief."

"It's all right. I wasn't going to eat anymore." Adaira had managed a bit of bacon, a couple of bites of toast, and a few strawberries to appease her mother's anxious promptings.

Isobel extended a fat strawberry. "Here's a nice, juicy one."

"No, thank you. I couldn't possibly eat another."

And if dear Seonaid didn't leave off brushing Adaira's hair and bumping her bruised scalp—

"Seonaid, I do believe there's nary a tangle left." Adaira broadly hinted.

"True, Addy, but your hair reeks of smoke and needs washing." After one last stroke, Seonaid laid the brush in her lap.

"A bath's been ordered, *chére*. We've only to send word once you finish breaking your fast." Mother took the cold washcloth Adaira held to her cheek. "*Zut*. The bruising isn't nearly as bad as I'd feared."

"That's because our Addy has a hard head," Isobel teased, handing her another cold cloth.

Adaira stuck her tongue out and grinned, wincing when her bruised cheek objected. She swept them with her gaze. "I thought I was going to die last night. I still cannot believe Seonaid had a vision. I prayed God would send help, and He did."

Seonaid nodded slowly, her soft brown eyes searching

Adaira's. She grasped Adaira's hand. "I saw Brayan and the fire. And Lord Clarendon lying on the ground. I was utterly terrified for you."

I was utterly terrified.

Seonaid's eyes misted with tears, and she trembled as a slight shiver shook her. Concern and a remnant of fear lingered in her gaze. "It was *one* of the clearest images I've ever experienced."

Ignoring the emphasis her sister placed on the word *one*, Adaira squeezed Seonaid's hand. Adaira suspected she knew precisely what other vivid vision Seonaid had seen recently and wasn't about to speculate on what she'd seen, or why this revelation had taken four years to manifest. Or why Seonaid was keeping silent on the matter. Most likely to protect Adaira.

Good Lord, unless she'd seen Adaira and Roark kissing?

To hide the blush staining her face, she bent forward and bussed Seonaid's cheek. "I'm most grateful, and I'm sure his lordship is as well."

Dropping her gaze to her lap, Adaira plucked at the coverlet's tatted edge. Her last memory of him was unnerving— hovering over her, furious and cursing. Did he believe Brayan's lies? She was a woman despoiled, albeit she'd been spared the memory of the worst of Godwin's attack.

Would Roark turn her, a woman disgraced, from his house? His strict adherence to respectability allowed him little choice. Society might recognize the difference between being compromised and willing participation, but the outcome for her was the same.

Shame and disgrace.

Cringing inwardly, Adaira closed her eyes and touched her sore lower neck. He'd tell her parents about Godwin.

She'd no doubt whatsoever. Roark was honor-bound to do so. Unless he thought they already knew.

What purpose would it serve to continue to conceal the assault from them? After last night, everyone would think the worst had occurred anyway.

She was thoroughly and completely ruined. She stifled a sigh. She supposed she could retire to a priory in France.

No. She couldn't.

She'd become corkbrained in a fortnight. Not that she didn't have a strong faith in God, but she didn't possess a docile or complacent bone in her body.

Hadn't yesterday proved that?

Truth be known, now that she was tainted, marriage was no longer an issue. Neither was becoming a lady of refinement. A smatter of silver glinted in the murky cloud fate had dealt her, after all.

Yes, after his lordship requested she leave his premises, she'd be free to do as she pleased. For certain, her parents wouldn't force her into marriage now. Who would have her anyway?

Some ancient lecher?

A doddering fool?

It mattered not that Brayan hadn't had his way with her.

Used goods. Soiled goods.

That was what the gossips would label her. So be it. Adaira could raise her horses, ride astride, and wield her riding crop until the snowdrops and heather carpeting the moors and hills near Craiglocky ceased to grow. She didn't need or want a husband.

Blue eyes, the color of the early morning sky, whisked across her memory. She sent her mother a sidelong peek. "How is Lord Clarendon?"

"He's fine except for a vicious lump on his head and a

headache to match." Mother rose from the bed, taking the cloth with her. "On his lordship's behest, his manservant came by earlier to check on your condition."

He had?

Adaira quickly hid the smile curving her lips lest she have to explain it. She wasn't precisely sure why Roark checking on her well-being please her so much.

She lifted her gaze. "What..." She licked her lips. "What of Brayan?"

"Oh, Addy." Isobel's lovely teal eyes pooled with tears as she grasped Adaira's hand.

Adaira dipped her chin to her chest, rubbing at the plump tears washing her cheeks. "I thought as much," she whispered. "He was such a good friend until—"

"No one knew Brayan was capable of such treachery." Mother hugged her. Angling away, she tucked a strand of hair behind Adaira's ear. Her mother attempted a smile, though her lower lip quivered the merest bit. Tears glimmered in her aqua eyes. "I'm praising God you escaped."

Brayan's betrayal had wounded them all.

"His poor mother. Has word been sent to her?" Adaira wiped her face with her sleeve.

Mother nodded. "*Oui,* Hugh sent McDonnell and Kirkpatrick before light this morning."

Adaira snuffled noisily.

"Here, Addy." Seonaid handed her a handkerchief embroidered with blue and white roses.

"Thank you." Adaira dabbed at her face, flinching when she brushed her cheek too hard.

Three sharp raps pattered on the door.

Maisey scurried to open it. She spoke softly with someone for a moment, then closed the door before turning with two notes in her hand. She passed Mother one and then handed the other to Adaira.

"That was Mr. Pepperhill." Maisey cast a glance to the door and flushed, her coppery freckles blending with the hue of her face.

Adaira hid a smile behind the handkerchief.

Was Maisey enamored with Pepperhill?

The notion was charming. Tall and solidly built, she was significantly larger than the diminutive valet.

With a final pat on Adaira's shoulder, Mother lifted the breakfast tray from the bed. Handing it to Maisey, she said, "Please take this below, and ask for Adaira's bathwater to be sent up."

"Yes, my lady." Maisey bobbed a curtsy before swiftly leaving the room.

Adaira unfolded the note. Scanning the contents, her heart tumbled over itself, then plummeted to her knees. It was a summons from Roark.

This soon?

She'd thought she'd have a bit more time before she was requested to leave. She raised her gaze to her mother.

Lifting her note, Mother said, "I'm to meet your father and Lord Clarendon at half-past eleven. I assume yours makes the same request?" She offered a small smile of encouragement. "*Oui?*"

Adaira nodded, incapable of forming words at the moment. She'd not expected to feel stricken. After all, wasn't this what she wanted? To be spared a month of tedious gatherings and social posturing?

To be rid of Lord Clarendon, Roark, once and for all?

Of course, it was.

She burst into tears.

Nearly two hours later, wearing a creamy gauze morning gown adorned with white lace and pale blue ribbons, Adaira stood beside her mother outside Roark's study. A lacy fichu was tied around her neck and tucked into her bodice, effectively hiding her bruises.

The door stood closed. Nonetheless, muted baritone voices rumbled from within. The temptation to lay her ear against the carved wood to hear what they said overwhelmed her.

On second thought, perhaps she didn't want to know. Smoothing her gown for the sixth time in half as many minutes, she twisted her lips at the irony. The simple gown suggested innocence.

Adaira knew otherwise.

As did Roark.

Mother touched Adaira's arm. "Are you ready?"

Best to get to it and get the worst over. With focused intent, Adaira swallowed the knot lodged in her throat. "Yes. The sooner we face the dragon, the sooner I can be on my way."

Mother sighed. "You're making an assumption."

Grimacing, Adaira shook her head. She glanced around the entry. After overhearing the unpleasant conversation last night, she was aware of how easily one could eavesdrop unnoticed in this house.

"Addy, you don't know what he'll do." Mother drew Adaira's attention back to the present.

Lowering her voice, Adaira said, "Don't I? I shouldn't have been outside last night. Once again, my impetuous behavior has caused a scandal, but in my defense, I was terrified for Fionn."

"I'm sure his lordship won't be overly harsh. He may wish to speak to you about the fire and Brayan, *non?*" Her mother smiled reassuringly. "While it's true you should've remained with the rest of the women, you did save the earl's life."

"Which wouldn't have needed saving if I hadn't been wandering the grounds last night. He's not likely to be gracious about that." A week ago, she'd have told him to go to the devil if he'd objected to her actions. She wouldn't have given a fig what he or society thought of her.

Now, it mattered. Roark's disapproval mattered.

Glancing down, she frowned, then adjusted the lace to cover a reddish-blue mark at the top of one breast. "You know how he responded when I kept him confined in the dungeon. Imagine what his reaction will be to almost getting killed because of me."

Her mother made a comforting sound in her throat.

Adaira cast a glance around the entry, fingering the familiar, comforting cross once more in its place. "He's a trifle hardhearted."

That wasn't altogether true.

She'd come to admire and appreciate the man under the stoic, severe exterior. She wouldn't let herself dwell on why. The cold fury she'd seen on his face before she swooned hadn't been the least bit encouraging. Ominous was far apter. Brayan's lies had prepared her to expect the worst.

Genuine shock flashed across Mother's face, and impatience edged her voice. "*Zut*, Adaira, surely you're not serious. You've seen his staff and the animals he keeps, *non?* Those aren't the actions of an unfeeling man."

"But," Adaira interjected. "He's a man ruled by rigid propriety and pride. I understand what he must do, and I appreciate why." That she did, surprised her. Mayhap her association with Roark had benefited her after all. She raised her hand to knock. "Can we be about it then?"

Grasping her shoulders, Mother turned Adaira to face her. "He could've had you imprisoned for abducting him. Instead, he invited us into his home to afford you a tremendous opportunity. That was the act of a compassionate man. Where is your gratitude, *chèri?*"

Wrapping her hands around her middle, Adaira nodded. "What you say is true, but has Roark ever defied conventionality when it comes to his expectations for women of his station?"

"Roark?" Disbelief, quickly replaced by a knowing, most unnerving look swept Mother's face. A smile pulled at the edges of her mouth. "Did he give you leave to use his first name?"

Tosh. Best to ignore that.

Rattled, Adaira forged onward. "True, he makes unusual concessions for his staff. He's compassionate and kind to his pets and other animals. And yes, he did make an exception to enforcing the law for abducting a peer."

Her mother merely looked at her, her expression understanding.

Adaira flicked her fingers at the study door. "He even makes allowances for himself." Gesturing across the foyer, she said, "For pity's sake, he has an owl in his library!"

Sophie took that moment to let out a haunting hoot.

Mother chuckled. "Do you think she knows we're speaking about her?"

"An owl, Mother. *Who* does that?" Adaira crooked an eyebrow. "I'll wager no one else in *le beau monde*. I confess his traits are charming and endearing. Those engaging qualities would touch any woman."

Mother raised her winged eyebrows but remained silent.

Drat, she has that I-know-what-you-are-thinking look in her eye.

Adaira rushed on. "Yet, I cannot recall a single instance when his inflexible adherence to social propriety and decorum for a woman of quality has been relaxed so much as a feather's worth."

Egads, she sounded as pompous as Roark.

No, as the Roark she'd first met.

Fisting her hands, she recovered, taking a calmer approach. "In that regard, when has he shown me the slightest leniency? It's as if he has a point to prove, and I'm how he intends to demonstrate it."

"You misjudge the man, Addy. From the onset, you determined not to like him, *oui?*" Mother peered at her, probing into her soul with her intelligent gaze. She murmured, "I don't understand why you disdain *every single* man."

Not every man. Not anymore.

The urge to burst into tears overwhelmed Adaira again. She was able to pretend her earlier outburst was a result of last night's trauma and Brayan's death. While those contributed to her uncharacteristic bout of sobbing, the thought of being sent away in disgrace from the one man who'd ever touched her wounded heart was what turned her into a caterwauling disaster.

It was of no matter. The noose was knotted. No sense in delaying the inevitable. Squaring her shoulders, Adaira lifted her chin. She raised her hand to the door once more, at the precise moment it opened.

Caught off balance, she pitched forward into Roark's arms.

Twenty-Seven

Adaira's nose pressed into Roark's solid chest, and he gripped her shoulders, steadying her. Well, this wasn't the entrance she wanted to make, to be sure.

Why does he have to smell so good?

"I beg your pardon." She shifted to move from his grasp. The fichu hung askew off one shoulder, and she sent a self-conscious glance to Mother, gliding by.

Were her lips twitching?

Roark continued to gently cup Adaira's shoulders. His penetrating gaze held hers. "Are you well?" Concern and something deeper simmered in his eyes.

She returned his regard, trying to read his mind. His focus sank to the marks on her chest, and shame sluiced through her, heating her face. Averting her gaze, Adaira stepped from his clasp.

She nodded as she adjusted the fichu. "I'm well, my lord. And you?"

Her parents conversed softly on the other side of the room, but the handsome man before her held her attention.

Through half-lowered lashes, she cast him a surreptitious glance. He looked splendid. Nothing like the fierce demon crouched over her in the coach house.

In point of fact, if she didn't know the sorry state he'd been in last evening, she'd be hard-pressed to believe he'd come close to dying mere hours ago. Except for a scratch along his left jaw, Roark appeared the picture of health.

Today he wore a deep blue jacket with a striped waist-coat in shades of blue and gray. Tucked into gleaming Hessians, his buff-colored pantaloons hugged his strapping thighs like a second skin. Certainly, they weren't the same boots from yesterday.

Had the lake debacle truly only been yesterday?

Either he or his valet had brushed his hair into the latest fashion, and a sapphire pin graced the impossibly compli-cated folds of his snowy neckcloth.

Adaira took a few steps farther into the room. Father, with Mother at his side, stood before slightly ajar French windows framed by heavy burgundy drapes. Her father didn't appear angry or upset. In truth, a cheerful smile tilted his mouth. If she wasn't mistaken, his eyes glinted merrily, too. It was difficult to be certain with the sunlight illumining him.

The smell of ink, leather-bound books, sandalwood, and barely a hint of tobacco lingered in the altogether masculine room. Several paintings, mostly sporting hunting scenes, dominated the wall behind an immense black walnut desk. One side of the room boasted a full but tidy, bookshelf complete with stuffed pheasants and quails on the topmost shelf.

Another wall drew her attention.

A pair of ornate swords, a shield with the Clarendon family crest, several small daggers, and a rather large, wicked-looking whip were attractively arranged against the paneled backdrop.

Roark approached her from behind. "If you'll have a seat, Adaira."

She barely kept her eyebrows from meeting her hairline at his familiarity.

He indicated a striped hunter green, maroon, and beige settee. "Lady Ferguson, please make yourself comfortable, as well. May I get you ladies anything to drink? Ratafia?"

"No, thank you." Adaira sank onto the settee and made a pretense of arranging her skirt.

Mother settled beside Adaira, poised and seemingly at ease. "I'm fine as well, my lord."

How can Mother appear so calm?

Adaira placed her hand on her rioting middle. It felt like camels and goats and frogs, and all manner of animals were doing their worst to her stomach, her heart, and her lungs.

"Lass, it's happy I am to see ye lookin' so bonnie." Father bent to kiss the crown of her head. In two long strides, he reached a brocade armchair, facing the settee and lowered himself into the cushion. His large form dwarfed the chair.

Adaira scrutinized Roark's face before running her gaze over the rest of him. How could she ever have thought him a trow? A glass of umber-colored liquid in one hand, he rifled through a short stack of papers atop his desk.

She detected no urgency in his mannerisms, and a small frown puzzled her forehead.

Perusing one document, he set it aside. After tossing back the contents of the glass, he raised his eyes and smiled. "Thank you, ladies, for your promptness."

Adaira canted her head but didn't speak. She'd the uncanny feeling everyone in the room knew something she didn't. Had he decided to press charges, now that she'd proven she couldn't ever be a proper lady? She squeezed her hands together, the nails biting into the soft flesh of her palms.

No, she wouldn't believe that of him. Not after the kisses they'd shared.

With a final glance at the documents on his desk, Roark came around to the front. Resting his hips against the edge, he crossed his ankles, folded his arms across his wonderfully muscled chest, and smiled again.

He does have nice teeth.

"I'm sure you want to know why I've asked you here."

"No, not especially."

"Adaira, hush," Mother admonished, though not unkindly.

Bother, I said that aloud.

Roark grinned unabashedly. Humor danced in his beautiful eyes. Now she knew how he'd felt muttering his thoughts for the world to hear. He seemed rather more chipper today than she'd expected. Didn't he have a vicious headache?

Meshing her lips together, Adaira determined not to speak her thoughts again. The man already read her mind half the time. She'd not be helping him by blurting them aloud.

She covertly eyed him. The lout was still smiling.

Must he be so cheerful?

She edged her gaze to the empty glass.

Cognac? Whisky?

This early in the day?

How much had he imbibed?

Perchance that was why he'd a constant smile plastered on his face. Or was he that pleased to be rid of her finally?

The gazelles flitting about her ribs bumped to an abrupt halt.

"But before we get to the matter, I'm afraid I have a confession to make, Adaira."

The menagerie started cavorting again.

"Indeed?" Why, she sounded quite poised despite the elephants playing leapfrog in her middle.

He nodded once before angling upright. He moved to sit in the chair beside Father. "Yes, I've misled you, although it wasn't intentional."

Was he referring to their kisses?

Surely he hadn't mentioned that indiscretion to her parents. She had no featherbrained expectations that their kisses meant anything more than shared passion. Roark was most skilled in the kissing department, and she'd been curious, that was all. She'd simply been experimenting.

Liar.

Adaira straightened her spine. He couldn't have told her parents about their kisses. Father wouldn't be sitting calmly. He'd be shaking Roark senseless.

"How so, my lord?" Adaira asked coolly. She was becoming quite accomplished at this playacting. Mayhap, she'd make a fine lady after all.

Shooting her father an unreadable look, Roark raked a hand through his hair. He winced. "Ouch. Forgot about that knot."

He gave her a rakish smile. "I gave you my word Fionn would only breed with horses of your choosing. Because of the fire last night, I've been lax with the horseflesh, and today he—erm—"

Was he blushing? He had to realize she'd seen horses mate.

A smile curved her mouth. "Yes? He...?"

He gave her a sheepish smile. "Tenacity is in season."

"Ah." She stared at him. She'd already decided the mare was a prime specimen. "The other matter?"

At once, the disarming smile faded from his face. "I know the events of last night are difficult for you to discuss, but—"

"My lord, let me save you a great deal of discomfort." Adaira folded her hands in her lap. After veering each of her parents a quick look, she took a bracing breath.

"I followed you into the carriage house after I thought I saw someone lurking there. However, due to the flames and the breeze flitting shadows about, I was unsure. When I entered the building, as you know, I found you alone."

"Lass, I told ye to return to the house." Father frowned at her, censure in his tone.

"Yes, I know, and I'm sorry I didn't obey. But I couldn't leave until I knew Roark wasn't in danger." She crossed her arms, then remembered it was unladylike to do so and uncrossed them. Drat, she'd addressed Roark by his first name, too.

Perhaps no one had noticed.

"Anyhow, Brayan followed me in. He was deep in his cups." She wasn't about to divulge the fervent kissing taking place before Brayan's appearance. She pointed her gaze at Roark.

"When he punched you, you hit your head on the barouche and were knocked unconscious. Brayan tried to force himself on me, but I smashed a whisky bottle over his head."

Her mother made a strangled sound and cut Father a distraught glance.

Last night she'd assured her frantic mother and equally worried father that Brayan hadn't had his way with her. It took some convincing, too. They'd difficulty believing she'd been able to overpower someone Brayan's size.

"Then someone heaved a lantern through one of the windows. The last thing I remember is trying to get you..." She tossed a look to Roark, then her parents. "Out of the building." Adaira sagged against the settee, her gown fisted in one hand. "There, that's the whole of it."

Do your worst, my lord.

"You weren't—" Roark paused and cleared his throat. "Unlike the other time, you were...left untouched?"

The gravelly timbre of his voice rang with deep concern. Almost as if he truly cared, and speaking of it was difficult for him.

Adaira stifled a chagrined groan.

"*Zut! Other* time?" One of Mother's hands clutched her throat, the other Adaira's forearm. Horror shone in the gaze she speared to her husband. "*What* other time?"

Leaping from his chair, outrage lining his craggy face, Father looked ready to throttle Roark. "What's he talkin' about, lass?"

Adaira threw Roark an accusing glare and lifted a trembling hand to her forehead. The onset of a headache pinched behind her eyes and forehead. What a blessing it would be if the floor would open and swallow her.

"I'm sorry, Adaira, I assumed they knew." Roark's voice rose in righteous irritation. "They're your parents, for God's sake! They have a right to know."

"My lord, I'm tryin' verra hard to maintain my temper. Ye'd best be explainin'." Father rarely got angry, but when he did, the outcome was most unpleasant for the target of his wrath.

Monkeys must be riding the rhinoceroses gallivanting around Adaira's insides. Queasiness rose and fell in undulating waves as a dread induced sweat-dampened pretty much all of her.

Splendid. Now, Adaira could add perspiring like a lathered horse to her list of ladylike attributes.

Roark met Father's gaze head-on, not the least intimidated. Or, if he was, he hid it superbly. "No, Sir Hugh," Roark leveled her an unreadable look. "That's your daughter's place."

Bugger it to Hades and back.

Adaira pressed her palms against her middle. *Stop, will you?*

With a resigned sigh, she closed her eyes, silently seeking the strength to voice what she'd been loath to entertain in her thoughts for so long. In the briefest manner possible, she told the sordid tale.

"You see," she said, staring blindly at the floor, "I blamed myself. If I hadn't been sneaking from the keep, Godwin never would have had the opportunity."

"How could you keep this from us?" Mother's voice cracked as she gathered Adaira in her arms, weeping softly into her hair. "For four years. Oh, how you must've suffered, *chérie.*"

Her compassion sparked answering tears, and Adaira found a degree of release from the burden she'd carried alone for so long.

"It's a good thing he fled Craiglocky." Father stomped back-and-forth before the settee, muttering under his breath. "If I ever find the *bastart,* I'll kill him."

Adaira jumped when he slammed his fist into his palm.

"That won't be necessary. Brayan broke Godwin's neck." Roark delivered the news calmly, though his voice held a steely note.

Mother's startled, "What?" was muffled by Father's, "What the bloody hell do ye mean, Brayan broke his neck?"

"How do you know that? You were unconscious." Adaira stared hard at Roark.

"I was half-conscious for a few moments before blacking out altogether. I heard Brayan's confession."

A fierce scowl on his face, his breathing labored and ragged, Father fisted and unfisted his hands. "Well?"

Roark could do the telling. Since she couldn't bear to relive the horror again, Adaira let her mind wander.

Visions of the priory she'd seen when visiting Tante Floressa as a child crept from the corner of her mind.

What was its name?

The white stone walls surrounding the abbey had been rather charming, as were the flower and vegetable gardens. And there'd been lovely singing.

Adaira wasn't gifted with a singing voice. Perhaps she could attend the livestock in the stables. Surely they had a horse or cow or two.

"Adaira, you said someone threw a burning lantern into the building?"

Roark's sudden change in subject jerked her out of her reverie, dragging her back to the present. Her head throbbed full on now. The instant they were through here, she was crawling into bed and burying her head under a pillow until the carriage arrived to haul her away.

She pressed a hand to her forehead. "Yes, the window at the back."

Roark joined her father in pacing the room. He paused in front of her. "I don't suppose you saw who threw it?"

Raising her gaze, she stared at him, dumbfounded.

It was dark outside. And it was at the rear of the build-

ing. And I had my head buried in my knees, crying my heart out.

He gave a curt nod. "No, I thought as much."

Roark had read her mind again. Or had she spoken out loud?

Heaving a gusty sigh, he plowed his hand through his chestnut hair. He winced again. The once neatly combed strands were disheveled, and a few flopped across his brow. "Well, let's be seated and get to the matter I wanted to discuss."

"Are you serious?" Adaira spread her hands, her voice raising an octave.

"This wasn't what you wanted to discuss? My God, what *else* is there? I've had to relive every atrocious thing that has ever happened to me, and you tell me there's *more?*" She hurled the last words at him. Gone were the tender thoughts she'd entertained of him upon entering the room. She itched to box his ears, the insensitive cur.

Fearing she was about to dissolve into a blubbering puddle, she leaped to her feet, then stomped to the window. She gazed out, wishing she could escape. Several guests mingled in the gardens she'd seen from her bedchamber. They strolled the well-tended paths or sat on benches arranged beneath flower-laden arbors.

Girding herself with anger, she pivoted to face him. "Oh, wait, how remiss of me. Of course, there is. This is where you tell me to leave your house because you cannot have a woman of my repute tainting the premises."

To her utter horror, the tears balancing on her lids, spilled over, hot and salty. They trailed down her heated cheeks. She'd cried more since meeting Roark than she had the entire rest of her life combined. And she couldn't abide weepy women. Her gaze trained on the floor, she dashed at the droplets. A pair of polished black boots appeared next to her gown's hem.

"No, Adaira, you have it wrong." Unbearable tenderness colored the timbre of his voice. Reaching into his jacket, Roark removed a neatly folded handkerchief. He handed it to her, waiting while she patted her damp face.

"I do?" She snuffled into the starched fabric, refusing to meet his unsettling gaze, and unable to face the censure she knew shimmered there. "What is it, then?"

"Look at me, vixen." Lifting her chin, he chuckled. His blue eyes deepened to sapphire when he laughed. Grinning lazily, he smoothed a thumb across her lips.

Drat, the elephants and camels were back, and from the feel of the obnoxious beasts, they were flipping cartwheels in her already unsettled stomach.

She peeped over Roark's shoulder. They were alone. "Where are my parents?"

Roark glanced behind him. "I imagine they thought to give us some privacy."

Adaira twisted her lips into a watery smile. "I'm quite certain that's not the least bit proper, my lord."

Neither was the hand cupping her jaw and chin, or the fingers caressing her cheek. This didn't seem like a man hell-bent on sending her on her way. She opened her mouth to say as much, but his mouth descended to claim hers.

Tender, but insistent, his lips skimmed hers. His tongue caressed the seam of her lips, bidding entrance.

Shifting in his arms, Adaira tilted her head and opened her mouth, granting him access. Warmth crested in dizzying waves, ever stronger and hotter, sending delicious sensations to her core.

Oh, but the man knew how to kiss.

He cupped her bottom, squeezing the fullness as he

arched his hips into her in a gentle, sensual rhythm. Her nipples tautened, her breasts swollen and weighty against her stays.

Roark trailed kisses over her eyes and cheeks, then nuzzled the sensitive spot behind her ear. "Do you know how much I've wanted to kiss you?" he whispered.

Gasping, Adaira sagged against him as pure desire sluiced to every pore. Should he attempt to lift her skirts and have his way with her, she wouldn't be capable of resisting. That knowledge astounded her, for she wasn't afraid.

How could that be?

Her desire for him had even pushed aside her unpleasant memories.

After several more tantalizing moments in which her entire body threatened to become a mass of jelly, Roark drew back. She mewed in protest, raising on her tiptoes and wrapping her arms around his neck. Their kissing couldn't end, not yet.

She felt the rumble of laughter deep in his chest as he eased her arms from him.

"No more. Not now, anyway." Holding her hands, he bent his lips into a smile.

Adaira returned it, a glimmer of hope dared to creep into her heart. "Now? Does this mean you're *not* sending me away?"

"Away? Why would I send my betrothed away, vixen?"

Twenty-Eight

Roark squelched a chuckle at the flabbergasted expression on Adaira's face. She blinked rapidly, and her perfectly sculpted mouth opened and closed several times. He'd rendered her speechless. Quite a feat, considering her quick wit and an even quicker tongue.

"You look like a trout gasping for air." He laughed aloud as temper immediately replaced the astonishment in her eyes. She wadded his handkerchief. For a moment, he thought she'd hurl it at him.

"Betrothed?" she finally managed to sputter in a strangled squeak. Yanking her fichu back into place, she swung away from Roark, pacing to the center of the room before spinning back around.

"Betrothed?" She spared a narrowed glance at the closed door. "They knew?"

He nodded, unsure why her response caused him a frisson of uneasiness.

"And *approved?*"

He bristled at the incredulity in her tone. Why

wouldn't they approve? Cocking his head, he nodded once, short and sharp. This wasn't the reaction he'd anticipated, not that one could be certain of anything with Adaira.

Tapping her foot on the floor, she planted her hands on her hips and muttered to herself, "Well, of course, they did, dolt." Her focus settled on his desk. "Those papers you were shuffling earlier—the draft of the marriage contract, I presume?"

He gave a cautious nod.

She marched to the desk, and after tossing the handkerchief onto the polished surface, snatched the terms of settlement he'd set aside. Without asking permission, she scanned the top page.

"Hmph." Adaira gave him a quizzical look before carefully replacing the document.

Roark approached the desk. "You're welcome to read the entire contract if you wish."

Her gaze briefly searched his, as if seeking something. Her gaze sank to the papers, and she flicked their edges. "Thank you. I'd like that, but not at the moment. Anyway, you know as well as I do, that ultimately, I have no say in the matter."

She started to turn away but froze. Rotating back, she faced him, and worry clouded her eyes. She pressed her lips together, her gaze swinging between Roark and the terms of settlement.

"Fionn?" She pointed to the papers. "He's...he's not part of that?"

Roark shook his head. "No, I insisted he remain your property."

Adaira's shoulders relaxed, and she exhaled a pent-up breath. For a fraction of a second, a smile teased the corners of her mouth. She spun away from him, and forehead furrowed, paced about the room.

He regarded her thoughtfully. What was going on in her impetuous, unpredictable mind?

Casting him puzzled glances every few seconds, she muttered beneath her breath.

What was she thinking?

She rubbed her hands up and down her arms before pressing them to her middle. A middle so small, he was sure his hands could span her waist.

Such a petite little thing, but in physique only.

Adaira had the personality and temperament of a behemoth. That brought a grin to his lips. Spirited, undaunted, and unintimidated, she reminded him of one of Aunt Beatry's pugs he'd seen trying to take on a boarhound once.

Adaira frowned at him, tromping to-and-fro across the Oriental carpet. Holding the cross at her neck, she slid the chain from side to side while rubbing the amber stones with her thumb.

Her skirts swished about her small feet as she marched. The white gown wasn't the least alluring, yet its simplicity enticed him, hiding curves he ached to hold. Curves he'd pressed against him or cupped in his hands minutes ago.

Roark's already aroused member pulsed at the memory.

Easy, boy.

She sailed across the floor, back-and-forth, reminding him of a caged lion.

His head throbbed unceasingly, which was why he'd indulged in a bit of cognac, hoping to take the edge off the pain. He eyed the cabinet containing his spirits. With a slow release of breath, he denied himself. He needed his faculties sound.

He regarded Adaira closely.

Was she angry?

Angling his head, he clasped his hands behind him. He rocked back on his heels.

No. He'd seen her infuriated.

Shocked?

No doubt. He'd expected as much.

But hurt?

Did she feel betrayed? Possibly.

She was much more sensitive then she let on, but not inclined to weepiness. Intelligent and perceptive, she must know her parents agreed to his offer because of their deep love for her.

But that wasn't what troubled her. Her lovely eyes were filled with confusion and doubt.

She marched to stand before him, then brazenly poked his chest. "Why?"

The pulse at her throat ticked rapid and uneven, and her breasts rose and fell with her agitation.

Reluctantly, Roark lifted his gaze from the creamy mounds and arched a brow. "*Why?*"

"Yes. Why would *you* agree to marry *me?*" Adaira's dark gaze dropped to his lips. She swallowed. "You cannot be pleased to be saddled with the likes of me."

"You think not?" He rubbed the side of his head in an effort to relieve the ache centered there.

"I'm not what you want in a wife. Not dignified and sophisticated, or... Or well-endowed." Adaira blushed furiously, coloring pink to the tips of her ears. Nonetheless, she valiantly plowed on. "Everyone knows it wasn't you who assaulted me in the carriage house. No one expects you to do the noble thing, least of all me."

Hesitation and wariness softened her tone.

"You're not pleased?" That stung. He touched the cross at her throat, feeling her raging pulse. "You don't wish to marry me?"

She cast him an astonished look, genuine surprise widening her beautiful eyes. "Truth to tell, I never thought to marry at all."

"Ah. But, if you had thought to, would I suffice for a groom?" He traced her collarbone with his fingertip.

She swallowed, then licked her lips, but didn't move away.

His groin tightened a fraction more. The pain in his head was fast becoming secondary to the unrelenting thrumming between his legs.

"I don't want you forced into a union, not of your choosing, Roark. You don't have to marry me out of pity. I know you're a compassionate man, but it's not your responsibility to save me or my reputation. It's too late anyway." She grasped his hand, forcing him to cease caressing her silky skin.

"I'm stronger than I look, Roark. I'll be fine." She shrugged her shoulders. The fichu slid askew. Adaira ignored the drooping lace. Smiling, a heart-wrenchingly sad smile, she said flatly, "I'm quite used to being the source of gossip and disapproval. One really does become immune after a while."

Her acceptance of the ridicule and censure directed at her tore his heart wide open.

Shoulders sagging, she dropped her gaze to her hands and fidgeted with a ribbon on her gown.

Like hell, one did.

People erected barriers and defenses and lived a lonely

life of isolation. Or behaved outrageously, keeping the company of those even more scandalous than themselves. Or they became bitter and unfeeling, afraid to hope for anything better than the harsh hand they'd been dealt.

He couldn't—wouldn't—let that happen to his free-spirited Adaira.

Stifling an oath, Roark straightened his shoulders. The infernal pounding in his head and throbbing in his nether regions affected both his patience and his ability to focus.

"You'd prefer censure and ostracism?"

"I prefer them over being compelled to marry a man who doesn't want me as I am." Adaira tilted her chin, meeting his eyes. "You have made it very clear you disapprove of everything about me. I'm not foolish enough to mistake your lust for anything more than what it is, pure animalistic drive."

She gave him a cynical smile and shrugged again. "You forget, my lord, I have a stallion that becomes crazed with the need to copulate. He doesn't give a rat's whisker about the mare he's mating. She's a means to an end. Humans are little better in my observation. At least the males of the species aren't."

By God, she'd compared Roark to her rutting stallion. He almost touched his jaw to make sure it wasn't sagging to his chest. Ire stung at her rejection, albeit he had to admit, she wasn't wholly off her mark.

"Adaira, the contract is already signed." He rubbed his forehead with two fingers. "While I understand your reluctance and had hoped for a bit more enthusiasm, rest assured, I fully intend to see this marriage through. I'll announce our betrothal at the ball tonight."

She stared at him for a lengthy, disquieting moment. A bluish tint ringed her eyes. Her slightly creased forehead hinted she struggled with her thoughts. Or perhaps, like him, she battled an unyielding headache. Finally, her expression softened, and she breathed out a slow breath.

"You're a fool, then, my lord. It's not necessary. Nonetheless, I shan't defy my father. I've caused him and my mother enough heartache. I hoped you had more sense than to be pressed into a marriage."

Adaira's gaze shifted past his shoulder. She gasped, her face turning ashen.

Whirling around, Roark glimpsed two women hurrying away from the French windows.

Helene and Lady Bradford.

"Bloody hell!" Roark stormed to the door.

Adaira fled the study after seeing Mrs. Winthrop's infuriated face glowering through the gap in the door. She'd heard every word. Adaira sprinted up the stairs, desperate to reach the sanctuary of her chamber.

Using her headache as an excuse to beg off, she hoped to be spared the ordeal of attending the ball tonight. She hastened into her bedchamber to find Seonaid and Isobel already present and beginning preparations. A new ball gown, admittedly the loveliest creation Adaira ever laid eyes on, lay across the bed.

Babbling and giggling nonstop, her delighted sisters flitted around the room, like a pair of colorful, inebriated butterflies.

Afraid to touch the delicate fabric of the gown, Adaira pointed at it. "Where did this gown come from?"

Seonaid lifted a pair of pearl beaded lavender slippers and an elaborately painted fan. "Oh, the first of Yvette's purchases were delivered. She sent Mother a note saying she and Ewan would be arriving in a few days. His business took longer than expected."

"But a new ball gown, for me? How?" Adaira dared to finger the delicate embedded lace overskirt's hem.

"We, Yvette, Mother, Seonaid, and me, planned it as a surprise," Isobel said, beaming.

Tears pricked Adaira's eyelids. They'd gone to such trouble to make her feel special and to show how much they loved her. Lord, she was grateful for her family, especially right now, when her world was fraying at the seams.

"And you've such wonderful news!" Swooping in for a hug, Isobel bussed Adaira's cheek. "Seonaid and I were returning from a walk about the greens when we heard word of your betrothal to Lord Clarendon."

Blinking back her tears, Adaira stared. Gads, if they knew, then every other soul within five miles was aware, as well. To be made a marriage offer solely to salvage her reputation was pathetic. The humiliation stung. She'd hoped to have a bit of time to adjust to the situation before others' tongues began wagging.

"Just think, our sister, the Countess of Clarendon." Normally composed and quiet, Seonaid giggled, her eyes sparkling with mischief. "Oh, Addy, everyone was whispering about your good fortune."

Good fortune?

Yes, Adaira supposed everyone would see it that way.

Everyone, but her.

She wandered to a table placed before the balcony window. A pitcher of water, glasses, fruit, and some sweets were arranged neatly atop it. Pouring a glass of water, she took a long sip. "Well then, there's no need to announce it tonight, is there? And thus, there's no need for me to attend the ball."

"But, Addy, you must. It would be a grievous insult to his lordship if you didn't." Seonaid's voice trembled with shock. Her uncertain brown gaze sought Isobel's.

Adaira grimaced. She cast her sisters each a glance. "You do know the circumstances, don't you? His offer was born of pity and honor to save my reputation. Not that there's any chance of repairing something so wretchedly tarnished. Blackened."

She flopped into an armchair, resting her head in her hand, her elbow braced on the chair's arm. After kicking off her slippers, she tucked her feet beneath her bottom. "Hardly cause for celebration, to my way of thinking."

Isobel and Seonaid exchanged worried glances. As one, they descended on her. Seonaid knelt on the floor before Adaira, and Isobel leaned on the chair's other arm.

"Dearest, you cannot mean to refuse him?" Isobel brushed a loose curl off Adaira's cheek before curving an arm around her shoulders. "That would make everything so much worse. Completely disastrous."

Seonaid laid her head on Adaira's lap and peeked at her sideways. "It's true, Addy. We heard—" She stopped, offering a timid smile. "Never mind. You've no choice. It's a brilliant match. He seems like such a nice man, and he's very fine-looking."

He is, at that.

"You have to admit he's devilishly attractive, Addy." She propped her chin on Adaira's knee. Seonaid nudged Adaira's knee. "Admit it. *You* think he's *handsome*," she teased in a singsong voice. "I've seen you looking at him."

Adaira relaxed into the chair, resting her head against the plush back. She patted Seonaid's shoulder while holding Isobel's hand. "Yes, he's sinfully handsome. Happy?" Adaira closed her eyes and sighed. "But the truth is, he doesn't want me. He didn't choose me."

That truth cleaved her heart wide open.

The tears she'd held at bay trickled dual paths down her cheeks. "I..." She couldn't tell them about Godwin. "I thought never to marry, that's all."

Truth be known, she was terrified of intimacy with a man. She couldn't explain her fear to her sisters or anyone else for that matter. It was one thing to share passionate kisses, but the rest?

A tremor shook her.

She'd no doubt, Roark would expect *that*. And often.

A knock sounded at the door, but before Adaira bid enter, Mother bustled into the room, holding her jewel case.

"Chére, you're as pale as fresh snow at dawn," she said. "Let me apply the tiniest bit of rouge to your cheeks and lips, *non?*"

To please her, Adaira suffered through the lengthy *toilette*. Yet, when she stood before the full-length cheval mirror, she stared in astonishment. She hardly recognized the elegant woman gazing back at her. She almost felt a proper lady.

Descending the stairs after her sisters, Adaira spotted Roark speaking with a group near the other stairway. She summoned a composed, if somewhat tremulous smile. Surreptitious glances, batting eyelashes, and covert whispers behind hands and fans greeted her arrival. Her sentiment transformed from happiness to indignation.

Grandmother's words, long forgotten, came unbidden to Adaira's mind.

When ye've made a mistake, lassie, admit your wrongdoin' and learn from yer poor choice, so you dinna do it again. But when others judge ye unfairly, which will happen in yer life, ye hold up yer chin, straighten yer spine, and spit in their eye.

Adaira smiled wryly at that last bit.

She squared her shoulders and lifted her chin, refusing to allow the gossiping or censure to determine who she was or how she would act. *She* was the victim, and Brayan and Godwin had wronged her. Society's hypocritical and judgmental attitudes compounded the offenses.

She'd heard whispers about the *tête-à-têtes* and dalliances prevalent amongst the *ton*. Cuckolding and adultery behind closed doors, or in garden arbors, was acceptable. But being set upon by nefarious blackguards against one's will was cause to shun the victim?

Preposterous claptrap.

Flipping open her fan, she painted her most dazzling smile on her face and entered the fray. Roark immediately appeared at her side. Despite her misgivings about their betrothal, she sent him a grateful look. He was a powerful ally, a reliable ship in this sea of duplicity she was about to set sail upon.

He bent over her hand, his lips grazing her fingertips before tilting into a rakish smile.

Lord, he was gorgeous. Adaira's appreciative gaze traveled from his shiny shoes, rested momentarily on his snug breeches, then journeyed upward to his coat and cravat. A happy little thrill shivered through her.

He wore an amethyst stickpin that matched her jewelry. Her breath hitched. Was it a coincidence, or had he donned the jewel on purpose? He would have had to consult with her mother about Adaira's attire.

What a delicious thought.

Diamond and amethyst earrings hung from her ears,

and a matching double-rowed necklace encircled her neck. The jewelry belonged to her mother. She'd lent them to Adaira in addition to the delicate amethyst and diamond tiara nestled atop her head.

She inched her gaze over Roark's strong, square jaw, the chiseled planes of his face, his perfectly styled hair, and at last, his sapphire eyes. Eyes that devoured her.

Twenty-Nine

"**G**od in heaven, that gown—"

Roark's warm breath caressed Adaira's ear, his awed voice wreaking havoc on her heart.

His gaze lingered on the generous expanse of soft flesh exposed above her gown. The worst of her wounds were well-hidden beneath the bodice—the one exception her mother had concealed with cosmetics. It could easily be mistaken for a shadow from the lace edging the neckline.

He swallowed, and when he lifted his gaze to hers, she recognized the blatant desire shining in his eyes.

"You look exquisite, vixen."

He wanted her. The knowledge astonished her. Yet, there was no denying the fire in his heated gaze. It thrilled and unnerved her.

No, the notion downright terrified her.

To hide her discomfiture, Adaira dropped her gaze to her skirt. She brushed her gloved hands over the fragile lace overskirt. The color of the softest heather, the bodice was shot with silver and gold threads. Beaded with pearls and lavender crystals, the gown shimmered in the candlelight.

"Thank you," she murmured.

The musicians struck a few chords, warming up for the long evening ahead. Roark placed her hand on his arm, possessively resting his atop hers. "Come, let me introduce you to a few of our neighbors and some of my friends before the dancing begins. I hope you'll reserve every dance for me."

Our neighbors?

He made it sound like they were already wed. The timbre of his voice, low and suggestive, curled Adaira's toes in her fancy new slippers.

"Not so hasty, Clarendon. I fully expect my cousin to grant me a dance or two." Flynn, his eyes shining and lips curled into a charming smile, sidled to their sides. He bowed smartly, winking at Adaira as he took her hand.

"Aye, yer lordship, I'll be havin' a dance with my daughter, as well." Father loomed behind Flynn for a moment before Dugall and the Earl of Ramsbury crowded in.

"I mean to share a dance with my brave-hearted sister, too," Dugall insisted with an affectionate upward sweep of his mouth.

Roark scowled like an intractable lad denied a pastry, and Adaira hid a smile behind her fan.

Dugall's smile widened into a grin.

Three calf-eyed damsels blatantly postured a few feet away, attempting to gain his attention.

Two matrons sailed to their sides, shooing the girls along while casting disapproving glances over their shoulders.

He boldly winked at the mother-hens.

Adaira quirked a brow.

He was fast becoming a man. Extraordinarily handsome —indecently so—the scallywag would leave a trail of broken hearts in his wake.

"Clarendon," Lord Ramsbury admonished. "You wouldn't deny me the honor of dancing with Miss Ferguson, would you? You'll have her to yourself soon enough. You mustn't be stingy, hoarding her company like treats from the confectionary, as you did at Oxford."

Covering half his mouth, Lord Ramsbury angled his head near hers, whispering in a *sotto voce*. "He always had a stash of assorted sweets and was *most* reluctant to share."

Mirth twinkled in his dark green eyes. He obviously enjoyed goading Roark, like intimate friends often do.

At the put upon look on Roark's face, Adaira giggled. His eyes glittered in a combination of incredulity and irritation at all of her dance requests. If she didn't know better, she'd think he was jealous. Oh, how she'd like to believe it was so.

"Of course, I'll dance with you, my lord. Roark knows it's bad *ton* to commandeer a partner, even if they are betrothed." She smiled, meeting Roark's eyes. "I wouldn't want to do anything to cause more whispers." Sweeping the room with her gaze, she inclined her head. "See, they need no excuse as it is."

The men looked to where she indicated, and several guests turned away swiftly. Lady Bradford plowed into Lord Bradford, spilling her champagne down the front of his breeches. Furious, he hissed something at her before clomping away, bowlegged. She shot Adaira a sour glare before scampering after her livid husband.

"*Touché*, vixen," Roark muttered beneath his breath. He squeezed her hand while turning her in the direction of the ballroom. "As your betrothed, I'm still claiming the first dance. No arguing or I'll kiss you into silence."

The strains of a waltz floated by on the overly perfumed air. Speechless, Adaira allowed Roark to guide her onto the floor. One of his hands rested proprietarily against the curve of her ribs. The room glowed from hundreds of candles resting in golden chandeliers and wall sconces.

Would he really kiss her in front of everyone?

Appalling.

And wonderfully delicious to contemplate.

She nearly giggled again, imagining the faces of his guests. Oh, that would give them a succulent morsel to bandy about.

"Did you truly hoard sweets?" she asked.

Suffering flashed across his face, quickly masked by a lazy smile. "I wasn't permitted bonbons or anything sweet tasting as a child."

"None? Whyever not?" Visions of Sorcha's shortbread, pasties, and clootie dumplings danced in Adaira's mind.

"My father thought them unnecessary." Roark lowered his voice to a rasping growl. "'Indulging in their consumption is a sign of a spineless coward,'" he mimicked.

She searched his face, seeking the deprived little boy buried inside the man. Hurt lay hidden deep within his eyes. Her heart contracted as a surge of anger heated her. "But that's completely ridiculous. Irrational. Abusive even."

Roark slanted his head. "An apt description of my sire."

"Roark?"

Adaira tightened the hand resting on his shoulder and felt the faintest ridge of a scar beneath her fingertips.

He flicked his gaze to hers for a moment before resuming his perusal of the room. "Yes?"

She had no right to ask. But her tongue formed the words even as her mind screeched for her to be silent. "The scars on your back and forehead. How did you come by those?"

He stiffened, and voice hoarse said, "You don't want to know."

But she already knew.

The whip in the study.

A ghastly reminder of what he'd been subjected to.

"*He* did that to you? His son? I'm..." Her voice caught, mere words insufficient to express her sorrow and regret. And outrage. How Roark must've suffered. Adaira inched closer, and although unseemly, wrapped her arm farther around his back in a comforting embrace. "I'm so sorry."

He responded by drawing her even nearer, holding her far too close to be acceptable. She didn't care, as long as it brought him some degree of comfort. He circled her around the floor, keeping excellent time, amazingly light on his feet. She managed a smile for Isobel as Lord Ramsbury twirled by with her in his arms, a rapt expression upon his face.

Another conquest for Isobel, it would appear.

Adaira was very aware of Roark's hand, pressing her against him. The light material of her gown was an insufficient barrier from his warm palm. He moved his thumb up and down her spine in time to the music. Her body reacted as if he were caressing naked flesh. Her breasts grew heavy, her breathing irregular. Unnerving, yet splendid, little quivers tingled in unmentionable areas.

He bent his neck and brushed her neck with his mouth before suddenly going rigid. "Blast and d—"

Turning her head, Adaira glanced behind her. She clenched his shoulder and hand, stumbling to a stop. Mrs. Winthrop and Count von Schnitzer stood at the ballroom entrance, a scowling Westbrook beside them.

"I cannot believe after I spoke with Helene today, she has the audacity to put in an appearance tonight," Roark muttered, urging Adaira back into motion.

Standing stock-still in the middle of the dance floor would garner unsolicited attention in addition to launching unwelcome speculation. A noticeable buzz began circulating the room when he'd entered with Adaira. The hum increased markedly in volume at the appearance of Helene and von Schnitzer.

Westbrook's face bore an uncharacteristic panicked expression. Roark knew the butler hadn't admitted Helene. She'd used one of the other unlocked entrances. No doubt the same one she'd used to pay her late-night visits to him. *Damnation.*

Adaira cast the pair a furtive peek. "But didn't you invite her?"

Roark shook his head. "Actually, no. She assumed she'd attend the events at Cadbury as she always has in the past. After the boating incident, I expressly told her Freidrick was no longer welcome in my home. I didn't think I needed to explain that meant she was no longer welcome, as well."

He presumed the obstinate woman would realize the obvious. Stupidity on his part.

Brazenness on hers.

There was no way in hell he was going to divulge to Adaira the details of his conversation with Helene terminating their association. He hadn't been intimate with her for months. After meeting the tempting armful he now spun about the room, any desire to bed the widow had flown.

Adaira turned her head ever-so-slightly to peek at Helene and von Schnitzer. They'd joined the rest of the dancers whirling around the sanded floor.

"She's glaring daggers at you. At us," Adaira murmured.

Roark lifted his focus from her face and met Helene's hostile glower. "She had a misconception about her position. I rectified that this afternoon."

And it had been most unpleasant.

The vulgarities spouting from Helene's mouth would have a hardened trollop blushing. She'd truly thought to lure him into marriage. He'd never remotely entertained the idea and had never given her reason to either. He determined his next wife would be of a different cut than Delia. Helene was too much the seductress to meet that requirement.

Adaira might not be an innocent, but she was chaste and modest.

And wholly desirable.

Helene's threats of retribution concerned him. And that viper of a cousin of hers... Slimy curs such as he were capable of innumerable reprehensible things.

"She believed you were going to propose tonight," Adaira said, no hint of retribution in her voice. She tilted her head, staring at him.

Roark missed a step but quickly fell back into rhythm. He met her gaze. When she was troubled, the brown of her eyes deepened. They appeared coffee black at the moment.

How did she come by that information?

She must've seen the question in his eyes.

She colored adorably, then peeked at him through thick lashes. "I overheard some guests last night, quite by accident, I assure you. It seems others have been anticipating a proposal as well."

"Indeed?" Roark drawled dryly.

The dance came to an end, and he scanned the crowd. Spying Sir Hugh and Lady Ferguson, he maneuvered Adaira in their direction. Roark kept an eye on Helene the entire time. "Adaira, stay close to your family. I don't trust either Helene or the count. I'm certain no good can result from their attendance."

He slanted his head in the direction of the disgruntled couple.

Lord and Lady Bradford, Lord and Lady Bellingsworth, and several other cronies of Helene's surrounded her and the count. Most likely squawking like distressed chickens in a henhouse with a fox.

Why had he invited any of them?

Ah, yes, it was expected and unforgivably rude not to.

Ludicrous, hypocritical rules.

Roark bowed to Lady Ferguson, then Isobel and Seonaid in turn as Luxmoore and Yancy dutifully returned the young ladies to their parents.

"Gentlemen," Roark said. "A word, if you please. Sir Hugh, might I speak with you as well?"

Yancy shot a perceptive glance to the group huddled and clucking across the ballroom. "Of course, Clarendon. We'll meet you on the terrace."

Sir Hugh patted his wife's shoulder and winked. "I'm not sure it's fair, leaving ye with three bonnie lasses and a roomful of smitten swains." Waggling his thick eyebrows, he eyed a pack of young bucks hovering nearby.

They darted frequent, hopeful glances at the Ferguson trio.

Roark turned and coolly assessed them. One look at his face, and the milksops scattered like cockroaches. "Perhaps someone should remain with you."

Where was Dugall?

He was just the thing to dissuade the moon-eyed beaux.

Lady Ferguson smiled, intelligence glimmering in her eyes. She met Roark's gaze. "No need to worry. We'll enjoy some lemonade or ratafia and wait for your return," she said in her soft French accent.

She perused the room. "Dugall is about somewhere."

Discerning woman.

She recognized trouble when it raised its bothersome head. Or, in this case, two heads. Although Lady Ferguson appeared the picture of composure, he was confident she was aware of the tension permeating the room.

Chuckling, Sir Hugh followed Luxmoore and Yancy through a pair of open French windows and onto the terrace, paralleling one side of the ballroom.

Lifting Adaira's hand, Roark insisted, "Promise me you'll not wander off alone. Not even to the retiring room." He met four pairs of eyes, noting the wariness reflected in each. "Stay together, please."

"*Zut,* my lord, I assure you, my daughters won't leave my sight. Your concern is very much appreciated." Lady Ferguson sliced a covert glance across the too warm room. "They're not here anymore."

Roark casually rotated on his heels, his gaze roving the ballroom. *Blast.* Where had they got off too?

"Please excuse me." Bowing once more, he strode to the terrace doors.

Adaira admired the impressive figure Roark cut as he nodded and smiled to his guests. He never slowed his stride.

She scarcely believed it. The same man she'd once disdained as a loathsome trow, had maneuvered his way past her carefully constructed barriers and had begun setting up house in her heart.

She turned to her mother. "Do you think they'll make a scene?"

Mother, a minute frown creasing her brow, searched the room again. At Adaira's question, she swung her attention to her daughters. "I'm sure I don't know, *chére*. How are you faring? These past two days have been trying for you, *non*?"

Trying?

Adaira bit back a sarcastic snort. "Yes, you certainly could say that."

"Mother," Isobel said. "I'm sorry, but my hem is torn. It needs to be mended at once, else it will rip further."

Seonaid nodded, a haunted glint in her eye. With a peculiar tone tingeing her voice, she murmured, "And I have need of the necessary."

Did she really?

Or, had she seen something?

"I would welcome a visit to the retiring room." Adaira stood, shaking her skirts. "My head aches a mite. A few moments rest and a cool cloth would be most appreciated."

As one, her sisters and mother rose to their feet.

"Let's use the one upstairs," Adaira suggested. "It will be less crowded than the two below, I think."

Mother linked her elbow with Adaira's. "Isobel, take your sister's arm." With a final glance about the room, she swept to the entrance. "To the retiring room, *mes chéris*."

Adaira breathed a silent sigh of relief. They'd reached the retiring room without encountering Mrs. Winthrop or the count. Thankfully, the chamber, which looked to be an unused sitting room given the connecting door, was unoccupied except for a maid.

One look at the chamber and Adaira grinned.

This must be Roark's Aunt Beatry's sitting room. It had

to be. She'd been a dog lover. Apparently, she had unusual decorative preferences, too.

A pair of rather garish orange and yellow floral settees faced each other. Two armchairs, each sporting black needlepoint poodles, were positioned between them at either end. A marble-topped table centered between the furniture contained a huge bouquet of flowers, a pitcher of water, and several glasses. Intricately painted screens situated on the far side of the room probably concealed chamber pots.

A shelf with various knickknacks, including truly hideous, cumbersome statues of dogs, stood to the right of the unlit fireplace. A life-size sculpture of a hound sat before it. More heinous dog statues and figurines were arranged neatly atop the mantle. All manner of fallalls and feminine whatnot covered a table to the left of the fireplace.

Another long table before French windows, which Adaira presumed opened onto a balcony, held mirrors, brushes, combs, pins, what appeared to be rosewater, and various cosmetics.

Isobel promptly removed her gloves. "I have need of a needle and thread. Oh, and scissors, please. I've torn the lace on my hem."

"I'd be happy to do it for you, miss," the maid volunteered.

"There's no need, but thank you." Isobel smiled kindly. "It's only a small rip. I shan't even have to remove my gown to repair it."

"The sewing supplies are over there." The maid gestured to a table beside the fireplace.

Isobel quickly set about mending her gown while Seonaid attended to her needs. Adaira removed her gloves, and after straightening the fingers, she draped the gloves on the settee's back. She turned to the maid. "I'm sorry, but I don't know your name."

The girl dipped a quick curtsy. "It's Clara, miss—er, my lady."

The poor servant had no notion who they were or how to address them. Although it wasn't customary, Adaira quickly made informal introductions.

"I'm Adaira Ferguson, and these are my sisters, Isobel." She indicated Isobel with a flick of her wrist, then pointed to the screen across the room, which hid Seonaid. "And Seonaid."

Taking a seat, she waved her hand in her mother's direction. "That lovely woman is our mother, Lady Ferguson."

Clara gawked at Adaira. "Coo, you're to be my new mistress."

Adaira squirmed on the settee.

Even the servants knew? Of course, they did. They were the first to know.

"Ah, yes. Well, um, as to that—"

"I think you are the bravest woman I've ever met! You saved his lordship's life." Clara stood, hands clasped and worship in her eyes, staring raptly at Adaira.

This certainly is awkward.

Adaira sent Mother a peep from beneath her lashes.

She'd settled in one of the armchairs and smiled tolerantly. Was there a twinkle of amusement in her eyes?

Adaira yanked a frilly pillow from behind her and tossed it on the seat beside her. "Um, thank you. Have you any headache powders? And might I trouble you for a cold cloth?"

If the servants were discussing her, she could be sure the rest of the household was as well. It came as no surprise, but disconcerted her, nonetheless. Egad, what else had the guests been discussing about her and Roark?

He knew she wasn't skilled in ladylike pursuits. Undoubtedly, he had no idea just how lacking in natural talent she truly was. Sewing, planning menus, diplomatic conversation, pouring tea, acting the part of a gracious hostess—her skills were nominal at best. *Atrocious* better described them.

And she didn't care much about improving her abilities.

Returning to the ball wasn't something she relished either. Mrs. Winthrop and her cousin lurked somewhere below. And there was still supper to get through.

Adaira almost groaned aloud.

"Here you are, miss." Clara handed her a glass of liquid and the cloth.

The girl's hands were deformed.

Clara's fingers were webbed together, and several were mere stubs, difficult to even identify as digits. Adaira met the maid's gaze. No sense in pretending she hadn't noticed. To do so would only embarrass Clara more. "Do you find it difficult to do things?"

Clara smiled and held up her hands. "I know they look odd, but I can do almost anything, even sew and cook."

Isobel giggled. "Addy cannot do either."

Adaira was fighting the urge to poke her tongue at Isobel when Seonaid reappeared from behind the screen, her face pale and anxious.

Mother promptly rose from her chair. She hurried to Seonaid. Laying one hand on her forearm, she pressed the back of her other hand against Seonaid's forehead. "Are you feeling unwell?"

She looked positively stricken.

Their mother hesitated for the briefest of moments. "Or...have you had a vision?"

"*Yes.* A vision." Seonaid scanned the room before marching to the fireplace. She grabbed the poker, then spun to face the door. "I'm afraid we're about to be interrupted."

Setting the glass and cloth on the table, Adaira threw Isobel a questioning glance. She stopped sewing in mid-stitch. They snapped their gazes to Mother and Seonaid. Their sister stared at the entrance, the poker angled like a sword.

Mother snatched the log tongs, her focus trained on the door.

Isobel snipped the thread before seizing a pair of scissors.

Adaira looked around frantically. Her gaze landed on a revolting pug statuette. Springing to her feet, she charged to the shelf. She grasped the bulky figure with both hands. No, it was too awkward. She whirled to the center of the room. There, in the corner by the wardrobe, rested an ancient parasol.

She dashed across the room. She'd barely wrapped her fingers around the worn handle when the door crashed open.

Thirty

Mrs. Winthrop sailed into the room, her thin lips twisted into a predatory smile.

Adaira edged closer to her mother and sisters. Each posed in a defensive stance before the cold hearth. Oh, to have her riding crop. Father had returned it to her this morning, but one hardly toted a whip around at a ball.

Poor Clara. She stood bug-eyed, mouth agape, gawking at the Ferguson women as if they'd all taken leave of their senses.

Stabbing them with a hostile glare, Mrs. Winthrop called over her shoulder, "They're alone."

Count von Schnitzer and his son appeared on either side of her.

When had Freidrick arrived?

He had the same sullen glower and perpetual sneer he'd worn when she'd seen him last.

Thank God Maisey had taken Kiki to the kitchen for the evening. If Freidrick tried to find the puppy, he wouldn't be able to. One of the lads who helped the cook had volunteered to take the dog to his quarters for the night.

Clara, taking her cue from the Ferguson women, laid hold of a battered cane. She scuttled to stand beside Adaira.

"What are *you* doing here?" Angling her chin, Adaira directed her comment to the count. "Men are not permitted in the retiring room. You must leave at once."

Chuckling, he moved farther into the room.

Freidrick remained at the door, checking the corridor every few moments.

The count's lewd gaze roved over her sisters and mother before sliding to Adaira. Invisible snakes slithered across her suddenly cold flesh.

"Who will make me? *Sie Frauen?*" He shook his head and ran a finger across his upper lip. Deviance and lust vied for supremacy in his piercing, rodent eyes.

"Look at them, Otto." Mrs. Winthrop raked them with her gaze and smirked. "Such a vulgar display of aggression. But one expects no more from barbaric, uncouth *Scots*."

Mother tilted her chin. "*Votre parodie d'une robe est beaucoup plus vulgaire,*" she said in her musical French accent.

Clara choked on a giggle.

Did she understand French?

Confusion flickered on Mrs. Winthrop's face, and she sent a desperate glance to von Schnitzer. He shrugged and continued his salacious leering.

"You don't speak French, Mrs. Winthrop?" Adaira chuckled. "Dear me, a social grace you're deficient in? *Tsk, tsk.*"

Clara giggled again, earning her a murderous glower from Mrs. Winthrop.

Glancing at her sisters, Adaira sighed. "I suppose I must

interpret. Never let it be said Scots are ill-mannered." She swung the parasol in a small arc. "Mother said, 'Your travesty of a gown is far more vulgar.'"

And indeed, the garment was a disaster. Pink and white, it quite obviously was intended for a much slenderer, considerably younger woman.

Mrs. Winthrop's bosom threatened to gush over the bodice and blacken both her eyes if she blinked too hard. That was, if the seams didn't burst first. Or the straining buttons pop loose and put someone's eye out.

Fury mottling Mrs. Winthrop's full face, she stomped to the center of the room. "Poke fun at me, will you? Not for long, I assure you. You see—though I cannot imagine why, you're such a shapeless stick—Otto finds you attractive. He has a splendid solution to end your farce of a betrothal to my Roark."

Her Roark?

Adaira twirled the parasol. "Indeed?"

Keep stalling.

Surely by now, Roark and the others had noticed the Ferguson women's absence from the ballroom. The men would search the lower levels first, of course. Did Roark even know this chamber was used for a retiring room?

"*Schnell*," Freidrick hissed, shuffling his feet. "Before someone comes."

"Otto has decided to leave sooner than anticipated," Mrs. Winthrop said. "He insists you accompany him. Roark will end this mockery of a betrothal once he learns you're in the count's company."

"How can you be sure? Roark's the one who insisted on asking for my hand, even though nothing untoward occurred." Adaira angled her head. "Did he tell you that? He can be quite determined when he sets his mind to something. He was most resolute that he and I should become affianced."

Mrs. Winthrop chuckled nastily. "Oh, I assure you, Roark will want nothing to do with you afterward. Otto has quite an *interesting* reputation, don't you, darling?"

A sinister smile curled von Schnitzer's mouth. "As you say. *Die Damen* are never das same."

"My daughter isn't going anywhere with him." Mother tightened her grip on the log tongs.

"I'm not setting foot from this room with your cousin. Not now. Not ever." Adaira lifted the parasol. If only it were her crop. She suspected the count was unhinged and didn't want to speculate what his last comment implied.

"Yes, you will, if you value their lives." Mrs. Winthrop wiggled her fingers at Adaira's family. A spiteful smile twisted the widow's lips, and she reached into her reticule and removed a small pistol.

Mother stiffened, and the others sucked in a chorus of sharp breaths.

Pointing the pistol at them, Mrs. Winthrop snickered. "In case you're wondering, I do know how to use the gun. And yes, it is loaded."

Thunder pounded in Adaira's ears, and fear replaced the blood in her veins. "One pistol for four—"

Clara made an inarticulate noise.

"Five of us?" Adaira shook her head. "I don't think so."

Roark, where are you?

"You don't truly think I'm that simpleminded, do you?" Mrs. Winthrop's malicious smile widened, crinkling her pudgy cheeks and the corners of her eyes. "No, Otto and Freidrick are armed, too."

A fiendish grin on his face, Freidrick removed a gun from the back of his waistband. He pointed the pistol at each of them in turn, jerking the weapon and making shooting noises with his mouth.

He's addled, too.

The count patted his lower back, then his breast pocket. "*Eine pistole und messer.*"

A knife, also?

Before the intruders showed their guns, Adaira had thought to have Clara run for help. That is, if the adjoining door was unlocked. That idea was soundly dashed. Adaira didn't doubt for a moment their guns were loaded. Neither did she doubt these vermin would use them.

Evidently, insanity ran in their family lineage.

"*Ich begann das* barn *feuers*," Freidrick bragged in a mixture of German and English. He waved his gun menacingly.

Mrs. Winthrop glared at him. "That was idiotic of you. Roark could've been killed, imbecile!" She whirled to the count. "You assured me the whelp had stopped setting fires."

Count von Schnitzer shrugged. "He was angry about *das hund.*"

Adaira clenched the parasol handle so tightly, it's a wonder the aged wood didn't snap. She took a step forward. "You filthy, coward. You're nothing but a—"

"Addy, *non*," Mother warned.

Adaira glowered at Freidrick, the despicable cretin. Willing to kill innocent animals because he'd been thwarted. She didn't want to imagine what the cur would've done to Kiki had she not rescued the puppy. Glaring at Mrs. Winthrop, Adaira lifted her chin, and challenged, "You cannot get me out of the house undetected."

"Oh yes, we—he can. I know several back stairways and passages. I've already shown them to Otto. We let Freidrick in that way." Mrs. Winthrop tittered, batting her lashes coyly. "How did you imagine Roark and I managed to be discreet?"

Adaira wished she could crawl in a deep hole. After vomiting first. It was galling enough she knew Roark's relationship with the widow. But to have the woman boast of it in front of Adaira's family was beyond the pale. Anger and mortification emboldened her.

"Why, I imagined you used the main entrance, as promiscuous strumpets with no concern for their reputations do," she said while casually twirling the parasol.

"Addy, *non*. Don't antagonize her," her mother murmured, her voice low.

Face pinched and eyes narrowed to slits, Mrs. Winthrop pointed her gun at Adaira's chest. "Otto, take the wench now before I truly lose my temper. Only use the passages I showed you. If someone comes upon you, pretend to be having a dalliance. I'm sure the chit can be persuaded to cooperate with a weapon pressed to her side."

The count removed his gun. He aimed the barrel at Adaira and motioned for her to move to the door. Still holding the parasol, she slipped around the edge of the settee.

"Addy..." Mother breathed.

Adaira glanced over her shoulder.

Terror glittered in her mother's and sisters' eyes.

Pale as milk, Clara swayed.

Gauging the situation, Adaira's mind raced.

There were five of them. Each gun only had one shot, and none of the hammers were cocked. If the women attacked in unison, caught the widow and the Austrians off guard, they might very well succeed in disarming the vermin.

"Can I at least say farewell to my family?" she asked.

Without waiting for permission, she moved to embrace her mother and sisters. As she hugged each one, she quickly whispered to them in French. She didn't hesitate to wrap her arms around Clara, giving her a swift command as well.

Dragging the parasol, Adaira made a pretense of moving with exaggerated reluctance toward the door. All the while, she assessed her abductors with covert glances.

Freidrick lingered partway in the corridor, nervously shifting from foot-to-foot.

Mrs. Winthrop stood with her hands resting atop the settee. The pistol loosely held in one, triumph lit her face.

Count von Schnitzer turned to follow Adaira from the room, and she caught him ogling her backend.

"*Schnell*," Freidrick growled again before poking his head around the doorway. "I think someone *kommt*." Panic laced his voice.

Adaira seized the opportunity and screamed, "Now!"

Hell broke loose.

Curses and shouts filled the chamber, and her mother and Clara flew at the count. Seonaid and Isobel descended on Freidrick, as Adaira sprang the parasol open in the widow's face.

Unprepared for the attack, Mrs. Winthrop stumbled backward, tripping over the rug. She landed hard on her ample arse, and her pistol skidded beneath the settee.

Adaira popped the parasol shut, and without a hint of hesitation or remorse, she walloped the hefty widow in the face. Bone crunched. Shrieking in agony, she clutched her gushing nose while struggling to her feet.

Breathing hard, Adaira pivoted to help her mother and Clara. There was little need. The count held one wrist firmly against his chest, no doubt broken. He sported a broad welt on his face, and his gun lay several feet away.

Mother kicked it under the armoire, grim satisfaction on her features.

Cursing, he made for the door, plowing into Adaira as he passed her. Sharp pain lanced her side.

Seonaid and Isobel had Freidrick well in hand. Swearing a string of German oaths, he held one hand to the scissors protruding from his shoulder. His other arm, limp and bleeding, dangled at his side. Isobel pointed his gun directly at his heart.

"Addy!"

Hearing the first distant yell, the villains tore from the room, moving amazingly fast, considering their injuries.

"Seonaid? Isobel?"

"Giselle, where are ye?"

"Adaira!"

Pounding footsteps reverberated as men thundered up the flight of stairs.

The women fell into each other's arms. Collapsing onto the floor, unmindful of the pools of blood, they hugged, laughed, and sobbed simultaneously.

Roark was the first to skid into the chamber.

Dugall, Yancy, Flynn, Father, Westbrook, Maisey, and a slew of others Adaira didn't recognize immediately followed.

Holding her ribs, she grinned up at Roark. Her hair plopped onto one shoulder. "Sometimes, unladylike behavior is most convenient."

His ice-blue eyes widened in shock, and the color drained from his tanned face.

Adaira dropped her gaze to her throbbing side and lifted

her hand. Scarlet stained her palm. "Will you look at that? I do believe I've been stabbed."

Thirty-One

Stockinged feet on his desk, a glass of brandy in one hand, Roark flicked his watch open.

A quarter past midnight.

He snapped the timepiece shut before returning it to his waistcoat pocket. Taking a long swallow, he welcomed the warmth heating his gut. He unbuttoned his waistcoat, then the top of his shirt. His neckcloth already lay in a heap atop his desk.

What a day.

His mind churned wearily.

He couldn't summon the strength to place his feet on the floor and walk upstairs. Tomorrow he'd have to find Helene and the von Schnitzers. They'd not returned to her house, according to her butler. Nonetheless, Roark's men monitored the premises around the clock. At least he knew who'd started the fires now.

Rage, second only to that he'd experienced when he'd learned of Adaira's ravishment, heated his blood and drove his thoughts. He'd sent for the local magistrate at once but didn't expect the official's arrival until midmorning. Roark's gaze prowled the room, passing the whip mounted on the wall, then snapping back to it.

For the first time in his life, he was sorely tempted to use the lash on someone.

He'd seen Doctor Thornton to the door over an hour and a half ago. The physician assured Roark, Adaira's wound was superficial. Her long stays had taken the brunt of the blow. She'd only required five stitches and now rested comfortably.

Although the ball had ended early, Roark insisted his guests eat before returning home or seeking their chambers. After all, Cook had prepared a succulent spread.

His betrothal went unannounced.

Little doubt remained that every soul in attendance was already apprised of the news. He smiled ruefully and lifted his glass, offering a silent salute to his affianced asleep two floors above.

Roark had planned to check on Adaira before he retired. His obligations prevented him from looking in on her earlier. Now, the hour was much too late to go tapping on her bedchamber door. Once again, duty took precedence over desire.

The responsibilities of an earl: never-ending, trying, and wearisome.

Sighing, he lowered his feet to the floor. Wrapped in weariness, he stood. After quaffing back the remaining mouthful of brandy, he placed the glass on his desk. Eager to find his bed, he grabbed his tailcoat from the back of the chair and quit the room.

Since he fully expected a long-winded lecture from Pepperhill reprimanding him for *gallivanting about the house half-clothed*, the valet could retrieve Roark's shoes and neckcloth in the morning.

Pepperhill was happiest when acting the role of a martyr.

Roark half-grinned, already hearing the valet's fussing and clucking.

Shoulders slumped and fatigue clouding his mind, Roark climbed the stairs. He found himself standing outside Adaira's door, seemingly born there on feet guided by his subconscious. Soft amber light glimmered in the crack paralleling the floor.

Was she still awake?

Perhaps she was in pain. Or was she afraid?

Given the past two days, she'd every right to be hysterical and that she wasn't caused him to admire her all the more.

In retrospect, placing guards about the house and grounds might be prudent. He didn't expect Helene's rashness to extend to another abduction attempt. Still, erring on the side of caution seemed wisest.

Hearing a soft cry from within Adaira's chamber, he tried the door's latch. Irritation gripped him when it turned in his hand. Why wasn't her chamber locked?

She cried out again, and he threw open the door.

A lamp burned low on the nightstand, wrapping the room in a comforting golden cocoon. Adaira, her petite form dwarfed by the bed, whimpered and thrashed.

Roark reached the bed in a few long strides.

Her face contorted. She swatted weakly with her hands. "No. Stop." Voice wavering on a sob, she begged, "Please stop."

Flinging his coat onto a nearby chair, Roark sat on the edge of the bed. "Adaira."

He touched her shoulder lightly with two fingers.

"No!" she cried, lurching upright. She scurried backward until the pillows and headboard prevented further retreat.

"Shh, vixen. It's me." Roark laid a hand on her leg to comfort her.

Confusion and tears swam in her sleep-heavy eyes. "What?" She closed her eyelids and drew in a tremulous breath, wincing slightly. She pressed a hand to her side. "What... What are you doing here?"

"I wanted to check on you before I retired, and I heard you shout." He adjusted his position on the bed, bending one knee to rest his thigh atop the mattress. "Are you all right? Was it a nightmare?"

A haunted look shimmered in her eyes, and she nodded. "Yes."

What he wouldn't give to go back in time and destroy the man who'd done this to her. "Do you dream of the attack often?"

"Not anymore." She brushed hair away from her face, flicking it over her shoulder. Relaxing a fraction, she said, "I haven't had that particular one in years."

Her lower lip quivered, and she sucked the soft flesh into her mouth, biting it with her top teeth.

"Come here." Roark extended his arms.

Adaira scrambled across the bed. She launched onto his lap and wrapped her arms around his neck so tightly, he doubted her brothers could've pried her off. Her nightgown, rucked to her knees, exposed shapely calves and ankles.

He shifted again, extending his legs before him and settled her more comfortably on his lap. He rested against the mound of pillows at the head of the bed.

"How's your wound?"

"A little sore."

"Want to tell me about your dream?" he whispered into her silky hair.

She smelled like a walk in the garden: lily, iris, lilac, summer sun, and morning breeze, condensed into one fragrant little bundle. He touched his nose to her hair and drew her sweet scent deep into his lungs.

She gave a watery chuckle against his chest. "Are you sniffing my head?"

His rumble mixed with hers. "Yes, I am. You smell wonderful."

"You always smell wretchedly fabulous, too."

"I do?"

"Uh-hum." Adaira sighed and nestled deeper into his lap and shoulder. One hand curved behind his back, the other lay dangerously close to his groin.

His member twitched, then twitched again, like a spoilt child demanding attention. He kissed the crown of her head once more. "The dream?" he coaxed.

She shook her head. "I don't want to talk about it."

A gusty sigh and a shudder followed her declaration.

Roark trailed a finger over one silky cheek before lifting her trembling chin upward. "It might help."

Her soulful eyes, pain and the remnants of remembered horror lurking in their depths probed his. "I don't want to remember. I want to forget it ever happened." Her focus shifted to his lips. "Will you kiss me and make me forget? At least for a while?"

Her eyes pleaded, even as her lips parted. She tilted her head, her lashes sweeping downward to caress waxen cheeks.

To deny her would be beyond cruel. Roark bent his neck, feathering the lightest of kisses across her mouth.

Sighing, she cupped the back of his head, urging him closer.

He deepened the kiss, angling his head and pressing his mouth harder against her velvety softness.

One tentative nudge and she opened fully to him, meeting his tongue with her own. Adaira moaned deep in her throat, one hand running over his shoulder and chest. Breaking the kiss, he lifted her off his lap and onto the bed. He cautiously laid down beside her.

Staring at him in wide-eyed wonder, she brushed a wisp of hair off his forehead.

"Do you want me to stop?" he asked, seizing her hand and kissing the palm.

"Nae, dinna stop," she whispered, a hint of Scottish brogue coloring her words. "Make me forget."

Roark gathered her in his arms once more. He kissed her forehead, her eyes, nose, cheeks, and finally settled on her sweet mouth.

Relaxing against him, she slid her hand inside the opening of his shirt.

A groan broke from him as she stroked and fondled his chest. Nudging her, so that she lay on her back, he pressed hot kisses along the slender column of her neck and her delicate collarbone. Her breathing quickened when he trailed his kisses gradually lower and untied the ribbons holding her nightgown closed.

"Oh, Roark," she breathed against his mouth.

Her sweet fragrance wafted from her exposed skin. The lone lamp cast her ivory flesh in ethereal light. Parting the fabric of her gown, he stared at the full, plum-tinted nipples thrusting skyward.

Brayan's marks had already begun to fade.

A fresh wave of rage crashed over Roark, but he forced it aside, concentrating on the trusting woman in his arms.

Adaira arched upward, instinctively asking him to take her into his mouth.

With a smile, he willingly obliged, laving the tip with his tongue.

She moaned, urging him closer.

"You like that, vixen?"

She nodded, restlessly moving her legs. Roark cradled her breast and lowered his mouth over the fullness, sucking and kneading. Adaira's breath caught, and a long, sultry moan floated from her mouth.

Turning his attention to her other breast, he edged up her nightgown. He skimmed practiced fingers along the softest skin he'd ever caressed. Roark teased her, adoring her breasts with his mouth, tongue, and teeth, while his fingers made a slow, sensual journey along the inside of her quivering thighs.

Adaira ran her hands over his shoulders and back, her movements urgent, almost frantic. "Roark—"

"It's all right, love. I shan't do anything you don't want me to." He nuzzled his face between her breasts, his hand nearly upon the black curls at the apex of her thighs.

"Trust me, Adaira. I'll stop the second you tell me to."

"Don't stop. *Oh...*"

He swirled a finger across her damp curls, gently flicking the bud of her femininity. She arched her hips into his hand as little whimpers of passion and want purred from her throat. Taking her mouth with his, he tasted her sweetness, while expertly stroking and plying her folds. He barely slid one finger, then two, into her hot wetness—enough to intensify her pleasure without frightening her.

Roark increased the rhythm of his fingers, amazed at the uninhibited response of the woman in his arms.

Adaira needed a powerful memory of passion and fulfillment to obliterate the horror embedded in her memory. Though he threatened to explode in his breeches, this night was for her. He'd not frighten her with his need. He wanted her feverishly, but if he took her now, he wouldn't be as gentle as she needed him to be.

She deserved to experience sweet release without a man's selfish demands overshadowing her pleasure. That would come later. After they were married, and she'd learned to trust him. He might be spending a good deal of time swimming nude in the lake in the meantime.

Her whimpers against his mouth deepened. She clutched at his shirt, her hips gyrating against his hand. Stiffening, she gave a gasping cry followed by a lengthy sigh. With a final shudder, she lay still. Roark caressed a plump buttock, then smoothed her nightgown over her hips.

"That was...amazing," she whispered against his neck.

He levered onto his elbows, smoothing back her hair before kissing her on the nose. "And that's just the beginning."

A frown flitted across her delicate features. "But you didn't..."

An adorable blush pinkened her skin.

He chuckled and sat up. No, he hadn't. His hard-as-marble, painfully throbbing member was none too pleased either. He hoped he'd be able to walk from her chamber with his dignity intact.

If he could manage to walk at all.

"Not this time, vixen. This time was for you." He stood, with his back to the bed. His attempt to adjust the protesting, ill-behaved monster in his breeches proved futile.

"Thank you," she whispered.

There was no help for it. Roark turned, ignoring the angry twitch in his groin.

Adaira's eyes widened at the eye-level lump before her.

"Oh, dear." She sent him a questioning look, a hesitant smile on her rosy lips. She stretched out her hand, her fingers grazing over him. "Does it hurt?"

Roark closed his eyes, gritted his teeth, and cursed the day he'd sworn to be a gentleman. "Not too terribly much," he managed, although even to his ears, his voice sounded strangled.

The serpent jerked angrily.

Bloody liar.

Roark tugged the covers over her. After tucking them snuggly around her shoulders, he bent and kissed her. "Goodnight, soon-to-be-wife."

Something flickered in her gaze before Adaira curled her mouth into a beatific smile. "Goodnight."

Roark swiveled on his stockinged heels. He snatched his coat off the chair. If he walked slowly, and if he was very, *very* lucky, and if God showed him the minutest amount of favor, he *might* make the door before he exploded.

The moment the chamber door clicked shut behind him, Roark collapsed against the carved wood. Eyes closed, he released a gravelly groan. He cracked open an eye, taking in his damp lower half, and groaned again—this time in chagrin, not satisfaction.

He'd never hear the end of this from Pepperhill.

Never.

Thirty-Two

Three days later, Roark at her elbow, Adaira made for one of the remaining barns, her well-used crop once more in hand. Fading hues of peach, pink, and lavender attested to the sun's recent arrival on the horizon. A riding tour of Cadbury Park was planned for those braving the early hour. Later, a visit to Ashby, a nearby village—to sample the best spice cake in all of England, according to Roark—was on the day's program.

Three blissful days of peace and quiet had passed. Well, as much peace and quiet as there could be with a house full of giddy guests. The worst disaster befalling anyone had been Sir Harrison's bout of gout and Lady Arterbury's tendency to spill whatever beverage she had in hand. Usually, on the unfortunate soul nearest her.

Roark sent to London for a special license just in case, but an intimate wedding was planned in three weeks. Adaira had stopped arguing against the match and reconciled herself to the inevitable.

Truthfully, she wanted the union. After Roark's visit to her bedchamber, her opinion on marital intimacies had improved dramatically, although she yet harbored a few qualms. Well, perhaps more than a few.

"Are you sure you're feeling up to a ride?" Roark eyed Adaira, giving her a smile that would melt the ice of Loch Arkaig in February.

Her pulse danced a distracting jig before settling into a steady rhythm once more. "I'm fine. The wound was scarcely more than a scrape. I never even—"

Pounding hooves and the creaks and groans of a fast-moving carriage interrupted her. Startled, she turned to look over her shoulder. "What in the world?"

Roark thinned his lips at the lathered horses. "By thunder, there had better be a good excuse for abusing horseflesh in such a manner."

He reversed their direction. With firm strides, he closed the distance to the coach. Adaira trotted beside him, striving to keep up with his long-legged gait. The door swung open before the driver alighted. Ewan jumped to the ground, then turned and spoke into the carriage. Swinging around, he loped to the house's granite steps.

"Ewan!" Adaira waved at him. "Oh, wait until he hears we're betrothed. He's not going to believe it."

Spying the dark look on Ewan's face, her steps faltered. Confused, she tossed Roark a glance. "Do you think something's amiss?"

"I'm not sure, but I've never known Sethwick to misuse horseflesh. He'll have a good reason for the team's condition."

As he spoke, the driver handed Yvette down. Instead of her usual cheerful smile, worry shown in her eyes and pinched face. She hustled behind Ewan, who, displaying uncharacteristic rudeness, didn't wait for his wife.

Ewan reached them, and without preamble blurted,

"Clarendon. Adaira. I don't know what the bloody hell happened here, but I've arrived three, perhaps four, hours ahead of the Bow Street Runners. And that's only because we traveled throughout the night."

"Bow Street Runners?" Adaira and Roark exclaimed at the same time.

A wicked suspicion niggled in the recesses of her mind.

"Let's go inside." Ewan plowed a hand through his hair. "We must come up with a plan and quickly."

Minutes later, Adaira and Yvette sat on the settee as Roark relaxed against his desk, watching Ewan pace. His long legs periodically disrupted the bright rays slanting through the windows onto the carpet. With each stride, Ewan absently slapped his gloves against his thigh.

"If the matter is urgent, shouldn't you get on with the telling of it, Ewan?" Running a finger along the corded braid edging the pillow in her lap, Adaira raised a brow. She sent her sister-in-law a questioning glance.

Yvette attempted a smile, but it failed to reach her troubled eyes. She obviously knew what the hullaballoo was about. Her serious expression spoke volumes, as did her hands clenched in her lap.

Unease flipped Adaira's stomach and tripped across her nerves.

Ewan planted his hands on his hips. "The head of the Bow Street Runners, Edmond Fletcher, has issued a writ for Adaira's arrest."

"Pardon?" She gasped, grasping the reassuring hand Yvette extended.

"The devil, he has!" Roark bolted upright, hands fisted at his sides. A ferocious scowl distorted his face. "On what charge? Who filed the complaint? When was it laid?"

"Roark, I'm capable of questioning my brother," Adaira said quietly, her mind reeling with shock.

"As your betrothed, it's my responsibility to protect you!" Roark thundered. He looked rather like a wrathful god glaring down at her.

"Betrothed?" Ewan and Yvette exclaimed simultaneously.

Adaira gave them a tight-lipped smile. Despite this appalling situation, the astounded expressions on their faces were priceless. Laughter from the garden wafted inside. She whipped her gaze to the French windows. *Closed.* There'd be no eavesdropping from that quarter again.

Roark, now pacing about the study, waved his hand dismissively. "Yes, she saved my life during a fire—after McVey attempted to ravish her. She was compromised beyond redemption, and a hasty betrothal was necessitated."

Adaira stared at him, pierced to the core by his flippant callousness.

How could he?

Struggling for composure, against the pain gutting her, she squished the pillow in a crushing grip. Icy disdain dripping from each word, she said, "Thank you, for that *concise* rendition, my lord."

His head snapped up. "I—"

He took in Ewan's disapproving expression, then Yvette's puzzled one before finally meeting Adaira's eyes.

She did not attempt to hide the wounded disappointment she knew simmered in her gaze. She felt it settle, a sickening glob, in the pit of her stomach as well.

Roark wiped his hand across his face exhaling a hefty puff of air. "Adaira, I didn't mean that the way it sounded. Please, don't take umbrage—"

"It doesn't matter." She'd been a fool. Shifting her attention to Ewan, she asked, "So, a complaint has been lodged against me? The charge?"

He spread his hands. "Take your pick: abducting and imprisoning a peer, assault, arson, robbery, attempted murder—"

God above. Complete fabrication— except for the first charge.

Roark scowled, his brows drawn into a tight line. "Seize it! Someone dared to lay a complaint on my behalf?" He jabbed his chest with his thumb. "What unmitigated gall."

Adaira held up her hand. "Let me guess. Where these charges brought by Helene Winthrop?"

The bloody, fat trollop.

"Her and a Count von Schnitzer, Lord and Lady Bradford, the Marquis of Hedonford, and Lord and Lady Bellingsworth." Ewan paused, closed his eyes, and pinched the bridge of his nose. "There were a couple more, but I cannot presently recall who they were."

Her heart plunging to her half-boots, Adaira slumped into the settee, hugging the pillow to her chest. "How can there be so many?" she whispered. "Why would they do such a thing?"

She'd just met Mrs. Winthrop and the count. The others couldn't even be claimed as acquaintances. Why would strangers bring such malicious allegations against her?

As if sensing her bewilderment, Roark rested his hand on her shoulder, giving her a reassuring squeeze. "Surely, Sir Lawrence didn't believe such claptrap."

"As a magistrate, he had no choice," Ewan said, disgust and regret making his voice rough. "He might've been persuaded to ignore one, or even two complainants if the charges had been less serious. But you know the English's hatred of the Scots. That many influential peers combined with those serious allegations, not to mention von Schnitzer's status as a foreign diplomat, persuaded Sir Lawrence."

Ewan shook his head, lines of tension bracketing his mouth. "Sir Lawrence couldn't disregard the complaints, especially after seeing Mrs. Winthrop's, 'pitiful swollen and bruised countenance.' Those were his words, not mine."

Adaira smothered a snort and pretended absorption with the weapons displayed on the wall. *Lying cow.*

Ewan folded his arms and cocked his head. "What exactly did you do to her, Adaira, if I may ask?"

"I hit her with a parasol. After she and those Austrian curs pointed guns at me, Mother, our sisters, and a maid." She lifted her chin defiantly. "I think I broke her nose. Badly."

"Well done, you, then." Ewan grinned. "I only wish I'd been there to see it."

Yvette clapped her hands, a broad smile lighting her face. "Me as well. Good show!"

Expecting censure, not praise, Adaira wasn't sure how to respond.

Ewan sent her an apologetic glance before meeting Roark's agitated gaze. "Sir Lawrence directed Fletcher to issue the writ."

"Speaking of which...," Roark said while stepping to his desk. "How did you come by the information?"

Withdrawing a key from his coat pocket, he proceeded to unlock a drawer. After removing a thick stack of sterling notes, he set them atop the desk. A pistol followed. He sank to the padded leather chair behind the desk before sliding another drawer open. Roark retrieved three crisp sheets of paper, and after placing them on the desktop, closed the drawer.

Whatever was he doing?

Adaira sent Ewan, now sitting on the arm of the settee beside Yvette, an alarmed glance.

Roark looked up to see everyone staring at him. "The information, Sethwick?"

Ewan took Yvette's hand in his. "Harcourt sought me out. If you recall, Sir Lawrence is uncle to Harcourt's brother-in-law. He let slip the news. Harcourt suspects the blunder was deliberate, to allow us a little time."

Dipping a quill in the ink bottle near his elbow, Roark nodded then began writing. The nib scraped across the page with his quick, deliberate strokes. Done with the first paper, he set it aside and scratched away at the second.

"Who is Harcourt?" Adaira asked softly. Must be a decent sort of fellow if he went out of his way to inform Ewan.

The men's gazes swung to her.

Roark answered. "His Grace the Duke of Harcourt, a chum from our university days."

Returning his attention to the paper before him, he signed his name. He sprinkled sand on the wet ink and, after setting it aside, began scribbling on the third sheet.

Adaira stood and shook out the folds of her pale blue riding habit. The forgotten pillow tumbled to the floor. She'd never been more frightened in her life, and she'd experienced a pair of colossal scares in the past few days. Clasping her gloved hands, she strove for composure. "What am I to do?"

After setting his seal on the pages with his signet ring, Roark scooted them to the edge of his desk before gathering the money and pistol. Stuffing the notes into the inside pocket of his coat and the gun into his waistband, he angled his head at the missives. "Sethwick, one of those letters is for Sir Hugh. One is for Yancy. The third is for my solicitor, which I hope Yancy will do me the favor of conveying, posthaste."

"As you say." Ewan gave a terse nod and searched Roark's face. "When should I deliver them?"

Roark approached Adaira and took her hand. "How fast can you change into your boy's garb?"

She gaped. How did he know she had it with her? Even Maisey wasn't aware.

"Umm..." She swallowed

Pressing her fingers, he cast a glance at Yvette. "How soon if Lady Sethwick helps you? I don't want your maid to know our plans. The fewer people who do, the better."

Adaira bit her lip. "Ten minutes?"

"Perfect. Sethwick, will you please see that my gelding, Atlas, and Fionn are saddled? Not a sidesaddle, either. Have the horses waiting in the stables."

"I'll see to it at once," Ewan said, pulling on a glove. "You're not riding Tenacity?"

Roark shook his head. "She's in heat. No sense in asking for more trouble."

Straightening his coat, he flashed a glance at the French window then spoke to Yvette. "Lady Sethwick, after your husband delivers my notes, may I impose upon you to inform my guests of my departure and offer my apologies? Those wishing to stay are welcome to remain and entertain themselves until my return."

Ever the gracious lady, Yvette smiled warmly. "Of course. I'm happy to be of assistance."

"As for the notes, wait thirty minutes after our departure before delivering them." He slanted a brief look at the desk.

A puzzled frown lining his forehead, Ewan gave one sharp nod. "What are you about, Clarendon?"

Roark smiled. He took Adaira by the shoulders, and pointing her to the study entrance, gave a little shove. "Go. Hurry. Meet me in here in no more than fifteen minutes."

She examined his face and recognized the determination in his eyes. "Not until you tell me what you're planning."

~

"It's to Gretna Green for us." Roark brushed Adaira's cheek with his thumb. "We cannot risk traveling to London for a special license when there's a writ for your arrest."

Eyes huge in her wan face, waves of emotion successively swept across her delicate features: fear, worry, disbelief, and astonishment.

With his forefinger, Roark edged her sagging mouth closed. "Once you have the protection of my name, none will dare attempt to take you into custody."

"Gretna Green," she choked, clearly on the verge of panic. "I cannot travel to Scotland with you unchaperoned!"

He had no doubt she couldn't bear any more censure.

"There's no other recourse. We must make extreme haste. We cannot afford the delay a carriage journey would cost us. And I don't know another woman capable of matching my pace on horseback."

Roark spoke soothingly, understanding the hypocrisy of his words. He had demanded propriety from her. Now, he insisted on heaving decorum aside to make her his wife.

Ironically, to protect her from the very type of person he'd attempted to mold her into.

Thank God Adaira had not succumbed to his misguided advice.

Catching Sethwick's eye, Roark received a tight smile and a nod of approval.

"Yancy, Lord Ramsbury, will hasten to London and contact my solicitor. My man will immediately refute the charges of abduction and imprisonment." He took Adaira's elbow. "I shall, of course, refuse to substantiate those charges."

He maneuvered her to the door. "The other allegations against you will be contested. We've witnesses aplenty to refute them. Lest an attempt is made to hold you until your innocence is proven, we must marry straightaway. Sir Lawrence will be most reluctant to jail my bride, I assure you."

His last few words were clipped. His ire begged for a measure of release. Helene had better pray he never encountered her or her cousins again. Roark abhorred violence, but at this moment, the generational rage he'd battled for years surged forth. It would take the mighty hand of the Lord Himself to restrain him if he ever faced Adaira's accusers. Or anyone who dared tried to harm her.

Roark couldn't bear to think of her in that cesspool, Newgate. His imprisonment was lavish compared to what she'd experience there. She'd not be able to defend herself against the guards or the riffraff who called the gaol home.

By God, it must not come to that.

A door slammed somewhere in the house. The clock in his study ticked unnaturally loud in the stillness permeating the room.

"Once again, this isn't fair to you. Required to abandon

your guests. To send Lord Ramsbury to London on my behalf. To flee to Scotland to wed me." Tears shimmered in Adaira's eyes, and she sniffed, searching for her handkerchief, which he'd wager was nowhere on her person. "I seem destined to cause you nothing but turmoil." A single tear slipped from the corner of her eye.

Roark smiled and caught the salty drop with a thumb. "What you fail to understand, vixen, is this is what I want." He lowered his voice and dipped his head. He needed Adaira to understand his commitment to her. "I choose to do everything you mentioned because you are more important to me than every one of those things."

Wonder, tinged with hope, brightened her eyes. "Despite my shortcomings and the havoc that seems to dodge my every step, you *want* to marry me?"

Roark cupped the side of her neck, caressing her jaw with his thumb. In a tender voice, meant only for her ears, he said, "Despite your shortcomings, and God help me, because of them. I wouldn't have you any other way. Forgive me for trying to change you. You're perfect just as you are. And yes, I do want to marry you, very much, in fact."

Two more plump tears toppled over the edge of Adaira's eyelids. From the joyous smile on her face, he was confident they were happy tears. His lips met hers in the most tender, sweetest kiss he'd ever experienced.

A noisy, rather exaggerated, throat clearing and soft snuffling reminded him of Lord and Lady Sethwick's presence.

Reluctantly, he released Adaira, and she jumped backward, a hand clasped over her mouth. She smiled warily at her brother and sister-in-law. Roark followed her amused gaze and chuckled too.

Sethwick and his bride, arms clasped about each other, stood grinning like cats with a canary.

"So utterly romantic." Lady Sethwick touched a frilly handkerchief to the corner of her eye.

A frown suddenly shadowed Sethwick's face. "Blast, I almost forgot the other unfortunate news I have for you."

"Indeed? And what other disheartening tidbits could you possibly have to convey, Sethwick?" Roark asked.

"I could be wrong, of course." The viscount scratched his head, then rubbed the back of his neck. "We *were* traveling at breakneck speed through Ashby. In dawn's muted light, appearances are often distorted—"

Shit. Shit. Shit!

Roark met Sethwick's troubled gaze squarely. "You saw my brother."

Thirty-Three

The setting sun illumed the unremarkable village Adaira and Roark approached. For all of its fame, she'd expected Gretna Green to be more pretentious. What was more, for the first time in her life, she couldn't wait to get off a horse.

She and Roark had left Cadbury yesterday morning, less than an hour after Ewan had arrived. They'd stopped only to catch a few hours' sleep at a small, out-of-the-way inn whose name she couldn't remember. When Roark knocked on her door well before dawn, it took a macabre vision of the bowels of Newgate to jostle her from the surprisingly comfortable bed.

Lord, she hoped this village boasted a decent inn.

A long soak in a hot bath was the first item on the agenda. And a warm meal. Having eaten nothing but a crust of bread midday, she was ravenous. Roark offered her other food, but anxiety and nerves quelled her appetite. However, her hunger had increased with each passing mile.

Perhaps the knowledge they neared their destination allowed her tenseness to abate.

For the past few miles, she and Roark had ridden in pensive silence. Her destiny collided with his the day she'd abducted him. Now, they were to wed. She'd been miserably wrong about him. Her offenses against him were more grievous than any wrong he'd done her. Yet, he maintained he wanted to marry her.

Why, she wasn't sure. She had much more to gain from this union than he did. He desired her. Of that, she was certain.

A sudden vision of him lying on her bed, his mouth and hands working their magic sprang to mind. Pinpricks of awareness and arousal had her fidgeting in the saddle.

Adaira sliced Roark a sideways glance to find him watching her. A slow, sensual smile curved his sculpted lips. She blushed as only he was capable of making her do.

When had she begun to care for him?

When she'd discovered he employed cripples and misfits? When he'd told her of the owl he'd rescued? When he'd approved her jumping into the lake to save Kiki? Or, had it been when she'd seen him standing forlorn in the carriage house?

She was still leery of sharing his bed. Tonight, she'd have to set her fears aside. She'd not deny him his husbandly rights. Not after everything he'd done for her.

"Look there." Roark pointed to a neat, white building trimmed in black. A sign proclaimed the establishment the blacksmith's shop.

"*That's* where we're to be carried?"

Adaira swallowed a chuckle. True, she'd never entertained girlish dreams of an elaborate wedding. But she'd also never envisioned reciting her vows attired in breeches and standing before an anvil.

A gust of wind blew past, depositing another layer of

road dust on her. Sneezing, she slapped at her breeches. Add two days' worth of travel grime to the things she hadn't expected to be wearing on her wedding day.

Roark laughed softly. "No, I was but showing you the renowned blacksmith shop. There'll be no irregular marriage for us. We'll be married properly in a church. No one will be able to contest the legality of our nuptials, here or in England."

"Oh." He'd thought this out, hadn't he? The knowledge comforted her.

Standing in the stirrups, he swiftly scanned the main street. "Yonder, at the end of the lane."

A quaint church, its white facade glowing in the last of the sun's rays, beckoned from the end of the street. Moments later, Roark dismounted. After loosely tying Atlas's reins to a post provided for that purpose, he turned to Adaira. Her breath caught at the glint in his eye.

"Throw your leg over," he commanded softly.

His large hands encircled her waist, and a ripple of awareness encompassed her. He lifted her from Fionn but didn't immediately release her. Pressed between the stallion and Roark's solid form, she raised her gaze to his.

He stepped closer until only the material of his pantaloons and her breeches separated them. His hands caressed the slope of her ribs. "If you truly don't want to go through with the ceremony, I'll find another way to protect you. I know you want to make decisions regarding your life. You've been denied that until now."

Fionn shifted and snorted, almost as if he'd understood Roark.

"This choice is yours." Gazing steadily into her eyes, no trace of irritation or manipulation belayed his words.

They'd ridden this distance, unchaperoned, and he was

willing to allow her to say no? Or, had he changed his mind, and this was his way of escaping the parson's mousetrap?

Stop it. He doesn't deserve your suspicious conjectures.

Adaira searched his eyes, seeking the scantest hint of subterfuge or reluctance. The last fragments of distrust crumbled under his tender gaze. Standing on her tiptoes, she brushed his lips with hers. "I want to marry you."

Roark hesitated, emotions warring in his eyes.

With a groan, he crushed her to him. He kissed her deeply as if she'd granted his greatest wish. Arms circling his neck, she met his unbridled passion with her own. She didn't know what the future held, but she did know it must include him.

A not so discreet cough interrupted them, and Adaira peeked over Roark's shoulder. A rotund, kind-faced cleric stood on the church's uppermost step, smiling.

"Perhaps, ye should commence with the ceremony first?" he suggested, a merry twinkle in his vibrant green eyes.

Fifteen minutes later, Adaira was Lady Clarendon. The reverend's housekeeper and a red-faced villager delivering vegetables had acted as witnesses.

"Please sign here, my lady." Reverend Gillies pointed to the line below Roark's boldly slanted signature.

As she handed the reverend the quill, her stomach gurgled, then growled loudly. She cradled her middle. "Pardon me."

"Can you recommend an inn for my bride and me?" Roark passed the cleric several coins. "One that serves a decent meal?"

"There's the Kirkhouse. The inn is spotlessly clean and well-tended." Tucking the money into the folds of his robe,

Reverend Gillies smiled. "It's owned by the Bowies, two of my flock. They cater to newlyweds. The beds are comfortable, and Mrs. Bowie is a wonderful cook." He winked at Adaira. "Ye havena lived until ye've tasted her clootie dumplin'."

Adaira's mouth watered. "Clootie dumpling? Truly?"

"Indeed," agreed the merry reverend.

"Oh, Roark. Have you ever tried the dish?" She touched his arm. "It's a marvelous dessert pudding made from oatmeal, bread crumbs, and dried fruit. Served with Devonshire or clotted cream, clootie dumpling is pure heaven."

She closed her eyes and licked her lips. Her stomach grumbled in protest again.

He gripped her elbow, steering her through the entrance.

"It's not clootie dumplings I have an appetite for, vixen."

~

"How utterly delightful." Adaira smiled at the tidy stone structure it had taken all of five minutes to locate following Reverend Gillies's directions.

The sun had disappeared below the horizon, and dusk hovered over the township. Nestled against a backdrop of towering trees, Kirkhouse Inn exuded a rustic charm. A profusion of colorful flowers spilled from vibrant red flower boxes flanking either side of the entrance.

Halting their horses at a well-ordered stable situated across the courtyard, Adaira and Roark dismounted. A lad of about five and ten rushed to greet them. He took both horses' reins. "Stayin' the night, are ye?"

Roark tossed him a coin. "Yes. Please rub the horses down well. If you've any oats, an extra ration for them both. There's another coin in it for you if I'm satisfied with their condition in the morning."

The boy opened his palm, and his eyes grew round as twin moons upon seeing the crown resting there. "Aye, sir. I shall be sure to take good care of 'em."

Adaira rubbed Fionn's nose. "Be a good boy, my friend." She pressed her forehead against his and chuckled when he snorted. "I know. You're tired and hungry. So am I."

With a final pat, she tucked her riding crop beneath her arm and turned to Roark. He'd already untied her small satchel and was attending to his. They'd traveled light, with naught but the barest essentials. The return trip wouldn't be as rushed. There was no need, thank goodness.

He took her arm and escorted her to the stairs. At the entrance, he held the door open, allowing her to step inside. A fresh bouquet of summer flowers dominated a shiny counter at the front of the common room. Four burly men sat at a table. Two young couples, their eyes only for each other, cuddled at tables beside the room's only windows.

Adaira sniffed. Something smelled divine. Her stomach thought so too, for it gurgled noisily.

"Good evenin'. I'll be right with ye."

A woman carrying a tray laden with full plates appeared from what must've been the kitchen. After delivering the food to the men, she set the tray on an empty table. Wiping her hands on her apron, she hustled behind the counter. A pleasant smile on her freckled face, she asked, "Ye need a room for the night?"

"Yes," Roark smiled. "Two, please."

Two?

Adaira didn't have to turn around to know every eye in

the room was trained on them. The innkeeper's gaze wavered between Adaira and Roark. Most likely, this was the first time a couple married in Gretna Green had *ever* requested separate chambers.

Roark lowered his voice. "I'd like to register one in my name and one in someone else's."

He winked at the holster.

Comprehension dawned on the woman's face. She narrowed her eyes. "Are ye married? I'll no' be havin' any havey-cavey under my roof."

Adaira felt a flush start at her toes and creep steadily to the roots of her hair. From the heat scorching her face, she'd no doubt her cheeks were the same shade of vivid crimson as the innkeeper's hair.

Blast, could this get any more awkward? Nary could a sound be heard from the diners. By the utter silence permeating the room, Adaira guessed they'd ceased eating altogether.

Roark shifted his stance, placing his back to the dining area. She concentrated on the suddenly intriguing scratches on the polished, but well-worn floor.

"Indeed, we're newly married by your very own Reverend Gillies. He recommended this fine establishment." Roark slid a substantial pile of notes across the gleaming counter.

Mrs. Bowie's eyes widened, her eyebrows nearly touching her hair. She scooted a quick peek at the diners before snatching the money. She rotated the ledger so Roark could register. He signed his name on one line, then, altering his handwriting, signed Flynn's on the next.

Flipping the book to her side once more, Mrs. Bowie gasped. "Yer lordship, it's an honor to have ye stayin' at my humble inn."

She bobbed a wobbly curtsy, and ducked her head, eyeing Adaira curiously. "My lady."

Adaira grimaced at her dusty breeches and boots.

Roark slung a look over his shoulder. The patrons immediately became reabsorbed in their food. He cocked a knowing eyebrow at Adaira, and she smiled up at him.

Returning his attention to Mrs. Bowie, he murmured, "We'll dine in our room. We require two baths as soon as we've finished eating. I'll take my bath in the second chamber I rented."

Passing him two keys, she nodded. "Yes, my lord."

"If anyone should inquire, we're Mr. and Mrs. Templeton. We'll be staying in the room registered in that name."

A confused frown settled on Mrs. Bowie's face. She sent a furtive glance to the other patrons before bending across the counter and whispering, "Ye want two rooms for baths? Only ye'll both be sleepin' in...," She perused the ledger. "Flynn Templeton's room? But ye're *really* Lord Clarendon?"

"Just so." Roark beamed and pressed several more notes into her hand.

Mrs. Bowie scratched her head, her gaze shifting between Roark and Adaira. With a shrug, she wrote numbers on a slip of paper. She handed the note to him. "Yer rooms."

After snapping the ledger closed, she lifted the book from the counter. Wedging it beneath her arm, she said, "I'll just put this someplace where pryin' eyes canna see."

"Most wise," he said.

Skirting the counter, she headed to the kitchen, tossing over her shoulder, "Dinner in fifteen minutes. Bathwater in thirty."

Adaira followed Roark across the lobby. They climbed the stairs, angled over an odd-shaped outer door.

"I'm sure Flynn will be thrilled you forged his name."

Two treads above her, Roark turned sideways. He grinned, not a trace of repentance on his face. "Cannot be helped, vixen. Have you forgotten? We've most assuredly been followed."

Thirty-Four

Wearing a cotton nightgown edged at the collar, wrists, and hem with Scottish lace, Adaira sat in the middle of the bed dominating the smallish chamber. Waiting for Roark's return, she brushed the snarls from her damp hair.

Her stomach twisted tighter and tighter with each passing minute. Spying her half-full glass of wine leftover from dinner, she scooted to the edge of the bed. She dashed to the table, and hefting the glass, downed the claret in one gulp.

Oh, the devil with it.

With a shrug, she brought the bottle to her mouth and tossed back several unladylike gulps. She banged the container atop the table a might more forcefully than she'd intended, causing the plates and serving utensils to rattle.

However, her nerves did seem the merest bit calmer. She returned to the bed and flopped backward, giggling when the fluffy folds of the black, primrose, and ruby coverlet swallowed her.

Kirkhouse Inn was everything Reverend Gillies had promised it would be. The charming chamber was clean, well-furnished, and tastefully decorated. The bed, a handsome solid structure made of some undeterminable wood, was flanked by two matching night tables.

A burgundy velvet wingback chair and footstool sat at an angle before the coal grate. A pair of high back chairs and a small table occupied the wall closest to the door. A washstand in the corner by the lone window, framed by a striped curtain, completed the room's furnishings.

After eating a generous portion of stovies, fresh bread, and cheese, Adaira had devoured the still warm clootie dumpling smothered in cream. Giving the bed a bounce, she giggled again. The key scraped in the lock, and she rose onto her elbows, her knees dangling off the bed.

Roark stepped into the room, his mahogany hair damp from his bath, and the air in her lungs hitched. He'd shaved, the subtle sandalwood scent she associated with him wafting to her. He only wore his pantaloons and an unbuttoned shirt. The white fabric contrasted starkly with the dark matting of hair exposed by his gaping collar.

Good God. He looked...delicious.

The silky curls tempted her from across the room. She itched to run her fingers through them or nestle her face against their softness. How much of Roark was covered with hair?

Embarrassed warmth suffused her at the thought.

"You look like a child caught being naughty." Wearing a sinful smile, Roark locked the door. He placed his bag on a chair, then walked toward her.

Adaira grinned. "The bed is wonderfully soft and springy."

"Let's hope it's not noisy." Roark waggled his brows.

"Not at all. See." She tilted her pelvis several times, bouncing the bed with her rear. "It moves, but doesn't make a sound." She gave one more forceful rock.

He made an odd sound in his throat, his focus riveted on her hips, and a muscle ticked in his clenched jaw. His perusal journeyed languidly upward, hovering on her breasts before his gaze met hers. Desire darkened his eyes to midnight blue.

She'd thought an aroused stallion a force to be reckoned with. The powerful man before her, his stance wide, shoulders squared, and hands fisted at his sides, shot a tremor clear to her toes. Whether her reaction was unease or awareness, she couldn't say.

Holding her attention, he lifted his shirt over his head. His muscles bunched with the simple movement.

Adaira's mouth went dry.

Roark's clothing hid a perfect, masculine form. His chest, shoulders, and arms were sculpted with well-defined muscles. A barely visible pinkish scar sliced across his rippled abdomen.

She hadn't noticed the mark in the dungeon's muted light.

Those fascinating hairs on his chest gradually narrowed into a dark strip disappearing into his waistband. Lord, but he was gorgeous. She'd been around rutting animals enough to know what the bulge straining against his pantaloons meant.

A thrill jolted between her legs.

Before Roark, there had never been a man who made her eager to join with him. At least she thought that was what the odd, intense urge thrumming through her was. Swallowing, she placed a hand on her quivering stomach, daring to meet his eyes. She'd never been more aware of herself as a woman.

A primordial grin tilted the corners of his mouth. She'd wager he knew exactly what she was thinking. Dropping his hands to his pantaloons, he unfastened them, and in one swift motion, he slid them off his narrow hips.

Like a proper lady, Adaira tried to look away. Her blasted eyes refused to obey. They feasted on the thick length, protruding proudly from a nest of blackish curls and the full, slightly darker-skinned pouch tucked below.

He stepped to the bed. "Your turn."

"*My turn?*" Adaira dragged her attention from his manhood. She cleared her throat, her gaze careening around the bright room. "With the candles lit?"

He nodded, a devilishly, sexy smile on his mouth. He flicked her collar with one long finger. "Now, off with it."

"I thought ladies left their nightgowns on during—"

"I want you naked. I've dreamed of seeing your delicious body." Roark angled his head. "I shan't be denied. Now, sit up so I can divest you of that entirely too modest gown."

She clasped his extended hand, allowing him to help her to her feet.

He must've felt the tremor that shook her, for he cupped her face. "Don't be afraid. I'll go slow. I promise. I'll not do anything you don't want me to. And I'll stop the moment you ask me to." He placed a soft kiss on her lips. "Will you trust me, vixen?"

Adaira searched his eyes. Patience and understanding loomed there.

"Yes," she whispered through quivering lips.

His strong fingers untied the ribbons holding her neckline closed. He loosened the row of pearl-sized buttons down the gown's center.

"Must they make these buttons so confounded small?" His warm fingers brushed the sensitive flesh above her breasts.

Yearning coursed through her.

"Do you wish me to do it?" Was that breathless voice hers? She sounded positively wanton.

"No, I have it." The last button sprang loose. Without hesitation, Roark gripped the material by her waist and hoisted the nightgown over her head. He sucked in a sharp breath, inexplicably motionless.

Adaira's flesh puckered, and her nipples tautened at the unexpected rush of cool air. She wrapped her arms around her shoulders and turned to crawl into the bed. Fear of the unknown rendered her uncharacteristically timid.

"No." He gently grasped her shoulders, preventing her from diving beneath the covers. His voice deep and seductive, he murmured, "I've envisioned you lying naked atop my bed with your beautiful hair surrounding you while I make love to you."

"You have?" She should be embarrassed—no, mortified—upon learning he'd entertained such shocking daydreams. Instead, another shiver of pleasure stole to her center, causing an unfamiliar edginess.

"Indeed, I have." Feathering his hands across her shoulders, Roark brushed her hair aside. He touched the topaz at the hollow of her throat.

"You always wear this."

"My grandmother gave it to me."

"It suits you. The gems match the amber flecks in your eyes." His sultry gaze met hers as he palmed a breast. "You're even more exquisite than I'd imagined."

Adaira gripped his biceps, closing her eyes and gasping. The sensation of his hand on her breast was sweet torment. Instinctively, she tilted her shoulders back, deepening the contact. "I'm skinny and not very buxom."

"Whoever said so is a liar." His touch feather-light, he brushed the wound on her side. "Does it pain you much?"

"No, barely at all. I'm sure my wound is much less than what you've endured."

His fingers teased her nipple as his mouth skimmed the juncture of her neck and shoulder. His warm, firm lips caressed their way to the breast he lovingly held with his hand. Fondling the other, he buried his face between their softness, lavishing both with hot, damp kisses.

Adaira's knees shook with the force of her newfound passion. She'd not expected every nerve in her body to be alight with sensation. Or to desperately yearn to feel his weight atop her, with her legs spread, him firmly between her thighs.

Roark's mouth closed over one aching nipple, and she moaned, collapsing against the mattress. He paused in his gentle assault to lay her on the counterpane before fanning her hair about her shoulders. Clutching the bedding, she resisted the urge to cover herself.

The bed dipped with his weight. He was so close, his body heat warmed her. The tempting shoulders and torso she'd longed to touch were right there. Mere inches separated them. She lifted a hesitant hand, then dropped it.

"Touch me, vixen. It's all right. I want you to." He carried her hand to his chest.

Once Adaira began, she couldn't stop. She glided her hands over his muscles and lovingly caressed his rough, scarred back. With her fingertips, she indulged the urge to feel the hairs shadowing his chest, even rubbing her face against them. They were a curious mixture of wiry crispiness and silky softness.

Fascinated, she watched Roark's body jerk and quiver with her inexperienced exploration. Were his nipples as sensitive as hers? Tracing the dark circle with her fingernail, she grinned as it rucked, and he made a strangled sound deep in his throat.

"Enough, I think. It's my turn." Tucking her to his side, one hand caressed her hip and ribs. He took her mouth in a searing, soul-wrenching kiss. Every doubt she'd harbored was whisked away by the blatant, consuming passion his lips and tongue created.

The trickles of sensations burgeoned. She panted and moaned with anticipation. "Roark—"

He didn't stop but continued to squeeze and caress, kiss and lick until she was so tense, she felt certain she'd burst.

"Roark..." she groaned again. "Please—"

Adaira reached to curl her fingers around his smooth shaft. The sensation of him in her hand spiraled her excitement to a higher level. With every stroke along his solid length, she became wetter between her legs.

His breath hissed between clenched teeth. He abruptly clasped her hand. "I don't want to rush you, but if you keep that up, I'll not be able to stop."

Releasing her hand, he skimmed his fingers, first over her ribs, then her stomach, and at last, cupped her between her legs. She shuddered against his palm. Her knees fell open in a blatant invitation, wanting the sweet release he'd brought her before. He knew her body better than she did, knew where to touch her to bring her the most pleasure.

"Roark, now please." Adaira grasped his shoulders, urging him to her.

He raised his head and peered into her eyes, his face

harsh with restrained passion. Nudging her thighs apart, he rested atop her, bearing most of his weight on his forearms. Adaira's gaze locked on the rigid flesh, ready to unite with her.

He kissed her shoulder, her chin, both eyelids, and finally, her mouth. "You know, I love you, don't you, Addy?"

Roark's words softly spoken settled in her fertile heart. Her love burst forth, finally ready to be shared. This marvelous, compassionate, handsome man loved her?

"You do? Truly?"

"Truly." He nuzzled her neck, breathing into her ear. Brushing a wisp of hair off her cheek, he asked, "Are you afraid?"

Shaking her head, she smiled. She caressed his cheek. "Not anymore. Not with you."

And to her joy and astonishment, she wasn't.

A possessive growl escaped his lips before he captured her lips once more. Spreading her legs, Roark eased into her. She felt pressure and fullness, but no pain. The pulsating ache inside demanded satisfaction. Gripping his rear, she tilted her hips to receive him. He withdrew until only his tip penetrated her, then lifting her hips, plunged into her.

Adaira jerked, gasping in unexpected pain.

"*What the hell?*" Roark froze atop her. Disbelief etched his face, and his pupils dilated in astonishment.

"Is it supposed to hurt?" she whispered, blinking away the tears that threatened. "Is it because you're quite large, and I'm small?"

It should only hurt the first time, shouldn't it? Surely, she wasn't too small to accommodate him. Was she? Was that possible? Mother would know, but there'd been no time to seek her counsel on such a delicate matter.

He closed his eyes and swallowed.

"No, love. You were a virgin." He moved against her, the smallest of movements.

Virgin? No, Godwin had...

Roark moved again, his size stretching her, but no longer causing discomfort. Tiny flickers of pleasure simmered and pulsed, where he remained embedded.

She blinked at him. "I cannot... Couldn't be."

Roark chuckled while rocking his hips, ever-so-gently. "Trust me, you were."

Then Godwin hadn't—

Joy consumed her.

There was only Roark. No other. Ever.

He rocked again, and then again. Each movement sent incredible sensations through her core. He began a slow, steady rhythm, muscles bunching as he flexed in and out. Adaira whimpered, the feelings he aroused almost frightening in their intensity.

Bending, he kissed her tenderly. "I'm sorry I hurt you."

"You couldn't have known." Her words ended on a low moan. Something was happening. Something exquisitely wonderful, but foreign and frightening in its newness. Desperation began to build with each strong thrust of Roark's hips. She lifted her legs, wrapping them around his waist. She clutched his back.

Roark groaned, burying his face in her shoulder. His movements quickened in speed and intensity. The urgency bubbled and simmered, rising layer by layer until she thought she could bear no more. She whimpered again, welcoming his weight and the pressure mounting within.

"You're almost there, love," he soothed against her lips. "Let it happen. Don't be frightened. I'll take you all the way."

Adaira barely heard his words, wrapped in sensations so overwhelming, cognitive thought was impossible. She surged upward, meeting his every stroke, passion coiling tighter and tighter, until all at once, she shattered into a thousand fragments of sensation, sailing on a sea of bliss.

In the recesses of her mind, as she floated back to awareness, she felt him pumping into her harder and faster. With a gravelly groan, he collapsed atop her, his face nestled in the crook of her neck.

His labored breathing blended with her soft pants. Long moments passed until her heartbeat returned to normal. Roark raised himself onto one elbow, his gaze burning a path straight to her unguarded soul.

She licked her lips. "Is it always like that?"

"Never before." A beautiful smile curved his mouth before he placed a soft kiss on her mouth.

He withdrew from her, and she almost cried out, suddenly bereft. As if sensing her need to be held, he wrapped her in his embrace, rolling with her until she lay across his chest. He traced her jaw with his finger, then trailed lower still to her breasts crushed against his chest.

"Pray, tell me, vixen, how I came to bed a virgin?"

Roark caressed her with his gaze.

Satiated, Adaira snuggled atop him, one slender leg wedged between his, a baffled look on her lovely face. "I can only think Brayan must've stopped Godwin before he finished." She shifted, folding her arms across Roark's chest. Resting her chin on them, she said, "I fainted and had always assumed he'd completed the act."

A shudder rippled through her, and Roark ran a soothing hand from her shoulder to hip.

"I shan't lie and tell you I'm not profoundly grateful he didn't because I'd never want you to suffer through something so horrendous." He trailed a finger across her lips. "But know this, Addy. Your lack of virginity was never of importance to me. When you love someone the way I love you, nothing else matters."

She kissed his fingers.

He focused his gaze on her breasts, squashed atop his chest while giving her *derrière* a firm squeeze. "You've such a deliciously lush body."

He brushed her breast with a fingertip.

"My *lush* body?" Adaira grinned at him impishly. "I thought you preferred *much* more voluptuous figures."

With a growl, Roark pinned her beneath him. "Shall I demonstrate exactly how delectable I find you?"

She curved her pretty mouth into a coy smile. Her pupils huge with desire, she purred, "Oh, please do."

Roark needed no further encouragement. His taking of her this time was swift and wild. He needed to mark her as his for eternity. Rising on his elbows, he watched her face as he brought her to ecstasy. Panting and her lips parted, Adaira threw back her head and stiffened. A guttural cry wrenched from her throat.

Her eyes flew open, her gaze meshing with his as she climaxed, convulsing over and over. Her passion-laden eyes widened when she felt him reach his apex.

"Roark!" she cried, gripping his scarred back, drawing him closer.

He ground into her, hands beneath her buttocks so she'd receive every bit of him. His hot seed spilled into her womb, toppling her over the edge again.

He folded her in his embrace, and within moments, sleep claimed her. She lay tucked beneath his chin, her head resting on his shoulder. Listening to Adaira's soft, rhythmic breathing, sleep beckoned Roark.

He refused to succumb.

They'd been tailed, he was certain of it, hence the two rooms. So, why hadn't the Bow Street Runners or Edgar shown their hands?

Thirty-Five

Content as a pampered cat, Adaira stretched and half-opened her eyes. Roark wasn't in bed.

"My bride awakens at last."

Fully clothed, he stood by the table, pouring steaming tea into a cup. Flashing her a dazzling smile, he rested his gaze on the flesh exposed above the sheet. "I was going to wake you in a moment. We need to be on our way as soon as you've eaten and dressed."

In four long strides, he crossed to the bed. He placed one knee on the mattress, then leaned over and gave her a very thorough kiss. "Good morning, Lady Clarendon."

He smoothed a finger along her collarbone.

She sighed, relishing his touch. "Good morning."

Roark stepped away.

"As much as I'd love to continue, we really must be off, Adaira. As you know, the Bow Street Runners are pursuing us."

A slight frown creased his brow. "Now that we're married, I'd prefer to deal with them on English soil. Truthfully, I expected them to overtake us sooner."

"Do you think they're close by?" A ripple of fear raised goose pimples across her bare skin.

He nodded. "It's unlikely we'll make England without encountering them."

Adaira flew from the bed. She scampered to don her clothing. Bending over, she searched for her short chemise in her bag on the floor. She snatched up a shirt.

Suddenly, strong arms encircled her from behind. Roark nestled his groin against her backside. "Don't tempt me, woman."

Spinning her to face him, he grabbed the shirt and yanked it over her head. The bottom edge barely reached the top of her thighs. He groaned, "If I stay here one more minute, we'll be between the sheets again."

He slanted his head in the direction of the bed.

"Would that be so bad? It sounds rather pleasant."

Adaira drifted her hand to the hard knot nudging her. She couldn't believe her boldness.

"Bugger it!" Roark jumped back as if stung.

She giggled. "My lord, are you afraid of me?"

"I'm afraid of what you do to me. I'm convinced something's afoot. I sense it. As much as I'd like to toss you on the bed and make love to you, wisdom dictates otherwise."

Feeling incredibly wicked, she let her shirt slip off her shoulder, exposing all but the nipple of one breast. "If you're sure..."

Stepping to the door, he grasped the latch, his gaze looking everywhere but at her. "I'm going to check on the horses and ask Mrs. Bowie to pack us a picnic. Can you be ready in twenty minutes?"

Adaira nodded, quite liking her husband's flustered state. "I'll be ready."

She bent to collect her breeches, deliberately giving him an enticing view of her bottom.

The door banging shut muffled Roark's, "Damn."

She grinned.

Once dressed, she made quick work of plaiting her hair. After stuffing her possessions into her valise, she placed the bag and her riding crop on the mussed bed. She made a visual search of the room.

Where was Roark's satchel?

He must've taken it with him.

Collecting a serviette and an oatcake in one hand, and the full teacup and saucer in the other, she made for the window. If the rays streaming in through the glass were any indication, the day would prove as warm as yesterday. After setting the cup on the ledge to allow the tea to cool, she undid the latch. Shoving the window open, Adaira welcomed the fresh morning air.

She nibbled the oatcake. She much preferred riding to being confined in a carriage, especially when the weather was warm.

Would Roark mind if they made a detour to Craiglocky before returning to Cadbury? She had something she wanted to show him—had only this minute realized how important it was that he see it. Chewing the sweet oats, she smiled, anticipating the look on his face.

The door swished open, and Adaira turned. The man standing there wasn't Roark, yet he resembled him greatly.

Edgar.

Forgetting the food in her mouth, she inhaled a swift gulp of air and choked on the oatcake. Eyes watering, she gasped and coughed.

Trying to remain calm, Adaira reached for the teacup.

From the corner of her eye, she scanned the courtyard below. Only the lad from last night wandered about.

Where was Roark?

Taking a sip of hot tea, she managed to wash down the chalk-dry glob wedged in her throat. She soundly burnt her mouth in the process.

Uncertain she could speak, Adaira swallowed twice.

Stepping across the threshold, Edgar nudged the door closed with a grungy, booted foot. He never took his hard gaze off her.

"So, you're the wench who thwarted my plans."

She eyed him, warily.

He shook his head. "You cannot imagine how irritated I was to discover my ever-noble brother intended to make an honest woman of you." His arctic gaze flicked to the bed. A suggestive grin twisted his mouth. "I assume the deed is done? Or, did he bed you before you were wed?"

Adaira didn't shift her focus from him.

Helping himself to a sausage, he took a bite. "It's of no consequence. You're excess baggage I can ill-afford to have interfering with my well-laid plans."

Facing him fully, Adaira judged the distance to her crop. Five feet. Perhaps a bit more.

"Why are you here? What do you want?" She sounded composed, but her hands shook so badly, the teacup rattled on its saucer.

"What do *I* want? Why, to ensure my dear brother never has an heir and denies me my inheritance."

Good Lord.

She took a tentative step forward.

Edgar seemed unconcerned that she might pose a threat and continued to stuff her breakfast into his mouth greedily.

"Just how do you intend to ensure you inherit?" She

took another step. "You cannot very well kill both of us in here." She flicked her hand in the air. Busy gobbling her food, he paid no attention to her movements.

Good.

Half a step more. "That's bound to be suspicious. The innkeeper knows we arrived alone. And Roark told her we might have unwanted company."

She edged forward a couple of inches.

Edgar shrugged his shoulders. With his mouth full of food, he mumbled, "She's easy enough to dispose of."

A half a foot more.

"You think you can kill Roark, me, *and* Mrs. Bowie and get away with it? Not likely." Adaira laughed scornfully.

Edgar stiffened. He faced her full-on, fury radiating from him, and her heart lurched to her throat. She'd made a strategic error. He didn't like being laughed at.

"Oh, I'll get away with it. You see, no one knows I'm here. I watched a stupid serving wench enter through an entrance by the stairs. Unsuspecting Mrs. Bowie will meet with my knife the next time she ventures outside."

The blood rushed from Adaira's face, leaving her light-headed. Following Roark upstairs last night, she'd seen the door. The entrance wasn't visible from the common room or kitchen.

"Your ashen face tells me you know which entry I mean. So easy to slip inside and sneak to the upper chambers unnoticed. Quite remiss on the innkeepers' part, really." He wiped away a crumb clinging to his lower lip.

Adaira squared her shoulders and jutted her chin out. "It won't be so easy to kill Roark and me."

Edgar shrugged and said in a sing-song voice, "They'll think you and Rory had a lover's quarrel."

Fear turned her blood to ice.

"I'll make it appear he killed you." He slipped a wicked-looking knife from inside his coat. "Then, overcome with remorse, he'll take his own life. He'll leave a note, of course. Terribly tragic, you being newlyweds and all that rot."

He would do it. She hadn't a doubt.

"Or perchance, you were robbed by some crazed fiend who carved the both of you up." Edgar lashed the air with the knife. "Harder to explain, but much more satisfying." A deranged chuckle escaped him.

He's utterly mad.

She didn't dare take her attention off of him.

Where is Roark?

Adaira was desperate for him to return, and equally terrified he would. She shuffled from foot to foot, moving toward the bed as she did. The crop was almost within reach. She slipped forward a hand's-breadth more.

"That's ridiculous," she scoffed, hoping to keep him off balance. "No one will believe such drivel. Your reputation precedes you. You're the first person they'll suspect. In fact, the Bow Street Runners should be arriving at any moment. They followed us from Cadbury, and my brother saw you in Ashby."

"Bow Street Runners? What for?" For a fraction of a second, uncertainty whisked across Edgar's face. The next instant, unadulterated madness replaced his confusion. He lunged for her at the precise moment she leaped for her crop. She instinctively hurled the remaining hot tea in his face.

He howled in pain and outrage, swinging at her blindly. "You bitch."

Whipping the cover off of her crop, she faced him, her blade at the ready. "You'll not kill me without a fight."

A malicious grin twisted his mouth. Edgar crouched and slid a second knife from his boot.

Mother of God.

"Do you know how many people I've killed with these?" He waved the blades in the air menacingly. "No?" His unhinged cackle filled the room, and he shrugged. "Me neither."

A commotion in the courtyard sifted through the open window, and Edgar charged at her. Adaira screamed and deflected his blows, short sword striking knife edge.

Relentless, he swung the knives with fluid determination. With every swipe, he cursed her.

Oh, God, where is Roark? He's been gone too long.

Her arm tired, deflecting his dual blows. She searched for an opportunity to strike Edgar. It took every bit of her concentration to keep him at bay.

A sly gleam entered his eyes just before he hurled one knife at her.

She leaped to the side, dodging it, but with a cry of terror, lost her balance. Tumbling to the floor, she lost her grip on the crop.

Oh, God.

Her chest ached as she struggled to draw air into her lungs.

Gasping for breath, Edgar stood over her, a sinister gleam of satisfaction in his eyes. He lifted his arm.

Her gaze locked with his. She was going to die.

Oh, Roark. I'll never be able to tell you that I love you.

A cry wrenched from Adaira's throat as she threw an arm up to deflect Edgar's blow.

The room suddenly erupted in chaos. A gun's deafening report reverberated in the small chamber, the explosion competing with several men's shouts and curses.

Edgar collapsed to his knees beside her.

Gasping and fear choking her, she couldn't tear her regard from him.

His unfocused blue eyes, so like Roark's, glassed over. He toppled onto her, pinning her to the floor with his weight.

"Get off!" she screamed, struggling to dislodge him.

She shrieked again as blackness threatened. The next moment, she was free of him, and Roark encircled her in his arms.

"Roark!" She buried her face against his chest, sobbing. "He was going to kill us."

"Shh, vixen. I'm here now. He'll never hurt anyone again." Roark scooped her into his arms. "I'm taking her to another room, Sethwick."

Ewan?

Was he here, too?

Adaira raised her head. He was.

He and four other men, dressed entirely in black, crowded the room. Two stood over Edgar, talking in hushed tones. Her gaze dipped to the smoking gun in Ewan's hand. "You shot him?"

She closed her eyes briefly, forcing the nausea billowing in her throat to abate. Her brother had killed Roark's brother.

"Aye, Addy." There was no victory on his face. He shifted his remorse-filled gaze to Roark's. His brogue thickened as it did when he was emotional. "I'm sorry. He gave me nae choice."

"I know." Roark released a trembling breath against Adaira's hair. He hugged her to him. "I want to get her out of here. Tell Fletcher we're in the room across the hall."

After Mr. Fletcher briefly, but had thoroughly questioned Adaira and Roark about Edgar, he turned his attention to their hasty marriage and the charges against her. "I regret having to press you, my lady, after what you've endured. As you know, rather serious charges have been leveled against you."

Roark stared the man down. "Given Mrs. Winthrop and her cousins' intent was to abduct my wife at gunpoint, not to mention threatening the other four women in the room, and the count stabbed Adaira, *I* insist they have charges brought against *them*."

Fletcher's bushy eyebrows kissed the top of his forehead. "May I presume what they claim was an unprovoked attack was actually self-defense?"

"Yes." Adaira nodded. "We—my mother, my sisters, and a maid—outnumbered them and thought an offense was my only chance of escaping the count."

Rubbing his chin, Fletcher assessed her. "Well, this does alter things." He gave her an apologetic smile. "You understand, the investigation must proceed? However, based on the information you've told me, I certainly see no need to take you into custody."

It was a full hour later before Adaira and Roark finally left Kirkhouse Inn. Mrs. Bowie had been profusely apologized to and generously compensated for the damaged chamber, as well.

A trifle sore from Roark's lovemaking, Adaira's discomfort wasn't enough to prevent her from riding. Slowly cantering their horses along the dusty lane, flanked on either side by flowing meadows dotted with wildflowers, Roark asked, "You're quite certain you're able to travel?"

His worried scrutiny hadn't left her for more than a few seconds since Ewan had shot Edgar.

She smiled. "I couldn't stay there another moment, and

I truly am fit for travel. Craiglocky isn't much more than two hours from here."

Roark cocked his head. "Why is it we journey to the castle rather than returning to Cadbury with the others? Your family will be worried." He chuckled, shaking his head. "They're at Cadbury, and we'll be at Craiglocky. Quite the reverse of how it ought to be."

Adaira raised her face to the sun. She relished the soothing rays on her cheeks, despite the freckles guaranteed to appear.

"Ewan will tell them where we've gone. I have something important I need to do at the castle." Adaira kicked Fionn's sides, surging ahead of Roark. She called over her shoulder, "Come along, then."

They made good time, alternating between galloping and walking the horses. The sun hung high in the cloudless sky when they trotted into Craigcutty. Adaira cast Roark a glance.

Did he remember the day they'd met?

He turned his warm gaze on her and smiled.

He did.

My, how her feelings for this man had changed in the span of a few short months. From loathing to loving. Adaira touched the cross at her neck. It was almost as if their meeting had been preordained.

She grinned at Roark. "I'll race you!"

Taking a shortcut through the woods, Adaira led him past the far side of Loch Arkaig, glistening aqua in the late afternoon sun. Bending low over Fionn's neck, she gave him his head. He'd missed these rides. Leaning to the side as the horse rounded a bend, she sliced a swift glance behind her.

Atlas thundered behind Fionn, Roark low in the saddle, grinning like a buffoon.

Adaira laughed.

He urged Atlas on, sending the cranes standing in the shallow water near the shore into panicked flight. Their great wings whooshed no more than a foot above her head.

She slowed Fionn to a trot, guiding him to an unimpressive grove of aspens a stone's throw from the dungeon entrance. The horses could rest in the shade and nibble on the sweet grass below the trees. Dismounting, she tied the stallion's reins to a stout branch. As she turned, Roark hopped to the ground beside her.

She almost laughed at the look of confusion on his handsome face.

After also tying Atlas to the tree, he encircled Adaira in his arms. "I've never seen you race." He chuckled and shook his head, then kissed her on the nose. "You're incredible. I confess I'd never have believed a woman could ride so superbly."

Dappled sunlight filtered through the trees, and a bird chirped a warning overhead. She angled away from him, arching a brow. "And why not?"

"Don't get your feathers ruffled, although you're adorable when vexed. I meant it as the greatest compliment. You sit a saddle as well, or better than any man I know."

A warm glow filled her at his praise.

With an arm cradling her waist, he turned them toward the castle. "Why are we here?"

Adaira grinned and grabbed his hand. "I want to show you something." She moved toward the keep, coming to an abrupt halt when Roark didn't budge. Sending him a questioning look, she urged, "Come along."

He stood his ground. "I'm not going in there." He pointed to the barely discernible door nestled in the time-worn grayish-brown stones.

"No?" She stood on her tiptoes. Holding his face between her hands, she kissed him, using every seductive wile he'd taught her.

He succumbed without resistance, enveloping her in his arms. She looped hers behind his neck. Several lengthy moments passed as they explored each other's mouths.

Adaira trailed kisses to his ear, whispering suggestively, "I thought I might attempt to seduce you."

"You don't say?" A lazy grin creased Roark's face, a dazzling contrast to the fire in his eyes. He marched to the entry, tossing over his shoulder, "Well, are you coming? Don't dally."

She snickered, pushing on the stone that exposed the latch to the door. "Now you're in a hurry? Help me, please. It's quite heavy. Watch that rose bush. It smells wonderful, but its thorns are wicked."

Roark pressed his shoulder into the stone, and with a protesting groan, the entrance swung open.

Adaira stepped inside, the familiar dankness enshrouding her. She lifted the lantern from a hook beside the door. Striking a flint, she swiftly lit the wick. "You can close the door."

The heavy stone slid shut with a soft thud. With an exaggerated courtly bow, he said, "Lead on, Lady Clarendon."

Curling her hand in his, Adaira led him through a couple of corridors and a set of doors. No rats scurried before them, but familiar weighty coolness permeated the air, causing her to shiver slightly.

"Where are the rats?" Roark peered about, seeking the vermin that had once populated the bowels of the keep.

"Gone, for the most part. A few weeks ago, Yvette gave kittens to two orphans who help in the kitchen. Shortly afterward, Seonaid rescued a mother cat and her older kittens from a villager who was going to drown them. They spend a few hours down here every day. They're excellent hunters, and the first couple of weeks, they left dozens of rodents on the landing atop the stairs."

Adaira didn't slow her pace. The only sound was their steady tread echoing along the stone tunnels. Her fear of the dungeon had diminished with the knowledge Godwin hadn't despoiled her. "Here we are."

~

Speechless, Roark stared at his former jail. The cell before him didn't resemble the chamber he'd been imprisoned within. Adaira rushed inside and set about lighting two lamps.

"What do you think?" she asked a trace of apprehension in her voice. "I hung tapestries along the walls, and with this carpet on the floor, much of the austerity is eliminated."

A narrow bed, topped with an indigo counterpane and heaped with mismatched pillows, rested against the far side of the tiny cell. A wingback chair and side table completed the decor.

Roark planted his hands on his hips, scanning the chamber. It held little resemblance to his prison cell. He crooked a brow. "Why?"

Adaira colored and fiddled with her cross. "I..."

Grasping her braid, she lifted it over one shoulder. She untied the ribbon and began to separate the interwoven strands.

"It sounds silly when I say it, but I convinced myself it was to banish your presence, and Godwin's, from this place. Truthfully, after I furnished it, I ventured here only once more." Her hair at last free, she ran her fingers through its length. Sitting in the chair, she pulled off her boots before removing her stockings. "It's odd, but I almost missed your presence."

She stood and unfastened her breeches. With a couple of hip wiggles, they slipped to the floor. Only her shirt and chemise remained.

"You missed me?" Roark grinned and untied his neckcloth.

She tossed her head. Tilting her chin upward, a spark of mischief glinted in her eyes. "Don't flatter yourself. I couldn't stand you, remember?"

His grin widened. "Yes, so you say, but you did this." He spread his hands. He ran an appraising glance over her shapely ankles and calves. "Do you mean to seduce me, vixen?"

Her eyes half-closed, she murmured, low and sultry, "I am trying, but you keep rattling on."

Roark moved to her. He loosened the laces of her shirt and drew the garment over her head. Adaira shivered, but from cold or arousal, he couldn't be certain. He reached for her chemise, but she swatted his hand.

With a giggle, she scampered to the bed, snuggling beneath the blanket. "Not until you're undressed, too."

He wasted no time obliging her. Within moments, he snared her in his arms and nuzzled her soft, fragrant neck. "We'll make new memories of this place. Ones to replace the tormenting ones we have, my love."

"Am I? Your love? Truly?" Adaira's eyes darkened. She traced his lower lip with her finger.

Roark raised himself slightly and kissed her palm before pressing it to his heart. "I didn't know what love was until you captured my heart. I'll live every day thanking God for bringing you into my life."

He lowered his head, kissing her tenderly.

"As will I." She graced him with a beatific smile. Adaira opened her legs. "Make a memory with me, husband, to carry with us for a lifetime."

And Roark did. More than once.

Epilogue

Late June 1818

Standing outside the paddock beside the massive new stables, Adaira rested her back against Roark. His arms encircled her extended belly. They watched Tenacity try to nuzzle her offspring.

Kiki ran in circles around their ankles, barking at the foal.

"She's beautiful, isn't she, Roark?"

The spirited silver-colored filly kicked up her heels and skipped away. Little puffs of dust stirred in her wake.

"Though she is a saucy girl." Adaira chuckled and caressed her stomach.

Roark's laughter joined hers. "Precisely why we named her Vixen."

Fionn neighed a greeting from an adjacent pasture. He tossed his head and pranced along the fence. The leaves on the trees bordering the meadow had begun their transformation to warm autumn hues.

"He doesn't understand why I haven't been riding him these past months," she said.

"I shan't risk either your health or our child's." Roark's arms tightened. "You rode him far longer than I was comfortable with as it was."

Vixen galloped to her mother. She circled Tenacity before dashing off to stop several feet away, taunting the mare to give chase.

Kiki yipped at the filly's antics.

The babe in Adaira's womb moved abruptly, and Roark rested a hand on her stomach. "I hope our son isn't quite as naughty."

Adaira sniffed in disdain. "Or our *daughter*."

"Or our daughter," he agreed, kissing the crown of her head.

"The babe cannot come soon enough for me," she groaned, rubbing her belly.

"I eagerly await our child's arrival, too," he admitted. "Sethwick is beyond obnoxious, toting Broderick about, showing him off every time we see your family."

She grinned, then winced as the babe kicked, especially hard. "He's a proud papa, and the bairn is a good distraction for Mother. She's been lonely with Dugall away at university and Seonaid's extended visit to Tante Floressa's."

Adaira shook her head. "I'd never have thought Seonaid would venture to France. Isobel, yes. Seonaid, never."

"I'm sure Yancy's frequent visits alleviate a portion of your mother's loneliness." Roark snorted. "I've never known him to be so eager for Sethwick's company."

Adaira chuckled. "You know as well as I do, discussing

politics and business with Ewan is only a ruse. Lord Ramsbury is determined to court Isobel."

Tenacity nickered, and Adaira cast a glance over her shoulder.

The breeze increased in momentum, scattering the crisp golden-brown leaves on the ground. They crackled in protest. She tugged her wool shawl tighter, and Roark turned her in his arms, hugging her close to his chest. She nestled into his welcome warmth, breathing in his familiar scent.

Canting her head, she murmured, "Even after everything Edgar did, you showed compassion and buried him in the family cemetery."

"He was as much a victim of my father's cruelty as I was." Roark rested his chin atop her head. "We responded differently to that abuse. Edgar became like our sire, while I did everything in my power not to."

"Mmm," she said, knowing memories still haunted him. Perhaps they always would.

He firmed his grip across her back for an instant before he rubbed the length of her spine in a soothing motion. "I'm sorry to say, I cannot be as forgiving of Helene and her cousins. I still don't know how they caught wind of the charges you and your family brought against them."

"We do not need to concern ourselves with them. They won't dare set foot on British soil again. Besides, I actually owe them a debt of gratitude." Freeing a hand from her shawl, she caressed Roark's cheek.

"Indeed?" Skepticism whisked across his face. "And pray, do tell me, how did you come to that conclusion?"

She raised her other hand, and looping it behind Roark's neck, she brushed his warm lips with her own.

"Because, dear husband, their trickery forced us together and brought about our hasty marriage."

A mischievous expression settled in his eyes, and he gave her a lopsided smile. "And here, I thought you were going to confess their abduction attempt forced you to admit you loved me."

Balancing on her toes, she pressed as close to him as her swollen abdomen would allow. The babe in her belly leaped.

"I already loved you, and will 'till the day I no longer breathe," she murmured against his mouth.

"And I'll love you until the oceans of the world cease to ebb and flow, Lady Clarendon."

Roark sealed his vow with a scorching kiss.

~

I hope you enjoyed
THE EARL'S ENTICEMENT
If you'd like to leave a review please,
I would be grateful.

Keep reading for a free preview of
TRIUMPH AND TREASURE
Book 4
Highland Heather Romancing a Scott: Castle
Brides Series…

Free Preview

TRIUMPH AND TREASURE
Highland Heather Romancing a Scot: Castle Brides
Book 4

Boston, Massachusetts

Late March, 1818

Angelina Ellsworth—no, she was Mrs. Moreau now—cast her husband of six hours a look of adoration as he escorted her across the marble floor of the luxurious Plaza Hotel. She resisted the urge to dance a giddy jig.

She was married.

She tried not to gawk at the immense glittering eight-foot crystal chandeliers, marble pillars, and life-size, almost nude—*er, make that entirely nude*—statues of mythical gods and goddesses. Cherubs, their chubby feet and legs immersed in the water, edged a towering fountain burbling cheerily in the lobby's center.

"Rather dazzling, *chérie, non?*"

Meeting Charles's amused expression, heat tingled her cheeks. She'd been craning her neck, staring at the *trompe l'oiel* ceiling depicting gods and other immortals—also bare as Norfolk dumplings.

Papa would've been utterly scandalized.

Nudity, mythical gods, vulgar displays of wealth. Blasphemous.

And utterly splendid.

She released a happy sigh.

If Papa had been alive, he'd never have consented to Charles courting her. Papa had been determined she marry a gentleman of his ilk: a staid, devout, *dull* fellow. Better yet, a man of the cloth. And with dowries the size of thimbles, Angelina and her sisters had few suitors, let alone debonair young men such as Charles.

Thank goodness, Mama entertained her ideas, and after his passing, had voiced and implemented them with complete disregard as to what her late husband would've preferred.

A romantic at heart, once Mama realized Angelina loved Charles, she readily consented to the match.

Angelina shook off her dreary thoughts.

This was her wedding day. A rush of excitement caused her breath to quicken. In two days, she and Charles would sail to the Continent for a lengthy honeymoon in Italy by way of France.

Prior to meeting him, she'd only dared hope that, perhaps, someday, she might visit her aunt and uncle, the Duke and Duchess of Waterford, in England. She'd never met them. Aunt Camille was her mother's twin, and they exchanged correspondences on occasion.

"Here's your room key, sir."

The skeleton key clinking onto the countertop reined in Angelina's ruminations.

"Thank you." Charles slipped the key into his coat pocket before taking her arm. "Is the room prepared?"

"Yes, sir. Everything is as you requested." The clerk's lips bent into a knowing smile. "May I offer my congratulations, Mr. and Mrs. Moreau?"

"Thank you." Angelina and Charles spoke simultaneously.

He patted her arm, giving her a crooked grin.

Her stomach wobbled with that peculiar flip-flop it did whenever her new husband smiled at her. She cast him a sidelong peek as he guided her toward the curved staircase. A mere three months ago, this splendid man had entered her life.

If it hadn't been for Mama's insistence that Angelina attend the Dennison's Yuletide ball, she might never have met him. She hadn't wanted to attend, aware her father's cohort—horrid yellow-toothed Abraham Stockton—would be there. The paunchy man always stank of garlic and sweat. And he was five and forty if he was a day.

Despite Mama's adamant refusal to allow him to call upon Angelina, he'd been trying to court her the three years since she turned seventeen. Mama claimed the man was dicked in the nob if he thought to marry Angelina.

For her part, Angelina suspected, had he lived, Papa would've arranged a match between her and Mr. Stockton. She shuddered at the notion. In fact, she'd been hiding from him in a curtained alcove at the Dennison's when a man darted into the enclosure.

Unaware she huddled on a sofa tucked in the corner, he peeked between the heavy velvet panels, muttering, "A more persistent match-making *maman* I've never encountered. And *zut*, four plainer, pudgier mademoiselles—"

Angelina had erupted into laughter. "Mrs. Twiggels and the quartet, I'd wager."

Charles had spun around, peering into the shadowy nook. He'd chuckled, a pleasant low vibration deep in his chest. "*Non*, Twiggels? Please tell me you jest."

Yes, indeed, God had smiled on her that evening, for Charles had arrived in Massachusetts that very day, brought to Salem on business. His presence at the ball had been pure chance. His associate had received an invitation and insisted Charles join him for the festivities.

Angelina swept Charles another love-filled gaze.

His lips skewed into a devilishly wicked smile, and the glint smoldering within his tawny eyes caused her heart to patter in anticipation.

With his black hair and high cheekbones, he cut a dashing figure. The navy blue of his coat enhanced his unusual brandy-colored eyes and emphasized the breadth of his shoulders. Shoulders, she itched to feel beneath her fingers.

Despite her gloves, her palms dampened. She brushed her hands against her champagne-colored silk gauze gown, allowing herself to imagine Charles's hands caressing her.

Soon they would be.

They'd shared several fervent kisses during their short courtship, and once betrothed, he suggested they become more intimate. Raised by her zealot father, Angelina couldn't bring herself to sin *that* way. Not that she wasn't anticipating the marriage bed.

She most definitely was.

Followed by four porters carrying their luggage, she and Charles climbed the arched risers. Their trunks had already been sent to the ship.

As they ascended the stairs, Charles's caressed her spine.

A delicious tremor spiraled outward from where his palm lingered. She suppressed a slight gasp. Something more than curiosity stirred, making her impatient for his touches and kisses.

And he was a *most* skilled kisser.

A widower, forced at the tender age of twenty to marry a much older woman to save his family's estate, in the seven years since, he'd made a fortune in commerce.

Angelina held no doubts his handsomeness availed him of many a willing bed partner, though she wasn't supposed to know of such things. If the Dennison's ball was any indication, women threw themselves at him in droves.

However, much to her astonishment and delight, he'd chosen to make her his wife.

Charles vowed he'd never loved another and that Angelina would be his until the day he died. She had no misgivings about his affection. A man couldn't pretend the warmth in his amber eyes or the husky timbre of his voice when he spoke of his adoration.

She pressed her fingers against the ruby and diamond ring encircling her finger.

Yes, this is real.

"Happy, *mon ange?*" He gave her waist a slight squeeze.

His angel?

Smiling, she nodded, releasing a contented sigh. "Yes, blessedly and deliriously happy."

How could she not be? She'd found love. Something her parents' marriage had always lacked. Until meeting

Charles, she hadn't been altogether certain love existed outside her novels.

"Here we are." Charles's rested his hand on the curve of her ribs, his thumb rubbing against her gown. It tickled.

To stifle her giggle, she bit her lower lip.

He waited for the attendant to unlock their suite, a glint of anticipation in his eyes. The door swung open, revealing a room resplendent with roses of every imaginable shade.

Stepping inside, she spun in a slow circle, her skirts swishing about her ankles. The heady perfume of a hundred fragrant blossoms permeated the air. She sniffed in appreciation. Surveying the chamber, she spied more flowers in the adjoining bedchamber and dashed to the parted door.

After peering within, she sent a glance over her shoulder. "What in heaven's name?"

Still speaking to the porters, Charles didn't hear her.

Untying the ribbons at her chin, Angelina breathed in the heady aroma before removing her bonnet. Her spencer followed. She placed the items on the table beside the bedchamber door, adding her reticule atop the pile.

She studied the bed dominating the room. A monstrous thing with carvings on the bedposts and along the canopy, from which hung scarlet bed curtains, it was a blessed wonder the frame supported the oversized mattress.

She stepped closer, inspecting the engraved posts.

Oh, my.

Nude forms entwined in various acts of intimacy coiled around the wood.

Good heavens.

Heat burned her cheeks.

Similar images of Greek and Roman gods adorned the walls and ceilings. Wicked as Sodom and Gomorrah. For the first time since entering the dazzling hotel, she experienced a tinge of discomfit. Though very luxurious, the chamber's blatant carnality embarrassed her.

She wandered to the bedchamber's entrance.

Charles finished speaking to the remaining attendant and passed the young man a coin.

"Of course, sir. Right away." The porter smiled widely and stepped into the corridor. He hesitated, staring at the luggage piled about the entrance. "Do you wish me to have a maid sent up to unpack your bags?"

Charles shook his head, a strand of midnight hair falling across his forehead. "*Non*, we're only staying two nights. We sail the day after tomorrow. I'm confident my wife and I can manage."

He turned to wink at Angelina.

She grinned in return. *Incorrigible rogue.* But he was *her* rogue.

He closed the door before crossing to her in several elongated strides. Sweeping her into his arms, he nuzzled her neck.

She adored how she fit beneath his chin. At five feet eight inches, she stood taller than most women of her acquaintance. Yet, within Charles's embrace, she felt dainty and feminine.

Angelina laughed huskily. "My goodness, why all the roses?"

"For you *mon ange* rose. I wasn't able to fill the room with angels, but roses? That I could arrange. I've imagined you naked, lying on a bed scattered with rose petals for weeks."

Should she be shocked? For the life of her, she couldn't summon a jot of chagrin.

My, I've become scandalous since meeting Charles.

He stepped away and unbuttoned his cutaway coat. The gleam in his eye caused her pulse to do all manner of odd things. Good Lord, he didn't intend to—

She glanced at the window, searching the sky. Enshrouded in a smoky violet-gray, dusk had scarcely fallen. Making love was most improper during the daytime. Wasn't it?

Charles wound his arms around her once more, reining in her wayward thoughts. He kissed her like a man long-starved.

Looping her arms behind his neck, Angelina returned the kiss.

He nudged his hips against her belly, his desire evident. "I must have you now, *mon amour*. I cannot wait."

She hadn't expected he would be quite so eager to bed her—and before dinner, it would seem. The knowledge both thrilled and disconcerted her.

"Help me with the hooks, will you?" She made to turn her back, needing his assistance to unfasten the gown.

"*Non*, that will take too long."

Before she knew precisely what he intended, he scooped her into his arms. In two strides, he reached the bed then laid her upon the lush counterpane. Charles shoved her skirts to her thighs, and after fumbling with the falls of his trousers, parted her legs.

Apprehension swept her.

"Charles, I'm not...This is so sudden. I don't—" She gasped on a choked cry.

"*Mon Dieu*," he groaned against her neck.

Blinking back tears and biting her lip against the stinging pain, Angelina stared at a lurid picture on the wall. Was the act supposed to hurt this much?

Charles stiffened, giving a final moan before collapsing atop her.

That's it?

All the whispered fuss was about *that?* Awash in disappointment and miffed at his callousness, she barely took note when he rose from the bed and fastened his trousers.

He chuckled, trailing a finger across her lips. "You resemble a *femme légère.* A wanton, lying there with your breasts revealed and your legs spread."

Shame and humiliation surged through her. She turned her face away, shoving the gown to her knees with one hand and tugging the bodice over her breasts with the other. She swallowed against the tears burning at the back of her throat.

How could he say that?

"*Chérie?*" Charles touched her cheek, turning her face and forcing her to meet his eyes. "Forgive me, *mon amour.* I'm a selfish oaf. I promise I'll take my time next go-round. You will see how wonderful making love can be."

He bent and kissed her.

Someone knocked on the outer door. Another rap immediately followed this time with more insistence.

"Ah, that must be our food." He gave her a boyish grin as he fastened his jacket. "I hope you don't mind. I requested an intimate dinner in our rooms rather than the noisy restaurant below."

After helping her off the bed, he placed another tender kiss on her lips. "I love you, *amoureux.*"

The outer door rattled once more. Someone was most impatient.

"I'll answer the door while you repair your appearance." Whistling, he left the chamber, closing the door behind him.

Repair her appearance?

She'd much rather take a hot, lengthy bath liberally dosed with scented oil. She'd been anticipating becoming a woman for weeks, and truth to tell, the unpleasant experience didn't measure up to her naïve expectations.

Something wet trickled down her thighs, and she rushed to the bathing chamber. After dampening a cloth from the washstand pitcher, she made quick work of cleansing herself, grimacing at the blood on the linen. After washing away the evidence of her virginity and Charles's virility, she smoothed her chemise and dress, shaking the fabric until the folds fell into place.

The pearl pendant above her breasts, a wedding gift from Charles, hung askew. She straightened the necklace, and then adjusted her bodice, wincing slightly. He had certainly been exuberant in his attentions.

Mama had explained what to expect, nonetheless...

As she tidied her hair, Angelina examined her face in the looking glass. Several curly tendrils had escaped the Grecian knot atop her head. Other than rosy lips and cheeks, she didn't appear different from the woman who had entered the chamber a few minutes ago.

Except, I am no longer an untried maid.

She trusted the next time would be more satisfying.

As she made her way through the bedchamber, men's angry voices clashed in the other room. She hesitated, listening.

"Up to your old tricks, Pierre?" an unfamiliar, slightly French-accented voice accused.

Pierre?

Angelina opened the door but stopped short at the threshold.

The man before Charles was no servant. Sporting a thin

mustache, the stranger stood attired in the latest fashion. From his gleaming Hessians and cream-colored pantaloons to his jade green coat and knotted neckcloth—from which a jeweled stickpin glistened—he exuded quality.

He was profoundly handsome. And extremely angry.

Another man stood by the entrance. Much less refined, he grasped the handle of a gun tucked into his waistband.

She slapped a hand to her mouth in an effort to stifle the gasp that tore from her.

Thieves?

As one, the men's gazes came to rest on her: Charles's worried and angry, the rough fellow's, aloof, and the handsome man's curious *and compassionate?*

"Whatever is going on, Charles?" To calm her tumultuous stomach, Angelina wrapped her arms about her waist.

Her husband's face had taken on a distinct greenish hue, and she feared he might cast up his accounts. He opened his mouth to speak, but no sound emerged.

The mustached man shook his head contemptuously. "*Charles?* How unoriginal."

He turned his attention to Angelina and into a formal bow. "Mademoiselle Ellsworth, allow me to introduce myself. I'm Jacques, Baron Devaux-Rousset."

Angelina didn't extend her hand. Instead, she tightened the grip around her middle.

Pale, his lips pressed into a thin line, Charles glowered at the Frenchman.

This man was no friend.

"My lord, did Charles not inform you? I'm Mrs. Moreau. We were married this morning. Please excuse my forwardness, but how are you acquainted with my husband? And who, pray tell, is Pierre? Him?" She pointed at the surly giant who continued to toy with his weapon.

The brute smiled, a humorless twisting of his thick lips.

Lord Devaux-Rousset speared Charles with an indiscernible glance before answering. "I'm his stepson. Though, paradoxically, we are the same age."

Oh, the older woman Charles married.

He hadn't mentioned she'd been a baroness or that she had children. Whyever was her son here? Boston was too far from France for Angelina to believe this was a chance encounter. Something was too smoky by far.

She sent Charles a sidelong glance.

Why didn't he say something?

He stood seething with silent fury and glared daggers at the baron.

Angelina angled her head in deference. "Charles told me of his marriage to your mother. Please accept my sincere condolences for your loss."

For a moment, the baron's composure wavered. He gaped at her before turning a steely glower on Charles. *"Vous avez dit que sa mère était morte?"*

Drat, she didn't speak French, but the baron had mentioned something about his mother's death. That much she'd gleaned. Perhaps, she shouldn't have offered her sympathies. The mourning period had ended months ago. At least she thought that was what Charles had told her.

Or, mayhap, it hadn't been that long, which explained the baron's annoyance at the news of Charles's nuptials.

"Charles, are you not out of mourning?"

"Merde." Charles stared at the floor and fisted his hands.

"There is a lady present, *imbécile*," the baron snapped. "Hold your foul tongue."

He turned his attention to Angelina, and his expression

softened. With a wave of his manicured hand, he indicated the ivory and gold striped sofa beside her.

"Mademoiselle, perhaps you should have a seat, and I'll explain."

"Thank you, no. I'd rather stand, my lord."

Why did he insist on calling her mademoiselle? Rather boorish of him. No, pointedly rude, truth to tell.

The baron regarded her for an extended moment. He gave a slight shrug. "As you wish."

He turned to the brute blocking the door. "Please wait in the corridor and deter any staff. I don't wish to be disturbed."

After perusing Charles contemptuously one final time, the baron's henchman gave a curt nod and exited the chamber.

Lord Devaux-Rousset sighed and slapped his beaver hat against his thigh. His gaze skimmed Angelina from her hair to her shoes, taking her measure. "You are lovely. I understand Pierre's fascination. Thank God, I arrived before he compromised you."

Angelina frowned, utterly confused. Was the man daft?

"Pierre? *Who* is Pierre? And how, in God's precious name, can my husband *possibly* compromise me?"

His voice very soft, and equally as gentle, Lord Devaux-Rousset murmured, "I sincerely regret having to tell you, but the man you call husband is the well-known slave-trader, Pierre Renault."

"What?" She blinked rapidly, certain she'd heard incorrectly. Charles couldn't be slave-trader. He wouldn't be a party to something so abhorrent.

Rousset leveled Charles a blistering glare. "And, I assure you, his wife, my *mère*, was very much alive when I left France."

Collette Cameron®

~

I hope you enjoyed this free preview of
TRIUMPH AND TREASURE
Book 4
Highland Heather Romancing a Scott: Castle
Brides Series.

From the Desk of Collette Cameron®

Dearest Reader,

Adaira is one of my more complex characters. She means well, but her actions land her in well-deserved trouble. I wanted her to grow as a person in the story, to see her own faults, and accept the flaws of others as well. She does that beautifully and matures into a lovely woman I knew she could be.

Roark is the typical wounded hero, having been scarred by an abusive father and an adulterous wife. He and Adaira are the unlikeliest of lovers, yet they both are motivated by their pasts. As you will learn, he is just a big softy who collects handicapped animals.

I found their happily ever after one of the most satisfying I've written.

I completed extensive research about horse breeding and types of horses for this story. Not being a horse person, I felt it important to get my facts as accurate as possible.

You can read Adaira's sisters' stories as well as Lord Ramsbury's, Dugall's, and Flynn's in other books in the Highland Heather Romancing a Scot: Castle Brides series.

Many of the characters in this series also appear in The Honorable Rogues® series. You can read the first chapters of all my books for free at **collettecameron.com**.

Hugs,
Collette Cameron®

~

If you haven't joined Collette's exclusive mailing list click on QR image to sign up! You'll get access to exclusive content, sneak peeks, contests, giveaways, and more…
(P.S. No spam!)

https://collettecameronbooks.com/freegift

**Collette loves to hear from readers.
You can contact her via her website:
collettecameronbooks.com.
Or email her directly at
collette@collettecameronbooks.com.**

**You can also follow Collette on social media:
Facebook:** https://www.-
facebook.com/ColletteCameronNovels/
Instagram: https://instagram.com/collettecamero-
nauthor/
Goodreads: https://www.-
goodreads.com/collettecameron

Social Media

Book Bub: https://www.bookbub.com/authors/collette-cameron

Pinterest: http://www.pinterest.com/colletteauthor/

YouTube: https://www.youtube.com/@ColletteCameronAuthor

Giggles are Guaranteed
Collette's Cheris Reader Group

https://www.facebook.com/groups/CollettesCheris/

If you love to chat about all things romance-book related and enjoy taking part in fun and engaging live events, contests, and giveaways join **Collette's Chèris VIP Reader Group, https://www.facebook.com/groups/CollettesCheris/,** my exclusive private book group on Facebook.

Giggles are guaranteed!

Hope to see you there,
Collette Cameron®

About the Author

COLLETTE CAMERON®

USA Today Bestselling author Collette Cameron® is renowned for her captivating, humorous, and heartwarming Scottish and Regency historical romance novels. With over 65 published titles, over 1.6 million books sold around the world, and multiple writing awards to her credit, Collette is a well-known author in the world of historical romance.

Readers love her witty and relatable characters including daring rogues, dashing scoundrels, and the strong and spirited heroines who capture their hearts. From the rugged highlands to the refined drawing rooms of Regency

England, Collette's novels will transport you to another time and place, where love and adventure are just a page away.

Collette's Sweet-to-Spicy Timeless Romances® are the perfect escape for readers looking for romantic escape, poignant inspiration, engaging humor, and entertaining stories.

Based in the Pacific Northwest, Collette is surrounded by the lush greenery and rainy skies that inspire her writing. She dreams of one day splitting her time between the Pacific Northwest and Scotland. In the meantime, she indulges in her love of all things cobalt blue, dachshunds, chocolate, and of course, crafting her next historical romance.

Blue Rose Romance® LLC
collette@collettecameronbooks.com
collettecameronbooks.com

Also by Collette Cameron®

BLUE ROSE ROMANCE® LLC
COLLETTE CAMERON'S® COMPLETE BOOK LIST

CHRONICLES OF THE WESTBROOK BRIDES
A Romantic Opposites Attract Mystery & Suspense
Family Saga Regency Romance

Midnight Christmas Waltz — Book 1

Mission at Midnight — Book 2

The Midnight Marquess — Book 3

Holly, Mistletoe, and Midnight Snow — Book 4

The Wallflower's Midnight Waltz— Book 5

Minuet at Midnight— Book 6

Kiss a Rake at Midnight — Book 7

Unmasked at Midnight — Book 8

Memories Made at Midnight — Book 9

Once Upon a Midnight Dream — Book 10

~

LADIES OF OPPORTUNITY
A Bluestockings and Rogues Opposites Attract
Regency Mystery Christmas Romance

The Wallflower's Wild Wager — Book 1

~

SEDUCTIVE SCOUNDRELS
A Sensual Marriage of Convenience
Regency Historical Romance

A Diamond for a Duke — Book 1

Only a Duke Would Dare — Book 2

A December with a Duke — Book 3

What Would a Duke Do? — Book 4

Wooed by a Wicked Duke — Book 5

Duchess of His Heart — Book 6

Never Dance with a Duke — Book 7

Wedding Her Christmas Duke — Book 8

The Debutante and the Duke — Book 9

Loved by a Dangerous Duke — Book 10

How to Win a Duke's Heart — Book 11

When a Duke Desires a Lass — Book 12

My Dearest Duke — Book 13

~

FOR THE LOVE OF AN EARL (Wicked Earls' Club)
A Humorous Aristocrat and Wallflower
Regency Romance Adventure

Earl of Wainthorpe — Book 1

Earl of Scarborough — Book 2

Earl of Keyworth — Book 3

~

DAUGHTERS OF DESIRE (SCANDALOUS LADIES)
A Romantic Class Difference Forced Proximity
Regency Romance with Aristocrats

~

THE CULPEPPER MISSES
A Humorous Wallflower Family Saga
Regency Romantic Comedy

The Buccaneer and the Bluestocking — Book 4

The Lieutenant and the Lady — Book 5

~

THE HONORABLE ROGUES®
A Second Chance Redeemable Rogue
and Wallflower Regency Romance

A Kiss for a Rogue — Book 1

A Bride for a Rogue — Book 2

A Rogue's Scandalous Wish — Book 3

To Capture a Rogue's Heart — Book 4

The Rogue and the Wallflower — Book 5

A Rose for a Rogue — Book 6

'Twas the Rogue Before Christmas — Book 7

A Rogue Worth the Risk — Book 8

9 781955 259866